MAINTENANCE REQUIRED

A SMALL TOWN ROMANCE

⚜

GIULIA LAGOMARSINO

Copyright © 2020 by Giulia Lagomarsino

All rights reserved.

No part of this book may be reproduced in any form or by any electronic or mechanical means, including information storage and retrieval systems, without written permission from the author, except for the use of brief quotations in a book review.

❦ Created with Vellum

For all the Millennials out there. I really tried to get your lingo down, but it was a LOT of research and I'm not sure how well I pulled it off. Eventually, I had to give up. I hope you appreciate the effort I put in. LOL.

FOREWORD

This series takes place in Indiana, just across the Illinois border, about sixty miles south of Chicago. Though some of the towns are real, most everything is fictional.

ERIC

"Eric, I'm telling you man, she's quiche."

I stared at him, wondering what the hell he was saying. My brother had a habit of talking like an idiot. He was part of the millennial generation that spoke in a completely different language. One that I would never understand. And if he wasn't speaking like an idiot, he had those damn earbuds in, constantly blaring music. And I never even knew he had them in because they were wireless. So, I would be talking to him for minutes before I realized he couldn't even hear me.

He rolled his eyes and sighed. "She's hot and totally perfect for you. Just go out with her."

I finished pulling the two by fours out of my pickup truck and slammed the tailgate. "I'm not doing it, Andrew. I've had a long day and more work still ahead of me. If you really thought she was so perfect for me, you should have given me her number, not set up a date for us for tonight."

Andrew ran behind me, ducking out of the way when I swung the two by fours to the side and almost knocked him in the head. Dumbass. He'd learn to move out of the way.

"Come on. Don't do this to me. I told her that you were a stand up guy and completely reliable."

"You said that?" I asked, not at all believing him. My brother didn't say anything unless he said it like a millennial, which basically meant that any normal person wouldn't understand a word out of his mouth.

"I'm translating for you. Please, man. Kelsey will be pissed if you stand her friend up, and then she'll never go out with me."

"So, this is really about you getting with the friend."

"Well, not totally. Man, don't be so salty. This chick is totally on fleek. I'm telling you, I can't even."

"Would you just shut the hell up? I can't talk to you when you get like this. I have no fucking clue what you're saying."

He groaned in frustration. "I'm saying that you need to 'chill out,'" he said using air quotes. "This woman is…" He scrunched his eyes as if it took all his willpower to come up with an English word. "Stylin'. She dresses nicely. She's the total package."

"See, why can't you just say that to begin with?"

"Because I sound stupid when I try to talk like you."

"No," I laughed. "You sound stupid when you don't finish your sentences because it's some secret language that you and your friends have. I'm telling you, if you ever get a real job and try to fit in with the rest of society, I'm going to have to send you to finishing school."

"I already finished school, you asshole."

I laughed again. I loved my youngest brother, but he was so out of touch with the rest of the world. He and his friends all reminded me of grammatically incorrect hippies, out to save the world one incomplete sentence at a time.

"Andrew, I have no desire to go out with a woman that you think is perfect for me. She's probably just like you, and I can't sit through a dinner where I have to decipher every word being said."

"Naw, she's nothing like me. She's actually more your age, so she's basic."

"Basic."

"Boring, like you."

"Andrew-"

"Please?" he pleaded. "I really like this girl. She could totally be my bae. Don't do this to me."

It was his eyes. Those damn eyes that looked so much like Ma's and every time he looked at me with those puppy dog eyes, I was a goner. I looked to the sky in frustration and yelled.

"Fine. When am I supposed to meet her?"

He did some kind of happy dance and then jumped into my arms hugging me. I shoved him back, uncomfortable with his weird version of a man hug. "Six o'clock at The End Zone."

"The End Zone? That's the place where I'm supposed to take this woman on a date? A dive bar?"

"Live a little, bro." He shook his head as he smiled. "You're totally going to slay it."

"Slay what? What the fuck are you saying?"

He pointed a finger at me, his head bobbing around as he laughed. "Don't do that, Hunty. You know! Alright," he said turning around. "I have to hit it. Just remember, pics or it didn't happen."

I stared at his retreating form, still trying to figure out what he said. "What was her name again?"

"Sandy or Mandy. Something like that."

He got in his car and drove away, leaving me standing there completely dumbfounded. What the hell had I just agreed to?

~

I walked into the bar dressed in jeans and a t-shirt. I figured that if we were meeting in a dive bar, I didn't need to get dressed up, which went against everything I believed about dating. However, since my brother set this up and basically coerced me into doing it, I wasn't too concerned how this whole thing turned out.

I glanced around the bar, seeing mostly scantily clad women and men dressed in biker gear with tattoos covering their bodies. I didn't care much for tattoos. I liked my body to be as natural as possible. Plus, I had seen way too many people that regretted things they had tattooed on their bodies.

The lights were dim and the bar was smoky. No one in this town cared about smoking bans in public spaces and nobody bothered to call the cops about it. I coughed from the stench in the air and waved my hand in front of my face to clear the smoke. I stepped toward the bar and gave a nod to the bartender, Jake. I knew him well from high school and still hung out with him occasionally.

"Eric, never thought I'd see you in here. What can I get you?"

"Just a beer. I'm supposed to be meeting someone here."

He pulled a glass and filled it from the tap, his eyes going to the corner table. "That woman came in alone. Keeps looking around like she's expecting someone."

"Thanks, man." I put some money on the bar and walked over to the table. She was about thirty, maybe thirty-two at most. She dressed nicely, I supposed, but definitely a little more…wild than I was used to. She had on short shorts and a plaid shirt that was tied at the waist. Her cowboy boots had splashes of teal in them and she had a cowboy hat that looked like it had seen a few rodeos. Compared to the other women in the bar, she was fully clothed.

As I got closer, I saw that her hair was brown and hung in loose waves down her back. Her large, green eyes flicked to mine and danced with a light I had never seen before. Her smile stretched wide across her face, shining so bright that it took my breath away.

She stood up and walked over to me, jumping into my arms and wrapping her legs around my waist. "Hey there, good looking. You must be my date."

I swallowed hard and cleared my throat, setting her down on the floor and taking a step back. "Eric, and you are?"

"Kiki."

Figures. Andrew couldn't remember her name and I get stuck with a Kiki.

"Kiki?"

"Well, it's Katherine, but that's so boring and I wanted something that was full of life."

I was already regretting stepping out of the house tonight. This woman was nothing like me. What the hell had Andrew been thinking setting me up with a woman that went by Kiki?

"Well, *Katherine*, how about we take a seat and I'll buy you a drink?"

"Sure. Let's get some food too. The nachos are amazing," she said, biting her lip as she rolled her eyes heavenward.

"I'm not sure I want to eat anything that comes from here."

"Oh, live a little. What's a little salmonella between friends," she grinned.

"I have a business to run and I can't afford time off because of food poisoning."

She threw her head back in laughter while I stared at her like she had a third head. What the hell was so funny about that? "You are so funny, Eric. Chrissy was right. You are definitely going to be a good time."

Was I in some alternate universe? What the hell was she talking about? I was probably the last person on the face of the earth that anyone would say was funny. In fact, my brothers always referred to me as a wet blanket. The only time I really let loose was when it was just the seven of us.

"Anyway, what is it you do, Katherine?"

"I work over at the Children's Hospital in Kankakee."

She signaled to Jake and he nodded back to her. "What do you do there?"

"I'm a nurse."

"Oh, I didn't expect that from you."

"Why? Because I'm out having a good time? Did you think all nurses were boring and stayed in on Friday nights?"

"Not at all, but when my brother set this up, I didn't know what to expect. He doesn't exactly have the same taste in women as me."

"I'll try not to take offense to that."

"Please don't. I'm sure you're lovely. I just don't think we'll have anything in common."

"Well, let's see, shall we? We can make a bit of a game out of it."

"And what would the game be?"

"How about every time we don't have a common interest, we take a drink."

"I think we'll end up very drunk by the end of the night," I muttered under my breath.

She smiled at me with a twinkle in her eyes. "Maybe this night won't be such a bust after all."

Jake brought over a bottle of vodka and two shot glasses. I raised an eyebrow at her. I definitely was not a shot guy. I hadn't had a shot in years. Beer was the most lethal drink I consumed at the end of the day.

"Live a little, Eric."

If there was one thing I never did, it was back down from a challenge. "Fine, I'll go first. Favorite color?"

"That's easy. Blue."

"Me too."

"Damn, I was so hoping you would say pink."

I shook my head and chuckled. The woman did have a sense of humor.

"Alright, my turn. Favorite sexual position?"

"Wow," I chuckled. "You really go right for the hard questions."

"I like the hard ones. In fact, the harder they are, the better."

I ran a hand across my jaw, scratching at the scruff I had forgotten to shave off after my shower. "Anything?" I asked.

"Anything," she whispered seductively.

"Doggy style."

She took a drink. "Damn, I like that one too, but not as much as the cowgirl."

My eyes dropped to her breasts that were peeking out from where her shirt was unbuttoned. I wondered what her breasts looked like as they bounced up and down while she rode my dick. My eyes flicked back to hers and she grinned at me.

"That's why I like it."

I drank my shot and cringed at the burn. "My turn. Favorite time of year?"

"Summer. Gotta love those men walking around with their shirts off." I watched as her eyes roamed over my body, taking in my muscles bulging from my arms. I worked hard, not at working out, but working with my hands and the rest of my body got a workout along with it.

I took a drink of my own. "Fall."

"It's a shame," she said as she drank her shot. "Swallow or spit?"

"Spit." I had never been one to go down on a woman. I didn't enjoy it and I didn't see what was so appealing about swallowing another person's bodily fluids.

"Swallow," she said before pouring another shot and drinking it down. I followed her lead and did the same.

The alcohol was going to my head already and at this rate, I wouldn't be able to drive home. I wracked my brain for something we might have in common. I had to slow this down.

"Pickup or car?"

"Pickup."

"Thank fuck. Me too," I said with a smile.

"Favorite feature of the opposite sex?"

"That's not a fair question," I countered. "There are too many different body parts."

"Such as?"

"Well, I'm pretty sure if I said that I was a breast man, your answer would not be the same."

"Okay, excluding obvious body parts, what's your favorite feature of the opposite sex?"

"On you? Your eyes. Definitely your eyes."

"Hmmm. That's a tough call for me." She looked at the alcohol as if she was weighing the alcohol into her answer. "I would say it's fair to say that your eyes are definitely my favorite feature."

We stared at each other for a minute, electricity zapping between us. I hadn't come here for anything more than a disappointing date, but this was fast becoming the most interesting date I had ever been on.

"Coffee drinker?"

"Tea."

I poured us more shots and we both took one.

"One night stand or relationship?"

"Relationship," I said, thinking that would be her answer.

She raised an eyebrow. "One night stand."

We both took a drink.

"Stay here and talk or go to my place and fuck?"

Did I just seriously say that? The alcohol must really be going to my head. She didn't answer, but picked up her purse and walked toward the exit, glancing over her shoulder and winking at me. I sat there for a few seconds, completely stunned that that had actually worked and quickly threw down some money. She was waiting for me outside and I grabbed her hand, dragging her over to my truck. She wasted no time crawling across the seat and licking my ear. I had to tighten my hold on the steering wheel to keep from driving us off the road.

When her hand snaked down to my package and latched on, my hips bucked in the seat, but not out of desire.

"Whoa! Hold on there, tiger. Wait until we get home."

She licked the shell of my ear and nipped at the lobe. "Why? Learn to loosen up and have a little fun."

"That-That's not safe. Distracted driving kills approximately nine people and injures at least a thousand every day in the United States."

"Then you're lucky no one's on the road with us."

Her hand moved down to my jeans and grasped at me again. I quickly pulled her hand away and set it on her lap, patting it gently. "Most accidents occur within fifteen miles of your home. We are well within that range, so let's just wait until we get to my place and then I'll let you have your way with me."

"Is that a promise?"

"If you let me drive us home without any more shenanigans? I swear it."

"I'm gonna hold you to that."

I recited the alphabet over and over in my head, but when that didn't work, I started listing all the states in alphabetical order. By the time we got back to my place, my manhood was a little more under control and I didn't feel like we would end this date in my pickup truck.

She hopped out before I could open her door and followed me inside. Luckily, my brothers were out for the night and there was no one to disturb us. They would definitely have something to say about me bringing a woman home since I was so picky with my selections. And Katherine definitely wasn't a woman I normally brought home.

Her hips swayed from side to side as she headed for the stairs and turned back to me tauntingly. I swallowed hard, trying to restrain myself from taking her on the stairs. I stumbled up after her and pushed her toward my door, slamming it behind me. I stripped her of her clothes and got mine off in record time. She jumped up into my arms and wrapped herself around me. I stumbled back, trying to balance us, but then overcorrected and sent us flying toward the bed.

We bounced off the edge and fell to the floor, her straddling my hips and grinding against me without even registering that we just fell off the bed. Her juices rubbed against my cock and before I could think about it, I was inside her and she was riding me hard. Fuck, she felt amazing. Her moans filled the room and it took every single memory of me and my brothers to keep from blowing inside her within a minute.

When I finally had myself under control, I rolled her over and took her hard. I felt like a deranged psycho going in for the latest kill. I had to have her. I needed to make her mine now. I had never let loose like this before. I was always the responsible brother that took a woman out on at least three dates before taking her home. This was so unlike me, but exactly what I needed right now.

I took her twice more that night and then fell back on the sweaty sheets with her laying on the other side of the bed. I shouldn't let her stay. I didn't even fucking know her, but she was already dead to the world. I rolled over and passed out, wondering why the hell I allowed myself to drink so much.

∼

The next morning, the sun shone brightly in my eyes, blinding me and letting me know that I had definitely missed my wakeup call and would be late for work. I threw the covers off, my head pounding and my stomach revolting. I was never drinking like that again. I stood and made my way to the bathroom, doing a double take when I saw a feminine foot sticking out of the covers. I leaned in close to examine it, as if I was seeing things. Her toe nails were painted a sparkly pink. I blinked several times, sure that I was imagining things, but the foot was still there.

I shook my head and looked up by the pillow. The woman from last night was most definitely in my bed. That hadn't been a dream, which meant the sex was very real also. I went into the bathroom and splashed cold water on my face and took a shower to wash the stench of sex off of me. I toweled off and saw that she was still sleeping in my bed. Not able to deal with her yet, I got dressed and went downstairs in search of coffee. Andrew was sitting at the kitchen table, doing something on his phone while Joe was making a smoothie of some kind. What ever happened to good ol' bacon and eggs?

"Morning," I mumbled as I poured myself some coffee.

"Morning. So, who's the lucky lady?" Joe asked.

"Shut up." I took a sip of coffee and cringed when he started the blender, making my head pound and my teeth clench painfully.

"Dude, it worked out?" Andrew said excitedly. "You brought what's-her-face home?"

"She has a name, asshole."

"I'm sure she does. I just don't give a shit what it is. Thanks again for that, man. Her friend was quiche AF." Andrew had a grin on his face that stretched a mile wide.

"She's here?" Joe asked, intrigue in his expression.

"Oh, yeah," Andrew grinned, holding his fist out for a fist bump, which Joe returned. "Upstairs in my room as we speak. She was so thirsty for me."

"Just once, I wish that you would talk like a normal person. I can't decipher what you're saying this morning."

"The friend was hot as fuck and she wanted my cock. Clear enough for you?"

"Crystal," I said, narrowing my eyes at him.

"Oh, God." I turned to see Katherine walking down the stairs, holding her head and wearing only my t-shirt, which barely covered her ass. I walked over to the coffee pot and poured her a cup, holding it out to her. She took a sip and then spit it out. "What is that?"

"Coffee."

"I don't drink coffee, remember?"

I searched my memory, but there were a lot of blank spots. I shook my head.

"We didn't drink that much," she said, sounding insulted.

"I only drink beer, so that was a lot for me."

"Who are you guys?" she asked as she looked at my brothers. I quirked an eyebrow at Andrew who looked completely unfazed by all this.

"You know Andrew and this is my brother, Joe," I pointed in Joe's direction.

Andrew shook his head slightly as he assessed Katherine. "Nope. Not ringing any bells." I rolled my eyes. Typical of Andrew to not recognize the woman he set me up with.

"Let me just eat some breakfast and then I'll drop you at your car. Do you want some eggs?" I asked Katherine.

"Sure. Do you have any cream to put in that black gunk you call coffee?"

"Nope. We drink it black."

"Savages," she muttered under her breath.

"Morning, everyone!" A perky blonde walked down the stairs and over to Andrew, straddling his lap and giving him one of the dirtiest kisses I had ever seen. I rolled my eyes and waited for her and Katherine to say hi to each other. They didn't really seem the type to be friends. The blonde looked like a slut and not all that bright. Katherine, while definitely more wild, for sure had more clothes on. Her face was free of makeup while the blonde looked like it was caked on her face.

The blonde came up for air and dismounted my brother. "Wow. Full house this morning. Are you going to introduce me, bae?"

Andrew gave her a strange look. "My brothers, Eric and Joe. You know her," he pointed at Katherine. She tilted her head and seemed to search her memory, but shook her head.

"No, I don't think we've met. I'm Sadie."

"Kiki."

"Wait," I pointed between the two of them. "You two are friends. Andrew said that he brought the friend home."

"No, I've never met her," Katherine said in confusion.

"But, I was supposed to meet Sadie's friend last night."

"Oh, Bethany," Sadie nodded. "Yeah, she took some other guy home."

"If I wasn't supposed to meet you," I said to Katherine, "then who were you waiting for?"

"I was waiting for a blind date also. I just assumed you were him."

"You didn't get a name?" I asked incredulously.

"In case you didn't notice, you didn't know my name either," she snapped back.

"That's because my dipshit brother couldn't remember your-*her* name. I just assumed when you introduced yourself as Kiki that you were the bimbo I was supposed to meet."

"Bimbo? Is that what I am now? Strange, you weren't calling me that last night when I was sucking your cock."

Joe cleared his throat," I think I'm gonna bounce. Way to go, Hunty," he whispered as he left.

I shook my head. It was too early for this crap. I finished making breakfast and unloaded it on plates. Katherine ignored me as she ate quickly, almost as if she wanted to get away from me. Which was fine because I was regretting our little rendezvous also. We got in my truck and I started for her car. I was trying to think of how to say this nicely, but there really wasn't a nice way of putting it.

"Look, last night was fun, but I don't normally do that kind of thing."

"What kind of thing?"

"Bring random women home from the bar. I usually date."

"So, what made you do it last night?"

"Alcohol. Lots and lots of alcohol."

"That's such a cop out. If you didn't want to have sex with me, you wouldn't have taken me home. I'm pretty sure you were a willing participant in what happened."

"I'm not saying it was wrong, I'm just saying I don't normally do that. It won't be happening again."

"Because you're too uptight?"

"Because you're not my type," I snapped. I wasn't uptight. I just did things a certain way and her way wasn't my way.

"And what is your type? Some Martha Stewart wannabe?"

"No, just not the type that goes home with men she picks up in a bar after just meeting."

"That's so hypocritical. Did you ever think that that was my first time doing something like that?"

I hadn't. It hadn't even been a consideration. By the way things went last night, I just assumed that was something she did on a regular basis.

"Well, it wasn't just that. You jumped into my arms when you saw me. You wrapped your legs around my waist! Who does that?"

"Oh, please. I had you pegged as soon as you walked over. The way you were looking around the bar in disgust, I knew you were too uptight to be in a place like that. I was messing with you."

"Can we just forget about last night? It happened, but it's not gonna again."

"Whatever," she huffed. We rode in silence the rest of the way to her car.

When she stepped out, she held the door for just a second. "See you around," and then she was gone.

That was one night that I wouldn't ever be repeating. Not only did I have a killer hangover, but I didn't particularly like dealing with women that felt they had been slighted. When I took a woman out on a date, I always made sure that we were on the same page before things went further. One night stands were just messy.

KATHERINE

This was really irritating. It had been two weeks since my night with Eric, but he still crept into my thoughts, and I wasn't sure why. He was rude and completely not my type, but the sex was good. I just wished I could remember more of it. The problem was, a lot of that night was a blur and I couldn't be sure if I was remembering what actually happened or if I was just remembering what I wanted to happen.

The images that scrolled through my mind were downright indecent. I swore I could still feel his lips wrapped around my nipple and the feel of his hands on my ass, but it wasn't crystal clear in my mind. More like something I really hoped was true. It was infuriating because in my mind, he was the best I'd ever had, and I couldn't help but want more.

I knew that would never happen though. We were nothing alike. In fact, when I saw him in the bar, I knew that the date would be a dud, but I decided to make the best of it. I toyed with him because it was my night off and I was desperate for some fun. He had surprised me when he asked me to go home with him. I really hadn't expected that. But then he was so stiff in the morning. It was like he couldn't believe that he had allowed himself to have fun for one night.

"Sorry I'm late!" Chrissy said, rushing over to the bar table and tossing her ten gallon purse on top, sloshing my drink all over the place. I sopped up the mess with some napkins as she pulled off her jacket and shoved her hair out of her face. "You are not going to believe what happened to me today."

"What?"

"So, I was getting ready to walk out the door when the hubby stopped me. Just came at me out of nowhere and totally attacked me. I felt like I was in one of those nature films where you watch the lion attack the lioness. You know where he mounts her and-"

"Yeah, I get the picture. And for all of us *not* having sex right now, this story really sucks."

"Hey, you just have to find the right man. Like that guy you met at the bar. Whatever happened with him?"

"You mean the stiff?"

"You said he was good in bed."

"He was. I think. I can't really remember, but the point is, he was a complete asshole the next morning."

"Was it because you stayed over? They always get pissed when you do that."

"No, he didn't seem to care. He even made me breakfast. In fact, most of the time he was a perfect gentleman. He just seemed to be pissed at himself for bringing me home."

"What outfit did you wear?"

I rolled my eyes. "It wasn't the outfit."

"I'm just saying, sometimes you dress a little slutty when you're feeling feisty. Maybe he just wasn't into that look."

"It wasn't the outfit," I stressed again.

"Alright," she said, holding up her hand placatingly. "So, if it wasn't the outfit, maybe it was the sex. Maybe you're not as good as you think."

I snorted. "Trust me, I'm that good."

"But was it good with him?"

I squinted, trying to remember as I dug through what I thought were memories. "Okay, I can't say for sure. I drank a lot and I'm not sure what was real and what wasn't."

"Well, there's your answer. I'm sure the sex just wasn't good enough. He realized it the next morning and didn't want to tell you how bad the sex was."

"But he made me breakfast and was pretty much a gentleman at the same time that he was an asshole. I'm not even sure how you pull that off."

"So, he was being sensitive to your feelings. Was he at least hot?"

"Eh. I guess. I mean, I remember that he had nice eyes. I guess he was good-looking, but when I was being shoved out the door, I wasn't exactly drooling over the guy."

"Well, what was he like when you were on your date? You said he was stiff. In what way?"

"Just…he called me Katherine."

She sucked in a breath, shaking her head. "Wow. That's…talk about uptight."

"I know," I whisper-hissed. "And he told me that he doesn't swallow. What kind of man expects blow jobs, but won't reciprocate?"

"Amen, sister. If he's not willing to lick my pussy and make me come all over his mouth, there's no way that I'm putting his dick anywhere near my mouth."

"We're talking about before your husband, right?"

"Of course. Darren goes down on me at least three times a week."

"Wow."

"I taught him early. He knows what I expect in the bedroom and what my rules are if he expects head."

I laughed a little. Leave it to Chrissy to have rules about giving head. "I've gotta hear this."

"Well, first, if head is given, I expect him to give me the same. Second, he must shower first. There is no way I'm going down on him and his sweaty ball sack. Third, he has to be trimmed. There is nothing worse than going down on a man and getting hair stuck in my teeth, or worse, down my throat! I won't gag on his cock, but I *will* gag if I have hair stuck in my throat."

"Completely understandable."

"Four, if he doesn't come in five minutes, I'm allowed to stop and we just have regular sex. But I still expect him to go down on me."

"You put a time limit on blow jobs?"

"Hey, my jaw starts to hurt, and trust me, I put in a lot of effort, so if he's not coming right away, I know it's because he needs more time. Besides, there's only so much my knees can take. You know, I'm in my thirties."

"You could always wear knee pads," I smirked.

"Right, that would really be a turn on."

"You could dress up as a volleyball player. Just tell him you're into role play."

"We already do role play, but I don't want him fantasizing about teenage girls. That's just gross."

"Point taken."

"You know, I think deep down, you're finding reasons not to date this guy."

My eyes widened in surprise. "He was the one that told me he never wanted to see me again."

"Yeah, but I can tell that you wouldn't have given him another chance anyway."

"You don't know that."

"But see, I do know this about you. You date men that will always let you down. Maybe that's why you don't want this guy. He sounds responsible, and maybe you don't want to date a guy that's responsible."

"That's ridiculous," I scoffed, glancing away. I didn't want to think that anything she was saying was true.

"You tend to date these guys that don't expect a lot from you, and then you're disappointed when they turn out to be losers."

"They weren't all losers."

"Cigarette man?"

"He wasn't a loser. He just smoked so damn much. I felt like I was suffocating just on his smell alone."

"And Marcus?"

"He lived with his parents. Come on, any woman would think that guy was a loser. He was thirty-three!"

"But you knew that when you met him and you still went out with him! See! You like being disappointed by men!"

"That's…" I scoffed, shaking my head slightly. "That's-"

"Ridiculous?"

"Yes! Why would I want to be disappointed by men?"

"Well, I'm not Freud. I don't have all the answers."

I thought about what she said as she rambled on about the graphic sex she had just had. Was she right? Did I really choose losers? This was a small town and the surrounding towns were small also. It wasn't like there were a lot of choices. But Eric was the exact opposite of a loser. He seemed very put together and if anything, too rigid. I'm sure to him I really did look like a slut. It was the one night that I had chosen to go out and have some fun, let my hair down and dress for fun. Had I actually known I was going to meet Eric, I wouldn't have dressed like that.

He was so intense and serious. The bar was too dirty and I was dressed too slutty. He didn't seem like he knew how to have any fun. Still, a man like him was probably a great catch. I shook off those thoughts. It didn't matter. It wasn't like I was ever going to see him again. He made it perfectly clear that I was not his type and we would never go out again.

ERIC

I got in late after another long day of work. I really needed to hire more help. The jobs were coming in faster than I could get them done. We did quality work at my company, but I was finding that the more work that came in, the more I had to delegate and not actually do the physical labor. And that was why I had gotten into home renovations to begin with. I loved to get my hands dirty, to create something amazing and see the finished project. I liked feeling productive during the day. I couldn't imagine ever sitting behind a desk like my brother, Robert, did. He loved being a lawyer, but the stress of the job was killing him.

My job was also stressful, but I had this cathartic release every time I ripped out a wall or framed in a new one. It was my passion, but that passion was waning the more that I had to sit behind a desk. I needed to hire a manager for the office to field the calls and do all the grunt work that I hated. I just had to find the time to do it.

I tossed my keys down on the side table by the back door and sighed when I heard grunting coming from the other room. There could only be two possibilities as to who was fucking in the other room, Andrew or Joe. I constantly wondered if I was always going to be living with them. As far as I knew, neither of them had a job, but they always paid rent. There was potential there for both of them, but for some reason, neither of them seemed to have any ambition. Andrew could have gone to college and gotten a degree in computer science or something. He was really great with computers, but he hated school. And Joe...I had no fucking clue what that guy was going to do. He just seemed to drift through life on beer and pretty women. I knew he made money, but he was pretty shady about it right now. I knew he was gone a lot at night, but I didn't know if that was from partying or some side gig that he didn't want any of us to know about.

I pulled open the fridge, not wanting to know what was going on in the other room. I didn't want to know who it was or on what piece of furniture it was happening. If they were even using furniture. I was tired of living with my brothers. It wouldn't be so fucking terrible if they actually had jobs and behaved like respectable, young men, but they were young and acted their age. I couldn't remember ever being as immature as they were. I always had goals in mind. I went to school for engineering and then opened my business with the help of my parents. They gave me a small loan, and when they decided to move to North Carolina, they basically handed over the house to me with the stipulation that I take care of my brothers. I never had to worry about Derek. He had a good head on his shoulders and had a woman he loved. I knew they would get married one day and he had a solid job. There was nothing to worry about there.

Robert was on his own in Chicago, taking care of himself just fine, but that didn't stop me from worrying about him. He worked long hours and the stress was obvious in his voice every time we spoke. I was more worried that he would have a heart attack more than anything.

Will taught a few towns over and he had his own house. I usually saw him on the weekends. He hadn't settled down yet, but I wouldn't be surprised if he did soon. As far as I knew, he wasn't a player. Well, I knew he dated from time to time. He taught history at a neighboring school district and seemed to be pretty happy.

I took a long drink of my beer and closed my eyes. That left Josh. I hadn't heard from Josh in years. He just disappeared one day and none of us had heard from him since. Robert had used his contacts to investigate anywhere he might be. We filed a missing persons report, but had yet to come up with anything. My parents were devastated. It hit my mom the hardest, but they continued to live their lives, pretending like he was just off on an adventure. It broke their hearts though. We dug into anything that might have been going on in his life at the time, but came up empty. He was just gone, in the wind with no trace left behind.

My brothers and parents didn't know it, but I had hired a PI two years ago. That's part of the reason I was working so much. It wasn't cheap to have an investigator constantly looking for someone, but Josh was my brother. I couldn't just pretend that he was okay. I needed to know for sure. But the longer he was gone, the more I worried that he was dead, just another unidentified body out there that no one claimed.

I slammed back the rest of my beer and tossed the bottle in the garbage, shutting down the thoughts of my brother being dead. If I thought about it too much, the guilt ate me up inside. I knew realistically that it wasn't my fault that he was missing, but I was the oldest brother. I should have seen something. I should have known that something was wrong, even though the last time I saw him, he was smiling and didn't seem to have a care in the world. What could have changed?

I walked into the living room, forgetting about why I had stayed in the kitchen, and was immediately hit with the sight of Joe bending a woman over the side of the couch, fucking her hard.

"Shit," I swore, quickly turning away. "Goddamnit, Joe. Can't you do that in your bedroom?"

"Hold on," he panted. "I'm almost finished."

The woman groaned and I heard a slap right before a low groan from my brother. I shook my head in disgust as I waited for them to cover up. I wasn't sure why I waited around other than the fact that this was technically my house and I didn't want to have to hide up in my bedroom.

"Let me give you a ride," Joe murmured to the woman.

"That's okay. I called an Uber before. It should be here any minute."

She strutted past me, wiping the lipstick from her lip as she winked at me. I shuddered and turned to my brother. "Nice."

"I know, right? She was totally on fleek."

"She looked like she was seventeen," I scowled.

"Whoa, swerve, man."

"What?"

"It's not like she's my bae."

I rubbed a hand across my forehead and took a seat far away from where he had just fucked that girl. If she was legal, it was definitely up for debate. "Can you just talk to me like a normal guy? How the fuck do you expect to get a job when no one can understand a fucking word you say?"

"I have a job," he said defensively.

"Right," I snorted. "I'd love to know what that is."

He glared at me and plopped down on the couch. "You need to get laid. You're way too fucking grumpy."

"I do get laid."

"Pics or it didn't happen," he shot back.

"You want me to take pictures of me fucking women? You're fucking disgusting."

He rolled his eyes. "I'm just saying that it's so rare to see you with a woman."

"Then why can't you just fucking say that?" I asked angrily. "Seriously, I'm fucking tired of trying to figure out what the fuck you're saying. I can't understand a damn word you or Andrew say."

"You need to get laid more often," he said, leaning forward and enunciating every fucking word. "What about that chick that was here a few weeks ago?"

I thought back to that very uncomfortable experience and grimaced. She was hot as hell, but I was so mortified that I hadn't remembered anything from the night before that I decided it would be best if we just never saw each other again. That wasn't me. I wasn't like my brothers. I was a one woman man, and when I met a woman, I dated her for a while before I slept with her. I didn't want there to be any miscommunication between us. I wanted her to know that I respected her for who she was and not what she could give me. It was the way I saw my parents' relationship and what I planned to have for myself.

"I haven't seen her since the next morning."

"She was thirsty," he grinned.

I quirked an eyebrow at him. "That morning?"

"Oh yeah. Totes."

I thought back to that morning, trying to remember if I wasn't a gentleman like I normally am the morning after. "I know we didn't have tea, but I offered her coffee."

He rolled his eyes at me. "You need to learn the language. She was fucking hot. She wanted you, but you were all *cancel*."

That I thought I understood. "We are completely different people. It would never work out between us."

"Only because you don't want it to. You could have asked her to Netflix and chill. I bet she would have gone for it."

"We don't have Netflix," I reminded him.

"The point is, she was into you, and you blew it. You could have had that woman in your bed every night, but you didn't want to adult."

I sighed and scrubbed a hand over my face. "I'm done with this conversation. I can't understand half of what you say and I'm tired of trying. I'm going to shower. I have an early morning."

"You don't have to be so salty. I get it, the struggle is real. But when you find that bae that you're looking for…" He nodded and grinned, shooting me a wink.

I spread my arms wide, frustration building at a rapid pace. "When I find her *what*?"

"You know. Goals AF. That's all I'm saying."

Apparently, he wasn't saying much of anything. I turned and stormed up the stairs to my room, slamming the door behind me. I really fucking needed him to move out so I didn't have to hear that shit every day. It's not that I minded him being here, but fuck, I couldn't stand the way he spoke. He wouldn't last five minutes in a job interview. They would look at him like he was a fucking idiot, and that was what concerned me most. I would never get rid of him, because he would never qualify for an actual job.

I pulled off my t-shirt and flung it in my laundry hamper, but then walked over and shoved it all the way in when I saw it was draping over the edge. It was bad enough that I lived with frat boys, my own room wouldn't look like that. Shucking my pants, I walked to the bathroom and turned on the shower, letting the steam fill the room. I was exhausted after such a long day. I hadn't even eaten dinner yet, but I was too tired to care. There was no way I was going back downstairs to deal with my brother.

I rested my head against the side of the shower wall and let the water cascade down my back. I thought back to my conversation with Joe and wondered if he was right. Was Katherine into me? Had I totally missed that? All I could think about was the mistake I had made, but what if it wasn't a mistake? I couldn't remember much from that night, but I did remember her waking me up several times during the night for sex. I just wished that I could remember the actual act.

My cock grew hard as I remembered her walking downstairs in only my t-shirt. I could still remember the way her tits looked in my shirt. I grabbed my hardening cock and gave a stiff tug. God, what I wouldn't give to get laid right now. And since I wasn't seeing anyone and had no chance of bringing a woman home anytime soon, I imagined Katherine as I stroked my cock.

My breathing sped up as a flash of that night shot through my brain. She was straddling my lap, her tits right in my face. I was tugging one of her nipples in my mouth as she rode me hard. I remembered squeezing her ass as she threw her head back and groaned. I could feel her fingers digging into my shoulders. I stroked myself faster, my cock growing fatter in my large hand. God, what I wouldn't give to remember all that happened that night.

I swore I felt her wet pussy grabbing my cock just before I shot off in my hand, spilling thick ropes of my cum all over the shower wall. I stood there panting, shaking my head slightly. Was it really that good that night or was I just imagining it? It was pointless in wondering. It wasn't like I was ever going to see her again. Even if I hadn't given her the shove off when I dropped her at her car, it wasn't like I had any way of tracking her down. Not unless I went to the children's hospital and searched her out, and I wasn't that desperate. She was just a really good memory. One that I would use every time I needed a release until I found the woman I was meant to be with.

∽

I unlocked the office and headed over to my desk that was filled with paperwork that had piled up over the last few months. I really needed to get started on this shit, but I had a job over at Mrs. Cranston's house. She called me over every few months to fix something. Sometimes it was fixing a screen in a window. Other times, I fixed a plumbing issue. I didn't normally do small jobs, but she never took no for an answer. The first time I tried, she just pushed on as if I hadn't told her I wouldn't take the job. She said she would see me soon and that she had a pie waiting for me. It's not like I could let her pie go to waste, so I headed over there.

Now, as I stared at the mountain of paperwork on my desk, I wished that I had just turned down the damn pie. It was really good pie, but I couldn't say no to it. I could call her up and tell her that she was going to have to find someone else for the job, but I knew that wouldn't work. Maybe one of the guys would come in and they could do it for me. Hell, I was the boss, I would just order one of them over there.

Nodding to myself, I pulled out my phone and dialed R.J. "Hey, I have a job for you."

"I'm kinda in the middle of a job, boss."

"This won't take long."

"Yeah, but-"

"R.J., just do what I fucking ask," I snapped.

"Okay, but then you're leaving Pete to drywall by himself."

Fuck. I scrubbed my hand down my face and sighed. I couldn't leave him to do the drywalling by himself. Not on that kind of project. It was too big.

"Never mind."

I hung up and dialed Mike. "I got a job for you."

"Yeah, I know you do, but that's not happening today."

I could hear the humor in his voice. Everyone knew that when Mrs. Cranston called, it was going to be a bad day for me. Nothing ever went right.

"Why the hell not?"

"Lacy has that doctor's appointment up in Chicago today. I'm afraid you're on your own, boss."

"What about Rex?"

"He's starting the Colson project today. It wouldn't look too good if he didn't show up on time on the first day."

I sighed and resigned myself to the fact that I would be the one to work for Mrs. Cranston today. Fuck, I really hated days like this.

"Yeah, alright."

"Relax, boss. What's the worst that could happen?"

I heard him snort in laughter before I hung up on him. Fucking dickhead. As much as I didn't want to admit it, I needed help, and there was only one person I knew of that could take care of this for me. I hated the administrative side of things, but finding a person that could deal with it was even worse. So, I swallowed my pride and called my baby brother.

"I'm just about to head into a meeting," Robert answered.

"I need your help."

The line was silent.

"Did you hear me?"

"Yeah, I did, but I just never thought I would see the day that you would come to me and ask for it."

Whatever. Robert could be the corporate dickhead all he wanted. I didn't want to suck it up and ask for his help, but I didn't have a choice at this point.

"Look, I need an office manager and you know I suck at this shit. Can you find me one?"

"I don't know. I'm pretty busy-"

"I really need this."

"And I've got meetings all day."

"You have an assistant," I pointed out. "Have her reschedule one of them."

"And this wouldn't just take one day. I mean, I would have to do interviews, which would probably take up my Saturday."

"You're always here on the weekends anyway."

"On Sundays."

"You're still here. Giving up one Saturday won't kill you."

"Not necessarily, but still, it's a big ask."

I rolled my eyes and sighed. "Fine, what do you want?"

"Who said I wanted anything?"

"Well, you said that you were heading into a meeting, but you suddenly have the time to sit here and bullshit with me."

"I don't want anything. Not right now."

"Fine." I gritted my teeth, hating that he was pulling this shit with me. He was a lawyer and would always think like a lawyer. "When you need something, all you have to do is ask."

"I'll start looking into it immediately."

He hung up without further discussion, leaving me no choice but to go along with his way of doing things. I tossed my phone on the desk and went over my meetings for the day. I had a few jobs that I had to go check out before the end of the day, but first I had to get out to Mrs. Cranston's house. Fuck, I really hated this part of the job.

I snatched my phone off the desk and walked out of the office, ignoring the mounting work that I had to do. I drove over to Mrs. Cranston's house and walked up to the front door, preparing to knock. She beat me to it, pulling the door open with a smile.

"Eric, thank you so much for coming over."

"It's no problem, Mrs. Cranston. What did you need done today?"

"Oh, please. Call me Jane. I've known you since you were in diapers. I used to give your mother tips on how to keep your little tushy from getting diaper rash."

I smiled uncomfortably at her. I really hated hearing these stories from her. Mrs. Cranston had to be at least seventy years old, but the way she spoke to me sometimes made me think of a perverted little grandma. You wouldn't think that her talking about diaper rash would be perverted, but if you could see the look on her face, you would realize there was a gleam in her eyes that said not only was she thinking about my tushy, but she was also planning out what kind of cream to use if she ever got my pants off me.

I walked past her into the house and made sure to put my backside to the wall. I always felt like she was checking me out, but I could never catch her in the act. She was a sly fox, a woman always on the prowl.

"So, what's the job?"

"Oh," she laughed lightly and shook her head, placing her hand on her forehead. "You know, I almost forgot what needed to be done. I guess I'm just more forgetful than I used to be. Next thing you know, I'll forget that I didn't put underwear on this morning."

The twinkle in her eyes had me shuddering slightly. I was all for cougars. She was just a little too much of a cougar for my tastes. "The job?"

"Right. Of course, you're a busy man. I can tell by the size of your muscles. You do a lot of work with those arms. I can only imagine what your hands have done."

I cleared my throat uncomfortably, kicking myself for not having delegated this job sooner.

"I just need a rusty pipe replaced under the sink."

"Alright, I'll take a look at it and see if I have what I need in the truck."

She led me back to the kitchen and picked up a pipe on the counter. "I picked up this pipe at the hardware store. They told me this was what I needed."

The way she gripped it and almost stroked it was just creepy. I tried really hard not to look creeped out, but it took all my effort.

"Right. Let me take a look."

I opened the cabinet door under the sink and laid down on the ground, checking what exactly the problem was. Upon closer inspection, I saw this was a simple fix. I just had to grab a few tools and I would have this fixed in no time. I heard a click and ducked out front the cabinet to see what the noise was, but all I saw was Mrs. Cranston sitting at the table, playing on her phone.

"I need to grab some tools and I'll have you fixed up in no time."

"No rush, Eric. Oh, and don't forget about my pie before you leave." She ran her hand along her collarbone, playing lightly with the pearls around her neck. "I made you French Silk."

I turned to leave, but did a double take when I thought I saw her lick her bottom lip. I swallowed hard and quickly made my way to the door, storming out to my truck. I just wanted to get this pipe fixed and then I would get the fuck out of here. This woman was giving me the creeps. I took a deep breath and started to grab my tools when my phone rang. It was Rex.

"Yeah?"

"Heard you had a date with Mrs. Cranston this morning."

"It's not a date."

"Sure," he chuckled. "Do you really think her pipes needed to be fixed?"

"I saw it. The pipe was rusted."

He barked out a laugh. "Under the kitchen sink?"

"Yeah, when you sent me out there last year, it was to replace the same fucking pipe."

"Are you saying she rusted her pipes to get me out here?"

"I'm saying she was disappointed when I showed up last year. Why do you think no one else will take those jobs?"

"So, this woman is hitting on me and you're just allowing it?"

"Hey, I'm not the boss. You run the company."

Damn, he had me there. "Well, what the fuck am I supposed to do?"

"Don't bend over," he suggested.

"Kinda hard when I have to fix a pipe."

"Look, I'm gonna give you a little advice."

"Alright, let me hear it."

"Don't take her calls in the future."

"And how the fuck does that help me now?"

"It doesn't. I never said I had a solution for right now."

"You prick. I swear to God, I'm giving you the shit jobs for the next two weeks."

He laughed out loud, not giving a shit at all. "It'll all be worth it later tonight."

He hung up, leaving me wondering what the fuck that was supposed to mean. How would this be worth it to him later tonight? I grabbed my tools and headed inside. Fuck, I was never doing these jobs again.

KATHERINE

"Shit," I said as I looked down at the little pee stick in my hand. Positive. That wasn't good. I had only been with one man in the past few months and he didn't really seem like the guy that wanted to be saddled with a kid that was from a one night stand. He seemed totally disgusted that he had even had a one night stand. What the hell was I going to do now? I had to get to work, so I'd think about it later.

I threw my stuff in my backpack and got in my Jeep that had seen better days and headed off to work. The one thing about working at a children's hospital was that it always gave me a new lease on life. Those kids were so young and dealing with some of the most horrible diseases, yet they were still so brave and optimistic.

I checked in at the desk with one of my fellow nurses and one of my best friends, Chrissy. There was a reason that we got along so well. We had similar interests, but we also both knew the demands of the job and had similar feelings on how to let go of the tension of working in the children's ward.

"How are the kiddos today?"

"Good. Casey's back."

My face fell. Casey was a little girl that had been battling cancer for two years now. She was seven years old and one of the strongest little girls I had ever known. If she was back in the hospital, that meant that either something had gone wrong with her treatments or she was no longer responding. My job was to take care of her and make sure she was comfortable and had everything she needed, but I was also there to care for her parents and guide them through this. They were scared for their little girl and though they wanted to be strong, it was hard to do after so much stress and frustration.

"That little girl is such a fighter. What went wrong this time?"

"Breathing problems. Her mother checked on her in the middle of the night and she was hardly breathing. They called 9-1-1 and rushed her to the local hospital, but she was transferred here once they had her stabilized. Doctor Wesley has been running tests since she got in."

"That poor family. They've been through so much already. I can't imagine being a parent and dealing with something like that," I said, absent-mindedly touching my stomach. When I looked back at Chrissy, her eyes were wide with shock.

"No."

I shook my head slowly.

"Don't do that. You tell me right now," she demanded. I swallowed hard and felt tears prick at my eyes.

"I'm two weeks late."

"Did you take a test?"

I nodded and sniffled. "Pregnant."

"Do you know who the father is?"

I slapped her on the arm and shook my head. "Of course I know who the father is. I'm not a slut."

"Sorry, it's just, you went through that whole 'I don't need a boyfriend' phase. I didn't know how many men you slept with."

"I slept with one and unfortunately, I was drunk and there's a lot I don't remember."

"Do you at least remember the good stuff?"

"I remember that he was the best I'd ever had. At least, I think so. Do you think when you're drunk sex just seems better, or it actually is?"

"I don't know. I've never had drunken sex."

"Really?" She had been married to a man named Tom for three years now and I had to hear multiple times a week about the wild monkey sex they had.

"What? Don't judge me. Tom says that he wants to be fully aware of everything he's doing to me."

That made sense. They didn't exactly have a conventional sex life. When the *Fifty Shades* movie came out, they decided to see if it spiced up their sex life. Apparently it had, and now I had to hear about their new found kink practically every week. Being a single girl, I really hated to hear about all that. It's not like I had anyone to try it out with. Not that I wanted to. I was all about the normal sex. Normal was good.

"So, who was he?"

"A guy I met at a bar. I thought I was meeting a blind date and so did he. We didn't find out until the next morning that we weren't even supposed to be meeting each other."

"Have you seen him since?"

I snorted. "Not this guy. Very stiff. Not exactly the type to go for one night stands."

"There are actually guys like that?" she asked, her mouth dropped open.

"I guess," I shrugged. "He drove me back to my car and made it very clear that he didn't normally do that stuff and we wouldn't be repeating it. He's definitely the family man type."

"Well, that could be good or bad. Good, because he's a family man, but bad if he doesn't want a family with *you*."

"I know. I haven't even thought about how I'm going to break it to him."

"Just rip the bandaid off."

I leaned on the counter and tapped my fingernails on my teeth as I thought about it. "Maybe I could send him an e-card or a bouquet of chocolates."

"Like, a congratulations?"

"Something like that. You know, if I get him chocolate, maybe it would soften the blow."

"I think that would only work for a woman. You would need to try something that would better suit him. What does he do?"

"I have no clue."

"You could send him a big box of condoms," she suggested. I narrowed my eyes at her and waited for her to connect the dots. "Right. Not really necessary anymore."

"Well, that's assuming we ever had sex again. He might not want any part of it. Or, he could want the baby, but not want anything to do with me."

"Well, then the condoms could be like a reminder. 'Don't knock up the next girl you sleep with' sort of thing."

"Yeah, because I'm sure as soon as I tell him I'm pregnant, he's going to go out and look for another woman to screw."

"You never know. You don't want to end up as one of the many carrying his child."

"You know, I really wonder about the way your mind works sometimes. I think I'll stick with the good old surprise factor. You know, show up at his house and say, *Surprise! I'm having your baby.*"

"I still think you should get him a box of condoms."

"I'll keep that in mind. I'm going to start my rounds."

I got started on checking on patients and by the time I made it to Casey's room, I had fully prepared myself to face the little girl. She was looking out the window, but when I entered, her face lit up.

"Kiki! I was hoping I would see you."

I smiled and walked over to the sink, washing my hands as I spoke to her over my shoulder. Her parents were standing by her bed, giving me a smile as I carried on with Casey.

"I was just telling Chrissy that I thought you came here just to see me. How are you feeling?"

She glanced over at her parents who were now talking in the corner. "Good. I think I just scared Mommy and Daddy a little."

I crinkled my nose and nodded. "Yeah, mommies and daddies tend to get scared easily. But you know what?"

"What?"

"I think we should make them feel better and wait to see what the doctor says. What do you think?"

"I guess. I don't want Mommy and Daddy to be scared."

"Me neither. Besides, if we wait to hear from the doctor, I get to spend some more time with you."

"Don't you have other kids to check on?"

"I already checked on all of them and I have my phone on me, so I'll get a call if someone needs me."

I got up from the bed and went over to the closet that held the games and got out *Shoots and Ladders*.

"You're going to play a game with me?" Her eyes grew wide as I sat down on the bed with her.

"Of course."

I nodded to her parents, letting them know that I would stay with Casey for a while. It was hard on parents to bring their child in and then wait around for answers. Sometimes they just needed a few minutes to talk to one another without worrying about being overheard by their child. Sometimes, they just needed a break from the stress of it all. That's what I loved about my job. I loved knowing that I was not only helping the child, but the parents also in whatever battle they were fighting.

⁓

When I got off of work, I still hadn't figured out how I was going to tell Eric about our little surprise. I had thought about waiting, but it would drive me crazy if I had to keep this secret to myself for another day. Besides, I wouldn't want to be kept in the dark if the situation was reversed. I stopped at the pharmacy on the way to his house and picked up a large box of condoms as a joke. Maybe Chrissy was right and it would break the ice.

I pulled down his long drive about ten miles outside the town limits and got a look at the house in the light of day. The last time I had been out here, I was hung over and wasn't paying attention too much. The house was old, but well kept. It looked like it had just been painted in the past year or two. There was a beautiful porch with a swing that I desperately wanted to sit out on with a cup of tea in the morning. I could watch the trees swaying in the breeze and watch the sunsets at night. I sighed because that wasn't my life and it wouldn't be. If I was lucky, my child would get to spend time out here with his or her father and get to experience the beauty of all this.

I parked in the back and got out of my truck with the bag of condoms. This was so stupid. Eric opened the screen door and stepped out onto the porch in jeans and t-shirt that clung to his perfect body. I may have been drunk the night we slept together, but one thing I remembered was his body. It was perfect in every way and the girl that snagged him would be one very lucky woman.

My eyes roamed over the muscles stretching his shirt sleeves and the slight sweat stain around his neck line. Some women might find that gross, but it was such a turn on to me. He was a working man, and it showed on every inch of his gorgeous body. And the way he walked out on the porch, his thigh muscles moving beneath his jeans had me licking my lips in anticipation.

"Katherine?"

"Yeah. Hi," I said awkwardly, as I pulled myself out of staring at his amazing body. I refrained from fanning myself and cleared my throat, reminding myself why I was here. I walked toward him and I could see the unease in his stance. He obviously thought I was here for more, something he already told me he couldn't give.

"What are you doing here?"

"Um, can we talk?"

The screen door swung open and one of his brothers walked out. He was obviously younger because he dressed like today's version of a hippie. He had this weird haircut that looked like the barber forgot to cut half his head. He wore tight jeans that were around the ankles, but baggy around the thighs, which I just didn't understand. And his shirt…It was like watching some crazy time warp.

"Hey, quiche girl!" The brother grinned, pulling his earbuds out of his ears. "Came back for seconds, huh?"

Eric narrowed his eyes, obviously wondering the same thing.

"Um, no. I didn't come back for seconds. I just wanted to talk for a minute and then I'll be on my way."

"You knocked her up?" the brother shouted.

Eric's head whipped around to his brother and he looked at him in confusion. "What the hell are you talking about?"

"She just came to talk? It's been, what, a month since she was here? Do the math, bro."

Eric slowly looked back at me and raised an eyebrow. I thrust the bag forward into his hands.

"Here, I got this for you. Kind of a joke present or whatever."

He opened the bag and pulled out the box of condoms. The brother started laughing hysterically, slapping Eric on the back as he bent over in laughter.

"That's woke AF. I bet you're turnt, man."

Eric stood there staring at me, totally spacing out as to what I had told him and the nonsense his brother was babbling on about. I watched Eric carefully, the color was slowly draining from his face and his right eye was twitching like crazy. He was losing it.

"Eric?" I asked softly, staring at his soft, blue eyes, wondering if he could actually see me.

His eyes glazed over as he stared off somewhere over my shoulder. I didn't know what was happening, but I had the feeling I had to move closer to him in case he didn't stay upright. I moved just in time.

"Catch him!"

His brother turned and caught him under the arms right before he collapsed to the ground. I knelt down beside him and checked his pulse, satisfied that I hadn't killed him with my news.

"That could have gone better," I muttered.

"Just give him a minute. I'm sure once he thinks it over, he'll be turnt."

"I'm not sure what that means."

The brother rolled his eyes. "He'll be excited."

"I'm sorry, I don't remember your name."

"Andrew."

"Nice to see you again, Andrew. I'm Kiki."

"Kiks. It's nice to see you again too. Especially now that you're going to be his bae."

"Bae?"

"His girl."

"Doesn't bae mean poop?" I asked.

"Only if you're Danish. This is so cool. I'm gonna be an uncle. I'm gonna have a little dude to teach things to. I can't even," he said as he stared off in the distance.

I stared at him, waiting for him to finish his thought, but when he didn't, I had to ask. "You can't even what?"

"Huh?"

"You didn't finish your sentence. You started to say something."

He smirked and winked at me. "Listen, I gotta bounce. Are you going to be okay with him?"

"Uh, sure. Maybe you could help me get him inside first?"

"Nah. I got this." He walked inside and returned a minute later with a bucket and upended it over Eric's head. He jerked and spluttered as the water poured over his face and sat up quickly.

"What the fuck happened?"

"Your brother informed you that I was pregnant and you passed out."

He started to sway again, but his brother held him up.

"Maybe I came at a bad time," I said standing. Eric shook his head.

"No, wait. We need to talk...figure out how this happened."

I tilted my head slightly, a smirk growing on my face. "There's not really much to figure out. We had drunken sex and now I'm pregnant. Mystery solved."

"Let's go inside and talk," he said, turning and opening the door for me. He was very much the gentleman, holding the door for me.

"Would you like a drink?"

"Water, please."

He nodded and got a glass of water for me, handing it over as his eyes flicked to my stomach. Self-consciously, I placed my hand there and then pulled on my shirt, like I could cover it or something.

"So, what are you planning to do with it…the baby…the fetus," he spluttered.

"I'm planning on keeping it. What you want to do is up to you."

"What I want to do," he said slowly. He nodded to himself and started pacing the kitchen. I could see this was going to take awhile, so I pulled out a chair and flung my bag on the kitchen table as I sat. I pulled out my phone and checked my emails, responding to a few from my family and friends. Then I took out a nail file and filed down my fingernails. They had been getting too long and were starting to bother me when I pulled on the latex gloves at work. When he was still pacing after that, I pulled out my buffing block and finished off my nails.

A half hour had passed and he was still pacing. I was getting hungry. My shift had just ended before I came here and I was tired and ready for food and my bed. But this had to be talked about at least a little bit. I stood and walked to his fridge, pulling out some ingredients to make dinner. He didn't even seem to notice. I was only going to make spaghetti, but glancing back at him, I figured I'd better make some meat for him. Guys weren't generally just carb lovers.

Another half hour later, I had spaghetti and Italian sausage plated and sitting on the table. Eric was still pacing, muttering to himself and lost in his thoughts. I started eating, studying him as I chewed my spaghetti. He was very handsome, not at all someone I would normally go for. Not because he was hot, but because he was obviously neurotic. I just wanted a nice, normal man. Was that possible? Did they even exist?

I shook my head and went back to my spaghetti. By the time I finished, I was getting a little irritated. If women waited for men to solve all the world's problems, we would die before they came up with a solution. I stood and walked over to him, tapping him on the shoulder. He turned to me, his eyebrows pinched in thought.

"Yeah?"

"Are you done?"

"Done?"

"You've been pacing the kitchen for an hour and a half. I made dinner for you, and while it's been fun to watch you wear a hole in the floor, I'd like to go home at some point tonight. So, would you like me to come back later or are you ready to talk about this?"

He glanced at the plate on the table and then back at me. "You made dinner?" He looked around the kitchen. "When did that happen?" he muttered to himself.

"Alright, well, this has been fun, but you're obviously still processing all this, so I'm gonna go." I grabbed a pen and paper from my bag and wrote down my name and number for him. "Call me when you've figured out…whatever it is you're trying to figure out."

I turned to go, but he grabbed onto my arm, stopping me in my tracks. "I've figured it out. Please, sit."

I pulled out the chair again and plopped down, ready to hear this brilliant idea he came up with.

"You're a man. I'm a woman."

I rolled my eyes. "I think you've got that backwards."

He frowned and bit at his lip. "That came out wrong."

"I got that much."

"What I meant was that a woman and a man will naturally follow their base instincts. It's a subconscious urge that's directed by primeval, animalistic motivations. It's self-serving, and unfortunately, selfishness is one of the base instincts that's ingrained in the human psyche."

I rolled my eyes, wondering if his scientific explanation was over.

"Our base instincts are the core of our very being. The foundation in which we relate to our most tangible desires. Obviously, we all desire love and meaning. Which for some could be just a taco, but in our case was more primitive. Ours was based on hunger, fear, love…"

He paced the room some more and I wondered why the hell I had chosen to sleep with this man. How was this the father of my child? Was he going to lecture our child about everything too? I was starting to see less of the sexy man that I fantasized about and more of a professor that was about to hand me a D on my psych paper.

"In short, our emotions are more direct and visceral. We use less of our minds, our control."

"So, you're telling me that we fucked because we wanted to and didn't have any control over our bodies, but we shouldn't be ashamed by this because we followed our base instincts?"

He nodded sharply.

"Where did you come up with that? *Psychology Today?*"

He shook his head and held out his phone. "Wikipedia."

I stood, sighing and throwing my bag over my shoulder. "It took you an hour and a half to come up with that?"

He frowned at me.

"Thank you, Freud, but I already figured that out."

"Where are you going?"

"Home. I worked all day and I'm tired."

"But we haven't finished talking."

"When you have a solution, give me a call."

"I do have a solution. We're going to get married."

I stopped and turned back to him, my mouth gaping. "Excuse me?"

"Katherine, it only makes sense. We're having a baby. A baby needs a stable, loving home and we can provide that. I won't have my child raised as a bastard."

"And I won't have my child raised listening to lectures on our base instincts. This isn't a solution."

"Yes, it is. You'll need help with the baby and I can provide a stable home. I already have the house and I have a successful business. I can provide for both of you."

"I have a townhouse and I have a steady job. I don't see the difference."

"Look, we did things all backwards here. A man and a woman are supposed to be married *before* they have a baby. We can rectify that now. We'll just go to the courthouse and get married. Our child will have two loving parents and everything will be fine," he said with a nod.

This man thought he had it all figured out, but he was forgetting one thing, we barely knew each other. I wasn't so naive to think that every marriage was based on love, but I believed that it should be. A baby was no reason to get married. He had the right intentions, but it would be a disaster.

"What about love?"

"What about love? I'm just trying to do what's best for our child."

"What's best for our child or what's best for you?"

"What are you talking about?"

I sighed and ran a hand across my forehead in frustration. "It's pretty obvious that you do things a certain way. You like everything to be in order, and that's fine, but I'm not going to marry you just so that it looks good to others."

"That's not what I'm suggesting. This is just what people do. It's the right thing to do. A child needs a stable home life. With us living together, we can give this child that."

"Not if I stab you," I muttered.

"What?" he asked, obviously not hearing me.

"I don't want to marry someone because it's the right thing. I want to marry someone because I love him. What you and I had was a good night of fucking." I tilted my head in thought. "At least, I think it was good. Frankly, I was a little wasted. How do you even know that we would be compatible?"

"I can pretty much guarantee that we wouldn't be if I remember the bar correctly," he muttered.

"Then why would you even suggest it? I'm going to go home now and I'll call you to let you know what's going on with appointments and whatever."

"That's it?"

"What do you mean?"

"I mean-" he shook his head and swore. "I mean that we're going to have a baby and you're just walking out of here. It feels like we should be doing something. Getting prepared or...I don't know. Something."

"We have nine months until this baby comes. There's plenty of time for planning. We don't have to solve everything tonight."

I kind of hated leaving him. He looked so lost and it made me feel bad for him. I had a next step. I had to get vitamins and start looking after myself better. I would have to start looking into what I needed to do to my townhouse to prepare. He just stood there with his hands shoved in his pockets like he didn't have a clue what to do.

I snatched his phone and called myself, then handed it back to him. "I'll call you, okay?"

He nodded and I got in my car, leaving the man to brood in silence. There was nothing I could do for him right now. It was exactly like he said, we probably wouldn't be compatible and pretending that this was more than a one night stand gone wrong wouldn't help either of us.

ERIC

I sipped my coffee on the front porch as I stared out at the countryside. It was peaceful out here, and that gave me time to think about my current predicament. A baby. God, I was so fucked. I wanted a wife and I wanted kids, but I never planned on having them like this. This was just fucked up.

A car pulled in the driveway and I sighed. Robert was here early for a Sunday. He was never up before eight on the weekends, so this made me nervous. It was barely six-thirty. He was dressed down today, wearing only jeans and a t-shirt instead of his usual suit.

"I see you lost the suit. Did you get fired?" I asked.

He climbed the steps and sat down in the chair next to me. "No, asshole. I'm here to do your fucking job."

"Which would be?"

"Find you an assistant."

Shit. I had forgotten all about that. "On a Sunday?"

"I couldn't get the day off yesterday, so I set up some interviews for today."

"You need me there?"

"Why the fuck would I need you there? I've gotten this far without you. I'm pretty sure I can handle the rest on my own."

"You're pissy this morning."

"Yeah, well, I had to get up at the ass crack of dawn to get here in time to help your sorry ass out."

"Any good candidates?"

He ignored me, just sat there staring off in the distance.

"Hey, did you hear me?"

He rubbed the back of his neck and sighed. "Look, there's a candidate, but I'm not sure how good she is. But I want you to give her a chance."

"And why the fuck would I do that? I need someone to make my life better, not worse."

"It's Anna."

"Anna? Anna who?"

"Anna Richards."

"Who the fuck is that?" The name sounded familiar, but I couldn't place it. Anna- "Anna, as in your high school girlfriend, Anna?"

A guilty look crossed his face as he shrugged and looked away. "Yeah."

"Why the hell would I hire her? Is she even qualified? Doesn't she work at the gas station?"

"She had some trouble finding work."

"She's been there for the last ten fucking years, Robert. Does she have any experience working in an office?"

"Look, she may not be the most qualified, but I need you to do this for me, no questions asked."

I choked out a laugh. He was insane if he thought I was going to leave my office in the hands of someone that didn't know how to run it. "No. I need someone that can organize the office. I can't just let anyone in there and have them fuck it up."

"She's been taking classes at the community college. Mostly computer classes. She at least knows how to work a computer."

"I know how to work a computer, asshole. I need someone that can run an office."

"She'll learn."

"The answer is still no."

"Look, you need an office manager and she needs a job. She's a hard worker."

"What are my other options?"

"Well, Mrs. Cranston came in and applied for the job."

I cringed and shook my head. "Who else? There has to be someone more qualified."

He sighed, running his hand across his jaw. "You said you would do me a favor-"

"No, you coerced me into giving you that."

"And I'm calling up that favor now. Look, I'm asking you to give her six months to figure shit out. If it doesn't work out, then I'll figure something else out."

"What am I missing here? Why do you need this so bad? Do you have a thing for this woman still?"

"Look, when I left town, I was shitty to her. The way I left things… I just need this favor."

I looked at my brother and tried to figure out what the hell was going on, but he had a good poker face. He wasn't going to tell me shit unless he wanted to. But this was obviously important to him. He wouldn't be asking me like this unless he really needed this.

"Fine, I'll give her six months, but I'm serious, I'll fire her if she doesn't do the fucking job."

"That's all I'm asking, man."

"Shit." I leaned back in my seat, a little pissed right now. I didn't want to take the risk right now. I had too much other shit on my mind and I needed the office to run smoothly, but I couldn't say no to my brother. I knew I was going to regret this, but family came first, and you didn't say no to family. "Don't make me regret this."

∼

I walked into the office Monday morning, still reeling from the bomb Katherine had dropped on me. I was fucked up all through the end of last week and the weekend. Everyone knew something was wrong with me, but I just ignored everyone and pretended that I was totally cool. It didn't go over so well. Luckily, Andrew had better things to do than out me to my brothers. I just needed a little time to figure shit out. I needed to know how to talk to Katherine and make this work.

First though, I needed to figure out this shit with my new office manager. She should be here by now. I had to get out on my newest job site and check in with the guys. At the rate this morning was going, I wouldn't be running on schedule today.

The door to the office was flung open and Anna walked in, trying to grab at the door as she ran into the office. Her bulky purse was flung over her shoulder, looking like it was weighing her down. Her dark brown hair was pulled back in a messy ponytail, making me wonder why she even bothered pulling it up. It didn't look like she had put in too much effort. Her clothes weren't professional, but that didn't really matter in this office. We were a construction company, not a bank.

"You're late."

"I know. I'm so sorry. My car wouldn't start this morning and I had to catch a ride."

I didn't say anything as I glanced at my watch. "Alright, for today, I just need you to organize the office. The filing cabinet is over there." I took her through the computer and showed her how I organized everything. "After the office is organized, I'll have the office number rerouted from my phone to here. But for now, let's just get this shit organized. If there's anything important for me, put it in this box," I pointed to my inbox. "Any questions?"

"Yes, where's the coffee?"

I looked at her in surprise. "The coffee?"

"You have a coffee maker, don't you? Isn't that a standard item in most offices?"

"Uh…well, I'm never here, so I always pick up coffee on my way."

"What about donuts?"

"Donuts?" I asked in confusion.

"You know, yummy goodness that you eat for breakfast? Although, I'm not against having it for a snack or a light lunch."

"I don't…"

She rolled her eyes and sighed. "Fine, no yummy goodness and no coffee. I can do this," she said under her breath.

I was confused. Was the woman actually demanding that I have coffee and donuts for her every morning? It was her first day on the job. I checked my watch again, and sighed. I was late.

"Right, I check in every morning, but I don't usually come back here at the end of the day. If you need to contact me, here's my number," I said, scribbling it on some paper. "Any questions?"

"Yeah, how have you run a business without an office manager up until this point?"

"Easy, I just shift everything from this pile," I pointed to the big stack, "to this pile." My hand rested on an even larger stack on the other side of the computer. "All the bills are taken out and paid, but everything else just kind of adds up."

"This should be fun," she muttered under her breath.

"Well, I can find someone else for the job if you're not up to it."

She looked up at me with a smirk. "I think I can handle it."

"Good."

I turned on my heel and walked out before I snapped at her. I was pissed that Robert had put me in this position, but I was even more pissed that she didn't have outstanding qualifications. I just needed something to go right today. I walked out of the office and headed to my truck, grumbling to myself the whole way. This was going to be a disaster and I knew it.

I was only halfway to my first job when she called. Rolling my eyes, I tried to answer nicely. "It can't be good if you're calling me already."

"I'm locked out of your computer. You gave me the wrong password."

"No, I didn't. I wrote it down for you."

"And I entered it exactly as you wrote it," she shot back.

"Then try again."

"I can't. I'm locked out."

"Then find someone that can get you back in."

"I would, but I can't get online to look up anyone that works with computers."

"Then use your phone."

"I don't have a smartphone, jackass."

I pulled over on the side of the road, my jaw clenching in anger. "What the fuck did you just say?"

"Not everyone has a smartphone. I don't have one."

"Did you just call me a jackass?"

"Well, if the shoe fits."

"Did you not want the job? Because I can find someone more qualified."

She snorted. "Good luck with that. Nobody else would touch this place with a ten-foot pole."

I clenched my jaw in irritation. Fuck, I already hated this woman and she had only worked in the office for a half hour. "Look, just figure it out. I'm trying to get out to a job."

"Right. Thanks for the help."

She hung up on me, leaving me fuming. I called Robert.

"How's everything going?" he asked hesitantly.

"Well, she's already called me a jackass, so how do you think it's going?"

He laughed slightly, but I could tell that he didn't know what to say.

"Look, I said that I would give her a chance, but she's already fucked up. She got locked out of my computer and can't get back in. If you want her to stick around, find someone that can go over and help her get logged back in. If this isn't fixed by the end of the day, she's fired. I need someone reliable, Robert."

"Alright, I'll take care of it. Just don't do anything drastic."

"I can't deal with this shit right now. I have a business to run. I can't afford fuckups."

"Yeah, I got it. I'll take care of it."

"Good."

I hung up and beat the shit out of my dashboard for a minute. I needed something to go right in my life right now. Between work and my fucked up personal life, things had to turn around for me now, or I was going to lose my shit.

~

My brain was going a million different directions the rest of the day. Anna kept calling with questions and problems. I was irritated as hell, but mostly because she kept calling when I was trying to figure out what the hell to do about Katherine. That was a problem that had to be solved immediately. I couldn't afford to just not think about it. I needed to find a solution and get it going.

I walked into the office at the end of the day and stopped right inside the door. My files were all over the floor, scattered in piles. Anna looked up from her spot on the floor, a pen stuck in her mouth and a notepad in her hands.

"Just chill. I've got this."

I ran my hand through my hair and stood there speechless. "What the fuck? I wanted this place cleaned up. You have the whole fucking filing cabinet emptied."

"Yeah, but I noticed something in one of the files and then I started looking at the others and-"

"I don't give a shit!" I shouted. "Fuck! I wanted this organized. I told you what to do." I glanced at the desk and noticed the stacks of paper still sat there. "You didn't even do the fucking paperwork."

"Hey, you asked me to organize this place. It's a mess, and I have a lot of work to do to get it in shape." I glanced toward the window and did a double take when I saw papers taped to the window. I stormed over and pulled one down, shaking my head at the sight before me. "What is this?"

"Okay, don't be mad, but I was going through some files and noticed these charges on the accounts, but I couldn't figure out what they were for. So, I started going through the files and found all these other charges that were similar. So, I started-"

"I didn't ask you to be Sherlock Holmes. I just wanted the office organized."

"At least let me show you-"

"Get out," I said tightly. I was barely controlling my anger right now. This was the last thing I needed at the end of the day.

"Excuse me? You're not even listening to what-"

"I said, get the fuck out."

She huffed and walked over to the desk, grabbing her purse and flinging it over her shoulder before storming out. Sighing, I walked over to the desk and took a seat. I looked down at the paper I had taken from the window and looked it over. At first, I didn't see anything. But as I looked at it again, I noticed a strange charge on there. The invoice was from one of my suppliers, and if I was guessing right, they were adding on charges and hoping I wouldn't notice, which I hadn't, because I never organized my fucking office. I stood and walked to the window, pulling down the other invoices. All of them had the same fucking charge on there. They were gouging me, and I had allowed it to happen because I was too fucking distracted with work.

Fuck. I pulled out my phone and dialed Anna's number. "Anna?"

"Fuck off, asshole."

She hung up before I could say anything else. I dialed again. "Just hear me out."

"Like you heard me out? I don't work for assholes."

She hung up again. Shit. This was going to take some finesse, something I didn't really have right now. I called Robert.

"What do you want, asshole?"

"I need a favor."

"I already did one for you."

"I'll owe you."

That got his attention. "What's the favor?"

"I need you to call Anna and convince her to come back to work tomorrow."

It was quiet for a moment. "Why would I need to convince her to go into her job?"

"Well, I was having a bad day and I sort of fucked up. Let's just say that she's not answering my calls."

"I don't know. It's gonna cost you."

"I already said I would owe you one."

"Yeah, but I'm not exactly her favorite person either. I'm not sure this is such a great idea."

"Then why the fuck did you hire her?"

"Because she needed the job and I knew she would do a good job. She just needed a chance."

"Well, I need you to get her back here."

"You're going to have to say please."

I gritted my teeth. "Please."

"Alright, I'll see what I can do, but if you fuck this up again, I can't do jack shit about it."

"Understood."

I hung up, then taped the papers back where she had them on the window. I had a feeling that I should bring by some donuts in the morning or something to make up for yelling at her. I was so lost in my head today about my situation with Katherine that I couldn't even concentrate on work. Then I snapped at Anna and fired her when she was just trying to do her job. Something had to give, and that something was my situation with Katherine. I needed to find a way to fix it before it ruined every aspect of my life.

I knew that was easier said than done. I was fucked. How had I screwed up so bad? Not only did I sleep with a girl that I had just met, but I got her pregnant. I wasn't even sure I liked her. She definitely wasn't a woman I would normally date. She didn't seem all that concerned with anything but having a good time. Then again, she did say she was a nurse. Maybe she was just trying to blow off some steam.

And then there was the way that she delivered the news. It was like she was totally cool with having a baby out of wedlock. What the fuck was that? Didn't all women want to be married before the kid came? My brothers were going to give me so much shit over this. I was always the responsible one out of all of us. I was the one they came to when they were in trouble and needed guidance. Who was I going to turn to? The only one that was even interested in a relationship was my brother, Derek, and he was almost five hundred miles away.

How would I even tell everyone? And my parents, God, they were going to be so fucking disappointed in me. When they heard about Derek and Claire, they flew out to meet her after we did. They fell in love with her instantly. What would they say about Katherine? She called herself Kiki. It sounded like a stripper name. What would I say when I called them?

Hey, Mom and Dad. I got this girl pregnant and I don't know anything about her other than her name and that she's a nurse. She refused to marry me and didn't even care if I was involved.

My parents were going to kill me. I could see my mom walking up to me and slapping me upside the head for not protecting *that young girl*. And my dad would chastise me for not being his responsible son. If there was one thing I couldn't stand, it was disappointing my parents. For as long as I could remember, I always did my best to make my parents proud. I never wanted to let them down and make them feel like they had failed. They already had one son that had gone MIA in the family. That was hard enough for my parents to swallow, but this? This would kill my mother for sure. I had to find a way to convince Katherine to marry me, or at the very least, get engaged.

I pulled out my phone and dialed the number she had given me. It rang a few times and then she answered, her sweet voice echoing through the phone. How had I not noticed that before?

"Hello?" she said again.

"Hi. This is Eric Cortell, the father of your child."

She chuckled on the other end. "Yes, Eric. I remember you."

"Right, well," I cleared my throat uncomfortably, rubbing at the back of my neck. I felt like a fucking idiot. "It's not like we've been properly acquainted. I wasn't sure…anyway," I said clearing my throat. "Um, I'd like to talk to you the next time you're available."

"Okay, um, I don't work on Wednesday. Will that work for you?"

"Sure, can you do breakfast?"

"How about afternoon? I work the night before."

"Would you like to come out here for dinner? I can cook and then we can talk in a more private setting."

"What about your brothers? Not that I mind them being there, but if they'll be listening in, it won't be very private."

"I'll make sure they make themselves scarce."

"Okay, I'll come over about 5:30."

"Great. I'll see you Wednesday."

I hung up and took a deep breath. This was all just so out of my realm of expertise. I didn't even know where to begin. The first thing I had to do was figure out how to cook.

~

I was scrambling. Dinner was a catastrophe. I burned the chicken to the point of it looking like charcoal, the mashed potatoes were soupy, and the asparagus was so soft that it hung limply from the fork. I couldn't serve this to her. She was going to be here any minute and I had nothing to feed her. I quickly rummaged through the cabinets and found a box of Macaroni and Cheese. It would barely be enough to feed me, but I would go hungry so that she had something to eat. It was the least I could do since I had promised her dinner.

I quickly got the water going and got to work on throwing away the chicken and asparagus. The mashed potatoes couldn't go in the garbage. They were pretty much liquid right now. The pots and pans were stacked in the sink and it smelled like there had been a fire in here. There sort of had been, but I opened the windows and hoped for the best. The macaroni was almost ready when I heard her knock at the door. Thank goodness she was running late.

I went over and opened the door, feeling nervous about all this. What I was going to ask of her was a tall order. I should have taken her out to a nice restaurant. I should have changed my fucking clothes. I still had on my work clothes and I smelled like sweat. I was already failing big time with my whole plan.

"Hi," I said, swinging the door open.

"Hi. Sorry I'm late."

"Not a problem." I gestured for her to enter and cringed when she started sniffing the air.

"Did something burn?"

"Uh," I quickly glanced at the sink and then back at her. "Yeah, sorry. Dinner is...well, it's in the garbage now. How does mac and cheese sound?"

She pulled her lips between her teeth and stifled a laugh. "That's fine. We could have just gone out to dinner."

"Yeah, I wanted to do this here. I thought I could make dinner and it would be more private."

"You don't actually know how to cook, do you?"

"I can cook," I said defensively. "I just usually grill out." I shrugged as I stared at the stove. "It's different *inside* the house."

She nodded, holding back her laughter. "Well, you're in luck because I love mac and cheese."

"Good." I went to the stove and finished making dinner and then served her a much larger bowl than my own.

"Why are you giving me more? Shouldn't you be eating more? You're a guy."

"Yeah, but you're eating for two."

"That doesn't mean I need two servings," she smiled.

There was no way I was taking food from a pregnant lady. I didn't care how hungry I was, there were just things that you didn't do and that was one of them.

I cleared my throat and swallowed a large gulp of water. "So, the reason I asked you here is for a favor."

"What kind of favor?"

"Look, I think that we both know that I'm not the type of guy to find myself in this position. I do things a certain way so that things always turn out the way they should. This is just so outside of anything I ever thought would happen to me."

"Okay, I'm not sure where you're going with this."

I took a deep breath and let it fly. What did I have to lose? "I want you to pretend to be my girlfriend."

She stared at me for a few seconds, her eyebrows furrowing as she tried to figure out my angle. "You want me to pretend to be your girlfriend when we're having a baby," she said slowly.

"Yeah. See, I'm always the reliable one in the family. I'm the one that doesn't screw up. I'm the one that's never let down my parents."

"So, this is because you don't want to disappoint your family?"

"Basically."

"What about your brothers? I mean, they already know that we had a one night stand. You can't hide this from them."

"It's for my parents' benefit. I can talk to my brothers and they'll have my back. I mean, I'm sure I'll owe them for the rest of my life, but they won't let me down."

"So, we pretend to be a couple for your parents. What happens when it falls apart? I'll look like the horrible girlfriend and you'll come off as the devoted father."

"Well, they live in North Carolina, so it's not like they'll be around to know if we're together or not."

"You want me to pretend indefinitely?" she asked, her eye widening in horror.

"Well..."

"What about when I meet someone and want to get married? Am I supposed to still pretend that I'm your girlfriend? Take off my wedding rings when they come to town? And what about holidays? Am I supposed to see your family all the time instead of seeing my own?"

I scratched my head, not really knowing how to answer that. "I guess I hadn't really thought of that."

"What part of this did you actually think through? Because it sounds to me like you don't want to be seen as irresponsible. But let me tell you something, I'm the one that's going to be showing in a few months, walking around without a ring. I'm the one people will judge. You're worried about your parents who are thousands of miles away."

"Look, I didn't say it was a great plan-"

"It's not a plan at all," she said, shoving back from the table and standing. "You know, if you wanted me to actually be your girlfriend, you could have suggested that we go out on a date and get to know each other or ask to at least spend some time with me."

"I'm sorry," I said sincerely. "I wasn't thinking." She rolled her eyes and picked her bowl up from the table, digging into her macaroni and cheese. "Would you like to spend some time together?"

"Seriously? *Now* you're asking me?" She shoved another spoonful in her mouth and set the bowl back down. "I'll call you when I have my first appointment," she said as she walked out the door.

"That could have gone better," I muttered. I sighed and leaned back in my chair, wondering how in the hell I was going to break this news to my parents. I was a grown man. I didn't need their approval. I just wanted it. As silly as it sounded, I wanted them to be proud of me.

KATHERINE

"So, did you tell the baby daddy?" Chrissy asked as she leaned across the counter of the reception desk. I hadn't been working with her this week, so I hadn't had the chance to fill her in yet. "Did he totally freak out? They always freak out."

"Well, it didn't exactly go the way I thought it would." I glanced around to make sure the she-devil, my boss, was nowhere in sight. "He passed out."

"No way," she said, her eyes wide.

"And then he paced his kitchen for an hour and a half muttering to himself."

"What did you do?" she asked, pulling out a box of Lemonheads.

I gave her a funny look. "This isn't a movie."

"It sure feels like one. So, what happened next?" she motioned me to hurry up.

"He went on some tirade about us following our base instincts and how what happened was perfectly natural."

She grimaced and popped another Lemonhead in her mouth. "Okay, this no longer sounds like an interesting movie. He sounds uptight. Is he a professor or something?"

I shrugged. "I'm not entirely sure. We haven't really covered all that stuff. In fact, the only thing we really covered that night was sexual positions."

"In the bar or at his house?"

"The bar," I said, rolling my eyes.

"And then he covered you with his body and pounded you into the floor," she smirked, tossing a few more Lemonheads in her mouth.

"How would you know?"

"Girl, this is my fantasy. Don't screw it up."

"And in your fantasy, did I end up pregnant?"

"I only daydream about the sexy stuff."

"And do you often fantasize about your friends having sex?"

She stared off into space, completely ignoring me. "You know, I bet he's like some really smart teacher. Does he wear glasses?" I shook my head. "I bet he does in class. And then when you go to visit him, he'll swipe all the papers off his desk and throw you down and take you right there on his desk. God, it'll be so hot."

"Did you not hear the part where he lectured me on our base instincts? Somehow I don't picture him as the type to throw me down and take me."

"Well, how was it that night? Did he feel stiff to you?"

"Of course he was stiff," I smirked.

"You know what I mean."

I thought back and shook my head slowly. "No, he let loose, well, with a few drinks."

"See? He was probably just really freaked out about the whole thing and that's how it came out. So, what happened then?" she asked, waggling her eyebrows at me.

"Well, then he told me we were getting married and that he would provide for me."

She fanned herself, grinning at me like an idiot. "That's so hot."

"No, it's not. If you met him, you would understand. He's not at all my type. It's not just that he's uptight about everything. He's just so...programmed."

"What does that even mean?"

"Like, he's got a plan for everything. He has too much order in his life. I mean, fine, but that's not for me. I have enough of that at work. I definitely don't need a man like that."

"Alright, you seem to be missing one very obvious point in all of this." I waited as she leaned in closer. "On a scale of one to ten, how hot are we talking?"

I shrugged. "Honestly, I'm not sure. I mean, I suppose he's good looking, but with all the crazy, it's kind of hard to focus on his looks."

She sighed, plopping her chin down in her hand. "So, no happily-ever-after?"

"I don't see how that could possibly happen. We're just too different. He wanted to meet up and talk last night and he suggested I be his fake girlfriend so that he didn't disappoint his parents."

She sucked in a breath and jerked back. "Ouch. Mommy and Daddy issues? Stay far away from that one."

"Kind of hard to do that now. What the hell am I going to do? I mean, it's not like he's a bad date I can just get rid of. I made a freaking baby with him. I'm linked to him for the rest of my life. He's completely neurotic and my kid could inherit those traits. How the hell do I deal with that?"

"Alcohol. Lots and lots of alcohol." I shot her a glare and she shrugged. "I'm not saying now. I'm saying when the kid is older."

"Thanks. That's very helpful," I said, snatching my chart off the counter and walking around. I had to get to work before my boss caught me talking. We had been standing there long enough. Any longer and I was asking to be caught.

"By the way, Casey's not doing so well. It looks like she's going to be here for a while."

My heart sank for that poor girl. Her parents were probably devastated. Sometimes it just killed me to work here, but I also knew that I was doing something really good. That's what kept me here. I took a deep breath and headed down the hall to her room. I checked over her chart on the way. Her white blood cell count was extremely low and her most recent scans showed that her cancer was spreading.

I put a smile on my face as I entered her room, but she didn't light up like she normally did. "Hey, peanut. How are you feeling today?"

"Not so good."

Her mom sat by her bedside, holding her hand and giving me a faint smile. Her dad stood by the window, staring out at absolutely nothing.

"Does anything hurt?" I asked.

She shook her head and closed her eyes. I walked over and checked her vitals and looked through all the notes that the doctor had left for monitoring. There wasn't a whole lot I could do for her. Sometimes, there were days like this. Medicine could only do so much. The cancer was slowly killing her, and if they didn't find something soon to help her, she would die.

Casey was asleep by the time I was done checking on her. I placed my hand on the mother's shoulder and gave a squeeze. "Is there anything I can do for you?"

She glanced down at her daughter and stood, walking with me out the door. She looked ragged, like she hadn't slept in a long time. "Mike has to go back to work. They said they understood why he was missing so much, but that they needed someone to fill in for him. If he's gone longer than this week, they'll have to hire someone to replace him."

I stared at her in shock. Mike and Cynthia lived three hours away. This hospital had a specialized cancer-treatment center. That's why they came here.

"I don't know how he's going to deal with leaving. He's devastated, but we can't afford for him to lose his job. His health insurance is all that we have."

I squeezed her hand in mine, feeling the tears prick my eyes. I quickly blinked them away. She didn't need my tears on top of her own. She needed someone to be strong for her. "It'll be okay. I'll be here as often as I can, and I'll help however I can. I know I'm not her father, but I can be here when you need a break. I can sit with Casey when you need me to."

"You're so sweet," she smiled. "I don't know what we would do without you."

I glanced past her into the bedroom at the sweet girl in the bed. Life wasn't fair, and as I watched her in that bed, I couldn't help but wonder what would happen if it was my own child in that bed. I prayed that I would never have to find out.

ERIC

I knew I had a lot of making up to do with Anna this morning. I had to get something to go right, and since I couldn't just magically make everything right with Katherine, I had to try with Anna. Shit, I never thought I would have two women in my life at once, let alone two women that downright hated me.

I walked into the bakery and studied the menu. There were so many donuts. What did women like? I glanced at the other side of the menu and saw they also made coffee. Maybe I should get some of that for her too.

"Eric, it's good to see you," Mary Anne said with a smile. "What can I get for you?"

"Um…I need to get some donuts and coffee."

"Sure, how many and what kind?"

I scratched my head. "Um…I'm not sure. It's for a woman," I said, as if that would clear up everything.

She raised an eyebrow at me, clearly not amused with my answer. "What does she like?"

I snorted. "Well, she breathes fire and spits nails," I laughed. When she didn't laugh along with me, I figured that joking around about this was not the way to go. "I don't know. I just met her."

"Lovers spat?" she asked with a smile.

"Not even close. She works for me, but she only started yesterday."

Mary Anne leaned on the counter, rapt with attention. "Anna?" I nodded. "I heard about her getting a new job. It was all around town that she quit on Earl. And it was about time she got a new job. That man worked her to the bone, but didn't pay her very well. I would have hired her here, but I don't have enough work to go around. Not that anyone in town is hiring."

While this was all very…not interesting, I didn't have time to stand around and gossip. "Right, well, I need a sort of makeup box of donuts for her. What would you recommend?"

She winked at me. "I'll put together something for you."

"And a coffee. Something she might like."

"You got it, sugar."

I waited as she gathered up an assortment of donuts and then blended some kind of coffee drink with whipped cream, drizzled with caramel. It looked disgusting. Who could drink that much sugar? What was wrong with just black coffee?

"Alright, sugar, that'll be seventeen-fifty."

I handed over a twenty. "Keep the change."

"Well, aren't you sweet."

I grabbed the donuts and drink off the counter and turned around, almost running smack dab into the town sheriff.

"Jack," I said with a nod.

"Eric," he nodded back, eyeing the drink in my hand. "Had a rough night?"

"It's not for me."

"Uh-huh. Look, son, there's nothing to be ashamed about. We all like different things, even if they are girly," he muttered the last part under his breath.

"It's not for me," I reiterated.

"Hey, what is that?" a woman behind the sheriff asked.

"I don't know."

"It's a caramel latte," Mary Anne answered.

"A latte?" the sheriff asked, chuckling under his breath.

"Jack, you know me. Do I look like the kind of man that would order a latte?"

"Well, you have one in your hand."

"It's not for me," I practically yelled.

"It's for a woman," another man said, hooking his thumbs in the loops of his pants. "He done pissed off a woman."

"I haven't *done pissed off* anyone," I said irritatedly, even though it was a lie. They didn't need to know that.

"Then, it's for a girlfriend," Jack surmised.

"Definitely not a girlfriend."

"Oh, for heaven's sake," Mary Anne said. "It's for his new office manager."

Jack raised his eyebrows in surprise. "You know, bribery is a crime." He leaned in closer so only I could hear. "And bribing her for sexual favors with a coffee isn't the way to go. Think jewelry."

"I'm not bribing anyone. Well, I sort of am, but not for sexual favors," I said a little too loudly.

The door clanked shut as a group of women from church entered, staring at me in surprise. One of them held her hands together and started praying.

"It's for my office manager, Anna. I was rude to her. This," I said, holding up the donuts and coffee, "is an apology."

"Anna Richards?" Jack asked.

"Yeah," I said warily.

He ran a hand across his jaw and chuckled. "Well, I don't suppose coffee and donuts will work with that one, but it's a start."

He clapped me on the shoulder and moved past me to order. I headed for the door, ignoring the women from church glaring at me.

"Womanizer," one of the women muttered under her breath.

I slowly turned to her, doing my best not to return her glare. "It's so nice to see you again, Mrs. Charles. How's Frank? Is he doing okay with the hip replacement?"

Caught off guard by my kill 'em with kindness attitude, she spluttered out, "He's doing alright. The stairs are a little hard on him, but he's getting by."

I nodded. "Let me know if you want a ramp put in. I'd do it at cost for you."

Her eyes widened in surprise. "You'd…you'd do that?"

"Of course. It's the *Christian* thing to do."

She gulped hard and nodded. "Thank you."

I tipped my head and walked out the door. Ma always said that you had to kill 'em with kindness. I never implemented that until this very moment, and I had to say, it was quite satisfying. Besides, seeing as how I knocked up Katherine, I was going to have to implement that tactic a lot. Might as well get used to it.

∽

I walked into the office, holding my proffered donuts and coffee out in front of me like they would shield me from her wrath. Anna was sitting at the desk, not bothering to look up when she heard the door open.

"Good morning."

She barely glanced up at me. "Is that a bribe?"

"It might be."

"What did you get me?"

"Uh, I got some of everything."

"And it's all for me?"

"Yeah."

She nodded. "Put it on the table over there and leave."

"Excuse me?" I asked, rearing back. Had I stepped in an alternate universe? Wasn't this still my office? "I don't really think-"

"Look, you kicked me out last night when I was trying to show you something important. I'm guessing you figured out what that was, otherwise, you wouldn't have had Robert call me and beg me to come back. So, the way I see it, I have the right to treat you the same way."

It was actually pretty logical. I just had to make sure this wasn't the dynamic every time I walked into the office. "Fine, just this once, but tomorrow, things go back to normal."

"I can deal with that."

I set the donuts and coffee on the table and turned back to her. "So, do you have any messages for me?"

"Nope. I'll let you know if I need anything. Otherwise, I should have all this organized by the end of the day. I'll need to see you tomorrow morning at eight to go through what I've found."

"Uh…"

"That wasn't a suggestion," she said, her eyes flicking up to meet mine. "You can go now."

I stepped back, taking the dismissal like a punch to the face. I was temporarily stunned and confused. Was I just supposed to leave? "Uh…okay."

I turned to leave, glancing back at her one more time. I shook my head and walked out of the office. That could have gone better. *It could have gone worse.*

My phone buzzed in my pocket.

Robert: Did she show up?

Me: She's here.

Robert: I wasn't sure she was going to listen to me. How'd it go?

Me: I brought her donuts and coffee.

Robert: You're real smooth.

Me: It seems to have worked.

Robert: And everything's cool?

Me: Um…Not sure. She kicked me out of the office.

My phone rang and I answered. "Yeah?"

"What do you mean, she kicked you out of the office?"

"She basically told me it was only fair and kicked me out. Honestly, I'm not sure what happened."

"So, you just let her kick you out of your own office?"

"Yes?"

"You don't know if you allowed it?"

"I'm not sure what the fuck happened."

He chuckled over the line. "You're a pussy."

I ran my hand through my hair, still trying to figure out what just happened. "That woman has some balls. Was she always like that?"

"Not at all, but I'm guessing she's changed a lot in the last twelve years."

"I'm not really sure what to do here."

"What do you mean?"

"She threw me out. And I'm her boss. That changes the whole dynamic in the office."

"Well, you just have to lay down the law with her."

I glanced back at the door and cringed. "I'm not seeing how that will benefit me. She ordered me into the office tomorrow morning. *Me*. I'm *her* boss."

"You could always fire her again."

"I need someone in the office. I can't afford to search for someone else."

"Then suck it up and deal with it."

"Do you think you could smooth things over for me?"

He sucked in a breath. "Look, I already did all I could. We didn't exactly end things on good terms. I'm not sure I'm the person to make this better for you."

"Then what the fuck do I do?"

"Bring her coffee every morning and pray that she doesn't fuck with your business."

"That's your advice?"

"Well, it doesn't sound like you have much of a choice."

"What happened between you two? Maybe she doesn't like me because of you."

"That's very possible, but it could also just be that you're an asshole."

"Whatever. She probably would have been just a normal woman if you hadn't fucked it up with her."

"Who says I fucked it up?"

I shook my head. "Really? You weren't always an asshole lawyer. If anyone fucked it up, it was you. Something changed when you went off to college. And you said that you didn't leave it on good terms. I'd bet my left nut that you fucked it up, and now she's in my office and

MAINTENANCE REQUIRED

she's going to have access to all my shit. I swear to God, if I come in and find she's erased all my files, I'm coming after you."

He snorted. "Yeah, I'd like to see you do that. You won't touch me because Ma asked you to take care of us. And you've always been more worried about what Ma and Dad think than what's normal for any grown man."

He was right there. "You may have a point, but that still doesn't change the fact that I'll be really pissed if she fucks my business up."

"Ooh, I'm really scared now."

"Fuck off," I spat, hanging up my phone. I glanced back at the door one last time and crept toward it. I would just check in really quick and make sure she wasn't spray painting the walls or something. I cracked the door, but didn't see her at the desk. I opened the door wider and ducked, but not fast enough when I saw the object flying at my head. Chocolate smashed into my face and raspberry filling oozed out and down my lip, onto my shirt.

"Didn't I say to get the fuck out?"

∼

I was out on a job, doing a home renovation. I would rather be doing my own home renovation, but time wasn't always on my side. Besides, now the things that I thought I wanted for my house had changed. I had a baby one the way. Would I have to install permanent baby gates? What about smaller tubs? I didn't want the kid to drown in an adult sized tub. At what age were they able to bathe on their own? There was so much that I didn't know and I didn't even know where to begin. All I knew was that I had to figure this shit out before Katherine decided to kick me out her life.

I had been a total douchebag when I asked her to be my pretend girlfriend. What kind of asshole did that? Apparently, I did. She was right. Asking her out on a date would have been the smarter thing to do. In fact, had she not been pregnant and I had been thinking clearly, that's what I would have done. But it seemed her pregnancy was affecting my brain cells. I had heard of baby brain. Was there such a thing as father brain?

It had only been a few days since the last time I spoke with Katherine, but I thought about her every day. It was strange, for a woman that I had known for such a short time, she was eating up all my thoughts. I was constantly wondering how she was doing or if she needed anything. I wanted to be there for her, mostly because she was carrying my child, but partly because I was intrigued by this woman. She had come into my house and basically told me how things were going to be. Usually I was the one that did that, albeit in a very respectful way.

I needed to feel like I was in control and right now, I wasn't in control of anything. I wanted to take care of her and make sure that her every need was met, but it was clear to me that she didn't see things the same way. She didn't seem overly independent, like one of those women that would kick me in the balls for suggesting she needed help, but she knew what she wanted, and apparently what I offered wasn't good enough. I could see that now. I had seen a problem and found a solution. But it was a terrible solution brought on by extreme fear of being a disappointment to everyone around me.

So, for the last few days, I had been doing everything humanly possible to figure out a way to get her on my good side. We needed to build a relationship so our child didn't grow up with seemingly strangers for parents. And I had to figure it out fast. Relationships took a lot of work and if I screwed it up along the way, which I was bound to, there would be setbacks. I just needed everything to go smoothly.

I put the finishing touches on the tile I had been grouting and stood back to inspect my work. This was a small job, so none of the guys were with me on this one. I was finishing up this renovation on my own, and I was just about done. My phone rang several times while I was cleaning up, but I couldn't answer it with my hands so filthy. When I finally checked my phone, I saw that Katherine had called, along with a few other clients. The clients could wait. I needed to know what Katherine was calling about. Taking a deep breath, I dialed her number and waited to hear her voice.

It was like a punch to the gut. I swore, every time I heard her speak, it got to me even more than the last time. How had I thought that she was just some slut in a bar? Well, I guess she still could be, but her voice was sweet and beautiful. Melodic…God, I sounded like a pussy.

"Eric?"

"Yeah, sorry about that. I was just finishing up some work."

"No problem. I just wanted to let you know that I have my first doctor's appointment tomorrow. You said you wanted to know, so I'm calling," Katherine said through the phone.

"Yes, of course. What time is it?"

"One o'clock. But they said it was more of an informational appointment."

"What does that mean?"

"I guess they're going to get my medical history and stuff like that."

"Well, then I should be there. In case they have any questions for me."

I could have sworn she chuckled over the phone, but chose to ignore it. "Yeah. Anyway, it's at the women's clinic. I'm supposed to be there at quarter to one."

"Okay, I'll see you then."

I hung up and grinned to myself. I was still terrified about this whole thing and I hadn't come up with any good ways to tell my parents about this, but I had made peace with the fact that I was going to be a father. I wondered how soon I could find out if it was a boy or girl. There had to be some resource that could tell me this information. I needed to be prepared going into this appointment for any questions I would have.

I had pretty much finished up work for the day and as I was on my way home, I passed a bookstore and thought I should stop in. They had to have some books on raising babies, right? I parked my truck in front of the store and got out. It was only when I opened the door to the bookstore that I remembered that my old elementary school librarian was now the owner of this shop. I would just turn around and leave. She would never know I was here. I headed for the door when I heard her voice.

"Eric? Is that you?" She came out from behind a bookshelf, smiling and holding out her arms as she walked toward me. "Why, I haven't seen you in ages."

"Hi, Mrs. Greene."

"Oh, nonsense," she said, pulling me in for a hug. "Call me Shirley. You're not my student anymore. So, did you come in here for a book or just to say hi?"

It would be weird if I came in here to say hi, but I couldn't exactly tell her that I was looking for a pregnancy book.

"Uh, I just came to browse. You know, just looking for something good to read."

"Oh, well, we have plenty here. What do you like to read?"

"Uh…" I blew out a breath, not able to come up with anything at the moment. "You know, I think I'll just browse."

"Okay, let me know if you need any help."

She walked away and started unloading some boxes, so I wandered around the store, trying to look inconspicuous. I made my way through the fiction section and over to the self-help section. I picked up a random book and pretended to flip through it as I scoured the section for baby books. When I found it, I started looking at all the choices and scowled. There were so many different books and I had no idea which one to go for. Half of them were listed as the number one baby book. They couldn't all be number one, which meant that most of them were lying.

"Did you find something?" Mrs. Greene asked.

I quickly straightened and cleared my throat, holding up the book in my hand. "I found what I was looking for."

She glanced at my book and then her eyebrows shot up in surprise. I finally looked at the book and groaned. *Rock on the Wild Side: Gay Male Images in Popular Music of the Rock Era.*

"Uh…" I laughed nervously, not sure what to say about that.

"You know, a bookstore is a lot like a therapist's office."

"In what way?"

"Well, I believe in doctor/client privileges. Oh, I'm not a doctor, but people shouldn't be judged for what they read." Her eyes flicked to the pregnancy books and then back to me. "Some people like erotica. Others like historical fiction. Who am I to judge? And then there are some that come in for purely informational purposes. Oh, I've had a lot of women come in and they always want this book," she said, pulling one off the shelf. "It seems to be the most popular pregnancy book I own."

I nodded as she smiled and walked away, taking the gay images book out of my hands as she left. I picked up the book she had pointed out and flipped through it. There was a lot of information in there, way more than I could take in just standing in the store. And the longer I stood here, the more likely it would be that someone would see me. I took the book to the counter and she immediately rang it up, then put it in a bag and slid it across to me.

"That's twenty-three ninety-nine."

I paid for the book, all the while watching her reactions. She didn't seem even the least bit interested in pulling any information out of me. When she handed me the receipt, she smiled.

"Thank you for coming in, and don't be a stranger."

"I won't," I smiled back. I turned for the door.

"Oh, and Eric-" I turned around, seeing her sincere smile. "Congratulations."

"Thank you, Mrs. Greene."

"Shirley."

"Shirley," I nodded and headed for the door.

KATHERINE

I rushed through the last of my patients and shoved the charts back in their respective spots. I was running late, and if I didn't hurry, I would miss my first doctor appointment. I checked my watch and saw that I only had a few minutes to get to the clinic across the street.

"Kiki, can you take the call for room 312?" my boss, Charlene, asked.

I wanted to scream at her in frustration. She knew that I had this appointment today. I had put in for the time off and she knew that I needed to leave. I had reminded her a half hour ago. But she didn't like me for some reason. If I spent too much time with the patients, she got angry with me. She said I wasn't doing my job, whereas I felt like I was helping them even more.

"I have an appointment. I have to leave now or I'll miss it."

She gave me a stern look and shook her head. "Fine, I'll just pull one of the other girls. At least they don't call off in the middle of a shift."

"It's the first time I've done it," I reminded her. "Besides, I'll be back when my appointment is done."

"Don't take too long. You know we're short-staffed as it is."

I refused to roll my eyes at her. I knew exactly how short-staffed we were because she was constantly loading me up on the schedule, even when it was supposed to be my day off. That was going to have to change soon. I had to get into the mindset that I was having a baby and I couldn't be working non-stop. I didn't have any idea what I was going to do for day care or how I was going to manage being a mother to an infant while working such demanding hours. I knew that Eric wanted to be involved, but I had no idea how much, and I was a little afraid to ask based on how he had reacted the last few times we talked.

I grabbed my purse and hurried to the elevator, taking it down to the ground level. I rushed across the street and ran through the door to check in, huffing and puffing as I ran up to the desk. The lady behind the counter barely looked up at me as she asked for my name. Then she couldn't find me in her computer and insisted there must be some mistake. Meanwhile, my appointment was about to start and this would all be for nothing if she couldn't find me in the system.

"Katherine." I heard the sexy, deep timbre from behind me and tried not to squeeze my thighs together. I spun around to see Eric approaching. His clothes were dirty and he smelled like sweat. The sound of his voice no longer turned me on as I stared at the man in front of me.

"We're at a doctor's office. You couldn't have cleaned up first?"

"I came right from a job. I had some issues and didn't have time to get home to change."

I shook my head. "I told you that you didn't need to come. This appointment is just medical stuff anyway."

"Well, I wanted to be here for it. Sorry if a little dirt is bothering you."

"Whatever," I mumbled, turning back to the woman behind the desk. "Can you please just look again. My appointment is supposed to start in just a few minutes."

"Ma'am, I already told you-"

"Is there something wrong?" Eric asked.

The woman behind the counter suddenly looked up and stared at the sexy man behind me. I swore she even batted her eyelashes at him. Um…

hello? I was here for an appointment with my OB-GYN. Why wouldn't she assume that I was here with my husband, or at the very least, my baby daddy, and that he was off limits? I glared at the woman, but she didn't seem to notice. She just kept staring at Eric, completely ignoring me.

"This woman says that she can't find my appointment."

The woman smiled brightly at Eric. "She's not in the system. I'm sorry, but we'll have to reschedule. What works for you?" she asked Eric.

My mouth dropped open and I blatantly turned to Eric with a scowl. He hid a smirk and wrapped an arm around my shoulders, pulling me in closer to his side. I flinched as I felt something wet touch my skin. Sweat, great, he was sweating and getting it all over me.

"Why don't you check again?" he asked. "Maybe you spelled it wrong."

She blushed and smiled, but glanced back at her computer. "Well, I guess it wouldn't hurt to check again. What was the name?"

I rolled my eyes, irritated that it took a hot man to get her to listen to reason. "Katherine Beck."

Her eyes narrowed in on the screen and then lit up. "Well, what do you know. It was right there!"

"Wow!" I said in mock surprise. "Imagine that."

Eric tightened his grip on me a little, giving the woman a charming smile. "Perfect. Should we just sit over there?"

"Yep. The nurse will call you back in a few minutes. Here's the paperwork you'll need."

She handed it over to Eric and I snatched it out of her hand before he could grab it. I glared at her one last time before turning to the seating area, but she only had eyes for my man. Well, my baby man. Baby daddy? Whatever. I shrugged Eric's arm off me and took my seat.

"You know, you'll catch more bees with honey," he said as we took a seat.

"Thanks, Grandma. I'll keep that in mind next time."

He held up his hands and chuckled. "I'm just saying, scowling at her isn't going to make her want to help you."

"I wouldn't have been scowling at her if she could just learn to read the damn schedule. And what was with all that charming bullshit you were laying on back there?"

"Charming bullshit?" he asked in confusion. "Oh, you mean the part where I was nice to her. Well, I'm a businessman and I know that being rude to people doesn't get you very far."

"Yeah, I got that with the whole bees and honey thing. What I don't get is why you were flirting with her."

He quirked his head to the side and his lips just barely tipped up. "Are you jealous?"

"Not at all. But you've already knocked up one woman this month. Maybe you should stop there," I said with a sweet smile.

"You know, it's not like this has happened to me before. I don't just go around knocking up women for fun. I already told you, what happened between us was a one time thing. I don't do one-night stands."

"Well, I don't either, so it seems we both got screwed over here."

He snorted beside me and I crossed my arms over my chest, glaring at him.

"What was that?"

"What was what?" he asked, not looking at me.

"That snort. What? You think I'm lying?"

"Look, I'm just saying, the way you were dressed that night and how you greeted me, it just screams that you're easy."

"Really? So, I get dressed up one night for fun and that makes me easy?"

He turned to me, resting his sweaty arm on the back on my chair. "You know what the problem with women is?"

"Please, inform me."

"You don't want to be objectified or judged based on your looks, but then you dress slutty and go home with a man at the end of the night. What else would I have gathered about you from that night?"

"Well, I guess I'll dress like a nun from now on so that no one mistakes me for a slut," I snapped.

"And maybe stop calling yourself Kiki. You sound like either a stripper or a parrot."

My anger boiled inside. This man was so rude and judgmental. "Seriously? Now there's a problem with my name too?"

"Katherine is such a nice name. Why would you think Kiki is the way to go?"

"Maybe because I didn't want to sound like an uptight bitch, *Eric.*"

We glared at each other for a moment, but then the nurse called me back. I almost told him to go fuck himself and leave me alone, but I didn't want to cause a scene in the middle of the sitting area. He got up and followed me back to an office. I really didn't see the point in him being here.

The appointment took about an hour, while a woman took down all my medical history and informed me about what kind of schedule I would have once I was seen by the doctor. My first appointment wouldn't be until I was three months along. And the whole time, Eric sat beside me and took notes in this little notebook. It pissed me off that he was taking such an interest in this pregnancy. Every time I saw him, I swore he pissed me off even more than the last.

There was nothing about us that was compatible. I just didn't see how any of this was going to work. Would we be those parents that shared custody, but could only barely be civil toward each other? And he was so judgmental. Would he be that way when we were raising our child?

We left after the appointment, neither of us saying a word to each other as we walked out of the building. The only thing I could hope for was that we would grow to be civil toward one another throughout the pregnancy.

"Katherine," he shouted as I headed toward the crosswalk to go back to work. I turned back to him with a raised eyebrow. "Call me if you need anything."

The thing was, he looked sincere, and that pissed me off even more. I knew that he would do whatever he could for me, but that didn't make me feel better. That made me feel worse, because that meant that deep down, all these issues were just surface problems. It meant that he really was a good guy. I nodded and turned away, but I noticed that he didn't walk away until I was safely inside the other building.

ERIC

I watched her walk across the street, pretending not to notice how great her ass looked in those scrub pants. I was in deep shit with this woman. She was such a pain in the ass and now I was stuck with her for the next nine months. And then twenty years after that. Fuck, I was screwed.

I ran a hand over my head as I turned and headed for my truck. I caught a whiff of myself and grimaced. Yeah, I looked like shit and smelled terrible too. This was not how I usually presented myself in a situation like this. Not that I had been in a situation like this, but if I was going somewhere other than a job, I tried to look nice. I most definitely did not look nice today.

I had problems on the job with the plumbing, and since the plumber didn't show up when he was supposed to, I had to try and find a quick fix. Let's just say that nothing had gone this morning as planned. I was lucky that I even made it to the appointment on time. Though, when I got there, Katherine made it pretty clear that she really didn't want me there.

My phone rang and I pulled it out, sucking in a deep breath before answering. It was my brother, Derek.

"Hey, man. What's up?" I asked, my throat cracking.

"Am I getting you at a bad time?"

"Uh, no." I glanced back at the hospital where Katherine had just walked in. Shit, I was going to have to tell him at some point. There was only so long that Andrew would keep this to himself. But now wasn't the right time. "How are things with you and Claire?"

"You know, wild and crazy. She had me do this thing the other night where I dressed up as Deadpool and she was-"

"You now, when I asked how things were, I didn't really need a description of what sexual acts you performed last night."

He chuckled into the phone. "Trust me, if you knew what happened, you'd want a description."

I headed for my truck, cringing at my own bad luck. "I've had enough of sex to last me a lifetime," I muttered, not really intending him to hear it.

"Uh-oh. That doesn't sound good. What happened?"

"Nothing, I was just…you know, it doesn't matter."

"Well, obviously it's something. No man says that he's had enough sex."

I sighed and got into my truck, not wanting anyone else to hear this conversation. "I met this woman last month at The End Zone."

"Nice," his voice grinned.

"Not nice. It was…a huge drunken mistake. I was in knots all night with this woman-"

"Oh, man, that sounds so dirty. So, you finally met the woman that would take you down."

"She's taking me down alright," I mumbled. I ran my hand across my forehead and sighed. "It was a mistake. We shouldn't have slept together. We're complete opposites. But then she showed up the other day and…"

"And?"

I shook my head. "Don't make me say it."

It was quiet on the other end for a moment while he put it all together. "Dude, did you knock up your one-night stand?"

I cringed. I hated the term one-night stand, but I hated the term knocked up even more. It sounded so crass.

"Holy shit, you did."

"What happened?" I heard in the background.

"My brother knocked up some chick in a bar."

"*In* the bar?"

"Not *in* the bar, you dumbass. It wasn't *in* the bar, right? I mean, you at least took her back to your place, I'm assuming."

"Hey, can you not discuss my personal issues with whoever the fuck you're with?" I asked. It was humiliating enough to tell him.

"No worries. It's just Hunter."

"Which doesn't mean jack shit to me," I snapped.

"So, am I right? You didn't fuck her in the bar, right?"

"Of course not."

"So, what are you gonna do?"

"Fuck, I don't know. I just found out. We just had our first appointment. It was just medical history and shit."

"Wow. I just….I can't even…"

"Don't you start that shit too. It's bad enough that Andrew and Joe can't finish their sentences."

"This is big," Derek said in awe. "I mean…holy shit."

"Tell me about it."

"You're gonna be a dad before I am."

"I'm aware."

"And I have a steady woman and everything."

"I know," I said testily.

"You don't even have that. She's just some woman."

I clenched my jaw in anger. "I'm aware."

"Dude, what the fuck were you thinking? Didn't you zip up?"

"You know, I didn't exactly record what happened that night," I said sarcastically. "We were drunk. What happened is still a little fuzzy."

He was quiet again and I waited for it. "Was she a good lay?"

I rolled my eyes and heaved out a sigh. "Does it matter? It's not happening again. She's made it pretty clear what she thinks of me and I may not have been too nice to her either."

"So, what are you going to do? I mean, are you going to see this woman again?"

"You mean besides at appointments? I have no idea. We're complete opposites. She's all carefree and shit and I'm-"

"An uptight asshole?"

"Thanks, man."

"Hey, you know I love you, but you have no clue how to let loose."

"Well, she's a little too loose."

"Ooh, I hope you didn't tell her that."

I didn't say anything, because that's pretty much what I had told her in the waiting room.

"Please tell me that you did *not* tell the woman you knocked up that she was loose."

"I may have implied that the way she dressed made men think of her a certain way," I said with a grimace.

"Dude, are you trying to ensure that you never meet your own kid?"

"I know that-"

"What the fuck were you thinking? It's not like you're perfect. She probably has all sorts of ideas about you too."

"Like what?" I asked defensively. "I'm responsible."

"Yeah," he snorted, "so responsible you knocked up a one-night stand."

"Well, aside from that."

He burst out laughing. "Oh my God! I never thought I would see the day that my big brother, the buttoned up, straight-laced, do-gooder would knock up a woman he wasn't even seeing."

"You make me sound like such an asshole."

"Because you knocked up a woman?"

"No, just the way you describe me," I grumbled. "I'm not that bad."

"Eric, you won't sleep with a woman until you've been dating for weeks. How the fuck did this even happen?"

"Alcohol."

He snorted and started laughing again. "Wow. You never even drink. Did she get you drunk on wine coolers?"

"Vodka," I corrected, needing him to know that I was a man and I didn't get drunk on wine coolers, although they were refreshing.

"You did shots? Are you fucking crazy?"

"It wasn't supposed to be like that." I groaned internally and explained what happened. "Andrew set me up on a blind date-"

"And you went? What the fuck were you thinking? You'd better get checked. She probably has a few venereal diseases."

I tended to agree. With Andrew, you just never knew what kind of women he was sleeping with. Though in this case, it didn't appear that it was an issue.

"She says she's not like that."

"Then how did she know Andrew?"

"She didn't."

I heard his sigh and could imagine him scratching his head right now. None of it made sense to me either. It was all one large clusterfuck. "If she didn't know Andrew, then how did he set you up on a blind date with her?"

"Mistaken identity. We both thought we were there to meet someone else, but didn't realize it until the next morning."

"Nice," I heard the grin in his voice.

"So, how did she get you drunk?"

"We were playing a game…about getting to know each other. Turns out, we don't have that much in common."

"So, a shot for every time you didn't have something in common? I gotta say, I didn't really take you for the type to play those types of games."

"Trust me, I'm not. It turns out, the one time that I threw caution to the wind, I ended up with a pregnant woman knocking on my door."

"How did she break the news?"

I grinned a little, finding it funny *now* how she had chosen to let me know. "A box of condoms."

"Oh, shit. I need to meet this woman. She's gonna have you all tied up in knots by the end of this pregnancy. She sounds just like what you need, someone to help you let loose."

"That's not likely to happen. Like I said, we're very different. I doubt she would ever go for a guy like me."

"So, what are you going to do?"

"I don't know. I offered to marry her-"

"Whoa, hold the fuck on. You can't just marry her because she's pregnant."

"It's the right thing to do," I shot back. "Not that it matters. She turned me down."

"And rightly so. You don't marry someone just because you knocked her up."

"Can you stop saying that?"

"What? That you knocked her up?"

I sighed heavily. I knew he was fucking with me, but I hated the term knocked-up. It wasn't supposed to be like that.

"Look, I know you. You're beating yourself up right now, but this doesn't have to be a bad thing. You're a good guy. Is she a nice woman?"

"She's different," I said hesitantly.

"That's not exactly what I asked."

"Well, what the fuck do you want me to say?"

"I was hoping for a description of some kind? Hot body? Beautiful eyes? Anything!"

"She had nice eyes," I said, recalling them from that night in the bar.

"Wow, what a winning endorsement."

"Look," I sighed. "It's just not like that. When I look at her, I don't see a woman that I want to date or even get to know. I look at the biggest mistake of my life."

"Ouch. You're gonna have to get over that. She's gonna be part of your life for a long fucking time."

"I fucking know that. I wish I could just go back in time or something."

"Have you told anyone else?"

"Andrew was there when she dropped by."

He snorted into the phone. "Well, if I were you, I wouldn't wait long to call Ma."

"I know," I sighed. "I just don't know how to tell them. They're going to be so disappointed in me."

"Oh, relax. You wouldn't be the first son to disappoint them. Besides, when Ma finds out that she's gonna have grandkids, she's gonna be thrilled."

"Why don't you knock up Claire and take the heat off me?"

"Yeah, I'm not seeing that happening anytime soon. Claire's not into settling down and I'm not gonna rush that."

"Thanks for the support."

"What are you so worried about? You know you're gonna be a great dad."

"It's not that. I just…don't want to be a dad that only sees his kid a few days a week," I said sadly.

"It doesn't have to be that way. You know, you barely know the woman. Why don't you try and get to know her. I mean, you have all this time before the kid comes along. Instead of just assuming that things won't work out with her, why don't you try talking to her like a normal person. Just be the man you are around us."

I snorted. "Should I invite you all along with me? Maybe then she'd see me as something other than an uptight asshole."

"Don't be a pussy. Man the fuck up and pretend like she's any other woman. You get to know her and if it goes well, seal the deal at the end of the night. It's not like you can knock her up twice."

"Thanks for that sage advice," I said sarcastically.

"Hey, you called me, asshole."

"I did not."

"Well, trust me, you will be many times over the next few months. Good luck," he laughed as he hung up the phone. I banged my head against the steering wheel and sighed. I had to figure out something. I couldn't just go around hating the mother of my child for the next twenty years.

KATHERINE

After another long day at work, all I wanted to do was lay down and get some sleep, but I wanted to check on Casey first. Her father had left two days ago to head back home for work. He wouldn't be back until the weekend, so the mother was all alone. I promised her that I would be here for her in any way I could and I intended to follow through on that.

I placed my hand on my stomach as I walked toward her room. I couldn't help it. I kept thinking about the fact that my child might be unlucky enough to go through that someday and that was a thought I couldn't stand. I put a smile on my face as I walked into the room. Casey was sleeping, but her mother was wide awake, just staring down at her little girl with a sad smile on her face.

"How's she doing?" I asked Cynthia.

She sat up suddenly, like she didn't want anyone to see her as anything other than put together. "Tired. She hasn't been awake much today. The doctors are trying a new treatment on her. This one has been harder on her than the others."

I had read in her chart that she had started a new treatment, and because of how weak she was, they wanted to keep her in the hospital to see how she responded to the treatment before they sent her home.

It was a last ditch effort to save her. All the other treatments hadn't worked. It looked like this was her last chance and her parents knew it.

"Have you eaten yet?"

She sighed heavily and smiled. "I didn't want to leave her."

"Go," I gave a small smile. "I'm off work. I'll sit with her while you take some time for yourself."

"Are you sure?" She glanced back at Casey, reaching out to touch her hand.

"I'm sure. I'll be here. You take as long as you need. Why don't you take a shower too. I'm sure you'll feel better once you're cleaned up."

I could see the hesitation on her face, but she nodded and walked to the door, lingering for a moment. "I won't be long."

"I'm not worried about it."

When her mom left, I took the seat beside her bed and held Casey's hand. There was something about this little girl that had captivated my heart. Maybe it was her beautiful face or her spirited personality despite what she was going through. I wasn't sure, but I knew what would most likely happen with this little girl, and I wasn't sure how I was going to deal with that. The odds were definitely against her, and while there were plenty of cases of people beating the odds, I couldn't help but wonder how much more her little body could take.

I sat with her for another half hour before she stirred, her eyes immediately going to where her mother would be sitting. "Where's Mommy?"

"She just ran down to get some food. I told her I needed some time with you anyway. I've missed you today."

A small smile curved her lips. "Will you read me a story?"

"Of course. What would you like to read?"

She lifted her hand weakly and pointed to a book on the table. It was an adventure book, probably above her reading level, but I knew she loved hearing stories about escaping to far off places. When she had been in the hospital last time, she had been reading the book

Zathura. I picked up the book and sat beside her, but she reached out her hand and tugged on mine.

"Sit up here with me."

I smiled at her. I could never say no to this little girl. "Well, we'll see if my butt fits on the bed with you."

She giggled as I pretended to wiggle into the spot beside her. I opened the book and started reading, but she didn't last long before she drifted off to sleep again. I didn't stop reading. I couldn't. If this was bringing her any comfort, I would read until my throat was sore.

"You're getting too attached," my boss, Charlene, said from the doorway.

I glanced down at Casey to make sure she was asleep before I spoke. "I'm just giving her mom a break. She's all alone now that Mike went home."

"I'm telling you, you can't stop by and visit like this. It makes it more difficult when they inevitably leave us. And you know she will. Her numbers aren't good. You're not her parent. You're not the one that needs to be fawning over her. Her parents are going to need you to be the one that takes care of Casey when she's in the final stages. How are you going to do your job when you're too busy crying over the little girl you fell in love with?"

I couldn't believe she could be so cruel. "Well, maybe it's hard for you and you don't like that, but I won't let this little girl feel anything but love while she's stuck in this hospital. If she wants me to sit with her and read a damn book, I'll do it."

Charlene pursed her lips and shook her head. "You're setting yourself up for heartbreak. Don't say I didn't warn you."

She turned and walked away. I glanced down at Casey again and wondered how my boss could be such a heartless bitch. Maybe I was getting too attached to her, but I couldn't help it. She was just too lovable.

Her mom returned fifteen minutes later and took a quick shower, then took her place beside Casey again. She didn't say anything about the fact that I was in Casey's bed with her, and I didn't offer any information. She didn't need to know that Casey woke up and wanted the comfort. It would make her feel bad that she hadn't been here.

"Is there anything I can get for you before I leave?"

"No," she smiled. "Thank you for helping out for just that little time."

"Anytime," I said sincerely.

I gathered my things and left, looking back at the little girl that stole my heart and her sad mother. If what Charlene was saying was true, I was in for a world of heartache, but I couldn't walk away. Not when I was already so attached to her.

∼

Tired and feeling emotionally exhausted, I climbed the steps to my townhouse and put the key in the door.

"Katherine!"

I turned to see Eric running across the street from where his truck sat. He looked like he had cleaned up, which was a hell of a lot better than I looked after my twelve plus hour shift.

"Yeah?"

He stopped at the bottom of the stairs, a little stunned by my cold attitude. I couldn't help it. I was tired and I wasn't in the mood to do this shit with him right now.

"Did you just get off work?"

I glanced down at my scrubs and then shot him a look. "No, I walk around like this all the time."

He shoved his hands in his pockets, tightening his expression. "I just came by to talk."

"You know, we have these things called phones. Alexander Graham Bell invented them well over a hundred years ago. I'm sure you've heard of them."

"Are you ever gonna give me a chance without being such a bitch?"

"Hey, you showed up on my doorstep at," I glanced down at my watch, "nine o'clock at night. If you really wanted to talk, you could have called me."

"I did. Several times, in fact."

Whatever. I hadn't checked my phone since my last break at the hospital. There was no point. It's not like there was anything pressing that I needed to be concerned about.

"Still, you couldn't have waited for me to call you back? I have a life, you know. If I'm busy, I'm not gonna answer just because it's you calling."

His jaw clenched in anger. "Well, I would answer if it was you, even if I was in the middle of the most important job of my life."

"Why?" I asked, a little baffled.

"Because, like it or not, we're going to be family. Maybe it won't be the traditional family, but we will be linked and I never ignore family."

I didn't know what to say to that. I hadn't really thought of us being family, and I hadn't realized that he would think of us that way either. We were just having a baby together, and we had just found out. It wasn't like it had been months and we'd bonded or anything.

"What did you want to talk about?"

"I wanted to try and work things out with you," he said harshly. "I wanted to try and find a way for us to get along, maybe get along better so that when we have this baby, we're not complete strangers."

I swallowed hard, fiddling with my keys a little. Okay, I felt a little bit like a bitch, but based on how things had gone so far, I just hadn't expected that. "How would I know that? We haven't exactly started off on the best of terms, you know, with you calling me a slut and all."

He huffed out a laugh, shaking his head. "You know what? I came here to make peace. Let me know when you want that too."

He turned and walked away, getting in his truck and slamming the door. But he didn't leave, not until I went inside and shut the door. Okay, I may have misjudged him a little. I just had to figure out how to get over that.

ERIC

I hammered the nail into the wood harder than necessary. I was still fuming over what happened last night. I was fucking pissed. The whole fucking thing had started off wrong between Katherine and me. It seemed the harder we tried to make things work between us, the worse things got. I just couldn't seem to do anything to get on her good side. Maybe I should have waited for a return phone call from her, but I felt the need to set things straight with us. Maybe if we just sat down and talked, things might be somewhat normal between us. And I needed that.

"Whoa, who pissed in your Cheerios this morning?"

I ignored Will as he walked up behind me. It was a Saturday, so he didn't have school. He usually swung by on the weekends to hang out and shoot the shit, if I wasn't working. I had jobs to finish, but I sent the guys out on them and took the day to work around the house a little. I had porch steps that needed to be fixed, and I needed them fixed before it got too cold. Besides, I had other projects that I wanted to finish up around the house before the baby came. It was time to stop putting off these jobs and get them done. There were no excuses anymore.

"I'm just trying to get some shit done around here."

"Work's been busy?"

"Yeah, and I don't have enough guys to finish up all the jobs I have coming in."

"So, why are you here instead of on a job?"

"Because I needed to get this shit done."

He walked up to the steps and tested the weight of one of the steps I had yet to replace. "It doesn't seem that urgent to me."

"Well, it needs to be done."

Will stood there watching me as I pounded in another board. "What's really going on?"

"Nothing," I ignored him, pretending everything was fine.

"Well, Robert's coming down in an hour. We can help you out with some of this shit."

I snorted, trying to imagine Robert getting off his fucking phone long enough to hold a hammer.

"Where are the Bobbsey Twins?" he asked, picking up a board and bringing it over to me.

"Probably still sleeping."

"It's eleven o'clock," he said incredulously. "I say we go throw water on them, wake their asses up. What do they do anyway?"

"Fuck if I know. They come and go as they want."

"You should charge them rent."

"I do. They buy groceries and everything."

"So…where do they get the money from? I've never seen or heard them talk about a job."

"Neither have I and I'm scared to ask."

"You don't think it's drugs, do you?"

I shook my head. "Nah, I would have noticed if they were into that shit."

"Huh. So, what else are we doing around here today?"

I stood back with a sigh and looked at the house. "I need to finish up these stairs and rip out the ones at the back. I need new supports in there. The roof has to be replaced before winter and I'd like to put in some new windows."

"Whoa, that's quite a list. Why does this all have to be done before winter?"

Before I could answer, a car pulled in the driveway, and not just any car. It was Katherine. Fuck.

"Uh, you want to go inside for a minute?"

"Why?" he asked curiously as he stared at the car. "Who is it?"

"Nobody," I said, hoping to kill his curiosity.

Yeah, that didn't work.

He threw down the hammer he had just picked up and started walking toward the car. When it stopped, he walked right up to the driver's side window. "Is there something I can help you with?"

The door opened and Katherine stepped out. She looked different today. She wasn't wearing her scrubs and she looked refreshed, like she'd gotten some good sleep.

"I just came to see Eric."

Will's jaw dropped and he looked back at me. "That asshole? Seriously, if you're looking for a good time, you're not gonna find it with him. He's about as boring and straight-laced as they come."

Her eyes flicked to mine in question and I shook my head slightly, letting her know that he didn't know yet.

"I'm Will," he said, holding out his hand. "The more handsome, devilishly charming brother. In other words, I'm what you're *really* looking for."

I sighed and walked over to her, deciding to save her from Will. He was a good guy, but he thought he was God's gift to women. I mean, he wasn't as bad as Andrew and Joe, but he could lay the charm on just as thick.

"Katherine, this is my younger brother, Will. Will, this is Katherine."

"And how do you happen to know my older, tediously boring brother?"

The porch screen door swung open and Joe stepped out looking sleep-ridden. That is, until he saw Katherine.

"Quiche-girl! You're back. See? I knew you'd be his bae."

"Quiche girl?" Will asked.

Joe plodded down the steps, his steps a little too jaunty for having just woken up.

"Man, I am so turnt to see you again. I thought for sure after my bro was all *cancel* that we would never see you again. And here you are!"

"Joe, don't you have someplace to be?"

"Wait, how does Joe know you?" Will asked Katherine.

"Um…"

"He was here one day when Katherine was here," I jumped in.

Joe laughed out loud, throwing his head back. "We're family. Can we just spill the tea here? Katherine is his bae, or should be. See, they had this Netflix and chill moment that wasn't at all Netflix, if you know what I mean."

Will stared at him, then looked to me for clarification. "Katherine was here one morning after…after we met in a bar."

Will looked to Katherine and then back to me. "You slept with her?" he said incredulously.

"Hey!" Katherine said indignantly. "I'm not that bad."

"Not you. Him," he pointed to me. "I don't know what's more unbelievable, that he was in a bar or that he took you home."

"Thanks, man."

"Sorry, not sorry," Joe interjected, "it's true. She's all on fleek and you're so basic."

I rolled my eyes. This was going nowhere fast. I needed to get my brothers away from Katherine. Obviously, she came out here to talk, and that wasn't going to happen if they were hanging around. I hadn't even told them about the baby yet.

The screen door opened again and Andrew walked out. Fuck, I was so screwed. "Will, can you guys give us a minute?"

"Holy shit! It's the baby mama with all the drama! How's my soon to be bae-in-law?"

"Your what?" Will asked. "What the fuck is he talking about?"

"Whoa!" Joe said, running his hand over his head. "Is he serious?" He glanced at Katherine and then back at me, his hand moving between the two of us. "This is so…I can't even…"

"Can't even what?" Will asked. "What are they talking about?"

"I'm pregnant," Katherine interjected, filling them in when I obviously couldn't.

Will's eyes flicked down to her stomach and then to me. "As in…"

"As in having a baby," Katherine clarified. "Your brother's."

"Are you sure it's Eric's and not Joe or Andrew's?"

She rolled her eyes, but I punched him in the face. I didn't need him implying that she slept around, let alone with all my brothers.

"Ow. What the fuck was that for?"

"For implying that she would sleep with that many of us."

"I'm just saying…I could see it happening with Joe or Andrew, but you? How the hell did that happen?"

"The way it usually happens," Katherine said.

"I know, but…seriously? I mean, it usually takes you forever to close the deal."

Katherine quirked an eyebrow at me. God, they were making me sound like a monk. A horn honked as another car pulled up the driveway. Great. Now Robert was here. He pulled up, eyeing Katherine warily as he got out. "What's going on?"

"This is Katherine," Joe piped up. "Eric knocked her up."

Robert's gaze shot to mine. I stared up at the sky, hands on my hips as I willed this day to just swallow me whole. It really couldn't get any worse.

"Uh…" He started chuckling and then he started laughing. "I'm sorry. I know this isn't funny, but…holy shit. When did this happen?"

"A little over a month ago," Andrew answered, a grin on his face. "You should have been there. He was all *cancel* and she was like *as if*. What did I tell you? Pics or it didn't happen."

"Obviously it did and we don't need pics," I said testily.

"Right, right," he nodded. "Well, now that everything's ratchet, I'm gonna bounce. Got my own bae that's fire."

Robert sighed, stuffing his hands in his sleek pants as Joe and Andrew got in Andrew's car and left. "Do you ever think that maybe they were adopted?"

"Nah, Ma would have returned them," Will said.

"So, you and my brother, huh?"

"You know, we're kind of working on that," Katherine smiled. "Believe it or not, I came to talk to him about the baby, and not all of you."

"That's cool." He pulled out his card and handed it over to her. "If you guys decide to get married, keep that on hand."

"Why?" she asked, staring down at his card.

"Because I'm a divorce lawyer."

∼

I had finally gotten rid of my brothers after convincing them that I couldn't tell them anything more until I worked a few things out with Katherine. Robert was pissed about driving the hour down from Chicago, but Will just shrugged it off and left like he had better shit to do anyway. Katherine and I just stood there for a few minutes in awkward silence, neither of us knowing where to go from here.

"What are you doing?" she asked, pointing to the stairs.

"Uh, I had a few loose boards. I have to rip out the set of stairs on the other end of the house and replace the whole thing."

"You know how to do that?"

I gave her a funny look. "Yeah, I know how to do that. I'm an engineer. It's sort of what I do."

Understanding lit her face. "Well, that explains the clothes when you showed up for the appointment."

"Yeah, I was running late because the plumber didn't show up."

"I didn't realize…we haven't really discussed anything about ourselves."

I laughed slightly. "No, we haven't."

"Do you have the time now? I mean, I don't want to interrupt your day, but…" She took a deep breath and blurted out, "I was a bitch last night. I had a rough day and I wasn't expecting that you wanted to get to know me."

"Sure." I held out my hand for her, helping her up the steps that were torn up.

"So, why does everything have to be replaced?"

"Well, it needed to be done, but now that the baby's coming…I just want to be prepared."

"Wow, you really are taking this seriously."

I was about to open the door for her, but stopped and turned to her, wanting her to see just how serious I was. "Look, I get that we got off on the wrong foot, but there's nothing I won't do for my child. No matter what our custody deal is, when my child is here, it will be a safe place for him or her. So, I'm doing what needs to be done to make sure that when the baby's born, I'm ready for it."

I watched as her throat bobbed and she nodded. I opened the door and waited as she walked inside. She looked around the place, like she hadn't seen it the first two times she was here. Although, the first time, she had been hungover and probably hadn't been paying attention. And the second time she was here…well, I wasn't really sure because I was too busy freaking the hell out.

"This is a big house."

"It was my parents'. They moved to North Carolina and left it to me, as long as I take care of my brothers."

"That was generous of them."

"Well, they didn't want to sell. There are a lot of memories here. They just wanted to live somewhere warmer."

She nodded to herself as she looked around a little more. "So, Eric, I know that you have four very nosy brothers and now I know that you're an engineer. I know that you like to do things responsibly, current situation aside, and that you're already preparing for a baby that won't be here for months. So, what don't I know about you?"

That could take a lot of time. We sat down at the table and I tried to think about where to begin. She had most of that right, but this was all backwards. We weren't at the awkward first date, but the awkward morning after, plus a few days.

"Uh…I actually have six brothers. One is out in Pennsylvania and he works at a security firm. He was in the Army for a while, but then he got out and bought into this security company. We don't see much of him, but he did just introduce us to this woman he's been seeing."

"Is that a big deal?"

I grinned. "Yeah. I never really thought he would settle down. He likes the danger, but it turns out that his girlfriend is a little crazy, so it works."

"And your other brother?"

My face dropped, along with my eyes. "We uh…we don't know where he is. He disappeared about six years ago. We haven't heard from him since."

"Disappeared, like something bad happened?"

"We have no idea. He was here one day and everything was good, and then…and then he was gone. We don't have a single lead on where he might be or if…if he's dead. He just vanished."

"Oh, I'm sorry. That must be very hard."

I shrugged, like it wasn't something I really thought about, but it was on my mind every fucking day. I wasn't sure how my brothers handled it. We didn't talk about it, but I felt it deep in my bones. I kept waiting for the day that he would walk back through that door and grin at us like he used to. I never changed the locks on the doors and the spare key was still hidden in the same fucking place, just in case he made it home to us one day.

KATHERINE

That was a great way to start off. I had gone and fucked up that conversation with one innocent question. No wonder he was the way he was. His brother had gone missing and he was the oldest. He probably felt some degree of responsibility for it, though he tried not to show it. I could see that darkness in his eyes though.

He quirked a small grin at me. "So, that's probably the darkest thing about me. Other than that, what you see is what you get. I work a lot. I'm trying to build my business right now, and it takes a lot of my time, but I'll always be there for you whenever you need me."

"I can see that now. I'm sorry I didn't before. I just…"

"It's not your fault. I think this whole situation is something neither of us was prepared for."

I laughed slightly. "Yeah, I definitely didn't think this was going to happen." It occurred to me that there were so many small details that I didn't know about him. "How old are you?"

"Thirty-six. You?"

"Thirty-one."

His eyes danced with humor. "I find it hard to believe that you're not taken yet."

"Well, honestly, I didn't want to get attached to anyone."

"Why's that?"

I shrugged slightly. "I saw all my friends running out to get married at such a young age. And I just kept wondering what else was out there. I sort of lied to you that night in the bar. I don't do one-night stands. I just don't tend to have long relationships. See, I have this theory that if you can't picture spending your life with someone after six months, then you shouldn't be with that person."

He nodded. "I could agree with that."

"So, I just ended it if I wasn't in love with the person, or if it just didn't seem to be going anywhere. I didn't want to waste my time on someone that I wouldn't stay with."

"That's actually very…responsible of you."

"I wouldn't go that far."

"No, really. You're not leading someone on when you know it won't work."

"And what about you? No big relationships? Were your brothers right? Does it take you a long time to seal the deal?"

I couldn't help but tease him. Obviously his brothers thought he didn't get laid enough.

He rolled his eyes slightly. "I don't just jump in bed with women. To them, that means that I'm too uptight and choosey. I just don't want the mess of a one-night stand. I want a meaningful relationship. Point in case, we had a one-night stand and look at us, pregnant and now trying to figure out how to navigate a relationship."

"So…" I glanced down, nervous to ask him this question. I was afraid he would respond in some outrageous way. But we needed real solutions right now. "How do you see us navigating this relationship?"

He chuckled slightly. "Well, since you turned down my marriage proposal and my offer for you to be my fake girlfriend, I guess we'll just have to do this the old fashioned way and get to know each other."

I nodded, relieved that he hadn't suggested that I move in with him again, or something equally crazy. "That actually sounds like a really good plan. So…"

And now it was awkward. I didn't know what else to say. Where did we go from here? Did we just sit here and talk? Or maybe we should just leave it at this amicable place before one of us inevitably said something to screw things up.

"So, what about you?" he asked, before I could stand up and leave. "Do you have any brothers or sisters?"

"Uh, two actually. My dad was blessed with all girls."

He huffed out a laugh. "Well, my parents were blessed with all sons. I'm not sure which is worse."

"I don't know. Can you imagine three teenagers in the house all at once?"

"Yes, but not girls. That…doesn't sound like fun at all."

"Well, apparently it wasn't fun for my dad. He walked out when I was sixteen."

"I'm sorry. Do you still talk to him?"

"Yeah." I shook my head at myself. I was being a little dramatic. "It wasn't the worst thing in the world that could have happened. I mean, my parents did the silent fighting thing. You know how you know that they're pissed at each other, but they won't argue in front of the kids?" He nodded. "It was usually about money. I'm not even sure what happened. They just told us one day they were getting a divorce. Of course, because my dad was the one that moved out, I was pissed at him. It wasn't until years later that I finally understood that sometimes things just don't work out. My dad's a good man, but I came to realize that they probably never should have gotten married."

He stared down at the table for a moment, like he was thinking about something important. Then his eyes shifted to mine.

"I know your feelings about getting married, and now that I know about your parents I won't push the issue. But I also want you to know that I want to be an every day part of my child's life. I don't want to be one of those part-time parents that only sees his kids on his days. I want to be there for everything. I don't want either of us to miss out on any of those firsts. I just…when I pictured having kids, I had this whole family and we were together, always supporting each other, and it was happy. I still want that, Katherine. I know I'm probably not your type. I know I can be an asshole and I'm not as loose as some other guys, but there's nothing I wouldn't do for my family. So, I'm asking that you give me a chance…give us a chance to see what could happen between us."

I was a little shocked by his speech. I hadn't been expecting that, not after how hard it was for us just the past few times we met. But the way he was looking at me, begging me to give him a shot, how could I tell him no?

"Okay."

∼

"Is this weird?" I asked Chrissy. "This is weird, isn't it?"

"Which part? Where you start dating your baby daddy to see if you can have a relationship after you both basically tore each other down? Or maybe you mean the part where you're talking about going out on a date with him, but you haven't once mentioned if you were attracted to the guy?"

"Both."

"Then you're right. This is weird. I don't understand why you're doing this. I thought you didn't like him."

"I know," I sighed, plopping my head down on my dresser. She had come over to help me get dressed for my date. "I went over there just to try and bury the hatchet. He showed up here the other night to talk and I was a bitch to him. So, I went over there, thinking that we would just find some kind of common ground. But then he told me that he wanted to be there full time for his kid, and that if we could make this work, he really wanted to try."

"Aww," she sighed holding her hand over her heart. "That's so sweet."

"I know! How was I supposed to say no to that?"

"I mean, it probably won't work, but I think it's sweet that he wants to try."

I plopped down on the bed beside her with a sigh. "I just have to make it through tonight. I'm sure that after one night on a real date, he'll see that we're just not compatible."

"That's giving it the good old college try," she said, slapping me on the back.

"What? It's so obvious that we would never work together. We're just too different. Even his brothers were shocked when they found out he had slept with me."

"Have you told your parents yet?"

I ran my hand over my stomach and grimaced. "I wasn't really looking forward to the conversation. I mean, my dad's gonna flip out and my mom's gonna purse her lips in disappointment at me."

"So, you were planning on telling them when?"

I shrugged. "When they meet the baby?"

She rolled her eyes at me. "Brilliant plan."

The doorbell rang and I glanced at the clock. "Shit. That's him."

"But you still have ten minutes," she shrieked.

"Not with him. He's super responsible, and apparently, very punctual."

"Doesn't he know that women are never ready on time? He can't just show up unannounced like this!"

"It's not unannounced," I reminded her as I pulled my dress over my head. "We had plans."

"But not for ten minutes," she reiterated. "In the female world, that's unannounced."

I shook my head and pulled on my shoes, trying to hurry up. I hadn't even done my makeup yet. "Can you get the door for me?"

Her eyes bugged out. "You want me to answer it?"

"I'm still getting ready!"

"But then I have to sit there and have the uncomfortable conversation with him until you're ready. You're asking me to give up like twenty minutes of my day for him."

"Chrissy, please," I begged as I ran into my bathroom and started rushing through my makeup. I heard her sigh and then stomp off downstairs to the living room. I heard him walk in, but then it was just silent. Like, dead silent. I strained my ears to hear anything, but there was nothing. I finished putting on my mascara and took a final look in the mirror. That was as good as it was going to get.

I turned to run out of the bathroom and ran right into Chrissy. She yanked me back into the bathroom and slammed the door.

"You didn't tell me he was hot," she hissed.

"What?"

"The man, standing in your living room at this very moment, the one that says he's your baby daddy-"

"He said that?"

"No, but that's besides the point. He's in there right now and he's so fucking gorgeous. How the hell could you leave out crucial information like that?"

"Uh….I guess I didn't notice."

"You didn't notice that the future father of your child is so smoking hot that he could light this whole place on fire? You didn't notice that his eyes are so piercing and gorgeous that I could melt just looking at them? I was captivated! Do you know how stupid that sounds? Me, a happily married woman, was captivated by a man the moment I opened the door. And you didn't notice?" she shrieked.

"I mean…I think he's good looking, but-"

"No, there are no buts. That man out there is something that every woman wishes she could wake up to every morning, and you're too blind to see it. Who cares if he's not as loose as you'd like! You can be the fun one and he can make up for it in looks!"

"So, you want me to be with him for his body?"

"Uh…am I having this conversation alone? Hello! Hot man alert in your living room. Yes, you should go along with this whole thing, and if he even mentions sleeping with you, you take him up on it because your vagina isn't getting any action for at least the next year."

"See, I thought you would be the rational one about all this. What happened to the woman that sat here just ten minutes ago and told me she thought it was ridiculous for me to go out with him?"

"I hadn't seen him then!"

I shushed her, sure that he could hear everything she was saying because she was being so loud. "Would you quiet down? I'm not sleeping with him again just because he's hot." When she opened her mouth, I added, "Or because I won't get laid for a year."

She closed her mouth and pouted. "You know, ever since you got pregnant, you really aren't any fun."

ERIC

I knew I was early. Hell, it had taken me fifteen minutes to pick out what I was going to wear. I felt like a damn chick, standing in front of the mirror and trying to decide what tie to wear. Finally, I decided on a gray tie. I wasn't sure if she liked a man in a suit, but this was what I wore on dates. I wanted to make a good impression for my date and let her know that I cared. If I showed up in jeans and a shirt, that sent the wrong message.

Originally, I was going to shave before I picked her up, but then I saw that I only had five minutes left before I had to leave. Technically, I had longer than that, but I had to plan for anything that could go wrong. A flat tire would make me late. I could run into traffic, though that was highly unlikely in our small town. Either way, I was not going to be late. I told her I was committed and wanted to be the best father. How would it look if I showed up late for our first date?

So, here I sat, waiting in her living room as her friend argued with her in the bathroom upstairs. I could barely make out what they were saying, but I smirked when I heard 'hot man alert'. I glanced around the room and noticed that all the pictures she had up were of her with her friends out having fun. One was at a bar, some kind of party. She was dancing with her head thrown back and a carefree look on her face. In another, she was getting ready to go bungee jumping. Didn't she know how dangerous that was? In another, she looked like she was about to go drag racing.

I shook my head as I continued around the room, looking at all the pictures. The woman was clearly insane, and I was trying to convince her that we should be together. How the hell was I going to do that? I would never do any of the shit she was doing in those pictures. Even when I got into trouble as a kid, it was well thought out trouble. If there was the slightest hint of something really bad happening, I was out. And as I got older, and the consequences of my actions became more clear, I became more rigid. I couldn't help it. It was like something flipped inside me and told me to always do the right thing.

Now I worried that I was never going to be able to make this work with this woman. She was sexy and fun, and I was…a wet blanket, just like my brothers always said. I heard her heels on the stairs, and then she appeared. My mouth dropped open. Holy shit. She was wearing a black dress that wrapped around the front her body, accentuating her tiny waist. The v at her breasts showed just enough cleavage to tempt me, but not enough to be slutty. And those damn heels, I swallowed hard as I watched those sexy legs make their way toward me. How had I not seen this before? Had I been blind? She was a knockout.

I felt like I swallowed my tongue as I stared at her. Clearing my throat, I stepped forward and held out my hand to her like an idiot, like I hadn't met her before. She glanced down and then her eyes flicked to mine in amusement. I dropped my hand and chuckled nervously. God, I had never been so nervous on a date in my whole fucking life. And I wasn't sure if it was because she was the mother of my child or because she was really that hot.

"You look…amazing. Beautiful."

"Thank you," she said, her face blushing slightly. I didn't miss how her eyes trailed over my body and lingered on my chest and arms. Good, that was a good sign. She was checking me out too. I just had to hope that she liked what she saw as much as I liked what I was seeing.

Her friend leaned over and whispered, "See? I told you, so fucking hot."

She slapped her friend and I pretended like I hadn't heard.

"Should we go?"

"Yeah."

Her friend walked out ahead of us, whispering something about seeing at the end of the night. I led her over to my truck and helped her in. I shook off my nerves and got into the driver's side.

"So, I thought we'd try that restaurant over in Cedar Lake. I made us reservations for six."

"The seafood place?"

"Yeah, but I know you can't have seafood. They have other things there."

"How did you know?"

I looked at her funny. "How did I know what?"

"That I can't have seafood."

"I read it."

She stared at me curiously for a moment. "Okay, well, that sounds good."

I started the truck and pulled away from her house. The silence was uncomfortable. I glanced at the clock, noting we still had twenty minutes before we got there. That was the bad thing about living in this area. There was at least a ten minute drive between towns, and further if you wanted to go to one of the bigger towns where you could go to nice restaurants or the local Walmart. We had a really nice restaurant in town, but I wanted to keep things private until we saw where this went. I tapped my thumb on the steering wheel, trying to come up with something to say, but I had no clue. What was I supposed to say?

"So, have you been feeling okay?"

"Yeah, pretty good."

"No morning sickness?"

"Not yet, but I hear that can come and go."

I nodded, thinking about some of the other things I had read. "No constipation?"

I heard it come out of my mouth. I knew I had said it and how fucking stupid it was to ask it, but it was too late. It was out there now, just hanging between us like a smelly fart.

"You know, I'm all about getting to know each other, but I don't think we need to know each other that well."

I cleared my throat again, feeling like an idiot. "Right, sorry about that."

Silence stretched thick between us. I felt like I was suffocating over here. This was torture. What would I say to any other woman on a date? It was like all the sudden, I didn't know how to talk to a woman. Her job. I could talk to her about that.

"So, you're a nurse, right?"

"Yeah."

"ER?"

"No, I work with kids."

"Oh, that must be fun."

"I work in the cancer ward."

Fuck, was there anything I could get right tonight? Seriously, this was going to be the longest night ever.

"That must really suck," I went for.

"It does. I mean, it can be really great sometimes, but then there are other times that it's really hard. Like, right now, I have this patient that's seven and she's been battling cancer for two years. She hadn't been at the hospital in a while, so I thought she was doing better, but then she showed up two weeks ago. Her cancer is getting worse, and it's really hard on the parents because they live so far away from the hospital."

"How do you deal with that?"

She shrugged. "Every time I think about how hard it is to see it, I imagine what they're going through. It kind of keeps things in perspective."

"Huh."

"What does that mean?" she asked.

"I was just thinking, it makes sense."

"What does?"

"You know, that night in the bar. You were letting off steam. I mean, after what you see all day, you probably need to let loose."

"So…I couldn't have been letting loose because I liked to, but because I have a job that's stressful?"

I did a double take, sure that I had mistaken the bite in her tone. She had an eyebrow quirked at me and her arms were crossed over her chest. Damn, I really thought I got that one right.

"That wasn't really…I wasn't implying that…" I sighed and settled further into my seat. "You know, I'm just going to shut up for the rest of the drive."

KATHERINE

Okay, I may have been a little hard on him in the truck. He was trying to understand me, but it felt more like he was trying to find an excuse for my behavior so he could say that I fit his normal. And even if I was trying to let loose because of my job, I didn't want him thinking that he needed to find a reason I was the way I was. Either he accepted me or he didn't.

So, here we sat at the table, him with his perfect posture and me slumped over slightly in the chair. It seemed to reflect who we really were. He was rigid and unmoving and I was more malleable. Although, I had to admit, Chrissy was right. How had I missed how hot he was? Was it just tonight or had he always looked like this? When I saw him standing in my living room in his suit, the first thing I thought was how sexy he looked in a suit. He still had a five o'clock shadow, but it looked good on him. And then I noticed how the jacket was straining across his biceps. I had never met anyone that had biceps that big. It made me wonder what the rest of his body looked like. I should have remembered from our night together, but unfortunately, it seemed like all the good stuff had slipped my mind.

Then we got in the truck and it was the usual uncomfortable presence that filled the air. Nothing clicked between us, and I started to regret coming out on this date with him. I had been hoping that something would come from tonight, but as of right now, it was looking like it would go down as the worst date I had ever been on, aside from the first one we went on where he got me pregnant. At least there was sex at the end of that date.

I watched as he cut up his steak. It looked so bland compared to my mushroom risotto. "Would you like a taste?" I offered.

He grimaced. "I hate mushrooms. It's fungus."

I huffed in irritation. "It's delicious in this. Just try it." I scooped up some and held it out for him. He pulled back, shaking his head.

"No, not a chance in hell."

"Seriously, you won't even try it?"

"No."

"God, why do you have to be so rigid all the time? You know, try something new. Experience life."

"Just because I don't want to eat mushrooms doesn't mean that I'm rigid and don't enjoy life," he shot back.

"Really? You're sitting there in a suit for our date. A freaking suit, and while it looks good on you, who wears a suit anymore?"

"You're wearing a dress. I don't see what the difference is."

"You're just so stiff. I mean, you're a good looking guy, but you dress like you're going out for a business dinner instead of a good night out."

"Wait, so I can't have fun because I'm in a suit?"

"Tell me, when was the last time that you actually went and had fun?"

I watched him thinking for a moment and then he shrugged. "My brothers come over for poker every weekend. That's fun."

"I'm not talking about doing the same old boring thing every weekend. I mean, go do something that's crazy and makes you feel alive."

"You mean like bungee jumping?" He smirked. "I saw your photos in your house."

"So, you're too afraid to try something like that?"

"I don't like heights."

I narrowed my eyes at him. "You're an engineer."

"And there are safety precautions in place to make sure that everyone is safe at all times."

"God," I groaned. "Do you hear yourself? Safety precautions and poker. Where's the fun?" He didn't say anything, just kept chewing. "Look, how about this, since we seem to have so little in common, how about we both try doing something that the other likes."

"You're not going bungee jumping."

"Obviously. I'm pregnant."

"And I'm not jumping. That's not safe. I'm not willing to risk my life for the thrill of falling to my death, only to be yanked up at the last minute. And that's if the cord doesn't snap. Have you seen the episode of *Fresh Prince of Bel-Air* where Trevor dies?"

"That was a TV show, and I wasn't recommending anything as *dangerous* as that."

He looked at me curiously. "Then what are we talking about?"

"I don't know. How do you feel about tattoos?"

∼

"This is ridiculous," he grumbled. "And completely unsanitary. Do you know how many people die from getting tattoos?"

"They don't die," I corrected him. "They might get hepatitis, but they don't die."

"And so you think I should do this?"

We stood in the entryway in the tattoo parlor and checked out the designs. I smiled to myself as he squirmed next to me. It wasn't asking a lot. Sure, it was permanent, but I wasn't asking him to risk his life.

"It's just..." he cleared his throat, pulling at his collar, even though it was unbuttoned. I turned to him fully and looked into his eyes. He looked scared.

"Are you afraid?"

"What?" He snorted and shook his head. "Why would I be afraid? It's just a tattoo."

"You look like you're going to puke."

He swallowed hard and shook his head slightly. "Let's just get this over with." He stalked forward to the counter and clenched his jaw hard. "I need a tattoo."

"Do you have a design in mind?" the woman behind the counter asked.

"No."

"Do you know where you want it?"

"No."

"Color or black and white?"

"I don't give a shit."

She leaned forward, resting her crossed arms on the counter. Her cleavage hung out of her tank top, but he didn't even seem to notice. "Is there anything you do know?"

I walked forward and slipped my arm through his, trying to comfort him. "We'll just look around at some designs."

She shrugged, like she really didn't care. "Fine, but he only has one opening for tonight, so you have about fifteen minutes to decide. Then you lose your spot."

"Fine, just give me that one," he said, pointing to the barbed wire tattoo image that was hanging on the wall. The woman glanced at it and then gave a bored look to Eric.

"Original. I'm sure Decker's gonna be thrilled to do that one. Again."

"What's wrong with it?"

She quirked an eyebrow at him. "Seriously? That was popular when I was in high school. *Twenty years ago.*"

He cleared his throat. "Whatever. It's simple."

I had to agree with the woman. It wasn't that it was a bad design, but it was so boring and unoriginal. I could remember half the guys in my graduating class going out and getting similar designs on their biceps. I really didn't want Eric walking around with a cliché tattoo, especially when I was the one that talked him into doing this. The point was to make him like me, not to make him hate me even more than he already did.

"Maybe you should look around a little more," I suggested.

"No, it's that one. It shouldn't take too long. Then we can get out of here and just end this night," he muttered under his breath.

We took a seat in the waiting area. His right eye was twitching, just like the day I told him I was pregnant, and his leg wouldn't stop bouncing. Maybe this was pushing him too far out of his comfort zone. Maybe this really was a bad idea. But before I could decide whether to call the whole thing off, we were called back and his arm was getting sterilized.

"So, DeeDee tells me that you want to go the boring route," the man sighed, tossing the paper aside. "Fine. Ruin your body with this shit."

"Wait, aren't you going to use the stencil?"

"Don't need to," Decker said. "I've done this design so many times, I could do it in my sleep."

He whipped out the tattoo gun and buzzing filled the air. Eric's eyes went wide and sweat coated his upper lip.

"Scared of needles?" Decker smirked. Eric turned his head, but as soon as the needle touched his arm, he passed out. Decker looked to me with a quirked eyebrow. "So, are we still going through with this?"

"Yes, but not that design."

ERIC

I woke up to something wet being brushed on my arm and then I felt tape. I glanced down and saw that my arm was bandaged. "Did you do it?"

"Yep. Here are the care instructions," Decker said. "Let me know how you like it," he smirked. He got up and walked out, leaving me alone with Katherine. She looked nervous, fidgety.

"What?"

"Uh, nothing. We should go."

"What happened?"

"Well, you passed out-"

I shot her an irritated look. "I know that." I glanced down at my arm again, noticing that the bandage was only on part of my arm. If he did the barbed wire tattoo, wouldn't the bandage go all around my arm? "The bandage doesn't go all around my arm." My gaze shot up to hers. "Why does the bandage not go all around?" I asked accusingly. "What did you do?"

She backed up a step, holding her hands up placatingly. "Now, Eric, just hear me out. You picked out that terrible tattoo and I didn't want you to hate it. This is permanent."

"So, you chose for me?"

"It's really good. I promise. You'll really like it."

I stood from the chair and stalked toward her. I felt like I was going in for the kill, which I very well could be, depending on what she had done. "What the fuck were you thinking? That's permanent."

"Which is why I chose a different design for you. The one you chose was awful. You would have hated it."

"I hate everything about this. I never wanted to do this. You're the one that insisted that I do this."

"Only because I was trying to break you out of your comfort zone a little. I mean, you're just so uptight."

"So, it's okay for you to permanently destroy my body to make you feel better about the way I look or how uptight I am?" I asked angrily.

"Look, I'm sorry, but I just wanted something that fit you-"

"Yeah? What did you get me? A tattoo of underwear wadded up?"

"No, but that would have represented you fairly well," she snapped.

"Look, you were right," I said, grabbing my shirt and pulling it back on. "We're too different. I don't know why I thought that we could make this work, but this right here shows that you have no respect for me, and you really don't fucking understand me if you think it's okay to pull this shit."

"I guess you're right," she shot back. "It wouldn't have worked. I only came on this date because you were all sad about wanting to be part of your kid's life. It was clear from the night we met that it would never work between us."

"Then I'll take you home and we can call this what it was, a sorry excuse for a date."

"Fine."

I grabbed my suit jacket and shoved the tie in the pocket. We walked out of the tattoo shop, but even then, I couldn't let my good manners slip. I held the door for her, and when we got to my truck, I helped her up into the cab. As I slammed her door, I shook my head. Sometimes I really wished that I could just be a complete asshole.

I dropped her off at her townhouse. She didn't say anything as she got out of my truck, and she didn't look back at me as she walked into her house and slammed the door. Fine. I didn't give a shit anyway. I was so fucking pissed. Who did she think she was to change the tattoo that I picked? She didn't know me. All she knew was that I was her child's father. We didn't have deep, meaningful conversation.

I sighed when I pulled in my driveway and saw that my brothers were home. They knew I was taking her out tonight, so they were probably going to grill me about it when I got inside, especially about the fact that I was home so early. Fuck, I didn't want to deal with this right now.

I walked up the steps and as expected, Joe stepped out with a huge grin on his face. "So, I'm guessing you didn't try to close the deal."

"Shut the fuck up."

I shoved past him, grimacing when my shoulder brushed against his. My hand instinctively went to my arm and Joe noticed.

"What happened? Did she beat the shit out of you or something?"

"No," I said tersely.

"Then what happened?"

"Nothing. Can we drop this?"

"You don't have to be so salty. I'm your brother. You can talk to me."

I didn't want to talk to him about this, but I also saw an opportunity for myself, a chance to not have to deal with his shit if I played my cards right.

"Fine," I said, crossing my arms over my chest. "I'll tell you what happened, but you have to talk like a normal person for the next month."

He glared at me. "Not cool, Hunty."

"See? Shit like that. My name isn't Hunter or anything close to it. Why the fuck would you call me that?"

"It's just a saying. Like when you walk around and call Will *bro*."

"I say that because he's my *brother*," I said testily.

"Whatever. Fine, I'll agree to speak like a normal person, *only around you*, for the next month, if you tell me what happened."

I noticed how he took the extra time to make sure that he didn't speak like a Millennial that whole time.

"Fine." I jerked my head for him to follow me. We went inside and Andrew met us in the kitchen.

"How'd the date go?" he asked, waggling his eyebrows at me. "It's kind of early to be home."

"She coerced me into getting a tattoo," I said angrily.

"And you didn't think that was a littles sus?"

I glared at Andrew. "What?"

"Suspicious," he said slowly. "She said she wanted you to get a tattoo and you just went along with it?"

"Look, it was obvious that we didn't have anything in common, so we made this sort of deal that we would do something the other liked, as a way to get to know each other."

"She totally played you," Joe grinned. "She was just trying to make you get out of your comfort zone. That's so-" he grinned wide, but when I shot him a death glare, he cleared his throat and thought hard about his next words. "Cool."

"Really?"

"What? You want me to speak like a normal person. I'm trying."

"Let's see it," Andrew said excitedly. "Man, it's like she put a tramp stamp on you or something."

"It's on my bicep. That's hardly a tramp stamp."

"Yeah, because getting tatted by a woman is so not cool, said no one ever!"

I took a deep breath and blew it out. I just needed to get this over with. Then I could get the fuck away from these morons and drown my misery in beer.

"Show us that tat," Joe urged. "What did you go with? I bet it's lit."

I unbuttoned my shirt and started to strip it off. "I don't know. I picked out a barbed wire tat, but apparently, she decided that it wasn't good enough."

"Wait, where did you go?" Andrew asked. "No tattoo artist is going to just ignore what you want."

"I don't know. Some place in Monee. The guy's name was Decker."

"Decker?" Joe's face lit up and then he started laughing. "Holy shit. She took you to a biker shop. Now I gotta see this tat."

I wondered how he knew who Decker was, but that was a question for another time. "I didn't actually see the tattoo getting done," I admitted after a moment.

"Because of the needle?" Andrew asked. He huffed out a laugh, pulling his lips between his teeth as he tried not to laugh. "Sorry, I forgot about your…aversion to needles."

"Look, I don't actually know what he did. All I know is that it's not what I picked out."

"Thank God," Joe snorted. "Barbed wire is so…old."

"The thing is, I'm scared to look at it," I admitted. "I mean, it's a permanent thing and…well, what if it sucks?"

"You can have it removed. I mean, it'll suck, but it's not like it can't be done." Joe reached forward and pulled at the bandage. I turned away, not wanting to see what it was. "Fire."

"What? She tattooed a fire on me?"

"No," he said frustratedly. "It's…awesome."

"Really?"

"Totally," Andrew agreed. "She did you a solid, man. Totally lit."

"Then just say it's really awesome," I snapped. "We talked about this," I said to Joe.

"Why doesn't he have to agree to it?" Joe argued.

"Because I just want to piss you off right now."

I walked into the downstairs bathroom and flicked on the light, taking my first look at the tattoo. I was shocked. It was completely badass, and was actually perfect for me. It was tattooed to make it look like my skin was peeled back and it was showing what was underneath. Inside were a bunch of cogs, just like in a machine. She had completely nailed down who I was with just this one tattoo. I was an engineer and she just showed me she knew exactly who I was. Fuck, I was an asshole.

"Damnit."

"You don't like it?"

I sighed, turning to Joe. "No, I do. I just realized how much of an asshole I really am."

"You could have asked me. I would have told you."

I flipped him off and walked away. Now I had to figure out how to apologize to her, and then, how I was going to make it up to her. I had a feeling that this would require a lot of begging, something I wasn't very good at.

KATHERINE

"You did what?" Chrissy shrieked.

"Look, I know it was kind of a shitty thing to do. I mean, when he passed out, I should have just canceled the appointment, but I saw this really awesome design and I wanted him to get it."

I took a bite of my sandwich and refused to look at her. The cafeteria was full of other things to look at. Things that wouldn't be judging me for the bad decision I made last night.

"Yeah, but he obviously didn't want it to begin with. A tattoo is permanent."

"I know, okay? I know I screwed up, but he didn't even bother to look at it before he got pissed."

Her eyebrows shot up. "Yeah, I gotta say, I'm on his side with this one."

"It was a really awesome tattoo," I grumbled.

"Look, I get that you were trying to bond with him, but you don't do that by forcing someone to go to the extremes you would. Men are like scared animals. You have to ease them into situations that they don't like. He actually seems to be handling the baby thing a lot better than the tattoo thing. Maybe it's for the best that this date ended so badly."

"Believe me, I know that and now so does he. Neither of us has to pretend like this might go somewhere because it's more than obvious that it would never work."

She shrugged a little. "Or it just shows how inflexible you both are."

"What does that mean?"

"Well, he did go there with the intention of getting the tattoo, but you didn't like what he chose."

"Because it sucked! It was barbed wire. I couldn't let him go through with that."

"He wouldn't have had to go through with it if you had just listened to him when he said he didn't want a tattoo."

I grumbled under my breath. She may have had a point.

"Look, you can't try to change the man. He's in his mid thirties. He's not going to change. You can either accept him for who he is or you decide he's not for you."

"My point wasn't to change him. I was just trying to show him some of my life. That was the whole point behind the whole thing, was to get to know each other better."

"But you're judging him for who he is. Have you tried to get to know him any? I mean, you have all these preconceived notions about him, but you really don't know anything about him, and frankly, with that attitude, you're never going to. And he's going to be in your life for a long time."

"So, you're saying I may have been too hard on him."

"Well, let's see," she said thoughtfully. "You got upset because he showed up to your baby appointment dirty, but then found out that he's a contractor and was out on a job. You didn't like it that he showed up at your house, even though he just came to work things out with you. And then there's the fact that you thought he was too uptight for wearing a suit on your date."

"Well, who does that? It wasn't like we went to a five star restaurant!"

"He was trying to look nice for you. Why is that so bad?"

I sighed, knowing she was right. "So, what you're saying is that I'm a bitch."

"I'm saying chill the fuck out and get to know him better. This doesn't have to turn into a romance, but maybe you should know who your baby daddy is before you decide he's a terrible person."

She stood from her seat and tossed her garbage. I followed, angry with myself because I knew she was right. I wasn't really giving him a chance. When he was saying all the wrong things in the truck, I wasn't trying to make him more at ease with me. Nope, I put on the bitch face right away. It wasn't like this was all my fault, but I was definitely playing my part in it all.

We took the elevator back up to the fourth floor and stepped out, but I was stopped by a hand across my chest.

"Holy shit."

"What?"

I followed her gaze over to the nurse's station and stared in shock. Eric was standing there holding a bouquet of roses, looking extremely uncomfortable.

"Yeah, he's a total dick," Chrissy hissed from beside me. As if Eric sensed my presence, he looked over to the elevators and stared straight at me. I swallowed hard, noticing that he was dressed nicely. He was clean shaven and based on the number of roses in that bouquet, he had come to make a big, fat apology. I felt Chrissy nudge me forward and I finally got my feet to work, moving over to him.

"Hey," I said hesitantly.

A small smile tilted his lips and he handed over the roses. "Hey. I came to apologize for last night."

"You mean, you came to apologize for me having Decker put a tattoo on you that you never agreed to?"

He laughed slightly. We both had fucked up last night. The difference was, he was standing here, at my place of work, apologizing when it should have been me that went to him.

"I, uh...saw the tattoo last night. It's actually pretty good. My brother informed me that it's *fire*. Whatever the fuck that is."

"So, you liked it?"

His eyes met mine, the intensity almost too much. I wanted to look away, but I forced myself to look him in the eye.

"It was perfect. I'm sorry I jumped down your throat about it. I mean, I'm still not exactly thrilled that I have a tattoo, but you were right. You saved me from making a huge mistake."

"Well, it just seemed to fit you."

"It does," he said, scratching his head slightly. "I'm not saying I'll be getting another one. I'm still not a fan of needles, but I'm glad I have this one."

I blushed for some reason. I knew my face was on fire, but I wasn't sure why. Did I really care that much about what Eric thought? I guess I did, because I found myself practically falling over myself at his praise.

"Thank you for the flowers," I said, finally realizing that I hadn't acknowledged them.

"You're welcome. Well, I just wanted to say I'm sorry for overreacting, so I'll let you get back to work."

He walked around me and headed for the elevator. "Wait!" I shouted, jogging after him. He turned to me, his beautiful blue eyes watching me questioningly. "You know, we made a deal last night."

"We did," his eyes lit with amusement. "But I'm not sure you're going to like what I have in mind."

"Well, I didn't exactly give you a choice, so I figure I have that coming."

"How about you come out to the house this weekend. Do you have any time off?"

"Sunday."

"Good. Bright and early," he said, turning and walking for the elevator.

"What should I wear?"

He turned back to me and lips spread into a slow, sexy grin. "Something to get dirty in."

I swallowed hard as I watched him get in the elevator. As he waited for the doors to close, he gave me a small wave, and I couldn't help but notice how handsome he looked today. He was just as sexy looking as last night, but something about him was different today. Maybe his eyes were a little softer, or he was a little less nervous. I couldn't put my finger on it, but something was different.

"So, he brought you flowers," Chrissy said, walking up to me as I continued to stare at the closed elevator.

"Yeah."

"Twenty-four red roses. That had to be expensive."

I nodded, lifting the flowers to my nose to smell them. "I know."

"Are you sure this guy isn't someone you could see yourself with?"

I couldn't say. If you had asked me this morning, I would have said there wasn't a chance in hell, but now? He made the effort to come down here and apologize. He brought me flowers and even told me I was right about the tattoo. I knew that wasn't an easy thing for a man to do, so the fact that he did it made him all the more attractive.

"Ladies," Charlene walked by, "staring at the elevator all day won't help the patients we have sitting in those beds."

I shook off my nerves as I pulled into his driveway. He hadn't said what time to come out, but I knew he was always up early. When I woke up at six this morning, with butterflies in my stomach, I knew that it was better just to get up. There would be no going back to sleep. I was excited for today, but also a little nervous. What if I did something stupid again? What if I snapped at him again and ruined everything? I couldn't afford to screw this up. I would be connected to this man for the rest of my life, so I needed to get to know him and stop judging him based on what I saw on the surface.

I got out of my car and shut the door, taking my next steps with confidence. I didn't even make it to the porch before Joe stepped out with a huge grin on his face.

"Hey quiche-girl," he said affectionately, walking toward me with his arms spread wide. My eyes widened in surprise. I didn't know what to do. Was he really going to hug me? He walked right up to me and wrapped his arms around me, squeezing me tight for a moment before stepping back.

"Uh…I didn't know we were at the hugging stage."

He gave me a funny look. "We're family now. You're my brother's bae."

"No, I'm not," I corrected. "We're just…getting to know each other."

His eyes softened a little and he wrapped his arm around my shoulder, walking me toward the porch. "I think we need to have a convo about what's really going on here."

"And what's really going on here?"

He pulled me down to the swing with him and placed his hand on my thigh. I quirked an eyebrow at him and he immediately moved his hand behind my shoulders on the back of the swing.

"I heard that he brought you flowers yesterday."

"He told you that?"

"Nah. It was all over Facebook. Everyone's trying to decide if you two are together or if the flowers meant something else."

"What do you mean *all over Facebook?*"

"The town page."

"There's a town page?"

He snorted. "Yeah, and when you start showing, that's going to be all over the page as well. People in this town are nosy and there won't be any escaping their questions."

"Perfect," I muttered. I thought I would just have to deal with their questions and stares, but apparently, I would also have to deal with my life being discussed on the town Facebook page.

"I know my brother is all basic and shit, but he's also the best man I know. He would do anything for his family, and that includes you now. Yeah, he's definitely a wet blanket, but he means well. He's just not as adventurous as the rest of us. But you should have seen the look on his face when he saw that tat. He knew he had fucked up with you, and I'm guessing that's what the flowers were all about."

"Why would you assume that?"

"Because, like I said, my brother's the best man I know. He admits when he fucks up and he always tries to right a wrong. There's nothing my brother won't do for you now that you're carrying his child. Even if this doesn't work out between the two of you, he'll still walk through fire for you. It's just the way he is."

"Why are you telling me all this?"

"Because I have a feeling that you don't have anyone in your life that has ever been that dedicated to you. But you do now, and every single one of us will be there for you, for anything you need. You just have to give him a chance to prove it."

I sighed heavily. I knew that I was judging him too harshly. That's why I was here right now. I wanted to get to know him. A man that brought you flowers when he fucked up, when he wasn't even fucking you, couldn't be that bad. So we were a little different. Wasn't variety the spice of life?

"He's in the shop over there," Joe nodded to a building across the lawn.

"Thanks."

I stood and walked down the steps, then headed across the lawn. My heart thundered louder and louder with every step I took toward him. It felt like something was shifting in that moment, like I was accepting something and now my heart knew it. I laughed at my thoughts and stopped outside the door. After taking a deep breath, I opened the door and stopped dead in my tracks. It was like a porno standing right in front of me. My very own personal porno that included only the man that knocked me up.

He was sawing a piece of metal and had a metal helmet pulled down over his face. Sparks were flying all around and all the noise started to fade out as I took in the man before me. He was wearing a white t-shirt and his jeans were slung low on his hips. His work boots sent tingles into my lady parts. Fucking work boots. They were so fucking sexy on him. My gaze trailed back up his body to his biceps. They were bulging, covered in a light sheen of sweat. Tiny droplets dripped down his arm, collecting at his elbow before dropping to the ground.

My mouth was dry, and suddenly all I cared about was walking over to this man and kissing him. I wanted to feel his hard body against mine and feel that bulge in his pants again. His arm flexed as he shut off the saw and lifted his helmet. Dirt was smudged on his face and when he turned to me, I could swear that my panties flooded with desire. Good god, what was happening to me? I just stared at him, my mouth hanging open as I tried to come up with something intelligent to say.

His eyes stared intently at me, like he could read exactly what I was thinking. Did he know how much I wanted him right now? Did he know I was thinking about what it would feel like if he wrapped his hand in my hair and pulled me into a kiss? I shook my head slightly as he walked toward me. He had a way of stalking toward me that I hadn't really noticed before. He didn't stop until he was right in front of me. His hand brushed against mine, then slipped around mine. His fingers intertwined with mine and my eyes dropped from his gaze to watch his hand linked with mine. My breath hitched slightly at the sight.

"Come on," he said, tugging me slightly toward him. I didn't know what he had planned for the day, but watching him in his shop working wasn't what I had expected. He led me over to a workbench where he had wood cut into long pieces.

"What is this?"

He looked up at me, his eyes bright with hope. "I'm building a crib for the baby."

I didn't know what to say. It was not at all what I expected when I came out here today. I thought he would take me to do some work on his house or something. I didn't know he even had the skills to do this sort of thing. I slowly looked away from his intense gaze and looked down at the pieces in front of me. It just looked like a big pile of wood to me right now, but I was eager to see how it all turned out.

"So, what do you need me to do?"

A slow smile split his lips. It wasn't much, but it was the most beautiful look I had seen in my whole life. Why had I not given him a chance before now? I didn't know how any of this would turn out, but it was clear that I had judged him too harshly. And it wasn't just the way my body was responding to his right now. It was the fact that he was so dedicated to this baby that he just found out about, that he was already building a crib for it. If there was any doubt in my mind that he would be a good father, it was wiped away in just these few minutes that I stood in his shop.

Over the next few hours, I watched as he made perfect spindles for the crib, his eyes watching carefully every last move he made. If something didn't work out right, he tossed it in the corner and started over. I asked him questions about what he was doing, and I was surprised at how easily the conversation flowed. He was in his element now, and there wasn't the pressure to perform.

I watched his large fingers move with the sandpaper as he smoothed the rough edges of the spindles. It was sexy to watch his hands at work. They were hands that built a crib for our child, and that was more amazing to watch than anything I had ever experienced before. It was a better rush than jumping out of a plane or whitewater rafting. And the longer that I sat there and watched, the more my heart softened toward this man.

"Do you want to try?"

I startled out of my fascination with his hands and looked up at him. He was staring at me, but if he caught on to me eye-fucking his hands, he didn't let on.

"Um, I don't really know what to do."

"I'll show you." He walked around behind me, his body brushing right up against mine. His left hand slid over mine, moving it until it wrapped around the spindle. I held it hard, my breathing turning slightly erratic with him this close. Then his right hand slid over my right hand and we picked up the sandpaper.

With his hand on top of mine, he slowly spun the spindle with his left hand while twisting the sand paper around the spindle as he moved our right hands up and down. He continued to move my hand along with his, practically stroking the wood with the sandpaper. It was the most erotic thing I had ever seen, though I wasn't sure he meant it to be that way.

Dust fell to the ground as we continued to work the sandpaper over the wood until the sandpaper needed to be changed. He tossed it aside and grabbed another piece, continuing the torment of being so close to him and feeling his body pressed up against mine. And then he leaned around my shoulder and blew the dust off the spindle as he examined it for anything left behind. My eyes were glued to his face as I watched his eyes moving along the wood. They flicked up to meet mine and time stood still. For a moment, we were locked together, neither of us breaking eye contact. For a moment, there was this electric spark between us that made me want him more than anyone else before him.

He shifted slightly and I felt a bulge press against me. My eyes widened, but he didn't move. He just continued to stare at me with lust in his eyes. I thought maybe he would make a move, try to kiss me or press himself further against me, but he didn't. He just stared at me, his eyes telling me how much he wanted me.

He slowly stood, his left hand still wrapped around mine as we held the spindle. His right hand slowly lowered with mine to drop the sandpaper on the table. His hand slowly slid up my arm, his touch burning like fire through my veins. His hand gently squeezed my shoulder and then slid down my back until it rested on my waist. I wanted to lean back into him. I wanted him to take me and make love to me, but I knew he wouldn't do it. He didn't move that fast with women, and I had already learned my lesson in trying to make him do something he wasn't ready for.

His left hand slipped from mine and slid around my waist, his large hand resting across my belly. I felt his breath hot on my neck, almost like he was trying to decide if he wanted to kiss me or not. My eyes slipped closed and I prayed that he would kiss my neck or give me some sign that he wanted me as much as I wanted him in this moment. I decided to take a chance and tell him how I was feeling. What did I have to lose?

"I want you," I whispered. His hot breath fanned out over my skin and his hand tightened on my waist.

"I want you too, but not like this."

I turned my head so I could see him. His eyes were tight with restraint and need. "Like what?"

"Do you think I'm not attracted to you? I think you're the most beautiful woman I've ever seen. But I don't want to fuck this up. There's too much at stake. I want to build something with you, and that means we have to take this slow." His hand slid across my belly again and his eyes slid shut. "I want all of you, not just the part of you that wants to fuck me."

I swallowed hard and nodded. I wanted him so badly right now. My heart was pounding out of control and his touch sent shivers down my spine. But he was right, there was too much at stake. We couldn't just fuck around. We needed to do what was best for our child. That meant taking things slow and seeing where they could go.

He stepped back from me, sucking in a breath like it pained him to leave me. For the first time since he had wrapped his body around mine, I felt like I could breathe again. I had been here for hours with him, but I knew that I couldn't stay with him any longer today if I had any hopes of resisting him. I didn't want to screw this up with him.

I turned toward him and raised up on my toes to press a kiss to his cheek. He had given me more than just the promise of what could come today. He had also shown me a side to him that made me weak in the knees. "Thank you for today."

He nodded slightly, his head down as he gazed at the floor. I turned to leave, but he snatched my hand, stopping me in my tracks. I looked back at him, but he was still looking at the floor. He squeezed my hand before dropping it. I walked out of the shop feeling like I had been hit by a truck. Holy shit, this man was shocking the hell out of me. One thing was clear, no matter what my initial thoughts were about him, if I continued to see him, there was a very good chance that I could fall for this man.

ERIC

I stayed in the shop for a good hour after she left, just trying to get my body under control. If I wasn't sure of my attraction to her before, I damn well knew that I wanted her now. It wasn't just because she was gorgeous. Although, now that I thought about it, I wasn't sure how I had been so blind before. Even when I was hit with the news that I was going to be a father, I hadn't seen it. Now, it was all I could see.

I tried my damndest not to stare at her as she watched me work today. Those gorgeous green eyes took in every last move I made. I could tell she was genuinely enjoying herself, just being there with me as I created the crib for our child. When I told her what I was doing, I could tell immediately how much that meant to her. She was choked up over it, and now that I knew how much she appreciated the gesture, I only wanted to make more things for her. I could make her a rocking chair for the baby's room. I could build a dresser for the baby. Hell, I would do anything she wanted if it meant she looked at me like that again.

But no matter how much I wanted her, I knew that fucking her would only make things messy at this point. The attraction was there, but I wanted to build a strong foundation for our relationship. I wanted it to be so strong that we had something unbreakable. We started out rocky, but I wanted everything moving forward to be based on something special.

I finally cleaned up the shop and headed inside for the night. I still had plenty of hours in the day, but for once, I just wanted to chill out and watch a game with my brothers. Tomorrow would come too quickly, and then it was back to the grindstone.

I walked in the house and took a shower, thinking about Katherine the whole time. When I was pressed up against her and I felt her curves against my body, I couldn't help the response my body took. It wasn't just my cock that wanted her. My whole body shook with a need that I had never felt before. My cock had pressed against my zipper so tight when it brushed against her. It would be nice for once to think that it was just my cock that wanted her, but I knew better. That just wasn't the way I was built. I wasn't like other guys that just got horny and wanted any woman they passed. Yeah, I still jacked off if I wasn't getting laid, but it was all using my imagination. But it wasn't like I walked around with a perpetual woody. My body responded when I was really attracted to a woman. That was why it always took me so long to close the deal with a woman. I needed to really want her. My body had to crave her.

Honestly, this was the first time that my body had ever craved a woman as desperately as Katherine. It was why I had a hard time pulling away from her, why I had snatched her arm when she tried to leave. I just needed to touch her one last time. It had taken everything in me not to kiss her when I wanted to. I had wanted to pull her hair off her shoulders and suck on her neck. I wanted to slide my hands under her shirt and palm her breasts in my hands and feel her soft skin under my calloused fingers. But that wouldn't have helped our situation any. No, I needed to be smart about this. I needed to make sure that we could be compatible in other ways, and not just in the bedroom. That wouldn't do our child any good.

"Hey," Will nodded as I came downstairs. "I didn't think you were ever getting out of that shower."

"I had a lot on my mind," I said, not really paying attention to him.

"Yeah? Anyone in particular?"

I glanced up and saw him grinning at me. "Don't be a shit head."

"What? It's nice to see my brother in love."

"I'm not in love."

"Right," he snorted, taking a sip of his beer.

"It's not love. It's…it's the possibility of more."

"Yeah?"

I nodded. I didn't know how to explain it, and I doubted my brother would understand. As far as I knew, he had never come close to being in love. He wasn't quite as discerning with who he slept with.

"Well, from what I've seen of her, she seems like a good match for you."

"A good match?" I asked incredulously.

"Yeah, I mean, she's hot, which is like ten points in her favor."

I rolled my eyes. "I wasn't aware that hotness points were all that mattered."

"It's not, but it's a great start. I mean, would you be so attracted to her if she wasn't so beautiful? Can you honestly say that it doesn't factor in at all?"

"No, I can't, but that's not all that matters in a relationship."

"Exactly, and that's where you and she fit. She's your opposite. She balances you out."

"How do you figure?"

"Well, she lightens you up. She makes you think about other things."

"You've met her once. How could you possibly know this?"

"Because I talked to Joe."

"Here we go," I said, snatching a beer out of the fridge. I leaned against the counter. I couldn't wait to hear this. "So, what does Joe say?"

"Well, he had a talk with her when she got here today." My fist tightened on my beer as I thought of my kid brother hitting on my woman. My woman? The woman I was…having a child with.

"And what did he say?"

"You should be happy. He talked you up, said what a great guy you are and she's the luckiest woman in the world, because she's got your devotion until the day she dies. Or something like that."

"That doesn't sound like Joe."

"No, but believe it or not, he's not just some idiot running around talking in incomplete sentences. He does pay attention and he sees what this woman could mean to you. And he has your back. You know that's always the way it'll be with us."

"I guess...I hadn't really thought about it like that. I just always pictured Joe as...Joe."

"That's because you only see what you want to see. It's the same thing with this woman. Where you see a chaotic mess, I see a woman that has the potential to give you the life you've always wanted, but like no other woman could."

I thought back to the shop, knowing that there was definitely potential there. "I just have to take things slow."

"That's always your problem, man. You take things too slow."

"Will, we're not talking about a woman I want to fuck. We're talking about the woman that's carrying my child. We've already had a rough start. I can't just go fuck her and not think of the consequences."

"That she might like you even more?" he laughed incredulously. "Come on, you need to take the risk now or you may miss out on the opportunity."

I shook my head. I didn't need my brother telling me how to play this. I knew deep down that I needed to proceed with caution. "I'm not in this just to see if we'll have a relationship. I'm in this for the long haul. She's carrying my kid and I want that kid to live with both his or her parents. In order to do that, I need to build something real with her. I know you don't understand that because you'll fuck anything in a skirt, but I have more at stake here, and I'm not gonna fuck it up."

"Alright," he said, holding up his hands. "I'm not trying to rush you, man. I just don't want you to miss out on something good with her."

I ran a hand through my hair in frustration. I knew that things were building between us, but what if it was all sexual? What if I couldn't convince this woman that I was the man for her? I understood now that she didn't want to marry me out of obligation to her kid, but I couldn't stand the thought of being away from my family. That just wasn't who I was. I needed to make this work.

"Look, I'm sorry. I didn't mean to make you flip out-"

"I'm not flipping out."

"Your right eye is twitching."

I slapped my hand over my eye, feeling it twitch beneath my fingers. Will smirked, trying to hold in his laughter.

"You're an asshole."

KATHERINE

This was ridiculous. If I wanted to see Eric, I would go see him. There was plenty to talk about with him. We were having a baby together, after all. I paced around my townhouse some more, wondering what I was going to talk to him about once I got there. I hadn't made any decisions on my living arrangements yet, so bringing that up would be pointless. And it's not like we needed to talk about baby names or anything. It was way too soon for that.

I groaned in frustration, pulling at my hair. I could still feel his body pressed against mine a few days ago. I wanted to feel that again. I wanted to be close to him and see where this could go. I had rushed my opinions of him in the beginning, but now that I had seen this other side to him, I wanted to know more. The problem was, he was taking things slow and I had to respect that.

I knew that part of it was hormones. I had read through some books, and they all talked about a heightened need for sex during the first trimester. Well, I was there right now, and it wasn't like I was going to go out and find someone else to sleep with while I was pregnant with another man's baby. Not that I even wanted to. I was attracted to Eric a lot more than I ever thought possible. It just took having my eyes pried open to see it. All the things that I thought I hated about him was just surface bullshit. I'm sure it would drive me crazy still, but now I could see the man underneath and he was definitely worth taking another look at.

"Screw it," I muttered, snatching my purse off the table and heading for the door. I wanted to see him, so I was going over there. I didn't really think things through until I was almost over to his house. I hadn't bothered to call first. I hadn't even sent a text message. What if he didn't want to see me? What if this was more one-sided than I thought? Maybe that moment in his shop was all my imagination. Maybe he didn't really feel the pull as strongly as I did. And if that was the case, I was going to make a fool out of myself by showing up at his house.

I pulled over on the side of the road and put my Jeep in park. What the hell was I doing? I could have called him or texted him over the past few days, but instead, I hid from him, afraid of what I was starting to feel for him. And now I was just going over there without calling. God, I was being stupid.

Headlights pulled up behind me and a bulky figure got out. I cursed at myself for being so stupid to pull over on the side of the road at night. I dug into my purse and grabbed the pepper spray, ready to use it if this was some psycho. The knock on the window startled me and I almost sprayed the pepper spray in my purse. I turned to the window, holding a hand to my chest. Eric's concerned face stared back at me, instantly putting me at ease. I rolled down my window and gave him a slight smile.

"Is everything okay? Did you break down?"

"What?" Shit. How was I going to explain this away? "Uh…no, I just…thought I saw a spider."

"So, you pulled over in the dark on the side of the road? That's not very safe."

"I have pepper spray."

He nodded slightly, but I could tell he wasn't too happy about what I was saying. "Were you coming to see me?"

I blushed in embarrassment, but he couldn't see that in the dark. "Yeah, I just thought we should talk."

"Alright, well, follow me to the house."

I nodded and rolled my window back up, shaking off the chills that ran through me when I looked at him. I pulled back onto the road, but as I started following him, I realized that now I had to think up something to talk to him about, since I had just told him I had wanted to talk. Shit. Why did I get myself in situations like this?

I pulled in behind him and got out of my car. I followed him up to the house and smiled when he held the door open for me. It didn't look like his brothers were there, so at least I didn't have to worry about that. On the other hand, now I was alone in his house, just he and I with no one around to stop the inevitable awkwardness that was about to drop in. I should have had a plan.

"Did you eat dinner yet?"

"No." I sat down at his kitchen table as he moved to the fridge.

"We grilled out last night. I have some leftover burgers if you want some."

"Sure, that's fine."

He got to work plating up the food, taking out some sides they had and dumping them on the plates also. He slipped the first plate into the microwave and turned to me, his arms crossed over his muscled chest as he leaned against the counter.

"So, what did you want to talk to me about?"

I blushed and ducked my head. It was best just to come clean about the whole thing. "I didn't actually have a reason for coming out here."

His eyes lit with surprise, but he didn't say anything.

"I was thinking about you and I wanted to see you. And then I thought, why shouldn't I come see you? We're having a baby together, and we're trying to see where this can go. So…so, I took a chance and drove out here, but then I realized that I was driving over and I hadn't even called you to ask if it was okay."

"So, you thought stopping on the side of the road was the way to go?"

"Well, I didn't see the big deal at the time."

He pushed off the counter and stalked over to me. He pressed one hand on the table and leaned on the back of my chair, putting his face right in front of mine. "If you want to come over, you don't need to call. You can come whenever you want, for any reason you want. I can't guarantee that I'll always be home, but that's the only reason you would ever have to text me first. Okay?"

The way he said it with such finality made me believe every word of what he said. It was like we were crossing another bridge in our relationship here. I nodded, my eyes flicking down to his lips. I wanted to kiss them, to know what it would feel like to be kissed hard by this man. Before I could make a move, he shifted away from me and back to the microwave. It was like he knew what I wanted and he was going to torture me until I was a quaking mess.

He pulled the plate out of the microwave and set it down in front of me, then grabbed some buns out of the cabinet, setting them on the table for me.

"Water okay?"

"Sure."

I watched as he moved around the kitchen, remembering how he did the same thing for me the morning after our one night stand. I put together my burger and started eating as he warmed up his own food. The burger was delicious, even if it was made yesterday. I didn't care. I hated cooking, especially after a long day at work. And the days had seemed longer than ever recently. This pregnancy was kicking my ass. Most days, I flopped into bed at the end of a shift, just showering long enough to be clean. What I really wanted was a nice, long bath.

"It can't be that good," Eric said as he sat down across from me.

"It's delicious. I usually have take-out for dinner."

"You don't cook?" There was no judgement in his voice, just curiosity.

"I'm just too tired when I get home. Before, I was just lazy, but now that I'm pregnant, I just don't have the energy at the end of a shift."

He nodded, his eyes boring into me as I ate. He watched my every move, eyeing how I took a bite of the burger and how I slowly chewed. I felt like I was under the microscope, but the way his eyes smoldered, I found that I didn't really care all that much.

"I could cook for you," he finally said, taking a bite of his own food. "What time do you get off work?"

Startled, I didn't know how to respond. He would cook for me? "I wasn't suggesting that you should cook for me."

He was about to take a bite, but paused, staring me down. "I know that. I was offering because I want to take care of you."

"Why?" I asked before I could think better of it. "I mean, you don't owe me anything."

He chewed slowly, wiping his hands on a napkin. I watched as his throat worked when he swallowed. He picked up his glass and took a long drink of water before he finally answered my question.

"This has nothing to do with me owing you. I don't keep points in my relationships. My offer is simply because we're family now, and I want to take care of you. You're pregnant with my child, and I want to take care of both of you. I don't like the idea of you being so tired at the end of work that you don't even want to make dinner. I'm usually in town until the evening. I can swing by your place and have dinner waiting for you. We can eat together or you can kick me out. Either way, it would make me feel better knowing that you aren't doing this all on your own. But I'm not making any promises on how good it tastes," he added with a smile.

Wow. Tears pricked my eyes at his statement. I never cried. Like, not even when I watched a really sad movie. It just never happened. The only excuse I had was that my hormones were out of control right now, and he had just said something so sweet that I couldn't help but be touched. I blinked back the tears and cleared my throat, trying to work past the hormonal outburst that I was suddenly struck with.

"Hey," he reached across the table, covering my small hand with his large one. "I didn't mean to make you cry."

I shook my head. "It's not that. It's just...stupid hormones," I muttered under my breath.

"So, is that a yes to dinner?"

I nodded, because I didn't trust myself to speak right now.

"Good. You can make me a copy of your key, if you're comfortable with that. Just send me your schedule and I'll make sure dinner is waiting for you every night."

"Thank you," I croaked out.

"No problem."

We finished eating in relative silence. I watched him as discreetly as possible as he ate, but he flat out stared at me. It made my body tingle. I had to get out of here before I jumped him. I was just about to thank him for dinner when his phone rang. His brows furrowed when he looked at the caller ID.

"Is everything okay?"

"It's my parents," he murmured, but didn't take the call.

"Have you told them?"

"Not yet."

I watched as his thumb swiped across the screen. He cleared his throat before answering. I thought maybe I should leave. It felt like this was a private conversation, but I also knew that he was worried about telling his parents, that he was worried about them being disappointed in him. It was like a bad car wreck, I just sat there and stared in horror at what was about to happen.

"Hey, Ma...yeah, I'm good. Business is good."

His eyes flicked up to mine and then down again. He rubbed a hand across his forehead as he nodded along with the conversation and put in the appropriate yes and no's. My heart was actually hurting for him right now. Watching him and knowing that this was going to be so hard for him was just killing me. When he first told me that he wanted me to be his pretend girlfriend and why, my immediate reaction was that he was being a pussy. But after getting to know him better, I didn't feel that way anymore. Hell, I was nervous to tell my parents too. That's what happens when you have parents that truly care about you. Being afraid of disappointing them is part of life.

"Yeah, can you put Dad on too. There's something I have to tell you guys...No, it's not bad."

He waited as his dad came on the line. His eyes slipped closed, and I knew he was gearing up to tell them.

"Uh...so, I have some good news to share with you. You're going to be grandparents…No, Derek and Claire aren't having a baby…I…it's me." He cleared his throat again as his right eye started twitching out of control. "I…"

I shoved out of my chair, unable to watch this anymore. Eric glanced up at me, confused by what I was doing. I grabbed the phone out of his hands and put it on speakerphone.

"Hello? Mr. and Mrs.…." My eyes widened when I realized that I didn't know Eric's last name. He quickly muted the phone.

"Cortell."

He unmuted the phone and I continued. "Mr. and Mrs. Cortell, my name is Katherine. I'm your son's girlfriend."

"Girlfriend?" his mom said excitedly. "We didn't know he was seeing anyone."

"It's new," Eric said quickly.

"But not that new," I clarified. He didn't want his mom to think he had just knocked me up after a few dates. "It's something that's been going on for a while now."

"Right after I last saw you," Eric said quickly. "And we're going to have a baby now."

"Oh my gosh!" his mom squealed. "I'm going to be a grandma!"

"Stop screaming in my ear," his dad said. "I'm standing right here. You don't need to shout at me."

"I can't believe it. This is so exciting. When are you due?"

"I'm only about eight weeks along."

"Oh, I wish I was there to help you out with everything," his mom gushed. "I'm sure you're going to have so much fun getting the house ready. Which room will you make the baby's room?"

"Uh…we haven't really worked out all the details yet," Eric said. I could tell he was calmer, knowing that he wasn't having to explain this on his own.

"I hope you're taking care of her, giving her foot massages every night and keeping the stress down."

"He's taking great care of me, Mrs. Cortell," I said as I stared into Eric's eyes. It wasn't completely a lie. He made me dinner tonight and offered to have dinner waiting for me every night. He stared back at me, affection bright in his eyes. His hand slid over mine and then he intertwined our fingers. I glanced down at our locked hands, thinking how nice this was. We were just two people taking care of each other. We didn't have any of the romance yet, but for now, this was really nice.

"Oh, please, call me Ma. Everyone else does."

I smiled, chuckling slightly when Eric rolled his eyes. "Alright, Ma."

She gushed on and on for a few more minutes, but all I could do was stare at my fingers interlocked with Eric's.

"What are you going to do about Joe and Andrew?" his dad asked. "The three of you are going to need your space, and their bachelor lifestyles are going to be a pain in the ass."

"We'll figure it out, Dad."

My eyes widened as I realized that they thought we were living together. It was an honest conclusion to come to. We told them we were together. Why wouldn't they assume that we were living together? When they hung up, I couldn't help the slight panic that shot through me.

"They think we live together. What are we going to do?"

He shook his head slightly. "It doesn't matter. We have plenty of time to figure that out."

I nodded, the panic easing some at his cool demeanor. I went to pull away, but he held tight to my hand.

"Thank you…for doing that for me. I know you must think that I'm pathetic, not wanting to tell my parents."

"Honestly? When you first told me, that's exactly what I thought. But I know you better now. I don't think it's pathetic that you want to protect your parents."

"But all this was pointless if we can't find a way to make this work," he said frustratedly.

"We just take this one day at a time," I said calmly. "There's no point in panicking over anything just yet. Like you said, we have time to figure all this out. And if it doesn't work, we're two grown adults. We'll figure it out, and I'm sure your parents will understand."

He nodded. "Why did you change your mind?"

A slight smile tilted my lips. "It was like watching cattle getting slaughtered. I just couldn't do it. Plus, now you have to do the same for me. And my parents are divorced, so we have to do it twice."

He paled slightly, but nodded. "I can do that."

"Oh, and my dad owns a gun."

ERIC

I had the keys to Katherine's place, but getting there by the time she got off work was going to be a problem. Everything that could go wrong today was going wrong. I just wanted to get over there and keep my word, that she wouldn't have to worry about dinner when she got home. It was my job as the father of her child to take care of her, but I was completely failing at that right now.

"Anna, just take care of it," I snapped as she tried to explain yet another thing that was wrong with my computer system.

"Wow, somebody's crabby today."

"Look, I have someplace I need to be. I hired an office manager to take care of this shit for me so I didn't have to deal with it. Are you competent enough to deal with this or do I need to find someone else?"

Anna's eyes narrowed in on me just as she picked up a mug. I knew she was going to throw it. I knew I deserved it. I was being an ass, and had been for the last half hour. I ducked right as she hurled the mug through the air. It smashed against the wall and fell to the floor in small pieces.

She got up from behind the desk and stalked around her desk to get in my face. I shrank back slightly, a little ashamed at how scared I was of this woman. I was going to have to have a serious talk with Robert about hiring this psycho. I took a step back as she approached, but I knew there was no getting out whatever was about to happen here.

"I want donuts tomorrow morning, or I'll let you find a new office manager. One that's *competent* enough to deal with your shit."

I swallowed hard and nodded. "Donuts. Got it."

I reached behind me and swung open the door, just barely slipping through as I saw her lips quirk up in a feral grin. When she dated Robert, I didn't remember her being like this. So, whatever that dickhead did to her, she was going to make my life hell until he fixed it. I got in my truck and pulled up his number as I headed to Katherine's place.

"Can this wait? I'm about to walk into a meeting."

"No, it can't wait, because whatever the fuck you did to Anna, she's taking it out on me."

"For no reason? You mean, she's just being nasty to you and it has nothing to do with you?"

I considered this for a moment. "Alright, well, I might not be helping, but she was not like this before."

"Like you would remember."

"Well, I don't remember the spawn of satan being around much when you were dating, so there's that."

He sighed heavily into the phone. "What do you want me to do about it?"

"Fix it. Whatever the fuck happened between you two, fix it so that she'll be nice to me again. Or…for once."

"Fine, I'll fix it."

"And you have to buy donuts for her. I'm going broke buying donuts."

"Yeah, you're broke and can't afford some fucking donuts."

"Not when she whips them at my head."

"Again, that's not because of me."

"Whatever. I expect donuts delivered tomorrow morning to the office. And they better be fresh."

"Fine."

"And nothing filled with raspberries," I added quickly. I had already learned my lesson with that one.

"Anything else, your Highness?"

"Fuck off."

I pulled up outside Katherine's townhouse as I hung up the phone. She wasn't home yet, so I quickly got out and pulled out my keys, flipping on the lights as I walked inside. She didn't have much for dinner, but I could make her something simple. I would have to pick up groceries the next time I came over.

I started on the chicken and then the potatoes when my phone rang. It was Will.

"Yeah?"

"Are you almost home? I'm hungry."

"So, make something to eat."

"I thought you were cooking."

"Will," I sighed, "you have your own place. Go make your own damn food."

"Where are you?"

"I'm at Katherine's."

"Why?"

"I'm making her dinner."

"Why?"

I rolled my eyes. "Because she works a lot and she's tired."

"*You* work a lot," he pointed out.

"I'm not pregnant."

"Thank God for that. You'd make a terrible pregnant woman."

"Is there a point to this conversation?"

"Yeah, what the hell am I going to do for dinner?"

"Well, just a guess, but you could make it for yourself."

"But I'm at your house," he whined.

"It used to be your house too."

"Doesn't matter. I'm at your house. You're supposed to do the cooking."

"I didn't invite you over, asshole."

"Since when have you ever invited me over?"

I squeezed my eyes shut, pinching the bridge of my nose. "I'm hanging up now."

"No, wait, what am I supposed to do about dinner?"

I ended the call without another word and finished up preparing the food. I made sure that I had everything right so I didn't destroy our food like the first time I told her I would cook for her. I was just sticking it in the oven when the doorbell rang. It couldn't be Katherine. She wouldn't ring her own doorbell. I wasn't sure that I should answer, but then again, whoever it was knew that someone was here. I walked to the door and pulled it open, seeing an older man at the door.

"Can I help you?"

He quirked an eyebrow and looked me up and down. I was in my dirty clothes still and I was pretty sure I smelled from my long day. "Who the fuck are you?"

"Eric. Who are you?"

"George. I'm Katherine's father. So, you're him."

By *you're him,* I could only take that to mean that he knew that I was the one that got Katherine pregnant.

"Yes, sir."

"Yes, sir," he scoffed, shoving me aside as he stepped inside. "Don't think those pretty manners are gonna make me like you any."

"Sir, I know that this isn't the ideal situation-"

"Let me tell you something, nobody is good enough for my little girl. Do you love her?"

"Love her? I barely know her."

His eyes narrowed in on me. "You're standing in her house and she's not here. I'd say you'd better get to knowing her a lot better than what you're doing now."

"Sir, your daughter is old enough to make her own decisions, without your input. Now, I understand that you might not be happy about the situation-"

"Not happy? Why the hell would I be happy that you're here?"

"Because I'll take care of her."

"Nobody needs to take care of my little girl. She doesn't need a man in her life. Especially not one that makes himself comfortable in my daughter's home. Do you even have a job?"

Anger flared inside me. I didn't need to take this shit from him. Things might not be perfect between Katherine and I, but I would never take advantage of her.

"Look, I get that you think I didn't protect her. It was a mistake, but I'm here to help make it right. From now on, we'll always be a family because of that baby. I don't shirk away from my responsibilities."

His face mottled in rage and his whole body tensed. "You got my little girl pregnant?"

I was confused. Wasn't that what he was so upset about? "Wait, why are you so pissed at me if you didn't know?"

"I heard that someone had been hanging around my girl. I was assuming it was you."

I swallowed hard, but stood my ground. It was too late to take back the fact that I had just outed the pregnancy to her dad. And then I remembered Katherine's warning. *My dad has a gun.* "You don't have a gun on you, right?"

"No." I sighed in relief. "But I don't need one for this," he said as he lunged at me. I tried to sidestep him, but he was too fast, catching me around the waist as he tackled me to the ground. I wiggled out easily from underneath him, but he came at me again. There were so many things around the house I could beat him with, but I couldn't hurt her father. That was just bad manners.

"Now, hold on, George. Let's just talk about this like calm, rational adults."

"You be calm. I'll be rational and kick your ass."

He swung at me and I ducked, holding up my hands placatingly. "George, your daughter is an adult. She can make up her own mind about who she sleeps with."

His face turned almost purple as he swung again. I stepped back, jerking my head away as his fist came at me. "Wrong. Fucking. Answer!"

He swung harder this time and almost got me. If he kept coming at me, I was going to have to figure something out. I could only back away so much. Maybe he would just wear himself down.

The front door opened and I turned to see Katherine walking in the door. I missed the fist coming at my face and felt the hard crunch against my jaw. My body jerked with the force of the blow, but I stayed on my feet.

"Dad!"

"You got pregnant by him?" George yelled.

"You told him?" Katherine shrieked at me.

"I didn't mean to!"

"Like you didn't mean to get her pregnant?" George asked, swinging at me again. I ducked, feeling the air whoosh over my head. Katherine dropped her things and rushed over, trying to get between us. My eyes widened and I shoved her to the side, just as her dad was going to swing again. His fist connected again, but I gladly took it if it meant that Katherine didn't get caught up in his rage.

"Dad, stop hitting him!"

"How many times did I tell you not to spread your legs for the charmers?"

"Trust me, he's not a charmer," Katherine muttered.

"He doesn't treat you right?" George fumed and turned back to me, getting in my face again.

"He does!" Katherine shouted. "He's just not the most…it doesn't matter! You can't just come in here and beat him up!"

"I think we all need to just take a step back and calm down."

George slowly turned to me, rage burning in his eyes. I guess that was the wrong thing to say.

                        ∼

I sat on Katherine's couch with two paper towels shoved in my nose to catch the bleeding. George sat beside me, icing his hand as Katherine moved around the kitchen, doing the job that I was supposed to be doing. But after George attacked me yet again,

Katherine told us that if we were going to behave like two misbehaving toddlers, then we were going to be put in a timeout like toddlers.

I glared at George and he glared right back at me. It wasn't like I meant to tell him about the pregnancy. I just thought Katherine had already done it. Stupid, I know, since she had told me that she was nervous to tell her parents. I had actually thought she was joking when she said I could tell her parents with her. Not that I wasn't up for it, but Katherine didn't strike me as the type of woman to shy away from that.

Katherine walked into the living room, carrying two beers and the dish from the oven. I stood immediately, reaching out to help her.

"I would have brought that in for you, Kat."

"Kat?" her dad snorted.

I glared at him. I hadn't meant to call her that. It just fit. It was a helluva lot better than Kiki.

"Dad, can you try for just two minutes to be civil?"

"I am being civil. Do you see my gun in my hand?"

"I thought you said you didn't have it?" I asked.

"It's in my truck. Do you want me to get it? I could give you a demonstration."

"Alright," Kat jumped in. "How about we put away the guns and the fighting words and talk about this like adults." She glared at both of us and then turned to her dad. "Dad, you already know. I'm sorry I didn't tell you sooner, but I knew you would react like this. But the fact is, Eric and I are having a baby and you need to deal with that. He's a good man."

George snorted. "He's filthy. What kind of man makes himself welcome in your home and doesn't even bother to clean up first?"

"The type of man that got off of work and came over here to make sure that I had dinner because I'm too tired to cook for myself," she snapped.

George's eyebrows shot up and he looked over at me. "You did that?"

"Well, yeah. She's pregnant and it's my kid. I told you, I'll take care of her."

"Well, somebody has to," he grumbled. "She's working too much and with a baby on the way, she's going to be exhausted."

"I know, and I offered to take care of her. I didn't want her working either, especially when she's going to be on her feet all day."

"Excuse me, but-"

George interrupted Kat. "And she's not taking care of herself. She looks tired and way too skinny."

"That's why I offered to cook for her. I don't like the idea of her going to bed hungry because she's too tired to cook."

"You know, I didn't allow you to do this so you could-"

"And that's another thing," George interrupted again. "What are you planning on doing once the baby's born?"

"Well, I wanted her to move in with me, but she didn't like that idea. I even offered to marry her."

"Let me guess, she said no," George huffed. "Stubborn, just like her mother."

"Can you please stop talking about me like I'm not here?" Kat said irritatedly.

"I just want to be a good father. I know she has reservations about marriage, so I won't push that issue, but I want us to be a family."

"See?" George turned to Kat. "Now, this is a good man."

Kat seethed next to me. "Two minutes ago you were saying he *wasn't* a good man!"

"That was two minutes ago," her father shrugged.

"You know, he wanted me to be his pretend girlfriend so his parents weren't disappointed in him."

George nodded with a grin. "I like it. It shows that he still respects his parents."

Kat screamed in agitation and stormed out of the living room. George turned to me with a grin. "She's got fire like her mother too. Don't let her push you away. She's one of the good ones."

"Trust me, George, I can see that."

KATHERINE

"Dad, I promise, I'm taking care of myself."

He stood by the door, looking at me in concern. I had been mad at him when he divorced my mom, but after a few years, I saw that he was still the same man, he was just happier not married to my mom.

"You should seriously consider what a life with that man could be."

"Dad, you hated him when you found out I was pregnant."

"And then I talked to him."

"For like five minutes," I said exasperatedly.

"It doesn't take more than that for a man to assess another man. I liked what I saw. He'll treat you right. You could do worse, sugar."

I glanced back toward the kitchen. Eric was in there doing up the dishes. I couldn't see him, but I knew he was doing all this willingly, and not because he was trying to get in my pants.

"Dad, I promise, I'm seeing where this is going, but I won't just jump into a relationship with him because of the baby. That won't end well for either of us."

"I understand. Have you told your mom yet?" I cringed. "You know she's not going to be upset."

"Have you met Mom?"

"Alright, well, she won't be mad for long. And she'll be disappointed more than anything. But you know your mother. She always comes around."

"Disappointment is worse than being upset."

"Honey," he wrapped his hands around my arms. "Just rip the bandaid off. You'll see. It'll be fine. Take that man with you, and that'll take the edge off. You know your momma has a weakness for handsome men. Just don't tell him I said that."

I chuckled. "Yeah, I'm not about to tell him my dad has a man crush."

"I never said I had a man crush. I said he was handsome. A man that's sure about his sexuality can say things like that."

I rolled my eyes and accepted the kiss on the cheek. After he left, I shut the door and made my way back to the kitchen. Eric had most of the dishes washed and I couldn't help but notice how much it made me tingle to see him in my house, doing domestic things.

I must have been staring for a long time, because he suddenly turned to me and grinned as he wiped his hands on the towel. I couldn't take my eyes off this masculine hands. The way they moved, the way they were so long and….

My eyes snapped up to his face when he cleared his throat. I blushed furiously, but only because of what I had been thinking, what I was hoping he would do to me with those fingers.

He glanced at the clock. "I should let you get some sleep."

"Right," I nodded, disappointed that he wasn't actually going to try anything.

"Was there anything else you needed before I go?"

"Uh…no. I'm just gonna sit down and put my feet up for a little bit."

His brows furrowed and he glanced down. "Do your feet hurt?"

I snorted. "My feet always hurt, pregnant or not."

He nodded thoughtfully. "Why don't you go take a shower and then I'll give you a foot massage."

"Really?"

"I wouldn't have offered if I didn't mean it."

It felt weird to walk away from him, knowing that he was sticking around to give me a foot massage. There were so many other things I would rather have than a foot massage right now, but if that's all he was willing to give, I'd take it. I went through my shower quickly, knowing that if I took too long, I might miss out on that foot massage. I threw on some pajama shorts and a tank top, then headed back into the living room. Eric was sitting on the couch, flipping through the channels.

I walked over to the couch and he immediately moved over, patting the couch for me to sit down. I did as he said, but was caught off guard when he hauled my leg up into his lap.

"Lay down."

"What?" I asked, my body tingling.

"Lay down. I want you to relax."

I swallowed hard, well aware that if I laid down facing him, he would most likely be able to see up my shorts. But I complied and got a small thrill when he realized his error. His eyes were glued to the space between my legs. I saw his throat working for control until he finally glanced away. He cleared his throat several times and snatched the lotion off the table.

Slowly, he worked the lotion into my foot. It felt so good as he applied all the right pressure. I wanted to say that I was relaxing, but the truth was, I wanted him, and having his hands gliding across my skin was more than I could take. It was like a lightning bolt right to my core. My whole body was starting to shake uncontrollably. It wasn't that noticeable, but if he kept going, kept rubbing his hands over my feet, I might just jump him.

Then his hands slid up around my ankles and over my calves. My eyes shot to his and what I saw could only be described as pure lust. He didn't take his eyes off me as he slowly worked his hands up and down my calves. I wasn't even paying attention anymore to whether or not it felt good. Slowly, his hands moved up my leg to my knee and then a little higher.

I saw the indecision in his eyes. I knew what he wanted. I spread my legs wider, hoping he would take my invitation. His hands moved higher until they were wrapped around my thigh. He bent over and slid his tongue up my leg. I gasped and moaned, sure that I was going to come just from his touch.

"Oh God."

His tongue slowly licked around my inner thigh and then he paused, just inches from the crotch of my shorts. His eyes slipped closed and I saw him sniff. His hands tightened around my thighs. I was sure this was it. He was going to rip down my shorts and tongue fuck me. Just the thought of it had me creaming.

"Christ," he murmured. Then he was on top of me, kissing me hard as his hand slid behind my head and held me to him. I wrapped my legs around him, pulling him tight against me. He groaned and his hips jerked against me. I gasped at the sensation, begging him to do it again. His hips bucked against me, his jeans pressing hard against my clit. I was panting hard, just barely hanging on when he tore himself away from me, panting hard.

He stood, not looking at me as he ran his hand through his hair. I was shaking hard, needing something only he could give me. I reached out for him, but he stepped away, shaking his head slightly. I opened my mouth to say something, but I didn't know what. Was he rejecting me? Did he not want me? Because it really felt like he did. Hurt washed over me and I covered my face, embarrassed that I had put myself out there and then failed so miserably.

I felt the couch dip beside me and then he was prying my hands away, pressing kisses to my cheeks and lips. "It's not you, Kat. I want you. You know I do. But we have to take this slowly. I want you so fucking much, but I don't want to screw this up with you."

His lips landed on mine in a gentle kiss, and then he was striding away from me and walking out the door. I laid on the couch in a sexually frustrated mess. I wanted him so much, but he was right. Did I want him because we connected sexually or because I wanted him? I wasn't sure, and until I figured that out, he was right, we needed to take this slow.

ERIC

I got into my truck and slammed the door. It took everything in me not to strip her shorts off and fuck her. God, I wanted her so bad. My cock was aching behind the zipper of my jeans. I knew she wanted me. I could feel it in the way her body shook when I touched her. I could smell her arousal. But dammit, that wasn't enough. I wanted more, so much more than just twisting up the sheets. I wanted her to want me for me, and not the orgasms I could give her. There was no doubt that she was attracted to me. She was writhing under my touch.

I slammed my fist into my steering wheel and took off. If I didn't leave now, I would change my mind and go back in and fuck her. That wouldn't help either of us. I drove home, determined to make my aching cock shrink to a normal size. But I knew that wouldn't happen. Not as long as I was thinking about the woman back there, laying on the couch looking like every man's dream.

I hit the brakes hard when I got home, barely shutting off the truck before I got out and marched up the steps of my front porch. I needed a fucking shower, and everything that went with it. I shoved the screen door open and stormed through.

"Hey-" Joe started.

"Shut the fuck up, asshole," I ground out.

"Ooh, someone's salty."

I turned and walked over to him, grabbing him by the shirt and slamming him against the wall. "You and I made a deal. Remember that?"

"You were serious about that?"

"Do you want a fist in your face?"

"Damn, fine." He rolled his eyes and sighed. "Someone's *grumpy*," he corrected himself with air quotes. "So, woman problems? Did quiche-girl leave you high and dry?"

I slammed him back again, and this time his head bounced off the wall. "Ow! Okay, okay. I get it. No more fun talk. Only boring, old people talk."

"And?"

"And no speaking about your bae." I growled and was about to punch him when he held out his hand. "Sorry! Your woman. Geez, don't fucking punch me."

"Just for that, you've added two more months to your sentence."

"What? You can't do that! You can't make me speak the way you want for three months!"

"Watch me."

I turned to leave, but he just wouldn't give in.

"You don't own me, fucker. I'll talk however I want, and there's not a fucking think you can do about it, *Hunty*."

I slowly turned, my eyes taking on a maniacal gleam. He just had to keep on pushing. Hell, I was horny and needed to release some tension. His face was as good as anything else. I swung at his cocky grin, getting him right in the jaw. He turned with the hit, grasping at his face as he looked up at me in shock.

"What the fuck?" he shouted.

"Now it's four more months. Fuck with me again, and I'll make you pay."

"You can't just keep beating me up. Eventually, I'll fight back."

I quirked my lips at him. "Remember what we did to Derek after we found out he screwed the math teacher?"

His face paled slightly.

"Do we understand each other?"

He nodded and wisely didn't say anything else.

I stormed upstairs and tore my clothes off. My cock was in literal pain right now. I didn't even bother with the shower. I grabbed some lube and slowly worked it over my cock. I groaned and started stroking. God, I could still smell her. I wanted to taste her and feel those pretty pussy lips quiver when I licked her. I started jacking myself harder, my breathing coming out in erratic bursts as I thought of the erotic sounds she made as I rubbed my cock against her pussy.

I shot off in my hand, shouting out as my hand filled with my cum. I had to lean against the bed to steady myself. The door flung open behind me and Joe stepped in, only to hold his hand up in front of his eyes.

"Whoa! What the fuck? I thought you were hurt."

I smeared my cum on my shirt and then yanked up my pants, fastening them in place. Then I took off my shirt and tossed it in the laundry basket.

"Get out of my room."

"You know, a little warning next time."

"You want me to tell you when I'm going upstairs to jack off? The shut door should have been enough."

"You don't have to tell me, but a little, *hey, I need some alone time* wouldn't be out of the question."

"I need some alone time? Do I look like a chick?"

"Fine, then say you need to do a manual override. Or you need to polish the banister."

"What? Am I twelve?"

"Rotating the drive head. Shucking the corn. I could keep going."

"Please don't."

"Fine, but the next time you come up here to yank the chain, you better find some way to let me know so I don't walk in on that white ass again."

"Or you could just find your own damn house and I wouldn't have to worry about you walking in on me at all."

"Cruel, man. Totally uncalled for. You'd miss me if I was gone."

"About as much as I would miss the clap."

He flinched slightly. "You…you don't have that, right?"

"No!" I practically shouted. "Could you get the fuck out of here now?"

"Fine, but just to be clear, that was a shout of ecstasy and not pain? I mean, it sounded kind of bad."

"Get the fuck out! Get out! Get out! Get out!"

He winced and shut the door behind him. I sighed and got into the shower to clean up. When I came out, there was a book sitting on my bed. I picked it up and sighed. *The Student's Manual of Venereal Diseases.* I didn't even want to know why he had that.

∽

The rest of the week went better. I got off work in time to go make dinner for Kat, and luckily, there were no more interruptions. Every night was a little harder and harder to resist her. We ate dinner together and talked, sharing little tidbits of our lives, but when all was said and done, we ended up on the couch watching tv, and she was just a little too tempting to resist. I made sure to stay on my side of the couch, even when giving her a foot massage. I never took the same liberties with her as I had that first night. And though I could tell she was disappointed, she never pushed for more.

But tonight was different. Tonight, I was going to take her out on an actual date. I made reservations in town for dinner, but I had a feeling that was a mistake. Everyone would be staring at us, and it wouldn't take long for the gossip train to start moving. But that was something I was going to have to start dealing with. I had been over to Kat's every night this week, and even if we didn't work out, they would still find out eventually about the baby. It was best just to rip the bandaid off.

I hurried down the stairs after checking the time on my watch. I was right on time for picking up Kat. I stopped in the downstairs bathroom to give myself a once over, even though I had just done that upstairs. I was worried. I wanted this to go right. The last time I took her out hadn't ended so well. Things were better between us, but I didn't want to jinx that.

"Whoa, where are you going? That's more than a Netflix and chill," Joe grinned. I glared at him and he quickly remembered our fight a week ago. "I mean, you look...nice."

"I have a date with Kat."

"Kat?" A grin split his lips. "So, *Katherine* now has a nickname. You two are getting pretty serious."

I rolled my eyes. "We're having a baby together. What did you expect?"

"Yeah, but this is like...serious."

"No shit."

"But a date...the last time you did that, you totally crashed and burned."

"I'm aware."

"And to go back for more...that's like asking for another kick to the nuts."

"She's not like that," I said irritatedly. "We got off on the wrong foot, thanks to you, but we're working it out now."

"You know, you should be thanking me. I should be the best man at your wedding. Just think, if I hadn't gotten you that date, you never would have met quiche-girl."

"You got me a date with a woman that ended up going home with another man."

He shrugged. "Thank your lucky stars that you didn't end up with that one. Not exactly wife material, if you know what I mean."

I was about to walk out the door, but stopped with my hand on the doorknob. I slowly turned, giving him the most sinister look I could muster. "You told me she was exactly my type." His mouth gaped as he realized his mistake. "You told me I would have a great time and she was just what I needed."

He scratched at the back of his head. "There was...and the bar..."

I slowly walked toward him and he backed up wisely. "I'm grateful that I met Kat and that I have this baby on the way, but this isn't how I would have chosen to go about it. You fucked with my life all so you could get laid?"

"I didn't tell you to impregnate her!"

"You had me meet her at a bar. And I don't even drink!"

"Hey, I didn't tell you to do shots with the woman. Besides, like you said, you're happy now. No need to kill off your last remaining brother."

"I have plenty more brothers."

He swallowed hard. "Right, well..." His eyes moved around in thought as he tried to think up another excuse why I shouldn't pummel his face in. "I can do your laundry for a week."

"Yeah, that should make up for your stupidity."

"And...I'll make you breakfast in bed. I'll even put a little flower in a vase for you."

"Do I look like the type of man to eat breakfast in bed?"

"Look, I really think you're getting too worked up over this. I mean, it's not nearly as bad as the time I de-pantsed you in front of the whole school." My face turned glacial. "Maybe I shouldn't have brought that up."

I took a deep breath and saw him visibly relax, his eyes slipping closed. I swung hard, dropping him to the ground with just one punch. He moaned and rubbed at his face. I smirked and headed for the door.

KATHERINE

God, I was nervous. I just wanted tonight to go well. This week had been hell on me and my hormones. I knew that I wanted this to be more than it was. I wanted to kiss him when I wanted, and I wanted to spend time with him more than just when I got home from work. I hated it that he left at the end of every night. And he always left early so I could get to bed. It was sweet of him, but irritating at the same time. I could still feel his body pressed down on mine. My body still throbbed in need whenever he came over. I had been a good girl the rest of the week, doing my best not to tempt him, but the gloves were coming off tonight. We had taken the time to get to know each other, and now it was time to get him into my bed again.

By the time my doorbell rang, I was a mess. I knew I was going to make an ass out of myself. I was a bundle of nerves. I just wanted this to work so badly. Which was ironic considering the way we started out. It was him who had wanted us to get together, and I had shoved him away. Now, he was taking it slow and I was the one that couldn't keep it together.

I swung the door open and took a deep breath as I took in his beautiful form. He hadn't worn a suit this time, and I was a little shocked by that. Then again, maybe he was just loosening up a little. His jeans hugged his legs just perfectly and that white button down hung just above his crotch, where I could still see the bulge in his pants. I swallowed past my desire and dragged my eyes away from his crotch. He had a slight smile on his face, but his eyes were roaming over my body too, taking in the curves from the tight wrap dress I wore. I figured I wouldn't be able to wear it much longer. Then I would start showing and this would no longer be sexy.

"You look amazing, Kat."

"Thank you. So do you."

He ran a hand over the scruff of his beard and sighed. "You're making it hard to take you out to dinner."

"We could stay in," I suggested.

He huffed out a laugh, shaking his head. "No, I promised you dinner. We'll figure out dessert later," he said in a low growl. He reached in and grabbed my hand, pulling me toward him. I stumbled into him, but then his lips crashed down upon mine and my body melted against his. His tongue slipped inside my mouth and his hand trailed up my back until he had a firm grip on my hair. My knees started to shake and my lady parts started quivering. And just when I thought we might take this to the next level, he pulled back and shook his head.

"That wasn't a good idea," he murmured, just inches from my lips

I wiped at my lipstick and frowned. "Bad kiss?"

"Good kiss," he grinned. "Very good kiss."

He reached up and swiped at my smeared lips with his thumb. "Gorgeous," he murmured under his breath.

I fixed my dress, sure that my boobs were about to pop out or something. When I was all set, he took my hand in his and led me down to his truck.

"So, where are we going this time?"

"Tria."

"In town?" I asked, a little baffled by that.

"Yep."

"You know that as soon as we walk in there-"

"The whole town's going to know about us? I'm aware." He yanked the truck door open and then stared at me. "I also don't care. And frankly, I like everyone knowing that you're with me."

My heart did a little happy dance that set my stomach fluttering. He held my hand as I stepped into his truck, and then shut the door behind me. I could see now that Eric did have game. It just took a while for it to come out. He wasn't overly confident when he talked to a woman. He just wanted to get to know her first. And I was that lucky woman. And now that we knew each other better, he knew exactly what he wanted and was going for it. I knew deep down that tonight was the start of something special.

When we walked into the restaurant, as expected, half the town looked up at us in surprise. I didn't know most of the people in here since I wasn't originally from this town. But they all seemed to know Eric.

"Who's this pretty lady?" an older gentleman asked.

"Gary, this is Katherine."

"Katherine," he said, smiling at me. "Beautiful name. I'm Gary and this is my wife, Alma," he said, gesturing to the woman across from him. "We've known Eric since he was a little kid. We live right down the road, in fact."

"Well, it's nice to meet you."

"You should stop by sometime. Alma will make her famous biscuits and tea, and then we'll tell you all about Eric when he was a kid."

"I don't think that's necessary," Eric cut in, glaring at the man good-naturedly. "You'll probably just tell her all the bad stories."

"Bad stories?" the old man scoffed. "Now, if we were talking about your brothers, I would have plenty to tell. You got the best one, here. Always kept his nose out of trouble and always a gentleman."

I wondered what Gary would think of Eric's gentlemanly behavior if he knew what we were both thinking about for dessert. My cheeks flushed slightly at the thought. Eric squeezed my hand and said goodbye to Gary and Alma. I barely nodded with a smile as Eric pulled me away. Eric pulled out my chair and then pushed the chair in after I took my seat. When he sat across from me, I could see the humor in his eyes.

"Shut up," I admonished.

"If I didn't know any better, I would think you were thinking some very dirty thoughts while we were talking with Gary."

I shook my head, but smiled at him. "I was thinking about how he said you were always a gentleman."

"And?"

"Are you?"

His face danced with humor as he stared at me. It was like the gloves had come off and our situations were reversed. When there was nothing on the table, I was confident and willing to take a gamble. But now that I knew exactly what I wanted, I seemed to have lost that confidence. Maybe it was because Eric was drawing this out, making me wait until he was sure we were both ready. Maybe it was because as time went on, he seemed to know exactly where this was going, while I was still questioning everything. Was he making me wait so long because he wasn't sure about us still? Or had he changed his mind? Surely if he had, he wouldn't be taking me out to dinner. Unless this was a pity date. He was taking his pregnant one night stand out for dinner, just to make sure she was fed. But the way he greeted me at the door made those thoughts immediately flee my mind. No, he was attracted to me alright, I just wasn't sure if he was as sure as I was.

"Your brain must be a fascinating thing to study," he said, a beautiful smile on his face.

"Why do you say that?"

"Because I can tell you're over there, analyzing every little thing that's going on. You're wondering what this date means. You're wondering if I feel the same way you do. And most importantly…" He leaned forward and lowered his voice. "You're wondering if I'm going to stay over tonight."

My heart thundered in my chest. "And?"

"And you already know what this date means. I wouldn't be here with you if I didn't want there to be more between us. And based on the kiss I gave you, I'm sure you know exactly how I feel about you."

He didn't say anything about the third. "And the other thing?"

His phone buzzed in his pocket, but he didn't break eye contact as he pulled it out. He barely glanced down at his phone before shoving it back in his pocket.

"What do you-" His phone buzzed again and he pulled it out, irritated this time. "Sorry." He sighed and answered his phone. "What, Joe?...Yes, I'm with Kat....At Tria. How did you know?" He sighed. "That's nice. Did you really need to call me about this?...Well, I'm trying to have a date...Whatever."

He hung up and slipped the phone back into his pocket.

"Sorry about that. Apparently, as soon as we walked into the restaurant, it was all over the town Facebook page. He says we're blowing it up."

"I didn't realize that we were such a fascinating topic."

"Are you kidding? This is a small town, and people love to gossip about who's dating who."

"Great."

"If it makes you feel any better, when you start to show, at least they won't be questioning who the father is."

"I suppose you're right." Not that it made me feel that much better.

"Now," he said, pulling my chair right up against his. "What do you say we give them all something to talk about."

And then he wrapped his hand around my head and pulled me in for an earth-shattering kiss.

~

He spun me around and shoved me up against the door just as I was about to put the key in. I wrapped my arms around his shoulders, pulling him in closer. I could feel his erection pressing up against me, and then I heard the urgency of him trying to unlock the door. The door swung open and Eric caught me just as I was about to tumble backwards. He picked me up bridal style and kicked the door closed with a wicked grin on his face. He took the stairs two at a time and marched right to my room. I wasn't sure he actually knew which room was mine or if he was just guessing.

He laid me down on the bed, immediately covering my body with his. His kisses were urgent and demanding, but it was his hands that were driving me crazy. His roughened palm was gliding down my side until he hit the hem of my dress. His hand slid up my thigh and then squeezed my ass lightly. He broke the kiss, moving his lips down my throat until he was kissing down between the valley of my breasts. I was on sensation overload, ever so aware of his hand sliding under my panties and skimming over my mound.

My breathing hitched from his touch, but his kisses kept me distracted. So many sensations rushed through me that it was hard to tell what I wanted from him right now. I spread my legs for him, moaning when his knuckles brushed over my clit. It seemed that Eric liked to take his time with every aspect of this relationship. He was drawing this out, teasing me and driving me crazy. I needed him. I wanted to feel his fingers on me and his cock inside me. When he pulled away and sat back to stare at me, I thought for a moment that he had changed his mind. But then he pulled me up and started pulling my dress over my head. His eyes narrowed as he took in my lace bra and panties. I watched as he swallowed hard, his jaw working as he fought for control.

But I wanted him to lose control. I wanted him to not be a gentleman with me. I sat up and crawled over to him, slowly undoing the buckle of his belt. He sucked in a breath as my hands skimmed his waistline. I could feel his ab muscles clenching as I brushed against them. When I pulled off his belt, I glanced up at him and then tossed the belt across the room. His eyes didn't follow, they just stayed locked on me and every move I made.

My fingers moved to his shirt, slowly unbuttoning every single button. I pushed the fabric over his shoulders, making sure that I brushed my breasts against his chest as I shoved the shirt down his arms. As soon as the fabric was loose, his hands clamped on the backs of my upper thighs and he lifted me in the air, tossing me back on the bed. He pounced on me, kissing me hard and rubbing his erection against me.

"Is that what you wanted, Kat? You wanted me to lose it?"

"Yes," I panted.

He kissed me hard, his hand cupping my breast through my thin bra. When his thumb brushed over my nipple, I arched my back and cried out. I was so sensitive right now, but it felt amazing. He ground his cock against me, continuing to brush his thumb over my nipple. My thighs quivered and my whole body shook as my orgasm washed over me. I gripped onto his shoulders as I clenched my thighs together, but he didn't stop teasing me, not until my body finally released and relaxed underneath him.

He pulled back, staring into my eyes as he brushed my hair out of my face. The way he was looking at me was intense, like he needed me right now, but was trying to hold back. I slipped my hands between us and undid his pants, working them down his hips.

"You need me, Kat?"

"You know I do. You've been teasing me all week."

"Not teasing," he murmured. "Just taking my time with you. I don't want to screw this up with you."

God, I had been so blind. How could I be so stupid as to think that this man wasn't right for me? He shifted away from me and pulled his pants off, stroking his hard cock before coming back to settle between my thighs. He pressed his lips to my neck, licking and sucking every inch of my skin. I spread my legs wide, begging for him to slide inside me, but he kept kissing my body. His fingers pulled at the cups of my bra and then his tongue was licking my nipples, sucking them into his mouth. I barely felt him undoing the clasp and sliding down the straps from my arms. I lifted my hips for him to slide off my panties, a thrill of excitement rushing through me that this was finally it.

My pussy was throbbing as I felt him sliding his cock through my soaking folds. He was groaning, but never slid inside. He just kept sucking on nipples and driving me crazy. After one more jerk of his hips, he slid down my body and kissed my stomach, leaving a wet trail as he made his way to my throbbing clit. My hips jerked involuntarily when he blew on my pussy. My whole body broke out in goosebumps as I waited for his lips to find mine.

I felt him spread my lips and then his tongue slid home. I cried out, jerking my hips up to meet his mouth. He gripped my hips and held me against his mouth as he tongue fucked me. Every moan felt like a ripple through my body. I was on edge and I couldn't hold on much longer. I slid my fingers into his hair and pulled him tight against me and bucked my pussy against his mouth, needing everything he was willing to give me. Before I could come again, he moved up my body and kissed me as he pushed slowly inside me. My legs shook as he slowly entered me and my breathing was erratic.

"Look at me, Kat."

I opened my eyes and stared at him as he pushed the rest of the way inside me. He slowly pulled out and then slammed back inside me. My body jerked back from the force of his thrust.

"Wrap your arms around me, Kat."

I did as he asked and wrapped my legs around him also. He started moving faster, his hips hitting me hard with every thrust. My nails dug into his back unintentionally, but that only seemed to spur him on. His cock pulsed hard inside me and I could feel him growing fatter inside me. I was on the verge of another orgasm when I felt his finger rub against my clit. I gasped, my body tightening around him as my body broke apart. My eyes fluttered, but then he leaned forward and kissed me hard, his hands threading through my hair on either side of my head.

"God, Kat," he murmured against my lips. He gripped my hip and thrust in several more times before settling deep inside me. He was panting hard as he rested his forehead against mine. I could feel his hot breath kiss my face. My body wouldn't stop shaking, and when I ran my fingers through his hair, I noticed that my hands were shaking just as bad as the rest of me. He kissed my forehead and then my nose, before kissing me softly on the lips.

He slipped out of me and then pulled me against him. I was laying half on top of him, feeling his heart pound beneath my chest. I sighed, content with laying beside him the rest of the night. But after drifting off to sleep, I realized that Eric had no plans to let me sleep the rest of the night.

ERIC

I was whistling as I walked into my house the next morning. I had to get changed and get to work. I knew I was running late, but I didn't care. After an amazing night with Kat, I was in no rush to do anything. I had woken her up two more times last night and made love to her slowly. And while I liked to fuck hard at times, it was different with Kat. *She* was different. She was the wild one, and maybe she expected something different from me, but I wanted her to know that this wasn't just fucking. It was so much more than that to me. And it was good.

"Somebody didn't come home last night," Andrew grinned, pulling his earbuds out.

"You know what? Nothing can bother me today. So, go ahead and talk in your weird vernacular or bug me about the fact that I didn't come home. It doesn't matter."

"Whoa, you…you really like this woman."

I laughed at him, clapping him on the shoulder. "Yeah, man. I really like her. I mean, I'm having a baby with her, but the rest is amazing."

"Shit." He sat down in a chair at the kitchen table, staring at it dumbfounded. "Does this mean that I need to start looking for a new place?"

"Why?"

"Well, you're sleeping with her. You're…happy."

"Yeah," I said slowly. "But she made it perfectly clear to me that she wasn't moving in with me. I don't know what's going to happen down the road, but for now, I'd say you're in the clear."

"Thank God. Just the idea of packing and then moving," he said as if he had a lot of shit to move. "And then there's the cooking on my own until I can find a woman to do it for me."

"Sorry, what?"

"Well, I can't do the cooking and cleaning on my own forever. I mean, I might survive for a little while, but eventually, I'll starve and the apartment would be a mess."

"And you think a woman is just going to move in with you and take over those duties because she's a woman?"

"Well, yeah. I mean, it's sort of built into their DNA or something."

I shook my head and laughed. "Man, I can't wait until you meet a woman." I changed my voice to sound like him. "Hey, babe, I thought we could Netflix and chill. I'm totally on fleek with you and I'm ready to clap back. But first, could you make me a sandwich and pick up my dirty clothes?"

He stared at me for a minute, his mouth hanging open slightly. "You should never try to talk like that again."

"Oh, like you sound any better when you say it," I shot back.

"First, I do. Second, do you actually know what you're saying?"

"No, but frankly, nobody else does either, so I figure it doesn't really matter."

"If you said that to a woman, she would run the other way."

I leaned across the table toward him. "Why do you think you're still living at home and you haven't had a steady girlfriend since high school?"

"Hey!"

I started whistling and walked out of the room. Like I said, nothing could touch me today.

Because I was late getting to work today, I knew that Anna would bitch at me as soon as I walked in the door. So, to cut her off at the head, I decided to pick up some donuts for her. I nodded to Mary Anne as I walked into the bakery. There was already a line of people, waiting on the deliciousness that Mary Anne created. I didn't have a huge sweet tooth, but even I had to admit that her creations were out of this world.

As I waited in line, I pulled up my messages on my phone. They were all from Anna. In every single one, she bitched at me for not being on time. There was something about RJ needing something, but I just deleted it. I would be at work soon, and then she could tell me in person what the issue was.

It was about three minutes into my wait that I realized that people were whispering and staring at me. I glanced down at my shirt, wondering if I had something on it, but there was nothing there. I glanced behind me, thinking maybe someone else had walked in and they were really staring at that person, but nobody was there.

That is, not until the group of ladies from church walked in. Mrs. Charles walked right up to me and smacked me with her purse. I winced when it felt like a ton of bricks was slamming into me.

"Ow! What the hell was that for?"

Her eyes narrowed in on me and she slammed the purse against me again. "Shame on you." She slammed her purse against my cheek this time, and I was sure she almost cracked my cheekbone.

"Christ, woman!"

Her eyes got wide and she slammed me upside the head again. "*That* was for using the Lord's name in vain."

"What the hell were the other ones for? I was just standing here!"

"That was for the sinful act you committed last night."

I stared at her, completely baffled. "How the hell do you know what I did last night?"

"Oh," a young woman raised her hand, like I was going to call on her. "Bethany Jones said that she saw you out to dinner last night with that nurse, Katherine. She works at Tria."

"Katherine?" another woman asked.

"No, Bethany. And she posted it on the Facebook page. Then pretty much everyone knew that you were out with her, but it was Alice Henderson that saw you leave her townhouse this morning. In the same clothes as last night, by the way."

"What, was she taking pictures?" I asked incredulously.

"So, then Mrs. Henderson called her daughter-in-law, Suzanne, and she told Stacey's mom, Tina, that you had spent the night over at Katherine's house. And Stacey was super angry because she's had a crush on you for the longest time. But you never noticed her before. Anyway, then Stacey was all pissed because you went home with another woman, so she posted on the page about you staying over at Katherine's last night. Now, pretty much the whole town knows about you two hooking up."

I just stared at the woman. I didn't even know who she was, but apparently, the whole fucking town knew all of my business now. "Don't you people know how to mind your own goddamn business?"

I turned for the door, but got a hard smack to the face that sent me to the floor. Twenty minutes later, I was holding an ice pack to my face while Mrs. Charles was explaining to Jack, the town sheriff, that I had used the Lord's name in vain in front of her several times, and that she was just trying to teach me a lesson. To make matters worse, Joe stepped into the bakery at that very moment, looking around at all the people standing around, and the sheriff talking to Mrs. Charles. Then his gaze landed on me and he grinned at the ice pack in my hand.

"What's going on here?"

"Hell if I know. Apparently, everyone in town knows my business."

"So, what's with the ice pack?" he nodded to my face.

"Mrs. Charles attacked me for using the Lord's name in vain."

He burst out laughing, clapping his hand on his thigh. I ignored him and listened in as Jack tried to talk down the crazy church lady.

"Mrs. Charles, you cannot go around assaulting people because you don't like the way they speak," Jack said calmingly.

"It's not just that. He brought a woman to her house last night and didn't leave until this morning!"

Jack snorted, but didn't say anything as the rest of the ladies fumed behind Mrs. Charles.

"Whoa," Joe said, stepping over to Mrs. Charles. "It's not what you think."

"Joe," I said in warning, but he just held his hand up as he continued toward Mrs. Charles. "It's not like she's just some random woman off the streets. You know my brother. He's a good guy. All of you know that. He doesn't just take women home and screw them."

Okay, well, at least he was trying to help.

"I mean, it takes him forever to close the deal with a woman. I was beginning to think his dick didn't work right."

I closed my eyes and groaned, shaking my head slightly. "Joe-"

"No, I'm not finished. You can judge all you want, but he really likes this woman. In fact, he got her pregnant after a one night stand and he's trying to make this work."

The whole room gasped and I dropped my head in my hands, wishing I could just disappear.

"You got that young woman pregnant?" Mrs. Charles screeched.

"Yeah, but he's totally all about her. I mean, at first he was so out of there, but when she came and tossed a box of condoms at him, that was the really funny part. Or so I hear. I wasn't there for it, but Andrew said it was hilarious."

"I can't believe you would sleep with a woman after just meeting her," Mrs. Charles said.

"Hey, it's called a one night stand for a reason," Joe argued.

"Jack," I pleaded. "Can we move this along?"

Jack was chuckling behind his hand, not at all concerned that all my secrets were being outed in front of half the town.

"So, are you together?" Mary Anne asked.

"Yeah, should I tell Stacey that she doesn't stand a chance?" the mystery woman asked.

"I don't even know who Stacey is!" I shouted.

"Well, as enlightening as this has all been," Jack grinned at me, "perhaps we should move this along. Mrs. Charles, please don't attack any more residents with your purse."

Mrs. Charles shoved her purse back on her shoulder and huffed in irritation. "Come on, ladies."

She turned on her heel and marched out the door, her crew of church-going thugs trailing along behind her.

Joe walked over and slapped me on the back. "See? All better. Everything's out in the open now and you don't have to worry about hiding it."

"I wasn't hiding it. I just didn't need the whole town knowing my business."

"But, they were all going to find out anyway. This way, it gives them time to adjust to the situation."

I stood and got in his face. "I don't need them to adjust to my life, Joe. It was none of their business."

He grinned wide and put his finger on his nose, pointing at me with the other. "Right, man. I totally gotcha."

I smacked his hand away from me, not even sure what the fuck that was supposed to mean.

"So, are you getting those donuts?" Mary Anne asked.

"Yes, and one of your lattes too."

"Oh," she exclaimed excitedly. "So, was the last latte really for Katherine?"

"No, it was for Anna."

"I can't believe you're two timing Katherine with Anna," the mystery woman said, stomping out of the bakery. I sighed and scratched at my forehead. Apparently, there *was* something that could ruin my good mood for the day.

Jack walked over and gripped my shoulder, still chuckling to himself. "Looks like you've got yourself in one hell of a situation."

"You know, it was actually working out pretty well until the whole town decided to stick their nose in my business."

Jack was a good guy. He was a few years older than me and had a wife and baby at home. I couldn't recall anyone getting this obsessive about his dating life when he met his wife.

"Can I give you some advice?"

"Sure."

"I would get over to the hospital and have a talk with Katherine. You don't want her to be blindsided by all this."

I groaned. I hadn't even thought about this getting to Kat. "Shit." I checked my watch. I still had to go to the office and there was bound to be a mess waiting for me there. "What are the chances that this new story will hold until the end of the day?"

"Well, considering that someone was filming the whole thing, I'd say it's already been uploaded on Facebook."

∼

I opened the office door and was almost run over by Anna.

"You knocked up Katherine Beck?"

I shoved the donuts and latte into her hands and stormed past her. "What are my messages for the day?"

"You have like twenty, but honestly, most of them are questions about you and Katherine. So, she's really pregnant?"

I sighed in irritation. "Yes, she's really pregnant. Yes, the baby is mine. Yes, it was from a one night stand. Yes, we are working on our relationship. No, this is not up for further discussion."

"Well, at least someone in your family takes their responsibilities seriously," she grumbled.

"What does that mean?"

"Nothing."

"It's not nothing. Is this about Robert?"

She ignored me and continued with her interrogation. "So, when is she due? Is she going to move in with you? I mean, I assume that you have some sort of relationship with her since you were seen leaving her house this morning."

"Did you not hear the part where I said this was not up for discussion?"

"I mean, I think I should know. As your office manager, what if she calls and needs something like your schedule? What am I supposed to do? If she's your girlfriend, then I should give it to her, but if she's just the woman you knocked up, then maybe you don't want her knowing your every move."

"If she calls, tell her what she wants to know," I snapped. "Now, can we move on?"

"Geez, fine. I was just thinking about what's best for your business."

"Focus on the business part and not my personal life."

She glared at me and moved to the table with the donuts. The office door swung open and RJ walked in, a shitty grin on his face.

"So, heard you're gonna be a papa."

"Does anyone in this town know how to mind their own business?"

"Mrs. Cranston called to offer her French Silk Pie as a condolence," Anna piped up.

"I don't need a condolence pie!"

"I heard the church ladies assaulted you at the bakery," RJ grinned.

"What? You didn't see the video?"

"Oh, I saw the video. It just didn't pick up recording until after she pummeled you."

"There's a video?" Anna asked.

"On the town Facebook page."

I threw my head back and prayed for this day to end.

"I don't suppose any of you thought to find the person that posted it and have it taken down?"

"It's on YouTube also," Anna exclaimed. "Wow, you already have one hundred and fifty shares. This thing could go viral."

"You know what? Fuck it. I'm done for the day."

"But you have jobs to go out on," Anna finally said, standing up from her desk.

"Obviously they're not that important if you can sit here and go over my relationship status on Facebook," I said to Anna, then turned to RJ, "and *you* are here instead of on a job."

"Should I do that?" Anna asked.

"Do what?"

"Update your relationship status on Facebook. It might help ward off the questions."

I stared at her, my anger reaching a boiling point. "No!"

I stormed for the door, only stopping when Anna called out to me. "Where are you going? What am I supposed to tell your clients?"

"Tell them I'm taking a sick day. I'm going home to drink."

"Just don't go to a bar," RJ said, tilting his head to the side. "That's sort of how this mess all started."

My phone rang in my pocket and I pulled it out, apprehension rushing through me when I saw Kat's number. "Kat-"

"Are you okay? I saw the post on Facebook."

I sighed, rubbing my hand across my face. "I'm sorry about that. I don't know what happened. Are you holding up okay? Anyone harassing you?"

"Uh...well, it's a mixture of dirty looks from women that I assume want you, and others wanting me to spill about how good you are in bed."

"I'm hoping you gave me a glowing review. I don't think I can take another hit right now," I grumbled.

"I didn't actually talk about it. Do you want me to?"

"Do you think it would help?"

"Eh, it's hard to say. I think the jealous ones might try to take me down, but the gossips will fall hard for all the details. And it might make up for the fact that Joe said he was worried about your dick."

I shook my head. I just wanted this day to be over. "As nice as it is of you to try and talk up my dick, I think it's best that we just let that ship sink."

"So, maybe we should take a few days to let the hysteria die down," she suggested.

"Not a chance. Just come out to my house tonight. You probably don't want to go home anyway. There are probably news trucks camped outside your townhouse."

"Funny."

"I want you with me," I said seriously. "I don't want to spend the night away from you just because people can't mind their own business."

"What about my stuff?"

"I'll send Joe to grab a bag for you. He owes me after he outed your pregnancy to the town."

"Fine, but tell him he's not allowed in my underwear drawer."

I glanced back at Anna and RJ, who were listening intently to my conversation. I moved further away and whispered into the phone so only she could hear. "Does that mean you're not going to be wearing any underwear to bed?"

"It seems counterproductive to put a barrier between us," she said, her voice low and seductive. That was all it took to swing my mood back in the right direction.

"I'll see you tonight."

"Tell that pervert to stay out of my underwear drawer," she said, right before she hung up. I chuckled to myself as I typed out a quick message for Joe to swing by and get the keys to her place. When I glanced up, both Anna and RJ were staring at me with gaping mouths.

"What?"

RJ shook his head slightly, leaning over to whisper to Anna. "It's like Eric has been kidnapped by aliens and replaced with this loose, almost fun version of Eric."

I glared at him. "Fuck off."

KATHERINE

I ignored all the looks I was getting. I had worried a little in the beginning about how people would treat me when they found out I was pregnant, but honestly, I didn't care that much anymore. People were so judgemental, and the fact was that I was an adult and I could take care of myself and a child, whether or not a man was in my life. But I did have him in my life, so they could all go jump off a bridge.

"Incoming," Chrissy hissed as she walked up with a chart. I finished making my notes on the chart I was closing out, and then I put it in a file holder.

"I heard that you're pregnant," Charlene said. "I suppose you're going to want reduced hours now."

"I've been working just fine so far," I said cheerily, not willing to give in to her petty tone.

"Well, just so you know, the hospital is making cutbacks. If you can't handle the work load, you'll be the first out the door."

She couldn't actually do that. You couldn't let go of a pregnant person just because they were pregnant. She had to have just cause, and I was one of her hardest working nurses.

"I'll be sure to keep that in mind," I said with a smile. Irritated that she didn't get a rise out of me, she walked away. Chrissy chuckled and grabbed her water from the other side of the counter.

"So, I heard you were outed on Facebook."

"Nobody can keep a secret anymore. You know, we should go back to the mafia days where you got your tongue cut out if you talked."

I pulled my buzzing phone from my pocket and grimaced. "My mom is calling."

"What's wrong with that?"

"She never calls in the middle of my shift." I chewed my lip as I considered answering or not. In the end, I decided to answer. "Hey, Mom. I'm working. What's up?"

"You're pregnant?" she screeched. "And I'm finding out from Facebook?"

I winced, pulling the phone away from my ear. "In my defense, I didn't know that was going to happen."

"Were you planning on telling me?"

"Of course. I was just waiting for the right time."

"And this is just some man you picked up in a bar?"

I glanced around, hoping Charlene didn't suddenly reappear. "Can we talk about this later? I'm not supposed to be on my phone at work. I really can't afford to get fired right now."

"Not with a baby on the way," she snorted. "I want to meet this young man. Before your father," she added.

"Uh…"

I could practically see her throwing her hands up in the air. "Of course, your father beat me to the punch on that one."

"It's not a contest, Mom."

Charlene rounded the corner, so I hid my phone behind my hair, turning away from her. "My boss is here. I gotta go. Love you."

I slipped my phone in my pocket just as Charlene walked up to me. "This isn't break time, ladies."

I glared at her retreating form. Chrissy shouldered up to me. "Well, look on the bright side, you'll have a break from Charlene after the baby is born. And then you can really piss her off by taking all those breaks to pump. She's gonna be so pissed," she chuckled.

"Yeah, that's just what I want. To piss off my boss who already doesn't like me."

"She doesn't like anyone. You just get the thrill of pissing her off when she has no recourse."

I grabbed my charts and headed off to my next patient's room, glaring at anyone who dared to give me a dirty look. They could all fuck off.

∼

I got off work and headed to Eric's house. He was right, there were people watching me everywhere I went. I stopped at the gas station and people started whispering. And when I drove down Main Street, there were people pointing at my Jeep. You would think I was a circus attraction. Seriously, I was pregnant, not a serial killer.

I pulled into Eric's driveway and parked, staring at the farmhouse for a minute. This would be my first time spending the night since the incident. It was strange. His brothers would be here and that was a little odd, right? I got out and headed for the door. Did I knock? I was invited here, so I was assuming that I was perfectly welcome, but what was the protocol for sleeping over at your baby daddy/boyfriend's house? I had never done this.

The door swung open and Eric stood there, leaning against the door frame with a grin on his face. "Were you going to stand out there all night?"

"I was trying to figure out if I should knock or not."

"Why would you knock?" he asked curiously.

"Well, I wasn't sure what the protocol was in our current relationship."

"Protocol?"

"Well, I didn't want to let myself in and make myself at home. That's a little too much like I'm your...your long-term girlfriend."

"As opposed to my short-term girlfriend?"

"Well, we just started being- you know, it's weird to call you my boyfriend. That's not a good term for me or you."

"I see," he nodded. "Well, you'd better come in so we can figure this out. I don't want you to stand on the porch every time you come over, trying to figure out what the protocols are."

He held the door open for me and then shut it behind me as I walked into the kitchen.

"So," he said, pulling out a chair for me. "I think we should establish this right now. I mean, the town is going to be talking about us a lot. I think I should know what to call you."

"Girlfriend and boyfriend sounds so…"

"Juvenile?"

"Yes," I said, thankful he understood.

"Well, I'm guessing I shouldn't walk around and call you my baby mama."

"And calling you my baby daddy feels weird. It's like a kinky version of a father. I don't know, it makes me feel like you're a pedophile."

"Well, I think it's safe to say that neither of us needs that added to the town Facebook page."

Footsteps pounded down the stairs and Joe walked into the room. "Hey, quiche-girl, how's it going? Were you attacked by the town?"

"Almost dragged through the streets. People had oranges to throw at me and everything. I barely escaped with my life," I grinned.

"Well, glad that you made it home. I have to say though, if you need me to go rifle through your drawers some more, I have no problem doing that."

I narrowed my eyes at Eric. "I told you not to let him go through my underwear drawer."

"I didn't," Joe insisted. "But you didn't tell me you had a drawer for lingerie." He winked at me. "Don't worry, I picked out something sexy for you to wear."

"Ew!" I shook my head in disgust.

"What? It's not like I've never seen lingerie before. Besides, since you already chose my brother, now at least I can picture what you'll look like in something sexy."

Eric slapped him upside the head. "Don't say shit like that. You're never allowed to think about her in lingerie."

"You know, we're gonna have a discussion about using your words instead of your fists."

"I didn't use my fists." Eric slapped him upside the head again. "See? Not my fist."

"Would you stop hitting me?" Joe said, rubbing the back of his head.

"That was a slap. Man up."

"I'm telling Ma on you."

"Yeah, you do that. And then I'll tell her that you were picturing my woman in lingerie and she'll tell me to slap you upside the head again."

Joe shook his head. "Brutal, man. I gave up my lingo for you."

"You gave it up because we made a deal and you kept fucking it up."

"I'm just saying, after I saved your ass today, you could at least lighten my sentence. You know, time off for good behavior."

"You told everyone that you thought my dick didn't work."

"Well, you should be happy about that. It makes you seem like less of a tool bag."

I watched the two of them bicker in fascination. My sisters lived further away and were married, so we didn't really get together that often anymore. But I remembered days like this. Only for us, it usually turned into a hair-pulling match.

"What?" Eric asked, turning to me curiously as I watched them.

"Oh, don't mind me. I was just catching the show. You know, you guys should turn this into a skit or something. I think the town would really like it. You could live stream it on the town page."

The door swung open and Andrew stepped inside with four pizza boxes. "Pizza's here!"

Joe stood immediately, grabbing the boxes from Andrew. "Thank God. I'm starving."

"Hey, sis," Andrew grinned, setting one box in front of me. "This one's for you."

"For me?"

"Well, sorry, not sorry, but I'm not sharing a pizza with you. I like you, and all, but even after you were outed to the whole town, that's still not enough for me to share my pizza with you."

I opened the box and smiled at the cheese pizza in front of me. "How did you know?"

"I called your dad," Eric said as he pulled pizza from his own box.

"Why didn't you just call me?"

"Because I wanted to surprise you."

"Hmm, well, now I really need to come up with a good title for you."

"A title for what?" Andrew asked.

"Well, I can't keep calling him my boyfriend."

"He's your baby daddy," Andrew said with a shrug.

"Which would make you the uncle daddy?" I grinned.

"Whoa, hold up a minute. There is no daddy anywhere in my name."

"Just call him your man friend," Joe suggested.

I wriggled my nose. "No, that sounds so…" I shook my head. "Too much like a sugar daddy."

"How about your live-in lover?" Andrew grinned.

"Yeah, I'm sure the church ladies would love that," Eric snorted. "Thanks, but I already got beaten with a purse multiple times today."

"And, we don't live together," I pointed out.

"Hang on," Andrew said, whipping out his phone.

"What are you doing?" Eric asked.

"Polling the town."

"You're what?" Eric asked, shoving back his chair. "Give me the phone."

"Just hang on. It's not like they don't already know."

Eric rounded the table, but Andrew anticipated this and took off into the living room.

"Give me the damn phone!" Eric yelled.

"Hang on, I'm getting some suggestions."

Joe and I continued to eat our pizza as Eric and Andrew fought in the other room.

"This is good pizza," I said.

"Yep. Best in town. You should really try their taco pizza."

"Ow! You asshole, I'm trying to help you!"

Something crashed to the ground and then there were loud footsteps pounding toward us.

"Suitor, worshiper, ooh... I like this one. Intended."

Eric crashed into Andrew, sending the phone skittering across the floor. Eric started smacking him in the face while Andrew tried to ward off his hands.

"I like *intended*," I said to Joe. "Maybe a little too medieval, but it could work."

"I can't believe you did that, fucker." Eric dragged Andrew off the floor and tossed him against the wall.

"Hey, I was just trying to help you out," Andrew argued.

I picked up the phone off the floor and started scrolling through the feed. There was no point in being mad. Right now, the whole town knew about us. I might as well go with it.

"Well, we could always go with the classic 'beau'."

Andrew threw a punch, clipping Eric in the chin. Eric ran at Andrew, shoving his shoulder into Andrew's stomach. They went flying through the screen door onto the porch. The screen door was ripped from its hinges, just barely dangling. Joe and I walked over to the doorway and watched as Andrew and Eric tumbled down the porch steps, kicking up dirt in their wake. I took another bite of my pizza, enjoying the delicious flavor.

"Is it always like this?"

"What, the fighting?"

I nodded.

"Nah. I mean, it depends on what's going on. When we were kids, we were constantly fighting."

"Do you fight Eric?"

Joe grinned, shaking his head slightly. "Eric may be passive, but you definitely don't want to get into a fight with him."

"So, you're saying he could kick your ass."

"Hey, I'm not ashamed to admit my limitations. But this is good for him. We like to push him into a fight every few months. It helps to loosen him up a little."

"Seriously? You do this on purpose to him?"

"Just think, when he comes back inside, you can play naughty nurse for him. I packed just the lingerie for you."

I smacked him in the chest and finished my pizza. I had to admit, it was a turn on to watch him fighting in the dirt. All that sweat and dirt caked to his body, it sent shivers down my spine.

I felt Joe's breath against my ear. "See? You're a dirty girl. Aren't you happy I packed that lingerie for you?"

I heard him chuckle as he walked away. He may have a point, but I wasn't about to tell him he was right.

ERIC

I shoved Andrew's face in the dirt and punched him in the side as I pressed all my weight on top of him. "Don't ever do something like that again. I happen to really like this woman."

"I know," he groaned.

"Then stop making shit more difficult for us. We have enough to figure out on our own without you involving the whole fucking town."

I pushed off him and watched as he stood, shaking out his arm. "I was doing you a favor, man. The more you try and keep your relationship with Katherine a secret, the more the town is going to gossip about you."

"You made me a laughing stock," I said irritatedly. "What goes on between Katherine and I has nothing to do with anyone else. I swear, between you and Joe, it's like you're trying to piss me off and make sure that you're permanently on my bad side."

He snorted, wiping off his clothes. "Like you have a good side."

I walked away. There was no point in arguing with him anymore. I'd said my peace and beat the shit out of him. Now, it was time to spend some time with Kat. I stomped up the porch steps where Kat was waiting for me, a sexy smirk on her face.

"You looked pretty hot out there, rolling around in the dirt."

"Rolling around in the dirt?" I puffed out my chest. "That was fighting."

Her fingers reached out and snagged my now filthy, white t-shirt and pulled me toward her. "Whatever you want to call it, it was totally hot."

"Yeah?" I grinned.

"Yeah."

She stood on her tiptoes, wrapping her hand around the back of my neck as she pulled me down to meet her kiss. I slid my hands around her waist and pulled her flush against me. The pizza, Facebook, my idiot brother- all of those things were forgotten the moment her lips pressed against mine. And now there was only one thing I wanted, and it involved her, me, and that sexy lingerie that Joe said he picked out. I slid my hands under her ass and hoisted her up against me. She wrapped her legs around my waist as I walked into the house.

"You're welcome!" I heard Andrew shout.

I kicked the door shut, wishing that my brothers weren't living with me. I would take her right here on the kitchen table if I didn't have to worry about them walking in on us. Her lips never left mine as I carried her upstairs. I wanted so bad to strip her down and take her, but I needed a shower. Hell, I was getting her filthy as it was, but I didn't want her to actually get dirty while I touched her. I opened the door to the bedroom and pushed it shut behind me. Her hands were digging at my scalp as she held me to her lips. I practically tripped over my own feet just getting her to the bed.

We bounced on the bed and I tried to pull back from her. "I want you inside me," she groaned, making it even more difficult for me to pull away. I took her hands and gently pried them from my scalp.

"I need a shower." She opened her mouth to argue, but I placed my hand over it and shook my head. "Kat, I want you too, but I'm filthy. When I get you in that bed, I don't plan on leaving for the rest of the night. I'll be quick."

"Then I'm joining you," she said, sitting up. "I've been working all day too. We can shower together."

This was such a bad idea. Just the thought of seeing water dripping down her breasts was enough to make me take her right now. If I got her in the shower, I wasn't sure how much cleaning would happen. I pulled back from her and pointed at her not to move.

"Stay."

Her eyebrows scrunched up and she opened her mouth to say something.

"No. I said stay. We both know that if we get in that shower together, neither of us is actually going to get clean."

"But-"

"No, Kat. I'm serious. I'm going to go in there and take a shower. When I get out, then you can get in. Do you understand me?"

She pouted and nodded. "Just give me a kiss first."

I looked at her warily. This just didn't seem right to me. There had to be some sort of trickery involved. Kat wasn't innocent or sweet. Well, I guess she might be, but in this moment, I didn't trust that she was playing fair. Still, the way she was looking at me, I couldn't just walk away without giving her a kiss. I leaned in and pressed my lips to hers. I fully intended to pull away, but then I felt her hands on my zipper, and then she was pushing down my pants.

My cock sprung out and then her lips were wrapped around my cock. I groaned and threw back my head. "Oh hell," I muttered. She moaned, sending shock waves through my dick. I was a goner. There was no point in fighting her at this point. She had me the moment she batted those eyelashes at me.

I pulled her off me and tossed her gently further up the bed, shoving my pants off the rest of the way and tearing my shirt over my head. "Alright, Kat. You want to play dirty? I can do that."

I crawled up her body and yanked her pants down her legs, panties and all. She gasped when I shoved her legs up and spread her wide. I looked up at her and grinned right before I shoved my face against her wet pussy. Her hips bucked and she cried out as I shoved my tongue inside her. She tried to move her legs, but I placed my arms over her legs, keeping her spread wide open for me. Her fingers gripped at my hair as she started spasming around me. I didn't let up. She didn't want to wait, and now she was going to pay for that.

"Eric! Stop, I can't take any more."

I sucked her clit into my mouth and gently bit down. She started writhing even harder beneath me, but I wouldn't let up. "You wanted this, Kat. I wanted to take things nice and slow. I wanted to see you in that sexy lingerie and take my time with you. You wanted this, and now I'm going to make sure that you feel me all night long."

~

I laid in bed, completely exhausted. I took Kat so many times last night. I just couldn't get enough of her. I couldn't keep my hands off her. We did eventually make it into the shower, but as I suspected, there wasn't a lot of cleaning going on.

I knew she had to get up soon for work, and so did I. After my day yesterday, I really needed to be on time today. But it was so hard to get up when I had her in bed next to me. She looked so peaceful next to me, not at all like the sassy woman that liked to push my buttons and drive me crazy. Our relationship was so strange. We had started off all wrong, but with a few minor adjustments, she quickly became a woman that I couldn't stop thinking about. When I first learned about the pregnancy, I made the rash decision to ask her to marry me. That hadn't gone over so well. But now that she was in my bed, in my house, I had to seriously think about a way to get her to stay. I didn't want her to leave. And maybe that was way too soon in our relationship, but I could see this lasting with us. I could see us raising our child together in this house and I knew we would be happy.

I would figure something out, but in the meantime, I had to get up and make her something to eat. I didn't want her going into work hungry. I leaned over and pressed a light kiss to her lips and then slipped out of bed, careful not to wake her. I pulled on my jeans and t-shirt and headed downstairs. I was shocked to see that Frick and Frack were already awake and eating cereal.

"Going somewhere this morning?"

"Got a job interview," Andrew said around a bite of cereal as he stared at the cereal box.

"What are you doing?"

"There's a puzzle on the back."

I snatched the box out of his hands and looked at the puzzle. "This is meant for kids," I said, tossing the box of Captain Crunch back at him.

"Hey, I can do these puzzles. All the adult puzzles are hard."

"You're a computer genius," I said, a little baffled.

"Yeah, but that doesn't mean that I like to use that much brain power at five in the morning."

"And what are you doing up?" I asked Joe.

"Just got home," he said, sipping his coffee.

"Of course you did. Why would you actually be home at a normal time?"

"Hey, I was working."

"What were you doing?" I asked accusingly.

"You know, what does it matter? You probably wouldn't approve. It most likely wouldn't meet your high standards that you set for everyone."

I was a little taken aback by that. "Seriously? Is that what you think of me? That I wouldn't approve of your job choice?"

"Well, yeah, Eric. You put all these expectations on everyone."

"All I expect is that you get a job and pay your own way. As long as that job is legal, I really don't give a shit what you do."

He watched me for a moment, like he really didn't believe me.

I rolled my eyes. "Just tell me what you're doing."

He sighed and pulled up the sleeve of his shirt, showing off almost a full sleeve of ink. "I work with Decker."

"That tattoo guy?"

"The same one that gave you that tat," he nodded to my arm.

"At a biker shop?" I tried not to let the judgement seep in, but obviously I didn't do a very good of it.

Joe shoved his sleeve down and huffed in irritation. "See? Apparently, that's not a good enough job for you. But I like it, and I'm good at it."

"Alright," I said quickly. "If that's what you like, then that's great. I just didn't know you were into all that shit."

"You know I like to draw."

"Yeah, but I thought you would…draw pictures and shit. Like… flowers or something."

"I'm not a teenage girl. I draw cool shit, and if you bothered to pay attention, I've been doing this for a long time."

Well, now I really felt like an asshole. "Look, I'm sorry. If this is what you like to do, then I'm glad you have it."

"Good, because I'm saving up for my own shop."

"Really?" I asked, a little surprised.

"Yeah, well, that's why I'm still at home. It's not like I stay here for your cooking."

"I'm a good cook," I said defensively.

"No self-respecting man lives at home at my age."

"Hey," Andrew snapped. "Why should I have to leave? Just because I'm a grown man doesn't mean I have to live on my own. Besides, he's still a bachelor," he jerked his head at me.

"Yeah, but not for long."

"Are you planning on marrying her?" Andrew asked in surprise.

"Well, it's still a little early for that, but I'm hoping it's going in that direction."

"Wait, so you proposed to her as soon as you found out she was pregnant, but now that you're dating her, it's too soon?"

I glared at Joe for pointing out the flaw in my logic. "Hey, I never said I was perfect. But she's pretty great, right?"

"Yeah," Joe nodded. "I mean, I don't know what she's like in bed, but-"

"Can you please knock it off with that shit? And stop going through her lingerie. It's creepy."

"I did that once, and I came upon it by accident. It's not like I was digging through her drawers and started jacking off when I found her lingerie. I was only thinking of you, man."

"That...doesn't make it any better," I grimaced, thinking of him picking out my woman's lingerie.

I walked over to the stove and started pulling out stuff to make breakfast. With a glance at the clock, I knew I didn't have too much longer before Kat would be up. I opened the cabinet to pull out the pan when a mouse jumped out at me. I fell back with a shout and watched as the little fucker ran across the floor.

"What the hell was that?" Joe asked.

"A mouse."

"It's by the fridge," Andrew pointed. "Quick, grab the broom!"

I snatched it from the corner and darted toward the fridge. Andrew grabbed the cereal box, like he was going to trap it in there.

"Here, I got this," Joe said, picking up the mop and turning it around. "Okay, I'll shove this under the fridge and chase it out. You be ready to either kill it or shoo it into the cereal box."

I nodded in agreement. Andrew got down on the ground, ready to slide the box in any direction the mouse ran. I got in a fighting stance, ready to beat the shit out the mouse.

"Alright, one, two, three!" Joe shoved the stick of the mop under the fridge and violently started swinging it from side to side. I watched, my heart beating out of control as I waited for the fucker to run out. But nothing happened.

"Damnit, it must have gone up into the fridge coils," I snapped.

"I got this," Andrew said, standing up and walking over to the fridge. He hefted the fridge back, getting it to tip back on its hind feet before letting it slam to the floor.

KATHERINE

I woke right before the alarm went off. I didn't want to get out of bed. I had been thoroughly fucked last night, and now I just wanted to call in sick and stay in bed all day. I moved my hand over to Eric's side of the bed and sighed, wishing he was still in bed with me. I heard a loud bang from downstairs and sat up in bed, brushing the hair away from my face. When I heard another bang, I got up and quickly threw on a t-shirt and raced to the stairs. When I got to the bottom, I saw something that made my eyebrows shoot up in surprise.

"Get it!" Andrew shouted. He was holding the fridge in a tilted back position, but let it slam to the ground. Joe started shoving the mop under the fridge while Eric was slamming the broom down on the ground.

"Right there!" Joe shouted, pointing to something. Andrew grabbed a cereal box that was laying on the ground and slammed it down on the ground.

"I got it!"

"Move," Eric commanded. He lifted the broom over his head and slammed the broom down on the cereal box over and over again, violently beating the box to death.

"I think you got it," Joe said, carefully peeking at the box.

Andrew released the box and Eric slowly lowered the broom to the ground. Andrew slowly lifted the box up and looked into the opening. He leaned in a little closer and shouted, jumping back from the box. A small mouse jumped out and landed on his face. Andrew screamed again, swatting at his face just as Eric brought the broom down on his head. The mouse jumped from his face and scurried across the floor, back under the fridge.

"Goddamnit!" Eric shouted, slamming the broom down on the floor. "That's three times that fucker has gotten away from us!"

"You didn't have to slam the broom into my face," Andrew groaned, holding his face. "I think that fucker scratched me."

"Well, if you had just taken the box outside, it wouldn't have jumped out at you."

"Hey, I thought that the man that swings a hammer all day could at least kill a rodent," Andrew argued.

"Oh, so this is my fault?" Eric shot back. "It probably got in here because you always leave the door standing open."

"Because I'm the one that always carries in the groceries and you guys never help," Andrew spat.

I could see this wasn't going to end anytime soon, and as much fun as it was to watch the inner workings of the male brain, I had to get to work. "Hey!" I shouted over the chaos.

All three of them turned to me, Joe and Andrew's eyes bugging out while Eric looked like he was ready to murder me. I glanced down, realizing that I had come downstairs in only Eric's shirt. Eric grabbed Andrew and Joe by the collars and marched them out onto the front porch.

"Don't look at my woman's breasts." He shoved them out and slammed the door, locking it behind him. The guys started banging on the door, but Eric only had eyes for me. "Could you please not walk downstairs anymore in just my t-shirt?"

"You don't like it?" I asked playfully.

"I do, but I don't need my brothers seeing you so...naked."

"I'm not naked."

He fingered the sleeve of the t-shirt. "This t-shirt hides pretty much nothing on your gorgeous body." His hand slid from the t-shirt to cup my breast through the fabric. He ran his thumb over my nipple and groaned. "Fuck it. I can be late again."

He grabbed me suddenly, lifting me off my feet. I screeched in surprise, but he didn't stop as he hauled me back upstairs to his bedroom.

"Eric! I'm going to be late for work!"

"You should have thought about that before you came downstairs looking like that."

"I heard banging. I thought something was wrong."

"And you were going to help in just a t-shirt?" He laid me down on the bed and lifted my shirt, sighing slightly. "And no panties. Yes, I can see how you would have been helpful."

I didn't have a chance to say anything. His fingers were on me, sliding inside me and filling me so quickly that all I could do was gasp. I was powerless against him, and when he slid inside me just minutes later, I decided that being late to work was totally worth it if I woke up like this every morning. Well, minus the mouse bashing.

∽

I rushed into the hospital and tossed my purse in my locker before hurrying to clock in. I was pulling up my hair when I saw Chrissy walking toward me, tapping her watch.

"I know."

"You're lucky that Charlene is in a meeting right now, or you'd be getting your ass reamed."

"I couldn't help it."

"Did your Jeep break down? I keep telling you to get a new vehicle."

"No, it wasn't that."

"You overslept?"

"Not exactly."

She put her hand on my arm to stop me. "You were playing handyman with Eric?"

I flushed bright red, but ignored her comment.

"I wouldn't have been late, but there was a mouse and then I'm not sure exactly what happened. One minute I was downstairs and the next I was upstairs with a huge dick inside me."

She grinned wickedly. "So, you're spending the night now. Two nights in a row, that's pretty serious."

"It's not serious. It's just…"

She quirked an eyebrow at me.

"Okay, it might be serious, but I don't want to jinx it."

"Right, because saying that you like the guy, the same one that is obviously obsessed with you, is going to make the whole thing go up in smoke."

"You never know."

"Mhmm," she smiled.

"Remember when he picked me up for our first date and you gushed over how hot he was? Remember how that turned out?"

"Yeah, but that was before, when you were both acting like assholes. Now you've found your rhythm."

"And I'd like to keep it that way."

"So, have you thought about it?"

I stared at her in confusion. She was biting her lip, like she was so excited that she just couldn't hold back whatever she was thinking.

"Thought about what?"

"Marriage," she said exasperatedly. "Geez, you're in love with your baby daddy-"

"My intended," I corrected.

"Your what?"

"Well, I couldn't just keep calling him my baby daddy. It has a weird vibe."

"Okay," she said slowly. "Anyway, are you thinking about marriage?"

"Chrissy, it's way too early to be thinking about something like that. Yes, I think I'm falling for him and he's so much more than I first thought, but this is still the honeymoon phase of the relationship. Everything's good now, but what about in six months? We already have a baby on the way. Eric was right, we need to take this slow. If we mess this up, it'll screw up our whole family."

She sighed and picked up her next chart. "Girl, sometimes you just have to take a chance on love. This might have started out as the date from hell, but you can't deny that you're building something amazing with him. And if you hold back too long, you could do just as much damage."

She walked away without another word. I wasn't sure if she was right or not, but I knew that I didn't want to screw this up with Eric. He was the first guy that I really wanted to be with, but with all our baggage, I just couldn't rush it.

ERIC

The last two months had been absolutely amazing. I went to the doctor with Kat and heard our baby's heartbeat, and that seemed to solidify something inside me. We were supposed to be together. She spent most of her time at my house, though there were times that I spent the night at her place just to have some space from my brothers. But they didn't seem to bother Kat. She actually enjoyed hanging out with them, which pissed me off. They would joke around and watch movies together. She was only supposed to watch movies with me. I knew that was a stupid way to look at our situation. My brothers really liked her, so I should be grateful they got along so well, but I wanted her to myself.

We both agreed to do something the other liked once a month. The first month, she made me try mushroom risotto. I think it was payback for that first date. I hated it, but I ate that whole damn thing just to prove to her that I could. I made her help me replace the windows on the house. She didn't actually do all that much because I was paranoid she would hurt herself, but I did make her stand and watch me work. I liked the way her eyes watched my body. It made all the hard work worth it when I took her upstairs and fucked her at the end of the night.

Last month, she took me to a fair and made me get on the freaking ferris wheel. I tried to argue that it wasn't safe for her. Pregnant women shouldn't go on rides. We both knew that a ferris wheel wasn't dangerous to her, and she argued the point in front of the whole damn line of people. By the time she was done, even the other guys in line were giving me crap. She grinned at me with satisfaction, knowing that the only reason I didn't want to go on the damn ride was because I hated heights. I squeezed her hand the whole damn time, terrified that we were going to plummet to our deaths.

Coming up with something to do with her was even harder. She didn't seem to mind watching me work. In fact, she liked it quite a lot. So, I picked something that I thought would drive her insane. I took her to a foreign film. Turns out, she loved it. I was bored out of my mind the entire night. The only good thing that happened was that she was so turned on by the French accents that she played out her own Parisian fantasy when we returned home that night.

So, now it was time for us to do it again this month. I had been wracking my brain, trying to come up with something that would get to her the way she got to me. It turned out, I seemed to be the only one that really had to step outside my comfort zone. Nothing seemed to phase her. It was like I was an old car that she was slowly fixing up.

She rolled over in bed and wrapped her arms around me, snuggling into my back. "Morning."

I rolled over so I could look at her and smiled. She was so beautiful in the morning. I could wake up next to her forever, and that thought didn't even scare me. I knew I was falling harder and harder for this woman every day, but I didn't say anything. I worried that she would run away as far and as fast as she could. I always managed to fuck things up when something big was on the line. I fucked up our first date and pretty much everything after that. Now that we had our rhythm, I was scared to death that something I did would tip the scales and she would slide away from me.

"Good morning, beautiful."

She smiled up at me brightly and slid her hand down my chest. "So, I was thinking…" Her fingers trailed further down my chest until they skimmed over my growing erection. Thinking was out now. There was absolutely no thinking once her hands were on me. "Today is the day."

She gripped my dick and squeezed slightly, stroking me up and down. I swallowed hard. "Uh-huh."

A wicked grin crossed her lips as she moved down the bed, shoving the covers out of the way as she took my cock in her mouth. The nerves in my brain were misfiring as the warmth of her mouth coated me. Up and down, her head bobbed, but her eyes never left mine. She pulled back, giving my dick one long lick.

"So, I've been thinking about your challenge for this month."

"Yeah," I groaned as she took me deep in her throat.

She stroked my cock, tilting her head to the side. "And I was thinking that I wanted to do something that would give you pleasure."

"Please tell me that my challenge is to see how many times I can fuck you in one day."

She chuckled and swallowed me whole again. "No, I was thinking that there's something you can do, something you might be uncomfortable with, but it would heighten your pleasure. And mine."

My hips thrust up as she took me again, sucking me harder this time. She was an evil seductress. "Tell me what to do."

She jerked me faster. My heart was pounding out of control. Whatever she wanted, I would give it to her.

"I want you to get a Prince Albert."

I moaned as she sucked me hard, working my cock with both her mouth and her hand. I was so close. Just a few more strokes and I would be coming hard.

"Is that a yes?"

"Yeah," I moaned. "Fuck, whatever you want."

She grinned wickedly at me and then took me in her mouth one last time, shoving my cock all the way down her throat. I shot off inside her, my hips jerking violently as she held me to her. I was panting hard as she slowly licked my cock clean, then sat up with a smile.

"I already made you an appointment for this afternoon, so you should shower and then we can get some lunch before we head over."

I snatched at her hand, wanting to return the favor, but she just gave me a saucy wink and strode away. I grinned, flopping back down in bed as I stared at the ceiling. I tried to remember what she had asked me to do, but I couldn't for the life of me remember. Something about a prince. It didn't matter. If she gave me head like that every morning, she would have me jumping out of a plane within a few months.

I quickly showered and dressed, then went downstairs for breakfast. Joe and Andrew were sitting at the table while Kat made breakfast. I loved seeing her in my kitchen. I had been doing most of the cooking, but every once in a while, she insisted on doing the cooking. And she was fantastic, even if she hated cooking. Hell, if she wanted to stay home and take care of our child, I would have no problem with that. She could do all the cooking and I could come home every day to images of this. I walked up behind her and wrapped my arms around her, kissing her neck as my hand slid over her very small bump. She was getting close to the five month mark and I couldn't wait until she was further along and showing more.

"God, are we going to have to watch this shit every morning?" Joe grumbled. "It's like a bad porno."

"How is it a bad porno?" Kat asked, sounding slightly offended.

"Well, first of all, there are no clothes coming off. First rule of porn is that clothes have to come off. Second, my brother is in this porno, which makes this disturbing. I'm not into picturing my brother having sex."

"We weren't having sex," I reminded him. "I was kissing my…Kat."

"Your pussy cat," Andrew chuckled.

"Hey," I snapped. "Don't say that shit."

"You're the one that named her Kat. You should have known it was only a matter of time before that joke came out."

"Well, this pussy cat is hungry, so scootch." I moved out of her way as she grabbed the pan and started scooping eggs onto the plates.

"You know, you don't have to feed my brothers."

"Yes she does," Joe said around a mouthful of eggs. "We'd wither and die without her cooking."

"I cook for you too, asshole."

"Yeah, but it's not like hers. Besides, your meals come with a lecture on learning to cook or taking responsibility for our lives."

"That's because you're twenty-eight years old and you still require someone else to do your cooking and cleaning."

Joe rolled his eyes and finished eating. Surprisingly, Kat was finished already also. She leaned over and kissed my cheek, then put her dish in the sink. "I'm gonna shower. We're leaving in two hours!"

Joe put his plate at the sink and walked out, leaving me alone with Andrew.

"Where are you going in two hours?"

I shook my head. "Out to eat and then…hell, I don't know. We're supposed to do our thing today."

He grinned. "What does she have planned for you this time?"

"Honestly, I'm not sure. She seduced me and then told me when she was giving me head."

"Nice," he grinned. "You know it's bad if she used head as a distraction. What did she talk about?"

I thought back, trying to remember actual words. I shook my head. "Something about a prince? Getting a prince?"

His brows furrowed. "Getting a prince?"

I shrugged. "Something about heightening sexual pleasure."

His face dropped as he stared at me, then he burst out laughing. "And you agreed?"

"Why? What is it?"

"Oh my god! I can't believe you agreed to that."

"What is it?" I asked again, my heart starting to pound.

"You are so fucked. She's definitely a seductress, giving you head while she asked you to do *that*."

"What is *that*?"

"Holy shit, I have to tell Joe."

I stood from my chair and walked around, slamming my hand down on his phone. "Just tell me what the fuck it is!"

He covered his mouth as he laughed. "Alright, keep an open mind."

"Just tell me what the fuck it is!" I roared.

"It's a barbell."

"A piercing?"

He nodded.

"Why would she want me to get my ear pierced? How is that going to heighten sexual pleasure?"

He chuckled, shaking his head. "She doesn't want to pierce your ear."

I frowned, not understanding where. "If not my ear, then where else would she pierce? I'm not getting an eyebrow ring."

He leaned forward in his seat and smirked at me. "Tell me, where is the place that you get the most pleasure from? And if you say your toe, I'm disowning you as a brother."

My eyes widened in horror and I stumbled backwards, knocking over the chair behind me. I shook my head violently from side to side. This couldn't be happening. My hand moved involuntarily to cover my dick. "This is so wrong. Why would she...Oh God," I said, swaying slightly into the table. "I don't feel so good."

Andrew chuckled, finding this whole situation so goddamn hilarious. "How did you not know what that was? And why would you agree to something without knowing?"

"I had my cock in her mouth," I whisper-hissed. "I wasn't exactly thinking about what she was saying. Hell, I would have agreed to a three-some with a guy at that moment."

He jerked back. "You aren't actually interested in that, are you?"

"No!" I practically shouted. "She tricked me. She used her powers to get her way." I shook my head slightly. "Well, I'm not doing it."

"Right," he snorted. "You go ahead and tell her that you weren't actually listening to her during sex and that you're not going through with it."

"She tricked me."

"Yeah, but she can turn this around on you, and you'll pay for it way longer than the recovery time of the piercing."

"No, I'll just explain to her that I didn't know what I was agreeing to."

"Doesn't matter. Besides, your woman is asking you to do this for her. Are you really going to say no?"

"You're damn right I'm going to say no. I don't even know where the damn piercing goes!"

"Right through the head of your cock."

I stood there for a minute in shock. I couldn't believe she would ask me to do this. It was insane. "Well, that does it. I guess I'm back to being single. Alone and single. Never to get married or have any fun sex ever again."

"Why?"

"Why? You want to know why? Because I'm not insane. I'm not going to let someone else touch my dick, let alone shove a piercing through it. That's insane, and one thing I'm not, is insane."

"But you are a wet blanket."

"I don't care."

"And the whole point of this was to try and bring you out of your buttoned-up demeanor."

"I like buttons. I like being able to squeeze a lump of coal out of my ass. Hell, I would rather wait for the most boring woman in the world to come along, than to have my dick pierced. It's not happening."

∽

"So, the process is pretty simple and only takes a few seconds to perform," Decker said.

"Do you have one?"

He smirked at me. "I don't talk about my junk with other guys."

I swallowed nervously. My hands were clenched tight in fists and I was pretty sure I was on the verge of passing out. The only reason I came was because I made a bet with Kat, and I wasn't about to back out of that.

"Look, I just need to know...something. Shit." He sighed and started undoing his belt buckle. "What are you doing?"

"Showing you what it looks like."

"Why, why, why….why would you do that? I don't need to see your dick."

"Relax," he said, shoving his pants down. His cock bounced up and I got a glimpse of silver before I averted my eyes. I looked up at the ceiling and took a deep breath. This was so wrong. "Just look at it. It's not like I'm asking you to touch it."

I shook my head, but he grabbed my face and yanked my head so that I was staring at his cock. "I've seen it."

"Any questions?"

"Does it hurt?"

He shrugged. "At first? Not really. Now? It's fucking amazing. Your lady is going to love it."

"So…you think I should do this."

"What I think is irrelevant. But imagine this, you're getting the best head of your life. She's sucking you hard, doing that thing that makes you want to blow on the spot, and then she hums."

"Huh?"

"That hum will send a thousand vibrations through your cock, making you shoot off faster and harder than you ever have before. Now, are you saying you want to pass up an opportunity like that for five seconds of pain?"

Well, when he put it like that…

"Trust me, this is something you don't want to miss out on."

He yanked up his pants and fastened the belt just as Kat walked back. "So, are you ready?" she asked with a twinkle in her eye.

"Yeah, I'm ready," I said with more confidence than I felt. I wouldn't appear weak to her again.

"Alright, drop 'em and we'll get you marked up."

"Drop…you want me to…"

"Well, I can't do the piercing through your pants," Decker retorted.

I huffed and yanked my pants down, my face beat red as another dude got down low and inspected my dick.

"I'm just going to mark you right now. We'll do the rest sitting down, in case you pass out again."

"I'm not going to pass out," I muttered.

He snorted. "Sure."

The door opened and I glanced up, shocked when I saw Joe walk through the door. He glanced down at Decker and then his eyes widened as he looked up at me. "Are you fucking serious?"

"Stop looking at it!" I shouted.

A sharp pain stabbed through my dick and everything went black.

KATHERINE

"I can't believe he did that before I was ready," Eric muttered as we drove home.

"He was taking advantage of the distraction," I said for the tenth time.

"I can't believe Joe saw my dick."

"Oh, relax. I'm sure he sees a lot of dicks working there."

"Yeah, but not mine."

I put the truck in park in front of his house and sighed. "Well, are you mad you got it?"

He shrugged, still refusing to look at me. "It feels weird. I have a fucking bandage around my dick."

"Well, it's like any other wound, you need to take care of it." I scooted across the seat and wrapped my arms around his neck. "Lucky for you, I'll happily be your nurse during your recovery."

"No," he said, dragging my arms off him. "You heard what he said, a six to eight week recovery time. I hope you remember that when you're horny and lying in bed, needing my cock. If I don't get any, neither do you."

"You'd really do that to your pregnant intended?"

"Yes, I would. I can't believe you tricked me this morning."

"I didn't trick you," I said indignantly. "I was trying to get you in the mood, to show you what it could be like!"

"And that might have worked had I known what the fuck it was."

I sighed, wondering how long this bad attitude was going to last. "You know, if you're going to get like this every time I try and get you to do something new, we're just going to have to stop doing new things. You're too grumpy."

"I come up with good shit," he shot back. "You come up with shit that's painful. Do you really hate me that much?"

"No, I lo-" I stopped myself from saying what I really wanted to say. It was too soon, but Eric caught on to what I was about to say and slowly leaned forward and kissed me on the lips.

"You what?"

I shook my head slowly.

"What were you going to say, Kat?"

I swallowed hard as I looked into his beautiful eyes. I couldn't tell him. It was too soon. "I...I was going to say that I love to drive you crazy."

His eyes fell slightly in disappointment. He took my hand and squeezed it slightly. "Come on, it's your turn."

"You're not going to make me bail hay are you?"

We climbed out of the truck and he slammed the door, heading toward the field.

"Wrong time of year and we don't actually farm any of this land."

"You don't?"

"Nope. We rent out the land to other farmers."

"Oh...I guess I just assumed you did it."

"Would you like that? To see me in tight jeans with a farmer's tan?"

I smirked at him. "You already have the farmer's tan."

"True, but you haven't seen me on a tractor yet. I bet that would drive you insane."

I had no doubt that if I saw him on a tractor, I would want to jump him immediately. All that bouncing on the seat could be a lot of fun.

We continued walking across the grass until we came up to a huge tree near the field. There was a hammock set up under it and as soon as we stepped under the shade of the tree, the heat melted away and the breeze cooled my skin.

"What are we doing here?"

"I need to rest my dick."

"Okay."

He sat down on the hammock and patted the spot next to him. "Come on, Kat."

I sat down beside him and we slowly maneuvered so we didn't tip over the hammock. We were swaying slightly with the breeze and it really was enjoyable, but this couldn't be all he wanted to do.

"So, what are we doing under here?"

"Relaxing."

"But, I thought we were going to-" He leaned over and covered my mouth with his hand.

"Just for a little while, I'm going to lay here with you and enjoy the peaceful day."

My brows furrowed in confusion. "That's it?"

"That's it."

"But... I had you put a barbell through your dick."

"I'm aware. I can feel the damn thing right now."

I laid there for a few more minutes, but the silence was killing me. "So, what does one do when lying under a tree?"

"You enjoy the quiet."

I had never done anything like this before. It was weird. Didn't he have things he wanted to do? I could be folding laundry or getting stuff ready for dinner. Hell, I could be catching up on my favorite TV shows. It seemed like such a waste to just lay here outside.

I shifted to my shoulder, allowing him to put his arm under my head. Then I did what I always did when lying with him. I brought my leg up over his.

A strained sound came from his mouth and he jerked away from me. "What's wrong?"

"Just brushed a little too close to the goods."

"Oh my god!" I shouted in horror. "What can I do? Are you alright? Should I-"

He wrapped his hand around my mouth and pulled me back down beside him. "You can lay down beside me and be quiet."

"But what about-"

"Woman, I just got my dick pierced for you. The least you can do is lay here with me in silence until I'm ready to move. Is that too much to ask?"

I shook my head slowly and watched as his eyes slowly slipped closed. I got comfortable beside him, sighing in contentment when his fingers started brushing up and down my arm lazily. The temperature was perfect and the breeze slowly pushed us back and forth. I could see the appeal of being out here. The sun peeked through the leaves above us, giving a serene feeling.

"If you want, I could get my clit pierced," I said, breaking the silence.

"Christ, you just can't stand to lay in silence, can you?"

"I was trying to be helpful," I said indignantly, leaning up on my elbow.

"By talking about getting your clit pierced? How is that helpful?"

"I thought it would make you feel better!"

"First, you can't get your clit pierced until after you have the baby. And second, why the hell would you think that talking about your pussy, when you know that I can't have sex, is helpful?" he shouted.

I shut my mouth, a small snort escaping as I tried to hold back my laughter. I really was being cruel.

"I'm glad you think my pain is funny."

"Not your pain. Just the situation in general."

"You're lucky that I like you. No sane man would put up with the shit you've put me through."

"No sane woman would walk away from you," I said quietly, staring into his eyes.

He brought his hand up to my face, brushing a strand of hair away. He threaded his fingers through my hair, gripping me around the back of the head as he pulled me in closer, just an inch from his lips. "No sane man could help but fall in love with you."

My breath caught in my chest just as he pressed his lips to mine. It was sweet, but demanding, sending me free falling in my love for him. My tongue slipped into his and my hands started skimming down his chest. I loved the feel of his hard body beside mine. My fingers barely touched his waistline when I heard his gasp of pain. I jerked back, my eyes wide.

"What? What happened?"

"Blood...rushing to the wrong place."

I burst out laughing, then kissed him hard. He pulled back and scowled at me.

"Not helping."

"Don't worry. I'll take care of you," I murmured against his lips.

"You're going to put me in an early grave," he grumbled.

"Not a chance. I haven't even gotten to try my new toy yet."

"Just so we're clear, none of your future challenges can involve anything with my body."

"You're no fun."

"I'm serious, Kat."

"Fine, but when you realize how good it's going to be, you'll be begging me to try something else. Maybe a nipple piercing."

"I can guarantee that I'll never beg you to have my nipples pierced," he said fiercely.

I smiled and snuggled back into his side. "We'll see."

ERIC

I limped along, my dick aching with every step. The damn bandage was uncomfortable, but the piercing was even worse. I wasn't even sure why I agreed to the damn thing. It was like learning how to do everything all over again. I had to sit when I took a piss, otherwise piss went everywhere, even from the second hole of the piercing. Was that going to happen when I ejaculated? God, this was a friggin' nightmare.

"Why are you walking like you just rode a horse for four hours?" Will asked as he brought me supplies to take up to the roof. I had to replace the roof before the baby came and my days of nice weather were running out. I was lucky that today was nice enough to do it. There had been rain in the forecast for the next week.

I ignored him and started hauling shit up the ladder. Each step was painful and I had to stop several times to take deep breaths. When I got to the roof, I bent over in and took several calming breaths, readjusting the way my cock was sitting in my jeans.

"Dude, what the fuck happened to you?" Will asked as he reached the top.

"You don't want to know."

"I kinda do. Did you get kicked in the nuts or something?"

I shook my head. "Kat," I said, as if that was all the explanation needed. He quirked an eyebrow at me. "It was that time of the month. You know, the challenge."

"Oh. Well, what did she challenge you to do?"

I grimaced and looked up at him. "You ever hear of a Prince Albert?"

His face dropped right before he burst out in laughter. "Oh my god. Please tell me that you didn't go through with it."

"Would I be bent over in pain like this if I hadn't?"

"Why the fuck would you do that?"

"Apparently I agreed to it during sex."

"So back out."

"I couldn't. I had already agreed."

He shook his head at me. "Yeah, because she would have held you at gunpoint and forced you to do it if you told her you really didn't want to do it."

"I don't go back on my word."

"This is a fucking cock piercing, not a proposal of marriage!"

"A promise is a promise."

He grinned at me, pointing his finger at me accusingly. "You like it."

"What?"

"You like that she makes you do these things that are outside your comfort zone."

"Yeah, I like having a tube shoved through the head of my cock and then a needle pierced through the skin, all to have a barbell shoved through."

"I knew it!"

"I was being sarcastic."

He shook his head and laughed. "No, you weren't. You *want* to hate it, but deep down, you love that she takes all your uptight shit and throws it out the window. She makes you live."

"You don't know what you're talking about."

"Yes, I do. She's the woman you've been waiting for your whole damn life. Remember that first date with her?"

"How could I forget?"

"You let your guard down with her. You took a chance and you loved it. That's why you pushed her away the next morning. You were scared. And that would have worked out for you if she hadn't shown up pregnant. That was the best thing that could have happened to you because it forced you to find a way to get along with her. Just think about it, if she hadn't shown up at your door a month later, you would have continued to go out on boring dates with boring women in your slick suit and your three date sex rule."

"I kept that rule with her."

"Just own it, man. She's everything you never knew you wanted."

"She's the devil that's turning me into someone I don't recognize."

He tilted his head and stared at me for a moment. "You love her."

"What?" I picked up my tools and pretended to get to work.

"You love her, so why are you so pissed right now?"

I started ripping up the shingles and tossed them over the side of the house into the dumpster I rented. "I don't know what you're talking about."

"You're pissed right now. The last challenge, as freaked out as you were, you still were happy the next day."

"Yeah, well, I have a barbell through my dick right now, so that could be what's making me so fucking crabby."

"No, that's not it. You need to tell her."

"And why would I do that?"

"Because you need to get it off your chest. The longer you let it simmer, the more it's going to drive you insane."

"No."

"No?"

"That's right. I said no."

"But you need to do this. You need to have it out with her."

"Will, just mind your own fucking business."

"What? Are you worried she won't say it back? Because I've seen the way she is around you. She's in love with you too. If you just-"

"I already fucking said it!"

He stopped his rambling and stared at me, his jaw hanging open. "What?"

"I told her yesterday, after my appointment. We were in the hammock under the tree and I told her that I loved her. Guess what? She didn't say it back."

"Maybe…maybe you said it wrong."

"Said it wrong? Are you fucking serious right now? How the hell could I have said it wrong?"

"I don't know, but guys screw this shit up all the time. What did you say?"

I shook my head and tossed the roofing shovel down. "I said that any guy would be insane not to fall in love with her."

"You prick, that's not the same thing."

"That's exactly the same thing."

"No, it's not! If you want to tell her you love her and get a response back, you need to be crystal clear. You take her hand in yours and cup her face with the other," he said, mimicking the movements on me. I rolled my eyes, but he continued. "You say, *I fell in love with you. Somewhere between the tattoo and the Prince Albert, I fell hard for you, and I want you for the rest of my life.*"

"Uh…are we interrupting something?" Robert asked, looking at me from his place on top of the ladder.

"What did I miss?" I could hear Joe ask from further down.

"It looks like Will is professing his undying love to Eric," Robert said, looking down the ladder.

I shoved Will's hand from my face and picked up my shovel, getting back to work.

"He told Kat he loved her, but didn't actually tell her."

"How do you not tell someone you love them?" Robert asked, picking up his own tools.

"He said it in a roundabout way."

Robert snorted. "Yeah, because women don't read between the lines enough. I can only imagine the shit running through her head right now because you weren't crystal clear."

"She probably thinks he was talking about another guy. She might even think you were trying to tell her to go for it with someone else."

"That's not what she thought," I finally said. "She knew exactly what I was saying. I could see it in her eyes. She just...I don't know. Either she doesn't feel the same way or..."

"Or what?" Will asked.

"Or she's not ready to say it."

He nodded and pulled out his phone.

"What are you doing?"

"I'm fixing this."

"What? I didn't ask you to fix this."

He shushed me as he held the phone to his ear.

"What are you doing?" I reached for the phone, but he smacked me away from him.

"Ma, it's Will."

I lunged for him, but he stepped away, picking up the roofing hammer and pointing it at me.

"Yeah, I was thinking that you and Dad should come out for a visit soon...Yeah, you know, meet Kat. She's really great."

I shook my head violently. The last thing I needed was Ma coming out here and putting all that pressure on us. I took another step toward him, but he swung the hammer toward my dick and I immediately cowered away from him.

"That's great, Ma. So, we'll see you next week? Alright. Love you too."

He hung up the phone and grinned at me.

"What the fuck were you thinking? You know how Ma is."

"Forget about Ma. I just did you a favor."

"No, you just made everything more difficult. Kat and I are just moving into a place that's really good. The last thing she needs is to have Ma hovering."

"No, he's right," Robert grinned. "He did you a favor."

"I'm not seeing the favor in all of this."

"Ma thinks that you live with Kat," Robert pointed out.

"Yes, and thank you for pointing out that Kat doesn't actually live here."

Joe grinned and nodded. "Right, and now she's going to have to move in. To keep up appearances."

"And with Ma visiting for a whole week, she's going to have to be the good little housemate," Will chuckled. "What I did was buy you enough time to convince her that living with you is what she wants."

I stopped and thought about that a moment. She *would* have to move in here. Ma already thought that she lived here, so if we told her that Kat had her own place, it would be awkward for both of us. And since Kat had already taken over telling Ma that we were having a baby, I knew deep down that she wouldn't want to do anything to make Ma look at her differently.

A small grin split my lips as I thought of all the possibilities. We would have to get her moved in quickly, and then I could start on my plan for making her admit to me how much she really loved me. Because deep down, I knew that she loved me, she was just scared to say it.

***

After putting on a new roof with my brothers, I was exhausted. We busted our asses to get it all done because the weather was expected to turn. Not only that, but we all had to get back to work the next day. My cock ached the whole day, and the sweat that built up throughout the day didn't help my situation either. I just needed a shower.

I groaned as I stepped under the warm water and it washed away the aches and pains. I leaned my head against the shower wall. I really wasn't sure I had it in me right now to do more than let the water do the work. The door opened and Kat stepped in, stripping out of her scrubs before she opened the shower curtain.

"You're home late today," I said, not opening my eyes again.

I felt her hands on me, running over my back lovingly. "The little girl, Casey, had some more breathing issues. I wanted to stay until I knew she was stable."

"What does her doctor say?"

I felt her huff out a deep breath against my back. "They don't think she's going to make it. Unless they find a trial she can get in, she's not going to survive. Nothing else is working for her."

I could feel her sadness leech into my skin. I turned and pulled her into my arms, rubbing my hand up and down her back. I couldn't even imagine what it would be like to have a child that young going through something like that. I wondered how Kat worked in that department now that she was pregnant. It must weigh heavily on her mind.

I pulled back and slid my hand down to her belly, feeling her growing bump beneath my hand. I would do anything to protect my child, but there were some things in this world that you couldn't control. And that was the hardest part to deal with.

Kat picked up the bar of soap and started to lather it in her hands. She slowly started washing my body, and I wasn't going to lie, it felt great. She delicately washed my dick, making sure not to be too rough with the piercing, and then she continued down my body. Not even the sight of her on her knees could get me hard right now.

She looked up at me with a raised eyebrow. "Not in the mood tonight?"

I huffed out a laugh. "Between my sore cock and working all day to get the roof replaced, I couldn't get it up if I wanted to."

"Well, I'll be sure to take extra special care of you tonight."

"Yeah? Are you going to make dinner?"

"I think that's only fair."

"And you're going to give me a foot massage?" I asked as I wrapped my arms around her.

"If you're nice to me."

I hummed low in my throat and pulled her tighter to me, sighing as I held her in my arms. I wanted to ask her why she couldn't admit that she loved me, but I knew that would only bring on awkward conversation and ruin the night. So, I held it in. My parents would be here next week and everything would change. I knew it.

I pulled back from her and grinned.

"What?"

"My parents are coming for a visit next week. They want to meet you."

Her face dropped in horror. "What? But…they think…oh my god, this is terrible."

"It's not that bad, Kat. They're nice people."

"But we practically told them we were living together."

I nodded, like I understood her problem. "Yeah, well, I guess we could always tell them the truth."

"What?" she shrieked. "You didn't want to tell them before, but *now* you think it's a good idea to tell them we had a one night stand?"

I shrugged lightly. "I was freaking out, but I've come to realize that no matter what, everything will be okay. My parents will understand, and they'll be fine with the fact that you live in your own place."

I was totally gambling here, hoping that she wouldn't be okay with this, and insist on moving in here. If the idea came from me, she would probably fight me every step of the way. This had to be her decision.

"How can you say that? Your mother will think I'm a whore!"

"Yeah, but you didn't care before. I mean, you were perfectly fine with telling them what happened before, so what's changed?"

"What's changed?" she shouted. "What's changed is that we already told them a lie."

"It's not a lie anymore. We're together now."

"But your parents won't see it that way. What will they think of me?"

"Kat, don't worry about it. Honestly, I'm not sure why you even care."

"Because I don't want them to think the worst of me."

I shook my head slightly. "Kat, it doesn't matter."

"Yes, it does. I will not have your parents thinking that I'm some whore that got pregnant and roped you into a relationship. I'll just move my things in here for a few days."

"They're staying the week, and in order to make it believable, you'd have to move in a lot of shit. I mean, you'd have to add stuff to every room of the house. No woman would live here with a bunch of men and not add her own personal touch."

"You're right. I mean, it'll be a lot of moving, but if your brothers help, we should be able to get it all done quickly." I nodded sagely. "But this is just for while they're here," she added quickly.

"I know."

She bit her lip. I could see the wheels turning in her head as she thought of all the stuff she needed to do.

"Honestly, Kat, if it's going to make you insane, we won't do it. I'll just tell my parents that you stay here sometimes, but you like your own space. They'll be fine with it."

"Well, I'm not!"

"Why? Why does it matter now?"

"Because I love you, you stupid jerk!"

I flinched back in shock. I had been hoping to push her into moving in with me, but I never expected that this would also convince her to open up to me in this way. My devious plan turned out to be brilliant. Well, Will's plan.

I smirked at her, shaking my head slightly.

"What are you smiling about?"

"It's about time you said it."

I bent down and kissed her, smiling against her lips as she wrapped her arms around my neck.

"I didn't want to jinx anything," she murmured.

"What would you jinx?"

"Us? We haven't exactly had the best track record so far."

"Well, if you would stop using my body as an art lab, we might be getting along better."

She slapped my shoulder, laughing lightly. "So, they're really coming?"

"Yeah, they're really coming."

She let out a long sigh. "Well, I suppose I have to meet them at some point."

"Kat, you have nothing to worry about. My parents will probably love you more than me."

"And what about you?" she asked nervously.

"What about me?"

"Do you…I mean, you haven't changed your mind about what you said yesterday?"

"Kat, do you really think I would have told you I loved you after you almost had me castrated if I didn't mean it?"

She rolled her eyes. "I didn't have you almost castrated. And you watch, you're going to love the way everything feels."

"And how do you know that?"

"I've done plenty of research."

I leaned in, kissing her lightly. "You're like a mad scientist or something." My lips skimmed hers and my fingers slid down her body between her legs.

"I thought you said that I couldn't have sex until you could." Her breath was heavy now as my fingers slid between her legs. She gasped slightly as I slid a finger inside her and slowly started pumping.

"I never said this was for you. I'm going to make you come all over my tongue, and that's all for my pleasure."

KATHERINE

"Be careful with that one," I snapped at Andrew. "I won't buy you pizza if you break my grandmother's vase."

"Jesus, it's just a piece of glass."

"It's an heirloom!"

He flipped the vase over and studied it. "It says it's made in China. And look, the price tag is still on it. She paid nine dollars for it."

"I don't care," I said, snatching the vase out of his hands, carefully placing it on the mantle over the fireplace. "It's special to me."

He sighed and left to get more stuff.

"Uh, where am I putting this thing?" Eric asked.

I looked at Fred, the elephant that my grandmother got on vacation. It was a porcelain elephant with a flat head, so it could be used as a side table. "Just put it next to that chair."

He raised an eyebrow. "You want to put an elephant next to the chair."

"It's not just an elephant. His name is Fred. He and Gertie belong in the living room."

"You named porcelain elephants," he said slowly.

"*I* didn't. My grandmother did. They're very special to me."

He just stared at me, obviously not sure what to say. Obviously he didn't get it, so I grabbed Fred from him. Men had no taste. I set Fred next to his favorite chair and stepped back to look at it. It was perfect. Gertie could go next to the couch.

Andrew rolled in my tea table and sighed. "I suppose you have a place for this?"

"What the hell is that?" Eric asked.

"A tea table."

"No. No, I draw the line at tea tables. If you tell me you're setting tea pots out in my living room, I'm going to lose my shit."

"They're beautiful. And I won't be setting tea pots all over the living room. Just on this table. It can go next to that window," I pointed to the far window. "We'll have to take down the baseball bat on the wall. It doesn't match at all, and I can't risk the bat falling on my tea set."

He looked over there and frowned. "But that's where my bat has always been. It's signed by Ryne Sandberg."

"I get it. That's a big deal, but my tea set needs to go there."

I watched as he clenched his fists and his jaw tightened. Will leaned over and whispered, "Remember the plan."

"What plan?"

Eric's eyes shot up to mine and he cleared his throat. "Uh...the plan to convince Ma that you live here."

"He's right. How is your Mom going to believe that I live here if I don't add my own personal touches?"

He gritted his teeth. "Fine." He walked over to the wall and ever so gently took down the baseball bat. "I'll just take this up to my room."

"Our room," I corrected. He glared at me. "We can't have your parents hearing you say that. They'll never believe us."

"You know, if you want the tea set here, that's fine, but doesn't it belong in the kitchen?"

My brows furrowed. "Why would it be in the kitchen?"

"Oh, I don't know, because that's where you make tea," he snapped.

My eyes widened in surprise. "Eric, that tea set is an antique. You don't actually use it for drinking tea."

"Then why the fuck would you have it?"

"For decoration!"

"For-" He chuckled low in his throat and twisted the bat in his hands like he was getting ready to swing. "Fine, we'll keep it out for *decoration,* but tell me, how much more shit are you bringing over that's just for *decoration.*"

"Well, there's my buddha and the metal spider in the spider web that goes in the corner, the coo coo clock-"

"Wait, you have a metal spider?"

"Yes. Herman."

He rolled his eyes and threw his hands in the air, almost losing his bat. "Of course, he has a fucking name."

"Stop swearing. It's not like you."

"Nothing's like me! You're bringing elephants and tea sets and metal spiders into my house that all have names!"

"That's not true. My tea set doesn't have a name."

"Un-fucking-believable!"

Will stepped in front of him, holding up his hands to calm him down. "Just relax, man. Keep your eyes on the prize."

Eric was breathing hard, like he was about to really lose his shit. But if he wanted to convince his mom that we were together, my stuff had to be here too. No woman would live in a man's house with his sparse furniture and lack of decoration. I mean, I liked sports as much as the next guy, but I didn't want team banners on the wall.

"Fine," he repeated again. "I'll just be up in *our* room, putting away my bat."

"Thanks, babe," I said sweetly. "Oh, and I'm going to have to move your recliner so I can fit my chair in here."

He slowly turned with murder in his eyes. "You're what?"

"My chair."

"Yeah, I heard that part. My recliner doesn't go anywhere."

"But it doesn't-"

"No," he said, steel slicing through the air. "Your chair can go by your tea set."

"But it won't fit over there."

"Then put it in the garbage. I'll give you the spider and the elephants and the damn tea set, but nobody touches my recliner. Understand?"

He looked so damn pissed...and it was so sexy. I grinned at him and nodded. "Of course." He nodded once and turned for the stairs.

"You know, you're just pissing him off."

I raised an eyebrow at Will. "You mean, by turning the tables on him?"

"What are you talking about?"

I smirked at him. "Do you really think I don't know what's going on here? *Keep your eyes on the prize. Remember the plan.*" His eyes widened slightly. I stepped forward and lowered my voice. "I know exactly what he's doing, what you all planned for me. Trust me, I'm not going to make this as painless as he hoped."

I walked past Will with a grin, knowing that I had them all. I didn't recognize it at first, but after our shower last night, I realized that Eric just wasn't being himself. And then it hit me, he was playing me. He knew that if he pushed moving in together, I would never go for it. He was trying to make me be the one that came to the conclusion that we should live together. It was true, I didn't want his parents to think poorly of me, but I also wouldn't be tricked by any man. So, if he wanted to play hardball, I would gladly play along.

∼

I was nervous as hell. I took the day off of work so that I could be here when his parents arrived. I couldn't spend the whole week with them, but they understood that. Still, I wanted to make a good first impression. I walked around the room, checking to make sure that everything was clean and in order. This had been their house, after all. I wanted to make sure that it lived up to their standards.

"Will you stop checking everything?" Eric asked. "They're not here to judge what kind of housekeeper you are."

"I'm not a housekeeper," I snapped.

"Exactly, and they know that. They know you have a hard job and that you're tired when you get home. Hell, you're pregnant. They don't expect you to keep everything clean all the time. Ma will probably take over when she gets here, because she wants to help out."

"But, she's our guest."

"Well, technically, she's my guest. Since you're only staying for the week."

I narrowed my eyes at him. He knew exactly what he was doing. Well, I wasn't going to let him get away with that shit.

"But while I'm here, it has to look like I'm the lady of the house, which means you have to do what I say."

"Really?" He stood and slowly walked over to me. "And what would that entail?"

"Listening to me, treating me like I already live here…"

"So, basically I'm your bitch."

"You asked me to move in with you. Let's just say that I'll give you a taste of what that would look like."

He smirked slightly, slipping his hand around my waist and pulling me in closer. "I already have an idea. I took my bat down for you, didn't I?"

I leaned in to kiss him, but pulled back when I heard tires on the gravel outside. "Oh god, they're here."

"You'll be fine. They'll love you," he whispered in my ear. With his hand wrapped around my waist, he led me over to the door and we stepped outside. I plastered a smile on my face that was way too big and way too fake to be believable. I felt a pinch in my side.

"Ow! What was that for?"

"You look like a demented ex-girlfriend with that smile."

"I'm nervous, okay?"

He turned me in his arms and stared down at me, brushing his knuckles across my cheeks. "They're going to love you as much as I do. So, relax, okay?"

His lips brushed across mine for just a moment, calming me instantly. When I looked up, his mom was standing in front of us, looking like she was ready to start gushing.

"Ma, it's good to see you." Eric stepped forward and wrapped her in a hug, then moved to shake his dad's hand.

"Mrs. Cortell-"

"Please, I told you to call me Ma," she said, brushing away my hand and pulling me in for a hug. "You look amazing. Look at that bump. Do you mind if I touch it?"

"Uh...sure."

Her hand moved to my belly and rested there for a moment. "I can't believe I'm going to be a grandma. I didn't think this would ever happen with my boys. Well, I figured it would happen with Eric eventually, but he has such high expectations that I never thought he would settle down."

"Tell me about it."

She looked up at me and winked. "Trust me, I know exactly what you're going through. Eric is just like his father." She took me by the arm and led me inside away from Eric and his father. "I bet he tried to move you in with him immediately and asked you to marry him."

My eyes widened in surprise. "How did you know?"

She raised an eyebrow at me. "Because his father did the same thing when I got pregnant with Eric."

My mouth dropped open in shock. "You were..."

"Oh, honey, it was another time, and of course I accepted. Things were different back then. Just don't tell Eric. He still thinks that his parents were saints."

"So, he doesn't know..."

"He would if he ever did the math."

"Did you love him?"

She tilted her head to the side. "We didn't know each other well enough to be in love. I was young and rebelling against my parents. My father was a minister, so I went through this stage of acting out. Turns out, I got in way more trouble than I bargained for," she laughed. "I'll never forget the look on my father's face when I told him I was getting married. Of course, it wasn't funny at the time. I was terrified, but Matthew was my rock through it all. He took full responsibility for me getting pregnant, even though it was just as much my fault. He told my father that he would do right by me and give me a good life, and he has. I never once regretted my decision to marry him."

Now that she was telling me all this, I felt bad. I was being deceitful when she was opening up to me.

"Mrs. Cortell-"

"Ma, or you can call me Elizabeth."

"Elizabeth," I smiled, glancing back at the door to check and make sure they were still outside. "I haven't been totally honest with you. Eric and I weren't dating when I got pregnant. It was just a fun night together."

Her face dawned in understanding. "Well, I can understand why you didn't want to accept his offer to run out and get married."

I smirked a little, thinking of his plan to get me to move in. "Of course, when he found out you were coming to visit, he played me, trying to get me to move in here so that you never knew we weren't together."

"So, you just moved in?"

"Yes, but I told him it was temporary. He's hoping I'll stay."

She looked at me with an expression I could only describe as twisted and calculating. "Dear, if you're not living together, but he planned on marrying you from the start, what exactly is your relationship?"

"We're taking it slow. He wants to do this right and make sure that we don't screw it up for our child."

"And you agree with this?"

"Yes, well, until I realized that he was trying to trick me into moving in with him."

"Did you know that Will called us and asked us to come?"

"When was this?"

"Last week on Sunday."

Hmm. That was interesting. "The same day that he told me you were coming, and then pretended that we should just tell you that we had been dating when I got pregnant."

"Yes, it seems they planned out this whole thing. Well," she grinned. "Why don't we have a little fun then."

"What do you have in mind?" I asked with an evil smile.

ERIC

"Katherine, I just love what you've done with the place," Ma said as we sat down to dinner. All my brothers were here, aside from Derek and Josh. I thought it was a little much to have everyone over for dinner tonight, but Katherine insisted. She said she wanted us to have a family dinner.

"Thank you."

"And I love that tea set out there."

Kat turned to me with a grin. "It was my grandmother's."

"And those elephants...so exotic."

"Eric doesn't really agree with my sense of style, but I convinced him that he couldn't just have sports memorabilia on the wall now that he's an adult."

I gritted my teeth. "It's a Ryne Sandberg baseball bat."

"Well, your sense of style is perfect," Ma beamed.

"Bullshit," Will coughed.

"William, nobody asked you," Ma scolded. She turned to Kat and smiled again. "So, have you picked out any dates for the wedding?"

I choked on my beer, almost spitting it out. Robert slapped me on the back, laughing under his breath. "Wedding?" I asked. We hadn't talked about getting married, and not that I was averse to the idea, but she made it pretty damn clear that we weren't there yet.

"I was thinking in the next month," Kat said, making my eyes bug out.

"The next month?"

"Well, I'm already showing," Kat said, turning to me with puppy dog eyes. "I don't want to be huge in my wedding dress."

I glanced at Robert and he shrugged. Maybe she was just putting on a show for my parents, wanting to play up our story to them. But then she stood up and walked out of the room, returning with a catalogue.

"I saw this dress the other day and thought maybe we could go check it out."

"I would love that, dear. You would look beautiful in that dress."

"What dress?" I asked curiously. Kat turned the book toward me and I grimaced. It looked like something out of the eighties with puffy sleeves and big bows. "That's…" Robert kicked me under the table. "Beautiful."

"I'm not sure it's exactly what I want, but I thought it would be worth checking out. Besides, we only have a short timeframe. Oh, and I need you to call Pastor Dave and see if we can book the church."

"The what?" I asked, growing more confused by the minute. Was she really going to take Ma dress shopping? And now she wanted me to book the church? I thought we were taking this slow and making sure this was going to work between us. Now she was involving my mother in this?

"The church, sweetie," she said with a smile. She smiled playfully. "I know it's asking a lot, but with our busy schedules, I really need help planning this all out."

"Oh, I can stay and help with the planning. If we're talking about this month, I could just stay the whole month!"

My eyes bugged out and I looked to Dad for help. "Isn't that going to be hard on you? I mean, to be gone that long?"

"Oh, your father can go home without me and return for the wedding. I can have my neighbor, Sue, look in on him."

"But..." I swallowed hard, unsure what to say. Was this really happening? And did I want it to happen? I mean, yeah, I wanted her to move in with me, but this was all moving a little fast. And if she was just trying to appease my parents, she just got a whole lot more than she bargained for. "Kat, maybe we should discuss the details privately, you know, before Ma moves here for the month."

"Oh, I think we've already talked enough about it. I'm sure I can get this planned in time with Elizabeth's help."

"But what about our *plans*?"

She tilted her head and smiled at me. "Oh, I can assure you, our *plans* are working out perfectly."

I watched the twinkle in her eyes and then it hit me. She was fucking with me. She knew my plans for her. That was what all this shit was about. The tea table, moving the bat, her metal spider. She was screwing with me because I tried to manipulate her. And now, somehow, she got Ma to go in on the whole thing with her.

I glanced at my brothers, seeing them all holding back their laughter. Dad was pretty much oblivious to the whole thing, too engrossed in his dinner to care.

"You're fucking with me."

Her mouth dropped open in shock. "Baby, why would I do that?"

Will snorted in laughter and Robert burst out laughing.

"How did you get Ma to go along with it?" I asked, leaning on the table.

"Eric, there's something you should know about your mother. She's the master manipulator. I'm just taking lessons," Kat said with a grin.

"So, you're not planning a wedding."

"That depends, are you still trying to manipulate me into living with you?"

"Ooh, busted," Joe muttered under his breath.

"How did you know?"

"Because the last thing you want is for your parents to know what really happened between us, which they do, by the way. But you went out of your way to tell me that it was no big deal if they knew about us. You had me fooled for a few hours, but once I thought about it, I realized that you were just trying to get your own way. And then your mother told me that Will called and invited them. The real question is, why did you think it would be so easy to trick me?"

I tossed my napkin on the table in irritation. "Well, I don't now."

She smiled triumphantly, laughing with Ma as she started eating again. My brothers were no help, laughing along as if it was the funniest thing in the world.

"So," my dad said, finally looking up from his plate. "When's the wedding?"

∽

I slid my arms around her, placing my hands over her stomach as she took out her earrings and placed them on the dresser. My parents left this morning and after a long day of work, we were both tired and ready for bed. I kissed her neck and ground my body against hers. I was still healing and wasn't supposed to have sex yet, but damn, I really wanted her.

"So, now that my parents are gone, are you leaving?"

"That depends."

"On what?"

"On how much you want to haul all my stuff back to my townhouse."

I stopped kissing her neck and turned her around in my arms. "Are you serious?"

She quirked her head to the side and smiled. "Well, we did just move everything over here, and it would be a huge pain in the ass to move it all back."

"It would be."

"And it's nice to not have to decide whose house we're staying at for the night."

"That would make things easier," I agreed.

"And it would help stop the gossip in town."

"Actually, I think it would fuel it. We haven't been giving them anything to talk about these past few months."

"Well, we wouldn't want to disappoint them," she said, wrapping her arms around my neck.

"We definitely wouldn't want to do that. Should I post an article in the morning paper?"

She grinned and pressed a kiss to my lips. "Nah, just tell Joe. It'll be on social media in two minutes."

"I like the way you think."

I slid my lips across hers and slipped my tongue into her mouth. I wanted her so bad, but I couldn't risk injuring my cock and being taken out of the running even longer than I already was.

"So, now that you're moving in with me, and you've already claimed me as your intended, what are we going to do about my brothers?"

"What do you mean?"

"Well, you have to admit, it's a little weird, living in a house with my brothers when we're about to have a baby."

"I don't know, I kind of like them here."

"You do?"

She nodded with a smile. "It's kind of nice. I'm not saying I want them to live here forever, but for now it's fine."

"What about when the baby comes?"

"Then we get to put them on diaper duty," she said mischievously.

"Yeah, I'd like to see you try that."

"Oh, don't worry about me. I'll use my hormones as a weapon to get my way."

"You're evil."

She shrugged lightly. "I do what's necessary."

She pulled back and finished getting ready for bed, but there was a lot on my mind now. Things were moving forward with us. We were living together, and that opened the door for so much more. Living together was just one step away from the big commitment, and I wasn't sure that we were ready for that yet. I had been foolish to suggest it when I first found out she was pregnant. I wasn't going to lie, I could see getting married to her, living with her for the rest of our lives in this house. I wanted that so bad, but I still needed to take things slow. This was all still new to us, and moving too fast would do more damage than good. But as I laid in bed that night, I couldn't help but think of what it would be like to see her walking down the aisle toward me and know that she was mine for the rest of my life.

KATHERINE

It was official. Over the past two months, I had officially gained more weight than any normal pregnant woman. It was all Eric's fault. Since we couldn't have sex, he was feeding me in other ways, plying me with all kinds of yummy foods to keep my sexual appetite under control. It had to come to an end. I knew that the end was coming. He was getting more and more adventurous every night, pushing himself to see what he could handle. Last night, he had ground himself against me until he came. He said it was weird, but I hoped it was weird in a good way.

"Earth to Kat," Chrissy said to me, waving her hand at me as we stood in front of the elevator.

I blinked and came back to the conversation at hand. She had been describing her kinky sex from last night to me and that was the point I had zoned out. It wasn't fair to tease a person that wasn't having sex.

"Since when do you call me Kat?"

"Since Eric calls you Kat. I think it's cute."

"You know, I was perfectly happy with Kiki."

She grimaced slightly. "Yeah, but he has a point. It does sound like you're a parrot."

I pursed my lips and glared at her. "Whatever."

"You know, half the staff calls you Kat now. Ever since it started circulating on the town Facebook page-"

"Where half the people that work here don't even live," I pointed out.

"But they all follow now. I'm telling you, you're practically famous ever since you were outed so publicly. Even Casey got a kick out of that video."

I gasped, smacking her on the arm. "You let her watch that?"

"Hey, she was feeling down the other day. I figured she could use some cheering up. Her last trial application was rejected," she said sadly.

I sighed, wishing there was something more I could do for the poor girl.

"Dr. Willis said that there's still one more trial he wants to try and get her into."

"Let's hope he's successful."

She studied me for a moment and then chuckled.

"What?"

"Nothing, you just look a little…frustrated."

I snorted. "You could say that again."

"So…are you into the homestretch?"

"God, I hope so. I mean, he's been great, but I need the real thing. I'm tired of waiting."

She pointed her fork at me accusingly. "Just remember, you're the one that wanted him to get this. You should be happy he's even taking care of you after the stunt you pulled."

"I know, but it'll be worth it. I've been reading up a lot on different things to do to make it pleasurable for him. I can't wait to try them out."

The elevator doors opened and we stepped inside. "What do you think is holding him back?"

I shrugged. "Maybe he thinks it'll hurt. I don't know."

"Well, make it good for him or he'll make you pay for the rest of your life." I nodded. "Hey, you didn't say what your other challenges have been."

"We haven't done any for the past two months. He said that we needed a break," I said with a smile.

She burst out laughing. "I can only imagine what he thought you would do to him next."

"Alright, I get it. I went overboard. Trust me, it's not going to happen anymore. I want Eric to like me, if only for our child's sake."

"That man doesn't just like you, he's in love with you."

I knew that. He had no problem telling me every day, and it was a great feeling, but I couldn't help but wonder when it was all going to fall apart. "You know, I just get this bad feeling every now and then."

"Like what?"

The doors opened and I stepped out, headed for the parking lot. "I guess…we're just so different."

"Yeah, but you guys have worked past that."

"I know, but this is the honeymoon stage. What happens after the baby is born and reality hits?"

"Um…I'm guessing you'll live a sickeningly happy life with one of the hottest men in the world."

I rolled my eyes. She made it sound so easy. "And when our kids get older? What happens then? What happens when I want to go have fun and my husband is wanting to stay home and build things?"

She put a hand on my arm and stopped me. "Okay, there are so many things wrong with what you just said. First, kids? As in, more than one?"

"Well, I would assume if we stay together that we'll have more."

"Right, so, you're also planning to marry him? Because you called him your husband."

"Look, I'm just saying it's the natural progression."

"Okay, but you're acting like Eric's boring."

"He is. I have to force him to do everything."

"Kat, you're being too hard on him. He's not boring. He's finding his adventurous side with you."

"He stopped that," I said indignantly.

"Only because you choose crazy challenges. You could have asked him to go canoeing or something that would lead up to the crazy, but you went right to crazy from the start. The man didn't stand a chance against you."

"Hey, I took him on a ferris wheel! That's the least crazy thing a person could do."

"I'm just saying, you're worrying about nothing. And who cares if he wants to stay home with you. I would kill to have a man that worshiped me the way that man worships you."

"You have a husband," I point out.

"Yes, and we have wild and crazy sex, but he doesn't stare at me like the world will end if I leave."

Maybe she was right. Maybe I was reading too much into all this, but I couldn't help but worry that this baby was all that was holding us together. I smiled at Chrissy and gave a wave.

"I'm going to have some wild, monkey fun of my own. I'll see you tomorrow."

"Hey, think about what I said!"

"I will."

"If you walk away from that sexy man, I'll refuse to be your friend anymore!"

I laughed and got in my car. I knew she would never stop being my friend. Instead of driving home, I headed for Eric's office. He said that he would be working late tonight, so I thought I would head over there and see if he was ready to go home yet.

On the way, I saw the bakery and remembered that Eric plied Anna with baked goods to keep her on his good side. I figured a little intervention on my part could only help. I pulled up to the bakery and headed inside. Mary Anne was wiping down tables and smiled when she saw me.

"Need a pre-dinner treat?"

"Actually, I was going to head over to Eric's office and I thought I might pick up something for Anna."

Her eyes lit up and she walked behind the counter. "I have just the thing for you. Anna comes in at least twice a week and she always gets the same thing." She put something in a box and handed it over. "Chocolate babka."

"Ooh, what's that?"

"It's a European coffee cake. It's so good."

"That does sound good. Can you box up one for me too?"

"Of course. Anything else?"

"How about two hot coffees."

"She likes cappuccinos."

I grinned. Mary Anne knew everyone so well. "Alright, two cappuccinos."

"Coming right up."

The door opened behind me and the sheriff walked in, tipping his head in my direction. "Katherine, you're looking good. How much longer?"

I sighed, rubbing my hand over my belly. "Two more months."

His smile warmed my heart. Everyone in this town was so nice. After the initial shock of the town heartthrob knocking up the nurse that was new to town, they all turned into a second family of sorts. Everyone smiled and asked about the baby. Of course, there were still people that gossiped, wondering when or if Eric and I would get married. I ignored them. Their opinions didn't matter to me.

"Do you have everything you need?"

"We're pretty much ready. Eric's been working on finishing up a dresser for the baby's room. As soon as that's done, we'll have everything we need."

"That's great. Oh, Ginny has some baby clothes that she never used. She wanted me to ask you if you wanted them."

"That'd be great. Tell her I said thank you for thinking of us."

"Any time."

"Mary Anne, can I get a black coffee?" Jack asked.

"Of course."

I paid her and then walked out with my purchases. Rubbing my hands together to ward off the cold, I started the car and headed for the office. When I pulled up, I was disappointed to see that Eric's truck wasn't there. I got out and headed up to his office. Anna was sitting behind the desk, completely engrossed in something on her computer.

"Knock, knock," I said in a sing-song voice. "I brought treats."

"Yeah," Anna said, still watching the screen.

"What are you looking at?"

"Uh…Eric had to go back to Mrs. Cranston's to repair something."

I walked around the desk and saw that she was looking at a page on Facebook and there were dozens of candid pictures of a man, but you couldn't see his face.

"What is that?"

"*That* is Eric."

I looked closer, taking particular interest in one where he was on his back under a sink. There was a closeup of his shirt riding up. I could see his ab muscles flexing and the obvious outline of his cock. My eyes widened in surprise.

"When is this from?"

"Um…about the time that you two met. Mrs. Cranston always requests Eric, and then she takes sexy handyman pics and uploads them to this special page she created for him. It's invite only," she grinned up at me.

My mouth dropped open in shock. "Why didn't anyone say anything to me?"

"Uh…because they probably assumed that you'd freak out like you are now and ask her to take it down."

"Freak out? Hell, I want to join the page. If anyone should be allowed access to these pictures, it's me!"

"Ah," she jumped, clapping her hands. "She just uploaded more pictures."

"Scoot over," I said, rolling her chair away so I could slide another chair over and get a better look.

The caption of the album said *The heater is acting up…*

I started drooling as I looked at the pictures of Eric sweating as he made the necessary repairs. It was obvious that it was too hot in the house. In one, he had his shirt lifted to his face to wipe the sweat. His full chest was on display, showing off every delectable inch of his body.

"Oh my god. This is like porn," I whispered.

"I know."

"How many people have access to this page?"

"Um...I think fifty." She scrolled to the group info and nodded. "Fifty-two."

"Huh. You'd think he'd have more followers."

She smiled up at me. "Mrs. Cranston is very picky about who she lets into the group."

"How do I get an invite?"

"You'll have to send a message to Mrs. Cranston."

"That old bat will never let me in," I grumbled. "She doesn't like me."

"She doesn't like you because you're with her boy toy."

I snorted in laughter just as the door opened. Anna tried to click out of the screen as Eric walked in, but ended up enlarging the image on the screen.

"What is that?" Eric asked. "Are you looking at porn at work?"

"Uh, no!" Anna said, trying to get out of the screen, but it seemed to be frozen. Her face turned beat red as Eric walked over, squinting at the screen. She dove in front of it, trying to block it from him.

"What is that?"

"Nothing!"

I laughed as Eric pulled her away from the screen and stared at the picture. "Is that...is that me?"

"Yes," Anna said, stepping away with her hands raised, "but don't freak out. It's all in fun."

"There's a picture of me on Facebook," he ground out. "That's from a half hour ago at Mrs. Cranston's house. Why are there pictures of me while I'm working?"

"Okay, don't freak out," I said, stepping up to take the heat off Anna. I was pregnant. He wouldn't flip out on me.

"Don't freak out?" he shouted. Okay, maybe I was wrong. "I'm running a business and there are pictures of me half naked on Facebook!"

"You're not half naked," I argued. "You still have your shirt on. It's just...showing a little skin."

He clenched his jaw in anger. "I want those pictures taken down."

"I didn't do it! If you want them taken down, you'll have to take it up with Mrs. Cranston."

He narrowed his eyes at me. "What?"

"You heard me. All these pictures were taken at her house. You should be flattered."

"Flattered that a woman is sneaking pictures of me?"

"Hey, you're man candy. Deal with it."

"The only man candy I want to be is yours!"

"You already are mine, and you'd better start proving it."

"What's that supposed to mean?" he shot back.

"It means that it's been months and I'm ready to try out what you're hiding in your pants!"

"Uh, I think I'm gonna go," Anna said, jerking her thumb at the door. "This looks like it might be..." She motioned between us and then gave a thumbs up. "Anyway, see you tomorrow."

She ran out of the office, slamming the door behind her. Eric turned his furious gaze on me.

"Was that really necessary?"

"Yes, it was," I said, throwing my hands on my hips. "You're healed, Eric. It's time to take that thing for a test drive."

My hands immediately went to his pants and undid his belt buckle. "Stop," he said, putting his hands on top of mine.

"No, I want this." I quickly unzipped his pants and yanked them down. His cock was hard and the piercing was calling out to me. Eric was breathing hard, his jaw clenched tight.

"We need a bed."

"We need your desk," I said, reaching behind him and shoving the papers off the desk.

"Anna's gonna be pissed at you," he murmured, slipping his hand into my hair. He pressed his lips to mine as he pulled me into him. His cock rubbed against my belly and he groaned as the piercing worked its magic.

"Do you really think I care?" I wrapped my hand around his cock and gently stroked up and down, careful not to touch his piercing yet. I wanted him relaxed before I touched it. His eyes slipped closed as I stroked his cock, up and down. I dropped to my knees in front of him and took a good, long look at his cock piercing. I smiled right before I licked the underside of his cock. He groaned and his fingers slipped in my hair.

"God, Kat…"

I added a little pressure and jerked him a little harder. I leaned forward and opened my mouth, but didn't take him in yet. I let my hot breath fan out over the tip of his cock, warming up his piercing. I flicked my tongue out, just enough to send a zap of pleasure through him. He groaned and tightened his hold on my hair.

Looking up at him, I could see that he was just barely holding on. I had him where I wanted him. I swirled my tongue around the head of his cock and then slowly slid my mouth over him, humming lightly.

"Shit."

I had read about humming during a blow job and how it sent vibrations through the metal and stimulated his nerves. He seemed to like it, so I did it again.

"Christ, Kat. That's so good."

I did it again, this time pumping him harder. He started jerking in my mouth, fucking me a little harder, something he hadn't really done before. I slipped my hand down to his sac and gently massaged his balls. I heard his intake of breath right before his hips slammed against my face and he shoved his cock deep down my throat. I swallowed, sucking him hard as he pumped inside my mouth, fucking me like he was on steroids. I moaned one last time and he lost it, shoving himself all the way in my mouth as he spilled his cum down my throat.

He tried to pull back, but I sucked him harder, taking every last drop from him. When I finally released him, he yanked me up off the floor and pulled me against his body.

"I'm so sorry, Kat. I lost control."

I pulled back and grinned. "That's what I wanted. So? How was it?"

He smirked at me and spun me around, lifting me up onto his desk. "Fucking amazing. And as long as I have you in here, I think I'll test out your theory of office fucking."

ERIC

I whistled as I made my way downstairs the next morning. Last night was amazing. Kat had been right about the piercing, but that didn't mean that I would ever get a piercing like that again. Once was enough, just like the tattoo. My brothers were right, I liked what Kat did for me. She opened me up to new possibilities. She took this rigid man and made him live, even if he was kicking and screaming along the way. When I thought back on my life without her, I wasn't sure what the hell I had been doing. It was like everything before her was mechanical. I was living life like a machine. Now my life was full of color.

"So, I take it all went well last night," Joe grinned.

I clapped him on the shoulder with a grin. "You know how you have these amazing mornings where the sun is brighter and the grass is greener and life is filled with possibilities?"

He looked outside and then back at me. "It's overcast and the grass if fucking dead."

I grinned wide at him. "And it doesn't even matter. This is life, my friend. It's what you make of it. So, where you see dead grass, I see spring just around the corner. Where you see clouds, I see the possibility of rain for spring, to bring everything back to life."

He stared at me for a moment. "What the fuck is wrong with you?"

"Nothing. That's the thing, Kat makes me see things I never saw before."

"She gave you an orgasm," he deadpanned.

"It's so much more than that. She breathed new life into this house the moment she stepped through that door. Everything is amazing because of her."

He stood slowly and took a step back. "Okay, where is my brother?"

"Right here, man. You know, I'm even missing that crazy language you and Andrew speak. Isn't that weird? Something that used to piss me off is something I want to hear."

"No," he said, chuckling slightly as he waved his finger at me. "I'm not falling for that shit. Do you know how long it took me to train myself *not* to speak that way?"

"Yeah, like six months."

"Exactly. I've gotten used to speaking this new way now and I'm not falling for your lines."

"What lines? Come on, throw out a *fire* or *basic*. It'll be fun."

"No," he shook his head. "Because in two months when you change your mind, I'm the one that has to deal with you getting all pissed again."

"Don't you see?" I said, rushing over to him. "I'm not going to get pissed. Life is amazing! And as weird as you sound when I can't understand you, it's who you are. Embrace it!"

His eyes narrowed and then his fist flew at my face. I didn't even have time to move out of the way. His fist was like a lead ball to the face. I dropped to the floor instantly. Since when did he learn to hit? He leaned over me, glaring down at me.

"Now, you listen here. I don't know what the hell you've done with my brother, but you return him to me by tonight, or I'll fucking punch you again. Understood?"

I opened my mouth to speak, but he held up his hand.

"Nope, you don't get to talk anymore. If you thought me talking was weird, this shit you've got going on is out of this world. Fix it. I don't like this version of you."

"Optimistic?"

"This isn't optimistic. This is sadistic."

"Why is Eric lying on the floor?" Kat asked as she walked into the kitchen.

"He was spouting weird shit about sunshine and grass, so I knocked him on his ass."

"Oh," Kat said, stepping over me to get to the coffee pot. "That makes sense."

I slowly sat up and rubbed my jaw. "You're okay with this?" I asked, getting to my feet.

She looked over at me and shrugged. "Were you talking about that stuff?"

"I was pointing out what a beautiful day it is. I was saying that we should embrace life. I told him he could talk weird again."

She nodded. "Yeah, he did the right thing."

"What?" I asked incredulously.

She walked around the counter and placed her hand on my face. "Baby, I love that you're doing all this new stuff, but I happened to like stuffy Eric too. You don't need to change everything about you." She took a sip of her coffee and headed for the stairs. "And I like that I can understand Joe now."

I was so confused. Wasn't this what they wanted, for me to loosen up? "I just don't get it. I thought everyone would be happy that I was loosening up."

Joe cleared his throat. "Let me solve this one for you. Man, your bae is all like *cancel* because she's totes on fleek and you're basic. Sorry not sorry, but let's spill the tea here for a minute. The struggle is real. You're all salty and she's thirsty. Goals AF, man. You need to Netflix and chill before you lose your bae."

I stared at him. "Did you just cram as much millennial shit into that little speech to piss me off?"

"Totes."

I nodded slowly. "You're right. That was…"

"Glad that I changed the way I speak?"

"Totes."

He punched me in the arm and laughed. "Maybe you're not so salty anymore."

He walked out the door and I rushed over, yelling at him. "This doesn't mean you should start talking like that again!" He waved over his shoulder. "It was a moment of insanity."

"Sure it was!"

"I'm serious. Let's go back to speaking like regular people!"

"Alright, Hunty!"

He got in his truck and pulled away. I slowly closed the door and rested my head against the door. "What have I done?"

KATHERINE

I took a deep breath and ran my hand over my belly. It had grown so much over the past month. I felt like I was close to popping already and I still had a month to go. My back was killing me and my ankles were constantly swollen. I hated wearing the scrubs at the hospital, but I had no choice, so when I was home, I always wore dresses. They were just more comfortable.

"Hey," Eric said, coming up behind me and wrapping his arms around me. His hands settled on my stomach and his lips immediately went to my neck, kissing right below my ear. I moaned slightly, not because I was turned on, but because he was there, I could lean back against him. He chuckled in my ear, knowing exactly what I was doing.

"I need a back rub."

"Yeah?" His hands moved slowly to my arms, running up to my shoulders. He slowly pulled the straps of my dress down my arms, the fabric stretching as he pulled it tight across my chest in his attempt to take off my dress.

"What are you doing?"

"You wanted a back massage."

He moved the straps slowly down my arms, giving a gentle tug when the front of the dress got caught on my breasts. His tongue licked at my neck and then his lips latched on, kissing at the base of my neck. I tilted my head to the side to allow him better access. His hands slid from my arms back to my belly, sliding under the dress that was now resting on my large stomach. He shoved the dress over my bump, letting it fall to the ground.

"Go lay on the bed on your side," he ordered.

I stepped out of the dress and walked to the bed, trying to look sexy as I waddled over there. I knew I failed, but when I turned to look at Eric, his eyes were burning with desire as he stared at me. He had this way of making me feel like a goddess even when I felt like a whale. It was empowering and gave me the confidence to get on that damn bed, even if I had to shuffle awkwardly. His eyes never left my body, taking in every inch of me, making me feel completely naked.

I watched as he stalked over to the bed and knelt down, slowly rolling me to my side. My eyes slid shut when I felt his wet tongue trail down my spine, stopping just above my underwear. His hand rested heavy on my hip, giving me gentle squeezes as he kissed his way back up to my neck. Then his fingers started gently massaging my back, hitting all the aching places, but now I had an ache between my legs that I couldn't ignore, and the more he touched me, the harder it was to talk my body down.

"You're so sexy," he murmured against my skin.

"I don't feel sexy."

I felt the tip of his nose running along my spine, sending tingles everywhere in my body.

"There's nothing sexier than you. It wouldn't matter if you were pregnant or not. I want you either way."

His fingers continued to dig into my back, taking away all the aches and pains, but his tongue never left my skin. After about fifteen minutes, his hand slid down to my hip and under my panties. His fingers moved down to my clit, brushing lightly over the sensitive nerves. I opened my legs, making room for his large hand. I was soaking wet from him touching me so much, my body just barely hanging on as he stroked me.

Then I felt his cock pressing against my ass. He slowly thrust forward as his fingers slowly swirled around my clit. With every stroke of his fingers, he thrust against my ass, a little harder each time. My breathing kicked into high gear as my orgasm built. I wanted him so bad, but I was powerless to even speak at the moment. Every time his cock pushed against my ass, my body started shaking even harder, until I was squeezing my thighs together from the massive orgasm that shook me. His fingers pressed against me, pushing my orgasm higher. I could feel his rapid breaths against my neck as he continued to grind against me.

"Eric," I breathed out harshly. "I need you."

My whole body was shaking as he pulled me toward him, kissing me hard on the lips. I got so lost in his kiss that when he pulled away, I felt a cold chill pass over my body. He dragged my underwear down my legs, getting a look at my soaking pussy. His eyes darkened, making me feel both wanted and vulnerable at the same time.

He stood up, dragging his t-shirt slowly up his muscular frame and pulling it over his head, tossing it to the ground. Then his fingers moved to his jeans and slowly lowered the zipper. I couldn't stop staring, my eyes never moving from the massive erection pushing forward. When he pulled his jeans down and his erection sprang free, I almost rolled over to grab him, but he stopped me with just one look.

He climbed back on the bed behind me and nestled right up against me until his cock was wedging itself right between my ass cheeks. His fingers moved to my bra, unhooking it and pulling it off me to toss on the ground. My nipples pebbled, pushing out into the open air, just waiting for him to touch. I didn't have to wait long. His fingers pulled at my nipples, twisting them lightly as he pushed his cock through my wetness. I groaned, widening my legs for him.

"Keep them shut. I like dragging my cock through your pussy juices."

I let my leg fall back down and laid there as he used my body, getting off on touching me. He hadn't even pushed inside me yet, but he was already breathing hard. With every thrust, his hands caressed my body. His tongue licked and sucked at my ear, driving me insane. I felt like I was on the verge of falling off the cliff again.

"Eric, I need you inside me," I pleaded.

"Be patient, Kat. I'll give you what you need."

I groaned in frustration, but he just chuckled in my ear. My heart pounded wildly as my body started to shake again. It didn't even take another minute before I was quivering from his touch and creaming all over his cock.

"That's it, Kat. Give me more," he whispered. He made everything sound so sexy. He made me need more of him when I thought my body was ready to fall asleep. I didn't think there would ever be a time when I didn't want this man.

His cock nudged at my entrance as he shifted behind me. He lifted my leg, nudging his leg between mine. Then he was pushing inside me, his hand gripping my thigh so hard he would leave a bruise.

"Fuck, I'll never get tired of you, Kat."

"I hope not." I grabbed behind me for his hair, running my fingers through the strands as he fucked me in long, slow strokes. He didn't fuck me hard like I thought he would. He just took his time, each thrust pushing me a little higher. I could feel my cum slipping down my legs and pooling beneath me on the sheets. I would be ashamed of how wet I was, but this man just brought out my sexual appetite.

"I'm gonna come," he whispered, his voice shaky and tight. His fingers slid to my pussy again, rubbing circles around my clit as his thrusts turned faster and jerky. I felt him jerk hard inside me just as my pussy clamped down from my third earth-shattering orgasm. His fingers stilled on me as he rested his head against my back. I could feel the sweat on his skin sticking to me. When he caught his breath, he slid in even closer to me, his cock slipping out of me as he softened. He stayed nestled up against me as we both started to drift off to sleep. His hot breath fanned across my skin as he held me tight. I knew in that moment that nothing could tear me away from this man. I could picture myself with him for the rest of my life, staying right here in this bed forever.

ERIC

Kat had been off for two days now. I could tell that something was bothering her, but she didn't say a word. She would feel her stomach and her eyes would squint, but she never said anything. But the more she tried to play it off like nothing was wrong, the more I worried about her.

"Kat, tell me what's wrong."

She turned to me, a hint of fear in her eyes. "I can't feel the baby move."

My heart stopped in my chest as I took in her words. My eyes flicked to her stomach and it took a good twenty seconds for my brain to kick online and my heart to start working again. I swallowed hard and gave a slight nod.

"Okay, let's call the doctor and see what she says."

She nodded and took a deep breath. I pulled out my phone and called the doctor's office. A nurse came on the phone and after I explained what was going on, she gave me a list of instructions to follow.

"You need to drink something with caffeine and lay down for a half hour. We need to count the movements that you feel in that half hour."

She didn't say anything. She just laid down on the couch as I went to grab her a coke. She drank it as fast as she could and we sat there, just waiting for something to happen. Her eyes kept darting to mine, panic and fear replacing the usually calm woman.

"Are you feeling anything, Kat?"

She shook her head slowly, tears filling her eyes. We waited another ten minutes, but when nothing happened, I decided that we were going to the hospital, no matter what the nurse said.

"Come on. Let's go to the hospital. We'll have you checked out."

I took her hand and pulled her up from the couch, not able to look at her. I was terrified. What if something was wrong? I couldn't stand the thought of something happening to our child. I had grown to love this baby more than anything.

"What if…"

I stopped and raised my eyes to look at her. I saw the same questions in her eyes, but I had nothing to say that would be helpful.

"Let's just get to the hospital."

Joe came tromping down the stairs and I could already tell there was a joke on the tip of his tongue. I shot him a death glare and he immediately stopped in his tracks, watching as Kat grabbed her stuff and headed for the door.

"What's going on?" he asked quietly.

"She can't feel the baby move. We're headed to the hospital."

He was quiet for a minute, but as I turned to leave, he grabbed my arm. "I'm sure everything's fine. But call me if you need me."

I nodded and headed for the door, placing my hand on Kat's back as we walked out the door and down the steps. It was quiet the whole way to the hospital. Neither of us knew what to say. I slid my hand across the console and gripped her hand in mine. I didn't know what the hell was happening, but it felt like something was shifting, and I was terrified that we weren't going to survive it.

We were taken back immediately to get checked out. Kat was given a gown by the nurse, and then we waited for her doctor to come in. I was a ball of nerves, my whole body shaking as we waited in the room. Kat just stared at the wall, her hands on her stomach as if she was trying to protect our baby from something. I couldn't take my eyes off her baby bump, afraid that if I looked away, the bump would disappear.

The door opened and the doctor came in with a smile on her face. "Hey, Katherine. The nurse said that you aren't feeling the baby move?"

"No. I noticed it yesterday, but I thought it was just one of those things. But then I didn't feel her moving today either and I got worried. Eric called the nurse and she said to try drinking some caffeine. We waited for a half hour, but…"

The doctor smiled at her and pulled a cart over with the ultrasound machine. "Well, babies like to give us scares. How about we check on that little peanut and see what's going on before we jump to any conclusions."

I breathed a little easier at the doctor's easy demeanor. It felt like a weight was lifted from my chest by her smile. Kat seemed reassured by that also. The doctor squirted the gel on her stomach and brought the wand to her belly, moving it around to find the heartbeat.

I stared at the screen, tears coming to my eyes when I saw our baby on the machine. She was there, so perfect and tiny, but there was no heartbeat. I could feel my heart racing and with every second that passed, Kat squeezed my hand tighter. The more time that passed, the more it became clear that we weren't going to find the heartbeat. I heard Kat sniffle and felt tears slip down my cheeks. I prayed hard as the doctor continued to look for the heartbeat. I prayed that my baby wasn't being taken away from us, but it was hopeless.

After another minute, the doctor shut off the screen and wiped Kat's belly. "I'm so sorry."

Kat gasped, tears spilling from her eyes. "Why?"

I gripped her hand tighter and stepped right beside her, leaning down to kiss her forehead.

"I don't know. I didn't see any complications during your pregnancy. We would have to run some tests to find out why."

We sat there for a moment, just taking in what the doctor just confirmed. Our baby was dead. We were so close to having her, but we would never see her beautiful smile or hold her tiny little hands in ours. She was gone before we ever got to meet her.

"What do we do now?" I asked.

"Well, you have a few options. We can wait until you go into labor naturally. That usually takes about two weeks after the baby has passed-"

"You want me to walk around, carrying my dead baby for two weeks?" Kat asked incredulously. Tears were streaming down her face and I could see she was on the verge of hysterics. I wrapped my arm around her, trying to give her some comfort.

"That's one option, Katherine. We could also induce labor. I would break your water and then it would take up to forty-eight hours for labor to begin. You would deliver the baby vaginally."

Kat gasped like she was being stabbed. I just stared at the doctor. I couldn't believe this was over, that we were standing here and the doctor was telling us our child was gone. I didn't know what to do. I didn't know how to handle any of this. All I knew was that the woman I loved was in tears and she was hurting. I couldn't stand to see her cry. I couldn't stand that I couldn't help her.

"I'll give the two of you a moment alone," the doctor said before leaving the room.

I sat on the edge of the bed facing Kat and took her face in my hands, forcing her to look at me. "Hey, we'll get through this."

"I don't want to get through this," she cried, her sobs breaking up her words so I could hardly understand her. "She can't be gone."

"I know, Kat. I know, this sucks." I pressed my lips to her forehead, trying to comfort her in some way, but I knew I was failing. There was no way for me to bring even an ounce of comfort to her. The child she had been carrying all these months was gone just like that.

"This sucks?" she spat. She shoved me back off the bed, her rage taking over. "We just lost our baby and you think this sucks?"

I was speechless. I didn't know what to say to her. It wasn't meant to be a flip comment. My ma had always told us that when something bad happened, it sucked, and it was going to continue to suck until it didn't anymore. Because one thing my family knew for sure, empty platitudes meant jack shit when you were hurting. There was no comforting a person that was hurting. There was nothing you could say to make it right. There was only acknowledging that the situation sucked and there was nothing you could do to make it not suck.

"Kat, that's not-"

"It's not like the Cubs lost the World Series; *that* sucks. This is our child." More tears spilled down her cheeks and her whole body heaved and shook. "She's gone and all you can say is that it sucks?"

I stepped back, running my hand along my jaw. I didn't know what to say to her.

"I want my mom. Can you please call her?"

"Kat-"

"Please," she whimpered quietly.

I stood there, my mouth slightly open as I tried to think of something else to say. But she rolled to her side, shutting me out. I swallowed hard and left the room, my whole body feeling like it was slowly shutting down. I leaned against the wall in the hallway and took in everything. I felt the tears building, but I refused to shed them right now. Kat needed her mom, and I would focus on getting that done. I just had to take things one at a time. I pulled out my phone and dialed her mom's number.

"Oh my gosh!" she answered excitedly. "Is it time?"

Pain ripped through me. Of course she would think it was time. I only had her number for emergencies. My throat constricted as I tried to get the words to come out, but nothing happened. I couldn't bring myself to say it. When she didn't hear anything, her voice grew quiet.

"Eric, what's going on?"

"She...We lost the baby," I croaked out.

I heard her gasp, but I shut out everything else. I couldn't sit here and listened to her tears over the phone. I was in my own kind of hell right now. I didn't have it in me to comfort her mother.

"We're at the hospital. We need to decide where to go from here, but she's asking for you."

"I'll be right there. I'll call her father and have him meet us there."

I nodded, then realized that she couldn't see me. "Thank you."

I hung up, sliding my phone into my pocket. I should make some more phone calls, but I was frozen. I didn't know what to do now. I didn't trust myself to go back in that room and not fuck it up again. But she was in there all alone. She needed someone, even if that someone was me.

I pushed the door open and went to her side. "Your mom is on her way, and she's calling your dad."

She didn't say anything. She just stared at the wall, facing away from me. She was blocking me out.

"Kat, I'm so sorry. I wasn't trying to downplay this. I just…" I sighed and sat down beside her on the bed, sliding my hand across her arm until I was gripping her hand in mine. She didn't squeeze mine back or even acknowledge I was there. "What do you want to do?"

"I want to be induced," she said after a minute. "I can't walk around with her inside me for two weeks. I can't…"

"I know," I said quietly.

"You don't know," she said in a low voice. It was like there was nothing inside her anymore. There was no emotion, no anger, just a blankness to her. I liked it better when she was pissed at me. She was no longer crying. I could see the tear tracks on her face where they had dried, but her eyes were dead as she stared at the wall.

"What can I do?"

"Tell the doctor."

I nodded, standing and giving her a kiss on the cheek before I walked out of the room. The doctor was waiting outside for me, a kind look on her face.

"Did you decide what you'd like to do?"

"She wants to be induced."

"Okay. I'll get a room for her. Do you have any family coming?"

"Her parents are on the way."

"Okay," she smiled slightly, her hand reaching out to touch mine. "I'll make sure that the nurses know they're coming. As soon as the room is ready, we'll put you in there and get started." She started to leave, but then turned back to me. "This is going to be very hard on all of you, and it can take some time once we induce labor. I would suggest once her parents get here that you go home and get anything you might want while you're here. Clothes for the baby, a blanket, comfortable clothes for Katherine…"

I nodded, but that was difficult to do. We already had a bag packed, but we had assumed that when we brought it to the hospital, we would be bringing our daughter home in those clothes. We had assumed that she would be wrapped in the blanket my mom had made. Now I was going to bring that to the hospital and put our dead baby in those things. I wasn't sure I could handle it.

I returned to the room and sat at her bedside, placing my hand on her hip. She stiffened at my touch, but didn't say anything. I wanted desperately to place my hand on her stomach, to feel the tightness of her belly, but I didn't think she would appreciate the gesture. In this moment, she hated me, and I had to let her have those feelings, because she was on overload right now. My feelings didn't matter. I may be the father, but I didn't carry this baby for almost nine months. I didn't feel all those kicks inside me or deal with the aches and pains. So even though I was dying inside, I kept it to myself and pretended like every moment of this wasn't killing me.

KATHERINE

I was numb. The initial pain I felt was gone and now all I felt was blank. I was choosing not to think about what was coming. If I thought about it, I would break down in tears again, and I didn't want to keep crying. I just wanted to space out and pretend like none of this was happening.

They moved me to a private room, and I knew that Eric was there, but my mind just wouldn't acknowledge him in any way. I didn't blame him for what happened. If anything, this was my fault. I was the one carrying our child. I was the one that was supposed to protect her. I had failed, and maybe that's why I was shutting him out. I didn't want to hear him tell me that I had failed, or worse, that none of this was my fault. Deep down, I knew that I had done something wrong. I knew that I hadn't done enough. Maybe if I had stopped working like he asked, everything would be fine. Maybe if I had removed all the stress from my life, she would still be here with me. But I hadn't done that, and now I was paying the price.

"Honey."

I heard my mom's voice, but I didn't react. Warmth flooded me momentarily, but then it was gone. My mom was here and she would know what to do, but I couldn't seem to actually function beyond acknowledging that she was in the room with me. She walked around the bed to stand in front of me. Pulling up a chair, she sat down and stared at me with a sad smile. There were tears in her eyes, but she didn't cry. Her hand stroked my hair, then moved to my back, rubbing up and down in soothing strokes. It was just like when I was a kid and I was sick. I would be leaning over the toilet and she would just stand there and rub my back. It was the most comforting feeling in the world right now.

My eyes slipped closed and I just focused on her hand moving on my back. As long as I focused on that, I wouldn't fall apart. But the more she rubbed my back, the more my feelings hit the surface. The first tear slipped from my eyes and then more. I choked on a sob and reached out for her hand, squeezing it tight. She didn't say anything. She just sat there with me as I fell apart again.

"Where's Eric, honey?"

I shrugged. I didn't care at this moment. I was still angry for his flip comment. I couldn't be around him. He once again proved that we're just too different.

"I think he should be here with you."

"I don't want him here," I mumbled, trying to hold back more tears.

"Did something happen?"

I refused to speak about it. I just wanted to lie here and forget this was happening. But that wasn't realistic. The doctor had already broken my water. Now I was just waiting for labor to begin. How long was I going to have to wait? I had tried not to think about what it would be like to go through labor, to deliver a baby that wouldn't be alive. It was heartbreaking to think about.

"What do you need, honey? What can I do for you?"

"Just sit here with me."

She nodded and stood when the door opened. I knew immediately who it was. I could feel him in the room, just like I always had. Only this time, instead of excitement, I just felt dead inside. I wasn't sure I could handle seeing him, so I didn't roll over or let him know I knew he was in the room. Mom's eyes flicked up to his and I watched as heartbreak covered her face. For him. I couldn't stand to see it, so I shut my eyes.

"The doctor said that I should run home and grab the baby's things, anything we want her to be dressed in or blankets." His voice broke and he stopped speaking for a minute. "I know we packed a bag, but is there anything you want me to get?"

I shook my head slightly. I couldn't think about that right now. I could barely even form a thought.

"Alright, I'll be back soon."

I felt him move closer and my body tensed when I felt his hand hover over my arm. If he touched me, I might just snap at him and say something I couldn't take back. I felt him move away and my body relaxed. When the door closed, Mom turned her gaze on me, confused and distressed.

"Honey, what happened? I thought things were going so well."

I didn't want to talk about it. I was afraid that she would get upset with me and think my reaction was stupid, and maybe it was, but this was how I felt right now. I needed to be angry at someone and with his stupid comment, he made it easy for me to take out my anger on him.

"When the doctor told us, he held me and…he said it sucked."

My mom didn't say anything, just stared at me for a moment. "I'm sure he didn't mean-"

"It doesn't matter. You should have heard how he said it. It was like his favorite team just lost a game or something."

"Honey, everyone deals with grief in their own way."

"Mom, we just found out our baby was dead. Hearing that it sucked was crossing a line. I don't care if he didn't know what to say. That was just…" I shook my head slightly and rested my head back down on the pillow. "I don't want him in here with me."

"Honey, he has every right to be in here. That's his baby too."

I knew she was right, but I just couldn't deal with him right now. Everything was falling apart. I couldn't deal with him on top of everything else. I knew that he had wanted this baby, but maybe he was relieved this happened. He wouldn't have to put up with me anymore. He wouldn't have to be stuck with a woman he never wanted. He would have a shot at his perfect family now, one that didn't include a woman he knocked up after meeting in a bar. Maybe this was all for the best. Maybe none of this was ever meant to be.

ERIC

I stepped out of the truck, slamming the door behind me. I was still in shock. Just yesterday, we were happy. We were making love and planning out our family. Now that was gone and Kat didn't want anything to do with me. I stumbled to the porch and took a seat on the steps, barely holding my head up as the heartache ripped through me. This house was supposed to be where we started our family, but instead, it was going to be empty. I already knew that Kat would push me away. I knew she never wanted to be here with me. It had just happened that way. But now that the baby was gone, she would leave me.

I hadn't realized how much I loved her until this moment. I always thought that fate just made our connection happen. I thought I was just destined to be attached to this woman, but I never expected that I would fall so deeply in love with her. I never thought that she would come to mean the world to me, that I would have trouble breathing when she wasn't around me. But as I sat here and realized that everything would change between us now, I couldn't help but think that there should have been something I had done sooner, to make her realize that I wanted her, and not just because of the baby.

The door opened behind me and heavy footsteps came down the stairs. "Is everything okay?"

Joe sat down beside me. He already knew something was wrong. I could tell in the way he spoke to me. Call him a pain in the ass or whatever, but he was family and he always had my back.

"We lost the baby."

I felt his hand on my shoulder and it almost broke me. I had to be strong for Kat, but here, sitting on the porch with my brother, I knew that it didn't really matter if I cried. I ran my hand over my face, catching the tears as they started to fall.

"I wanted that baby so much."

"I know, man. How's Kat?"

I huffed out a laugh. "She kicked me out. I told her that this sucked and she took it as me not thinking this was a big deal. Now she won't talk to me."

"Did you explain?"

"Would it have mattered? She needs someone to be angry with."

"Yeah, but that's harsh. You should be there with her."

"I needed to get our bag," I said, swallowing down my tears. Sitting here crying about this wouldn't make any difference.

"Have you talked to Ma?"

"No, I called her parents. I just...I couldn't..."

"I'll take care of it. I know they'll want to be here."

I didn't say anything. I just stared at my hands, thinking about how I would be holding my daughter soon, but then I would have to say goodbye. All my hopes and dreams had just gone up in smoke in the blink of an eye. I pushed off the stairs and headed inside. As much as I wanted to hide out and pretend like none of this was happening, I had to get back to the hospital. Even if Kat didn't want me in the room with her, I would still be there.

I walked upstairs and into the baby's room. It was like a sledgehammer to the chest, walking in there and seeing everything we had planned. The room was ready. *We* were ready. But none of that mattered anymore. There would be no child to rock at night. There would be no reason to have the baby monitors anymore. The clothes in the drawers would never be used.

I grabbed the bag off the floor and set it on the dresser. I opened it and went through everything we packed for our little girl. There was a pretty dress for her to wear home, but as I looked at it, I hated that dress. I dug through the drawers until I found the pink swaddle sack. That's what I wanted her to wear. I wanted her to be wrapped in warmth. I never wanted to think of my baby girl being cold. I packed a onesie that said Mommy and Daddy's little girl. She would have a piece of us with her always. Then I packed the blanket my mother had made. She would be wrapped in the love of my family and she would always feel all the love that we had for her.

Next I packed the rattle I had made for her. It was just a wooden rattle, but I had handcrafted that for her. I couldn't stand to look at it every day. If it was with her, she would have a piece of me with her at all times. The last thing I grabbed was the giraffe that Kat had picked out for her. She had said that she didn't want our daughter to have the typical teddy bear. She wanted something fun for our daughter, so that she always knew wild and adventurous things.

I went to our bedroom and picked up the bag that Kat had packed for herself. I wasn't sure what she had packed, but if she had intended to wear it, that's what I would bring for her. When I packed it all in the truck, I stopped when I realized that the car seat was already installed in my backseat. I stormed to the back and tore it out of my truck, throwing it across the yard as I screamed out my pain. Next was the cradle for the car seat. I yanked that out and flung it as hard as I could, heaving hard as I stood there and watched the thing plop on the ground.

Shaking my head, I took a deep breath and got back in my truck. I had to get back to the hospital. I knew it would be a while. They said it could take up to forty-eight hours for labor to start. The next few days were going to be painful.

I pulled up to the hospital and grabbed the bags out of my truck. I couldn't just walk up to her room. I had to check in first. It was required before entering the hospital. The nurse looked me up, smiling as she saw the bags in my hand. I just stared at her numbly. Her smile disappeared when she looked at the screen. That's what the rest of my life would be. People looking at me with smiles on their faces until they realized the truth. They would ask about the baby, and then immediately give their pitying looks when they realized our little girl was gone.

"You can go on up."

The door buzzed and I walked through the doors, knowing that the next time I walked through them, I would be heading home, without my daughter. I took a deep breath and made my way to the elevator. The ride up took forever and was way too fast all at the same time. When I stepped out onto the floor, the nurses all glanced at me with pitying looks, but tried not to stare. I felt like everyone knew exactly what was happening, and they probably did. I wondered which of them drew the short straw and had to be the nurse that would be there with us as we delivered a baby that would never take a breath.

I walked down the hall to our room, but when I got there, Kat's dad was waiting outside the room, his arms crossed over his chest. I could tell by the look on his face that he wasn't going to let me in.

"Sir, I know you're just doing what she asked, but I need to be in there with her."

"She doesn't want you in there. I can't let you in."

I clenched my jaw and tried to be patient. "With all due respect, that's not just her child. She's mine too, and I deserve to be in there with her, dealing with this loss with her."

He looked down and sighed. "I know you have the right to be in there, but my baby girl is hurting right now, and there's not a damn thing I wouldn't give her right now to make the pain go away. I need you to respect her wishes. Please don't make me call security on you. You can wait in the waiting room and I'll keep you updated on everything that's happening."

I shook my head slowly. I couldn't believe this shit was happening. I wanted to storm in there and demand that she let me be there with her. I wanted to wring her neck for denying me what was rightfully mine. But I also couldn't stand to be the one that caused her even an ounce of pain. I knew this was killing her, and if me not being there helped her in any way, I had to give it to her.

I held up the bags for her dad to take and swallowed my pride. "If she needs anything…"

"I'll come get you," he promised.

I nodded and turned for the waiting room. I sat there for hours, just waiting for any word of what was happening. I looked up when footsteps approached. My brothers, aside from Derek and Josh, were all there. My hands shook as I stood. My heart started thumping hard in my chest. I took deep breaths, trying to control my erratic breathing. Robert pulled me in for a hug and I broke, gripping the back of his shirt and pulling him tight against me. I buried my face in his neck when I felt my other brothers place their hands on my shoulders and back. Everything was falling apart, but even with all that, I knew I would be okay because I had my family with me.

I stood there, surrounded by my brothers for a good half hour. I couldn't pull away. I couldn't speak or do anything. I wasn't even sure if I was holding myself up or if they were doing it for me. When I finally pulled back, I had to clasp my hands together to try and stop them from shaking. I swiped at my face, removing the tears from my face.

"Mom and Dad are on their way," Joe said.

"Thanks," I croaked out.

"Why are you out here?" Will asked.

I shook my head slowly. "She doesn't want me in there."

"Bullshit," Robert spat. "This isn't just about her. You're the father. You have every right to be there. Hell, I'll find a judge that can order you in the fucking room if need be."

"And accomplish what?" I asked tiredly. "Make a suffering woman feel more pain?"

"But why doesn't she want you in there?"

I shook my head slowly. "When we found out, I didn't know what to say, so I said what Ma always used to say to us. I guess I should have explained, but I'm just so used to hearing it that I didn't think. She took it the wrong way. She thought I was saying it like our baby didn't really matter. And she's in too much pain to try and understand. So, I'm out here and the woman I love is in that room hurting."

"I'm sorry, man," Andrew said. "What can we do?"

"Nothing. There's nothing anyone can do."

~

Five hours later, Derek stepped off the elevator and rushed over to me. He stopped in front of me, unsure what to do. I tried to think of something to say. I tried to figure out what I was supposed to do, but I had nothing.

We weren't a family of huggers, Derek least of all, so I was shocked when Derek stepped forward and wrapped me up in a hug. He patted my lightly and I felt him shaking his head.

"I'm so sorry, man."

I nodded, not able to speak.

"How's she doing?"

"Not good."

"Then why the fuck are you out here?"

I sighed heavily. I was tired of explaining why. I walked over to the windows and stared out at the people below. Someone was walking out of the hospital on crutches. There was someone beside him, holding flowers that were probably meant to cheer him up. I wondered if they worked. Another couple was leaving the hospital. I could see the woman laughing. Everyone down there was just going about their day. They had no idea that we were up here, that Kat was losing her baby, that my life felt like it was being destroyed. Everyone just moved on with their lives, because this didn't touch them, and I hoped nothing like this ever did. I rested my head against the window and let my eyes slip closed.

"Eric?"

I turned around to see Chrissy standing there.

"What are you guys doing here? Is Kat in labor?"

I tried to muster up some kind of response, but I couldn't. I just stared at her. It was like the life had gone out of me. I couldn't even answer a fucking question anymore. My eyes drifted away from her face until I was just staring off into space. I heard one of my brothers come over and fill her in, but I wasn't listening. I felt her squeeze my arm and then she was gone.

Hours passed, but I didn't hear anything from Kat's dad. I was tempted to go back there, but numbness had set in. Suddenly, not being in there seemed like a really good thing. I wasn't feeling anything right now. It was like I was immune to the world around me. I mostly stared off into space, not even thinking about anything. I could almost imagine that I didn't even exist as the rest of the hospital continued to move on around me.

"No!"

The piercing scream cut through the haze I was in. I looked over at the hallway, my heart beating a little faster as I replayed that scream over and over again in my head. Had I imagined it? Then I heard it again. It was a gut-wrenching, terrified scream that had me pushing out of my chair and running down the hall to Kat's room. Her dad stood at the doorway, blocking it, keeping me from getting to Kat. I could hear her sobs through the door, each one ripping through my heart and shredding me wide open. Her dad fought me off, struggling to keep me from getting in the room, but I was no longer myself. Kat was in there and she needed me.

"Get off me!" I shouted, fighting to get her dad out of the way.

"She doesn't want you in there!"

"She needs me. Can you hear that?" Her moans were digging into me and piercing my soul. I couldn't respect her wishes anymore. I needed to get in there and hold her.

"She doesn't want you," her dad spat. Then Derek was there and he was pulling her dad off me, tossing him up against the wall like a rag doll. I didn't pay attention to what happened after that. I shoved inside the room and took in the sight before me. It broke my fucking heart.

KATHERINE

I had refused an epidural. I wanted to feel every ounce of this delivery. I wouldn't have the beautiful moments every other mother would have. There would be nothing to wipe away the pain of delivery, ensuring that I would remember this moment for the rest of my life. The nurse urged me to have the epidural, saying that the delivery for a stillborn baby would be much harder on my body than a regular delivery, but I just ignored her. I had been in labor for most of the day now. I didn't know how long it had been since the doctor told me she was gone. Everything seemed to be a blur, except for labor. That was so intense that it was crystal clear in my mind.

My mom hadn't left my side since she got here. My dad came in to check on me from time to time, but he mostly stood outside my door like a guard dog. Part of me wondered if I should let Eric in. I needed him, even if I couldn't admit it out loud. But I was scared. I was afraid that he would blame me for losing our daughter. I was afraid that he would be angry with me for basically ignoring him since we found out. There were so many things I was afraid of that I just couldn't handle thinking anymore. So, I focused on labor and let everything else slip from my mind.

Another contraction hit and I started breathing through it. Since I didn't have an epidural, I could get up and walk around whenever I wanted. I paced the room, my hands gripping my back as the pain tore through my abdomen. I breathed in and out slowly, taking deep, cleansing breaths. With every hour that passed, the contractions got worse, and with it, a deep ache that settled in my chest. I wanted this to be over, but as soon as it was over, reality would hit. My little girl would be born, but she wouldn't be coming home with me.

A sob ripped through me and I leaned on the counter, trying to hold myself up. My mom rushed over to me, placing her hands on my shoulders.

"It's alright, honey."

I shook my head, knowing nothing about this would ever be right. My baby was gone. Eric and I were torn apart. No, there was nothing in my life that would ever be right again.

The door opened and Chrissy walked through, a sad expression on her face. As soon as I saw her, I started sobbing again. She rushed over to me and wrapped me in her arms. This was really happening. The more people that showed up, the more real this became. It wasn't just happening to me, though it really felt like it.

She didn't say anything. She didn't try to smother me with placating words. She just held me as I cried. But she wasn't really who I wanted. I just couldn't admit it to myself.

I didn't say anything for a long time. Chrissy just sat with me and watched me with every contraction. I knew that she couldn't sit here all day with me. She probably had to get to work. I finally turned to her and gripped her hand.

"Thanks for coming."

She knew I wasn't asking her to stay. She gave me a hug and made me promise to call her when the baby was born. It stung, but what else was she supposed to say?

The pain got so much worse over the next few hours. I was beginning to regret not getting the epidural. I thought I wanted to feel all of this, but now I wished I was just numb. I walked as much as I could, but eventually, I was too tired and had to lay down. Every contraction hit harder than the last and the tears that I was trying to keep at bay were now streaming down my face. I knew I was close to delivering this baby.

When the nurse came to check on me again, she gave me a sad look and told me it was time to push. That was when I lost it. Pushing meant my daughter would no longer be inside me. It meant that I would have to say goodbye. It meant that I would never feel her inside me again, but I also wouldn't get to take her home.

I started shaking uncontrollably and when the nurse started shifting me into a new position, I lost it. I started screaming and yelling, anything to get her to leave me alone.

"Katherine, if you can't calm down, I'm going to have to sedate you."

But I couldn't hear her. I saw the needle that she was holding and I knew she was going to put it in my IV. I started writhing around on the bed, tears streaming down my face as I fought to keep her away from me. The door flung open and Eric rushed into the room, a look of horror on his face when he saw what was happening.

He rushed to my side and grabbed my hand, yelling at the nurse to stop. I was sobbing so hard, sweating from the hours of labor. I was a mess, but he was staring at me with all the love in the world.

"Kat, listen to me." He cupped both sides of my face and forced me to look him in the eyes. "You can do this, okay? I'm right here and I'm not going anywhere, okay?"

I sobbed harder, gripping onto his shirt. He pulled me against him and stroked my back. I tensed as another contraction hit. It was the most painful one yet. Eric gripped my hand and brought it to his mouth, giving my hand a kiss.

"I've got you. We're going to do this together, okay?"

I nodded against him, still sobbing into his shirt, but he didn't seem to care.

"Katherine, I need you to get ready to push, okay?" the doctor said. "I know this is terrible and I know you don't want to do this, but I'll be with you every step of the way. We all will. We're going to deliver your beautiful girl and then you can hold her."

Hold her. I could hold her. I nodded and let them shift me into position. When they told me to push, I did as they asked, but it hurt too much.

"Eric, why don't you sit behind her to support her?" the doctor suggested.

Eric climbed onto the bed behind me and pulled me back into his hard chest. I instantly felt comfort wrap around me, and I felt like I could do this. Eric's hand moved to my forehead and he pushed my hair out of my face. Then he gripped my hand in his and we prepared for the next push.

"Alright, when you feel the contraction, start pushing."

I nodded and when it hit, I pushed as hard as I could. The nurse nodded and told me I was doing well, but it didn't feel that way. I waited for the next contraction and pushed again. Over and over, I pushed, praying for the agony to end. My body hurt, but my soul was crushed. I started crying, not feeling like I could do this anymore. I was exhausted and my heart hurt so bad.

"One more push, Katherine," the doctor said encouragingly.

I nodded and pushed one last time. It felt like the baby just slid out of my body. Silence filled the room. I closed my eyes and cried as Eric wrapped his arms around me. Where there should be a baby's cries, there was only deafening silence. My body shook with sobs, but Eric was there, holding me close to him.

The nurse took our child over to a table and cleaned her, then wrapped her in a small blanket and put a hat on her head. My face crumpled as I watched her treat my baby with all the gentleness of any other newborn. She picked her up gently and walked over to me, a slight sheen of tears in her eyes.

"Katherine, meet your baby girl. She's so beautiful."

She lowered her down into my arms and I held her for the first time. I wasn't sure if I was holding her properly or not. The first time I was holding my child, and she wasn't even really here. I smiled down at my precious girl, tears pouring silently down my cheeks.

"She's so beautiful," I whispered.

Eric was pressed tightly to my back, looking over my shoulder at our little girl. "She's got her Momma's beautiful face."

I had thought of this moment many times over the past few months. I imagined holding her hand and having her squeeze it back. So, even though I knew nothing would happen, I picked up her tiny hand and pushed my finger into her hand. She didn't squeeze me back like I had imagined. There was no cooing or weird baby noises. There was only silence.

I was barely aware of the doctor still working on stitching me up or finishing up with everything else. I just sat there in Eric's arms and held my little girl.

"What should we name her?" Eric asked.

I shook my head slightly. I had thought about names for months, but I knew I wouldn't be able to decide until I saw her. Now that she was here, there was only one thing I could think of.

"It's not a name, but I think we should call her Angel. Because that's what she is now."

Eric kissed my cheek and then brushed his knuckles down her little face. "Angel."

I could feel his chest shaking behind me. He was hurting too. "Do you want to hold her?"

I looked back at him, the tears soaking his face, but he shook his head. "Take your time. I can hold her later."

So, we sat there, our family of three that would never be whole. We stared at our little girl, knowing that soon we would have to give her up.

"I think she would have been an artist," I said after a minute. "A painter."

"Yeah?"

I nodded. "She would have sat on the porch at the house and painted sunrises and the snow on the ground in the winter."

"And she would have been the kid that came home with scraped knees every night and her hair a mess," Eric smiled. "But she would have grown up to be one of the most beautiful women in the world. And she would have met a man that was smart and cherished the ground she walked on."

"And he would have been responsible," I smiled up at him. "Just like you. Because she would have been a daddy's girl and she would want someone just as amazing as you."

His eyes were intense and he swallowed hard, leaning in to press a kiss against my temple. Then he leaned his head against mine and together we watched our baby sleep. Because that's how I had to see it. She was sleeping, and she would be for the rest of her life.

ERIC

"Here," Kat said quietly. "You can hold her now."

"Are you sure?"

She nodded. "I'm tired. I need to lay down."

"Do you want us to lay in bed with you?"

A stuttering breath left her chest and she nodded. I helped her shift into a more comfortable position and then laid down beside her on the small bed. I rested our Angel on my chest, just like I thought I always would. I stared down at her, wondering what it would be like to feel her chest move up and down on mine. I would never know. I rested my large hand on her back, shifting my eyes to the ceiling as I felt my eyes filling with tears. I swallowed hard, trying to hold it all in. Kat had just started to calm down. I didn't want her to start crying all over again. There would be enough of that when they took her from us.

Kat wrapped her hand around mine and gave a gentle squeeze. I took a deep breath, choking down the sob that was rising in my throat, but the more she held my hand, the harder it was to keep those feelings at bay. I wanted my child. I wanted the life that we had planned. How was I supposed to just let go of all that and pretend like none of this ever happened? How would I walk into work every day and do my job?

"I always pictured this," I choked out. "I imagined laying on the couch at home with our baby on my chest. I thought about those first two weeks at home with her after she was born. You would sleep in after the baby kept us up all night, and I would sneak into her room in the morning and take her downstairs so she didn't wake you up. And I would have this time alone with her, where I could just hold her and feel her tiny body on my chest."

I closed my eyes and felt the weight of her on my chest. But it wasn't anything like I had imagined. She wasn't wiggling around or making little noises. I would never see her face scrunch up when she was about to cry. I would never hold her over my shoulder and walk around with her when she couldn't calm down. This was the only moment I would get with her.

Hours passed with Kat and I staring at our Angel. I knew they would be coming soon. I knew we couldn't stay like this forever. I wanted our parents to get a chance to meet their granddaughter before they took her away.

"I should get everyone. I think they'd like to meet her," I croaked out.

She sniffled and nodded slightly. "Okay."

I gently moved her onto Kat's chest and pressed a kiss to her tiny cheek, my tears slipping onto her tiny body. I glanced up at Kat, pressing a kiss to her forehead before I walked out the door. Once I was in the hallway, I leaned against the wall and took a deep breath and then another. I didn't want my family to see me crying like this. The pain was overwhelming. I just stood there, breathing in and out, trying to regain some sense of control.

I felt a strong hand on my shoulder and looked up to see my dad standing in front of me, tears in his eyes. He gripped my shoulder tightly, pulling me toward him. I wrapped my arms around my dad and broke. The tears fell heavily and chest constricted with the pain. He just stood there holding me as I fell apart again.

"I want her back," I cried.

"I know, son. I know."

After a minute, I pulled back and swiped at my face. "I was coming to get everyone. I thought...you'd like to meet her."

My dad nodded. "I'll get your mother and Katherine's parents. When we're done, I'll send in your brothers."

"Thanks," I said, still trying to dry my face.

"You'll get through this," he said after a minute. "You're the strongest man I know. It may feel like you're broken now, but time will heal that pain."

It didn't feel like that would ever happen, but I nodded anyway. When he went back to the waiting room, I opened the door to our room and watched Kat as she stood by the sink, giving our child a bath. She was running the cloth over her body, taking extra care with her little toes and belly button. When she was done, she took a towel and gently dried her off. Then she pulled out a bottle of lotion and started rubbing it into her skin. When she was all done, she put a diaper on our baby and then gently put on the onesie I had packed. She leaned down and pressed a gentle kiss to her forehead. I could see the tears slipping down her face and the way her body shook. She looked like she was barely hanging on. I walked into the room and wrapped my arms around her from behind. Her hand gripped my forearm, as she cried.

"I didn't see the dress," she cried.

"I took it out," I admitted. "I wanted her to be in something warm. I didn't want to think about her being cold."

I felt her nod. "Thank you."

"Let me help you."

Together, we put her in the swaddle sack, leaving her little hands out for now.

"There, now she'll always be warm." I picked her up and held her against my shoulder, cradling her head in my big palm.

There was a knock at the door and our parents entered. Now that they were here, I didn't want to give her up, not when I had so little time left with her. But they needed this as much as Kat and I did. We weren't the only ones losing Angel.

Ma walked forward first, her cheeks a little red from crying, but she was smiling at me. "Look at you. I always knew you would be a great father." It felt like a punch to the gut. Ma wrapped her arms around Kat and me. "It may not feel like you're parents, but you are, and you always will be. You're just parents that had your baby taken from you way too soon."

She stepped back and placed her hand on Angel's back, right by my hand.

"She's absolutely beautiful. May I hold my grandchild?"

I nodded and passed her over, then pulled Kat into my side. Both of us watched as my mother lovingly held our daughter, staring at her as if she was the most precious thing in the world. When she was done, Kat's mom came over and held her, pressing a kiss to her cheek. One by one, everyone took their turns holding our little girl. Kat's dad started tearing up when he realized how tiny she was in his big hands. My dad gripped my shoulder while he held her in one arm. When they were done, my brothers came in, each taking a turn holding their niece. I could tell that Kat was overwhelmed and needed some space.

I turned her in my arms, wrapping her up and rubbing her back. "Do you want to lay down for a little bit?"

I felt her nod against me and led her back to the bed, helping her in and then pulling the blankets up over her. She looked so fragile right now, like one more thing would break her, and I had a feeling that when they took Angel from us, that would be what did her in.

"Rest, baby."

I kissed her forehead and then turned back to my brothers.

"You're one lucky man," Robert said. "She's beautiful. I'm glad you got this."

"But I don't have her," I croaked out.

"You know what it's like to have the most beautiful thing in the world. I know she's gone, but you got to feel that love. That's something that no one can ever take from you."

He was right, and I knew eventually I would feel that way, but right now, the pain was too intense. I backed away and watched as they all took turns holding her, pointing out her cute fingers and her little nose. As much as I didn't want this to end, I needed it. I wanted to take Kat home and…I wasn't sure. I just couldn't stand the visitors anymore. I was emotionally drained and so fucking tired. I had been awake for days, waiting for labor to kick in and then for Kat to deliver. Something had to give.

The nurse came in a little later. It was time. I knew it before she said it. Ma came back with her, a small smile on her face. She walked over to Kat, placing her hand on her arm. Kat turned from where she had been staring out the window.

"Sweetie, it's time, but I thought that before they…before they take her, we could get some pictures of all of you."

Kat nodded slightly, but didn't look too happy about any of it.

"I know this doesn't sound like something you'd want, but you're going to want to remember this day and look back on Angel. And one day, you'll be able to smile when you look at her picture."

The photographer came in and positioned Angel in Kat's arms, showing me where to stand. Picture after picture, we looked down on our little girl, knowing these pictures would only bring us sadness. It felt like torture. But Ma was rarely wrong about anything, so I went along with it, even though it was tearing my heart out.

KATHERINE

I was drained. Wrecked. Destroyed. I was tired of the company. My body was begging for sleep, for me to drift off and just forget all of this. I was sad and angry at the same time, and I never knew from one minute to the next which feeling would take over. I wanted to just get this over with and say goodbye. Delaying the inevitable almost made this more painful, but I also dreaded saying goodbye.

I wanted to have a private funeral for our little girl, so the hospital would have the funeral home pick up her body and prepare her for burial. But I couldn't stand the thought of her being buried across town, away from us where I couldn't watch over her. She should be close to us.

"Eric." He turned to me, taking his eyes off Angel. "I want her buried under the tree in the back yard. I don't want her to be alone."

"I don't know that that's possible, but I'll have my dad look into it."

I nodded. "Thank you."

I rested my head back on the pillow and closed my eyes. I was so tired. It was already late afternoon. It seemed like I had been in this hospital already a week. I had no concept of time. I wasn't sure when the last time I had eaten was. There was nothing but the deep ache in my chest. Would it ever go away? Would I ever feel like myself again, or would I always feel this empty?

"Kat, it's time," Eric said quietly.

I sat up in bed as he placed Angel in my arms one last time. I wasn't ready to let her go, but I also felt like there was nothing more I could say to her. I had spent hours thinking of her, talking to her, wishing that this was different. But nothing would ever be the same again. There were no words left to tell her. So, I stared at her. I said a prayer that she would be taken care of and feel no pain ever again.

"I love you more than anything in this world," I whispered. I kissed her cheek one last time and lifted her up to Eric. I watched as he held her, but he seemed to feel the same way I did. It was time and we both knew there was nothing more to do or say. He pressed his lips to her cheek, brushing his knuckles along her cheek one last time.

"I love you, Angel."

He handed her off to the nurse, who put her in a bassinet and rolled her out of the room. I watched as Eric seemed to deflate right in front of me. It was over.

"I want to go home," I said quietly.

Eric nodded. "I'll go tell the nurse."

He walked out of the room, leaving me alone in the room. Instead of laying in the bed any longer, I got up to pull on some clothes, but my body was so exhausted that I couldn't do it. Frustrated, I sat on the edge of the bed and started pulling on my pants. I was tired of being in the hospital gown and sitting on the bed. I never wanted to see another hospital room again. I sighed as I thought of going back to work, seeing all those little kids in the hospital, in there waiting to die. Because, let's face it, most of the kids that came to the hospital for extended periods of time never left. But I couldn't think about that now.

Eric came in, seeing me struggle to get on my clothes and rushed over to help. His face was emotionless and cold. Throughout the day, I could see everything he was feeling, but it was like the moment they took Angel, he just turned blank.

"Katherine, are you sure you want to go home tonight?" the nurse asked as she walked into the room. "You've had a long day. Maybe you should stay one more night. The grief counselor hasn't been by yet and-"

"No offense, but I've seen enough of this hospital. I want to go home and sleep in my own bed. I don't want the reminder of the place where I lost my child. I don't want to see any more nurses or be looked at with pity. I just want to go home."

The nurse nodded. "I'll have the discharge paperwork ready soon."

I packed up what little I had, all the while Eric sat in a chair by the window and stared outside. His finger ran across his lip, like he was thinking about something, but I had no idea what. This past day, I had seen more emotion out of this man than ever before. I was pretty sure that when we left this hospital, he would no longer be so open with his feelings. Everything would change now. Would I continue to live with him? I had just sold my townhouse. I didn't have anywhere else to go. I wanted to stay with Eric, but I wasn't so sure he felt the same way. After all, we were only together because of the baby, and now she was gone.

The nurse brought a wheelchair for me, and as much as I didn't want to sit in it, I also knew that I was too exhausted to walk. I sat down and Eric wheeled me through the hospital. I saw people that I worked with. It must have gotten around the hospital that I lost the baby. Everyone was looking at me with sad faces. That's what this would be like for me now. I would never escape this. I would always be the woman that lost her baby.

I leaned my head on my palm as we made our way out to the front. Eric locked the wheels on the wheelchair and came around in front of me.

"I'll grab the truck and bring it here."

I wanted to argue with him, but I didn't have it in me to walk across the parking lot, let alone five feet in front of me. I nodded as he walked away. Someone walked past me, giving me a faint smile and a wave. They were probably being polite, but it pissed me off that someone would be smiling at me right now.

The truck pulled up and Eric rushed around, grabbing the bags and tossing them in the back. Then he helped me stand, but when my legs shook and I almost collapsed, he swiftly picked me up and carried me to the truck and set me inside. When he got in, he sat there for a minute, like he was waiting for me to say something, but I had nothing to say.

I could tell he was watching me, so I looked out the window. I couldn't stand him staring at me, wondering if I was okay. I wasn't okay, and I doubted I ever would be again. The motion of the truck had me slipping off to sleep. I didn't wake up until the truck stopped outside the house. I was so tired though. I didn't think I could wake up enough to get inside, but it didn't matter. Eric opened the door and slid his arms under me, cradling me against his body. I took his strength, wrapping my arms around his neck and burying my face against his shoulder.

When we stepped inside, I heard Andrew and Joe asking if I was okay, but I ignored them and so did Eric. He took me upstairs and shut the door behind us once we were in the bedroom. Instead of setting me down by the bed, he took me into the bathroom and started stripping off my clothes after setting me on the toilet. This wasn't like the other times he saw me naked. Everything was different now. I had the belly of a woman that just had a baby, but no baby to show for it. I felt ugly and disgusting.

Eric stripped off his own clothes and pulled me into his arms. He wasn't hard like I expected, and I couldn't help but wonder if that was because he didn't find me desirable or because of what happened. Even though I knew that he was hurting, my mind was telling me that it was because he didn't like what he saw.

"We're gonna get through this, Kat."

My eyes slipped closed as I snuggled further into his body, taking his warmth. He pulled me into the shower, but I didn't feel like cleaning up. I was exhausted. I just wanted to go to bed. As if he sensed that I just didn't have it in me, he started rinsing my hair and then shampooed it. His gentleness was touching. The way he ran his fingers through my hair made me feel like I was something to be cherished, to be cared for. When he started washing my body, the tears started. They silently trailed down my face as I stood under the water and Eric took care of me. When he was all done, he shut off the water and wrapped a towel around me, drying my hair as best he could. He even attempted to brush my hair.

When I slipped into bed, the overwhelming grief settled inside me again, but I didn't feel like crying anymore. There was just a numbness to it all. Eric laid down beside me and pulled me into his arms. I settled against his chest, hearing the steady beat of his heart, and fell asleep.

ERIC

A whole day passed with us just sleeping. We were both exhausted and drained. Kat slept harder than me, barely waking up when she had to go to the bathroom. When she stood and wobbled on her feet, I jumped out of bed and helped her to the bathroom. She looked paler even after all that sleep. I was worried that the trauma of it had been too much for her, that something else was wrong. Had we left the hospital too early? What if something was wrong and I missed the warning signs?

Kat didn't speak to me at all, not even when I asked direct questions. She nodded or shook her head, but no words left her lips. I was worried about her, but I didn't know how to make any of it better for her.

On the morning of the second day, I got up and made some breakfast. I wasn't really hungry, but Kat needed to eat. I had no idea when she last ate. I made some eggs, bacon, and toast for her, then brought it upstairs. As I was climbing the stairs, I realized that it was unusually quiet in the house. Joe and Andrew weren't here.

I pushed the bedroom door open and saw that Kat was awake, just staring at the wall. "Hey, I made you some breakfast."

She didn't say anything. She just stared off into space. I set her breakfast on the nightstand and got down on my haunches in front of her, so she could see my face.

"Kat."

Her eyes flicked to mine, but they didn't acknowledge me in any way. It was like she could see me, but she was looking right through me. I brushed her hair out of her face and then shook her lightly.

"Kat, you need to eat."

"I'm not hungry."

It was the first thing I had heard her say since the hospital. Part of me was relieved, happy that at least I heard her speak and knew that she was still here with me. But a bigger part of me was sad. She was hurting and there was nothing I could do to fix that. But I could make her eat. I had to do something. I couldn't just sit by and watch her melt away. I couldn't make her heart stop hurting and I couldn't make those terrible memories slip away, but I could make sure that she got stronger.

I gently pushed my hands under her body and lifted her into a sitting position. She didn't respond in any way. I sat on the edge of the bed and started shoveling eggs onto the fork. When I held it to her lips, she didn't move. She stared at my shirt, just a blank stare.

"Kat, I need you to eat at least a little bit."

It took a few minutes, but she finally opened her mouth slightly, allowing me to feed her. After three forks of eggs, it was clear that I wasn't going to get her to eat anymore. I had to hold the bottle to her lips to get her to drink water. Sighing, I set the tray aside and helped her to lie back down. I kissed her on the cheek and brought the tray back downstairs. I stared out the kitchen window, just staring at the muddy yard. I felt like a failure. I couldn't protect our baby and I couldn't help Kat. I didn't even know where to start.

I ate some breakfast and then cleaned up the kitchen. I didn't want to go back upstairs. I didn't want to see the shell of the woman I loved. But she didn't have anyone else. I was the only one here for her right now. I wanted to call her mom, but I wanted to give Kat a chance to be alone and deal with this. Maybe tomorrow would be a better day.

I walked back upstairs to check on her, but she was sleeping again.

MAINTENANCE REQUIRED

I took a seat in the room and spent the day keeping an eye on her. I stared out the window from my chair and watched the sun slowly sink in the sky. After days on end of crying, I was exhausted. I never thought I would see the day I would cry. I wasn't an emotional person, but losing Angel had been too much. But I couldn't afford to just lay around and think about what I had lost. Crying wouldn't make this better. It wouldn't bring her back and it wouldn't help me get through my days. I had to get to work. I had to keep my business functioning. I had no idea when or if Kat would ever want to go back to work, so I had to make sure that I could support both of us. And we would have hospital bills coming soon, and I had no idea what was covered under her insurance.

I slipped out of bed, making sure Kat was comfortable before I left the room. I shut the door quietly and sighed when I saw the baby's room door was standing open. I stood in the doorway, staring at the crib I had made and the dresser that was on the far wall. I had just finished it last week. We hadn't even put clothes in it yet. The rocking chair was waiting for a mother and child, but we wouldn't be using it. I shut the door to the room. I couldn't see this every time I came up here. I walked downstairs and into the kitchen. Joe and Andrew were sitting at the kitchen table talking, but they shut up as soon as I stepped into the room. So, they were talking about me.

"Don't you guys have anything better to do?"

"We were just waiting to see if you needed anything," Andrew answered slowly. I glanced back at him and frowned. He was wearing his usual weird clothes, but he had a suit jacket thrown over his bright purple shirt, which made the whole ensemble even weirder.

"What's going on?"

"What are you talking about?"

I waved at his clothes. "What's with the clothes?"

"I always dress this way."

I crossed my arms over my chest and glared at him. "No, you don't normally wear a suit jacket. And you look like you tried to actually style your hair like a normal person."

He rolled his eyes at me.

"Look, if you're trying not to piss me off, I'd rather that you just be yourself. I can't stand everyone walking on eggshells around me."

"It's not you," he sighed.

"Then what is it?"

He picked at something on the table for a moment. "I...I applied for a job a week ago at this computer company."

"That's great."

"I didn't get the job," he said defeatedly.

"Oh...Was it because you didn't have the education? Because you could go back to school-"

"It wasn't that. They said...they said I didn't fit in with the company. Apparently, I'm too "hipster" for them. They said that I dressed too funny. They didn't think clients would take me seriously dressed like this."

I stared at him, trying my best to hold back the laughter that was bubbling up inside me. I nodded, trying anything to not laugh at what he was telling me. But there was no holding it in. I burst out laughing, running my hand over my face as tears poured from my eyes. God, I hadn't laughed like this in...My laughter slowly died down until there was nothing left. The pain returned, and when I looked at my brothers, it was like they knew exactly why I had stopped laughing.

Was this the way it would be from now on? Would all happy moments be killed by the pain of losing her? I stumbled over to a chair and plopped down, resting my head in my palms. I couldn't do this. I couldn't be this lifeless human being. I needed something to push me on, to make me feel even an ounce of something other than the pain.

"Is there anything we can do?"

I ran my hand over the beard that had grown in the last week. "I just need to get back to work. I can't...I need to work."

"Are you sure you don't want to take some time off?" Joe asked. "We can fill in for you."

"That's nice of you guys to offer, but what would I do all day? I can't just sit around here."

"What about Kat?" Andrew asked. "Are you sure you should leave her?"

"I'll talk to her mom. Maybe she can stay here for a little bit."

"What about the funeral?" Joe asked. "Maybe you should wait until after that."

I nodded. "Maybe. I have to at least check in at the office tomorrow. I don't have a fucking clue if anyone's even going out on jobs."

"RJ's running things," Joe supplied. "I called him after we found out about…Anyway, I figured you weren't really thinking about that stuff. I've been checking over there every day to make sure there's nothing that needs to be taken care of."

I didn't know what to say. I knew Joe was working toward having his own tattoo parlor, so I knew he wouldn't want to help me out in the long term. I had offered him jobs before, and he never took them. The fact that he stepped up and took over like that just shocked the hell out of me.

"Thank you," I choked out.

"I can help out, you know, until you're ready to get back to full time."

"I appreciate that."

KATHERINE

"Katherine?"

My mom was here. I stared at the wall, but I didn't say anything. I couldn't. The only thing I could do was replay the events of the last week in my head. Everything from the last time Eric and I made love to leaving the hospital. That was really the last thing I remembered. I slept a lot over the last few days. Getting up to go to the bathroom was a chore. The nurse had told me that delivering a stillborn baby was nothing like delivering a newborn, but I didn't want to hear it. She was right though. My whole body felt like I had just been in a car accident. I ached in places that I didn't know I could ache. But nothing hurt more than the pain in my chest.

I finally shifted in bed to look at my mom. She was dressed all in black, like she was going to a funeral.

"Is it today?" I asked, my voice nothing more than a whisper.

"Yes, honey. I thought I could help you get ready."

I nodded and allowed her to help me with everything. It took a long time, but after an hour, I was finally ready. I walked out of the bedroom to the top of the stairs, but that had been enough to do me in. I knew I couldn't make it down the stairs. As if on cue, Eric appeared at the bottom of the stairs and rushed up to get me. He must have seen my legs shaking.

"I've got you," he murmured, lifting me in his arms. I didn't protest, even as he walked past all of our family with me in his arms. His dad held the door open for Eric and he took me outside to the big tree where I wanted Angel buried. There was already a hole in the earth, waiting for the casket to be lowered.

My breath stuttered in my chest as I thought about my little girl being buried in the ground, all alone and cold. It didn't matter if she was already gone. She would be alone in that tiny grave. I didn't want that for her. I knew I could visit her every day this way, but no child should be so alone.

"Kat, it's okay."

"She's alone," I cried.

"No, she's not. We all have something for her, so she'll never be alone. She's going to have a little piece of all of us with her."

I swiped at my tears and nodded. Eric set me down in a chair and nodded to the funeral director. He opened the casket for us, and my heart stopped. She looked just as peaceful as she did in the hospital.

Derek stepped forward first, pulling out a gun. "Hey, princess. I got you a gun. I would have taught you to use it when you were older, but now you'll have it with you, to protect you from anything." He set the gun in the bottom of the casket and took a step back.

Then Andrew stepped forward, holding an iPod and earphones. "I don't want you to get lonely, so I brought you some of the best music. I even uploaded some of your dad's music, even though it sucks. And I know your mom really likes country music, so I put plenty of it on there." He set it down in the casket and moved for Joe.

"I made a drawing for you. I would have taken you to get this tattooed on your body the moment you turned eighteen. I'd probably have to do it behind your dad's back, but you would have loved it."

Eric's mom stepped forward and gently pulled a hat onto Angel's head. "I made this for you, sweet girl. Now, you'll never be cold."

She pressed a kiss to Angel's face and stepped back. Then Robert came forward. "So, if Derek's gun didn't scare off the men, and you ended up marrying one of those jackasses, you might need me someday." He placed a phone in the casket. "I programmed my phone number in there, so you could call me. I'll always answer."

Will placed a small history book in the casket. "This is a book, *Helen of Troy*. You're so beautiful, that I know you could have started a few wars."

I turned to Eric, tears in my eyes. "I didn't get her anything."

He knelt down beside me and pulled something from his pocket. "I took care of it." He opened a jewelry box and inside was a tiny bracelet with the letters E, K, and A dangling from the chain. "This is from us."

He walked to the casket and placed it around her wrist. I wasn't sure what happened after that. I knew I was crying, but everything was a blur. When they closed the casket, I started sobbing. When she was about halfway into the ground, I lost it.

I started sobbing, gripping his shirt and yelling at him for allowing them to bury her. I knew it didn't make any sense, but I couldn't stand the thought of her being alone. Eric lifted me in his arms and carried me back to the house while I sobbed against his shoulder.

"How could you do this to me?" I started hitting him, but he just held me tighter, hurrying toward the house.

"Kat, we have to bury her. You know we have to."

"No," I choked out. "She needs her mother!"

He shoved the door open and walked through to the living room, setting me down gently on the couch. He crouched down in front of me, holding onto my hands as I tried to get in a few more swipes.

"Kat, listen to me! Listen to me." I stopped swinging at him and looked into his eyes. There was pain there, just as intense as it was in the hospital. "She doesn't need us anymore. She's gone. She's not hurting. She's at peace."

My lip quivered as I stared into his eyes. I knew he was right, but my heart couldn't understand it right now.

"Eric, why don't you take her upstairs?" my mom suggested. "I'll stay with her."

Eric nodded and picked me up. Part of me just wanted to stay with Eric, but the other part of me was angry with him for allowing our daughter to be taken away. I knew it wasn't rational, but grief never was. When he set me down and walked out the door, I felt like a door was shutting on a chapter of my life. It felt like nothing would ever be the same again.

At some point during the night, I finally accepted that what happened was necessary. There was no point in being upset about it anymore, and I couldn't just sit here and cry anymore. I had nothing left to give. I was emotionally spent. It was like as soon as I accepted that she was really gone and I would never hold her again, my emotions just dried up. I didn't feel a thing. I wasn't sad. I wasn't angry. I just existed.

Eric came to bed that night, but neither of us said anything. I didn't know what I would even say if he spoke to me. I drifted off to sleep at some point, and when I woke the next day, I just laid there staring at the wall. Nothing existed around me. People moved in and out of the room, but I hardly noticed them. I did everything on autopilot. I went to the bathroom when I needed to, but I mostly just laid in bed. It was like I was on life-support. My body was alive, but nothing about me functioned like normal. And the only good thing about any of it was that I didn't feel anything. And if I didn't feel anything, I couldn't be hurt.

ERIC

I walked into the office the day after the funeral, ready to get back to work. I just wanted to bury my head in something, to accomplish something. I didn't want to think about the child I lost or the woman at home that couldn't function. Her mom was there with her during the day so I could get back to work. I had no idea how long that would last. Everyone else had lives to get back to. My parents were leaving tomorrow and heading back to North Carolina. Derek had headed back home after the funeral yesterday. He had already been gone for almost a week. He couldn't take off any more time.

Joe was in the office, arguing with Anna over something when I walked in. They saw me and instantly got quiet. I stood there in the doorway, pissed off. It was starting already. Irritated, I tossed my bag on the ground and stormed over to the desk.

"What's going on?"

"Nothing," Joe said quickly, narrowing his eyes at Anna. She pursed her lips, but didn't say anything.

"Look, this is still my business."

"It's nothing you have to worry about," Joe said. "You just…this isn't something you need to deal with."

I sighed heavily, shaking my head. "Look, I don't need time off or for you to coddle me. I don't need everyone to stop talking as soon as I come in the room. I need to get back to work and get back to normal, so tell me what the hell is going on so we can fix it and move on."

Anna turned to me and handed me a piece of paper. "Uh...Mrs. Cranston is requesting service. She said that her roof is leaking. Everyone else is out on a job right now. I can't get anyone over there for a few days."

"I told you, I'll take care of it," Joe hissed.

"No, I'll do it," I said. I needed the distraction, and getting up there with a hammer and nails would feel good. I could do something other than sit around and think. This was just what I needed.

"Eric-"

"Joe, you've never repaired a roof. I can't send you over there to do it."

"I helped with putting in the new roof on your house."

"That's not the same thing."

"Then I'll come along and watch. I need to learn, right?"

I eyed him warily. "Are you planning on sticking around?"

He shrugged one shoulder, not really looking at me. "Maybe. It was nice working here, you know, having a day job."

"You love your job," I pointed out.

"How do you know?"

"Joe, you're saving for your own shop. You wouldn't be doing that if you weren't serious about it."

"Well, maybe I'm not so sure anymore."

I couldn't tell if he was being serious or not. I had a feeling he was only doing this so he could keep an eye on me, and I wasn't sure how I felt about that.

"I've been doing this for a week now. It's not so bad. I figured I could try it out for six months and see if it works."

"Fine, you can come, but you do everything I tell you to."

"Fine."

"Alright, call Mrs. Cranston and let her know that I'm coming by. Joe, let's go load up the truck."

We worked in silence, me handing him things we would need and him putting it in the bed of the pickup. I couldn't be sure that we had everything we needed, but if it was just a small job, we should have everything we needed. When I pulled up to the curb, Mrs. Cranston wasn't her usual jovial self. It was fucking depressing.

"Mrs. Cranston, you have a leak?"

"Yes, I'll show you where."

The pity in her eyes killed me. I just wanted normal. Was that really too much to ask? I didn't want everyone looking at me like some charity case. We got to work on finding the leak. I walked Joe through the process of assessing the damage and how to replace everything properly. To my surprise, he paid attention and dug into the work, doing everything I asked and actually did a good job. By the time we were done, I felt lighter than I had in days. I was sweating and dirty, but it felt good. I could deal with this. I could move on as long as I kept putting one foot in front of the other. Life would continue. It wouldn't be as bright as it would have been with Angel in the world, but at least the pain wouldn't be so intense.

I stayed at the office later than I should have, but getting wrapped up in work had helped so much that I just couldn't stand the thought of going home. Once I was home, there would just be an emptiness there. I knew that I should be there for Kat. I knew that she was hurting. But I couldn't just sit around and feel sad. I needed to do something that would make my life feel like it meant something again.

But it wasn't as easy as just staying at the office. Anna was pretty much running everything now, and she kept reminding me that she didn't need me going over every last detail. After her fifth glare, I finally left the office. I noticed she left right after me. I drove home and with every mile I felt a little more like I was returning to hell.

When I pulled into the driveway, I just sat in my truck for a good ten minutes, trying to will myself to go inside.

Sighing, I grabbed my stuff and headed inside. Kat's mom was at the kitchen table, a cup of tea in her hands. When she saw me, there was a sad resignation in her eyes.

"How's Kat?"

"Sleeping."

"Did she get up today?"

Her mom shook her head. "I could barely get her to eat anything. I was going to have her take a shower, but I knew I couldn't do it myself."

"Why?"

"She's too weak. I'm not sure if it's from the delivery or if…if she just doesn't have it in her. I can't hold her up in the shower."

Shit. Now I felt like crap that I had been gone all day and her mother was having to deal with this. I knew she didn't mind taking care of her daughter, but she wouldn't be able to stay here forever. Besides, it wasn't her job to take care of her anymore. That was my job, and I was failing at it. "I'll take care of it."

"I'm going to head back to the hotel for the night. I'll be here in the morning bright and early."

"You can stay here," I reminded her.

"I know, but you two need this time together. And Katherine doesn't need me hovering over her night and day."

I wasn't so sure about that. From what I had seen, that was exactly what Kat needed. I said goodbye and headed upstairs to see Kat. If she wasn't asleep, I was going to have her take a shower. If she was, it would have to wait until morning.

"Kat?"

She didn't respond, but that didn't mean much. She had barely spoken since she had been home. The most I heard out of her was when she was yelling at the funeral. I walked further into the room and bent down in front of her. She looked peaceful as she slept. Her face wasn't sad and she didn't look defeated, but I knew that would all change the moment she woke up. I kissed her on her forehead and went into the bathroom to take a shower. When I came out, she was still asleep, but she had rolled over to my side of the bed. I slipped under the covers and pulled her in close to me. This was the first time since the night we came home from the hospital that she was laying on my chest. It felt right to have her with me again, to have her body draped over mine. It only took a few minutes for me to fall asleep.

When I woke in the morning, Kat was staring up at the ceiling as she laid on her back. I watched her for a few minutes, but she showed no signs of recognizing that I was in bed with her. She was just blank.

"Kat."

I got no response.

"Kat."

Still nothing. I shifted closer to her and gently tilted her face until she was looking at me. She blinked, but her facial expression didn't change.

"How about we take a shower?"

"I'm tired," she said quietly. She returned to staring at the ceiling. I almost let it go, but then I thought of her mom, being stuck here with her all day and not able to get her to do anything. I had to do my part to try and pull Kat out of this state.

"I know you are, baby, but you have to get cleaned up. I'll help you, okay?"

She didn't respond. I got out of bed and pulled back the covers, sighing when I saw that she had bled through her pad and it was all over the bed. Thank God I had a water-proof mattress pad. I lifted her in my arms, but she was like dead weight. She didn't try to wrap her arms around me or even lean her head against my chest. I brought her into the bathroom and set her down in the shower, stripping her nightgown over her head. It was covered in blood, but I couldn't deal with that right now. I tossed it onto the bed and turned on the shower, then stripped my own clothes.

"Kat, I need you to hold yourself up." She ignored me, or maybe she didn't hear me. I wasn't sure which it was. I bent down and forced her to look at me again. "Kat, listen to me. I need you to help me out here. I'll get you cleaned up, but I need you to hold yourself up, okay?"

She finally looked at me, like it finally clicked with her that someone was there with her, talking to her. She nodded gripped the shower bar with a shaky hand while I got to work. After cleaning her up, I knew that I didn't have time to shower myself. Her legs were shaking bad, so I got out and wrapped her in a towel. After wrapping a towel around myself, I grabbed a pair of pants for her and a t-shirt, along with some underwear. As I dressed her, I heard her shaky breaths, like getting dressed was too much of a struggle for her.

I still had to make the bed and there was no way I was letting her stay in bed all day today. She needed to start getting up and moving around, even if her body and her mind were telling her not to. Just as I was bringing her downstairs her mom walked through the door. She looked happy to see her downstairs, but when I shook my head, her smile dropped. I set her down on the couch and knelt down in front of her, once again bringing her face to meet my gaze.

"Kat, I have to go into work, but your mom is here, okay?"

She just stared at me. I couldn't stand to see that blank expression. She could see me, I knew she could, but it was like she was looking right through me, as if my voice was just some distant sound.

"Kat, I know you're hurting, but you can't do this to yourself. You need to try and do something today. Anything. Sit with your mom and watch TV or talk to her as she makes breakfast. Can you do that?"

She nodded slightly.

"Good. And I need you to eat something for me. Can you do that?"

She nodded again and then leaned back against the couch, like she was too exhausted to do anything else. I sighed and met her mother in the kitchen.

"She doesn't look any better today," her mom said worriedly.

"She's not. She just stares off at nothing. She was wide awake this morning, just staring at the ceiling. When I went to get her up for a shower, I noticed that she had bled through her pad. It's all over the bed. I have no idea how long ago that happened. I don't know if she doesn't care or if she just can't deal with it." I ran my hand over my jaw and sighed. "I have to go clean up the bedroom and get to work."

"I'll take care of it. Where are the spare sheets?"

"In the hall closet. Thank you."

"Maybe she'll be better now that she's not in bed."

"God, I hope so. I don't know how to get through to her."

"Maybe she just needs some time," her mother said hopefully.

"Yeah, maybe."

I hoped she was right, but I had a feeling that if I didn't pull Kat out of this soon, I wouldn't ever be able to reach her.

KATHERINE

"Honey? Chrissy is here to see you."

I stared off into space from my spot on the couch. I heard her. I knew that I had to sit up and participate. I just didn't want to. I saw her walk in front of me and I gave a smile, though it was really only for her benefit. I had nothing to smile about.

"How are you feeling?"

"Fine, for the most part."

And I was fine. My body was healing and I didn't really hurt anymore, but the ache in my chest was devastating. I hadn't cried since the funeral and I wasn't sure I would ever cry again. There was nothing left in me. My mind flashed back to the funeral, seeing my baby girl being lowered into the ground. I think that was the moment that I knew I just didn't have it in me to feel anything. That was the absolute worst thing that could ever happen to me. Nothing would ever be as painful as that. So, I shut down and refused to acknowledge anything except the very basics. I knew my mom was worried about me. I heard her whispering with Eric, asking him to do something to pull me out of this blank state. It was almost funny to think that they thought they could fix me.

It didn't escape my notice that Eric seemed to be just fine. He was kind and gentle with me, but aside from me being an annoyance to him, he seemed to function fine. He went into work every day and carried on conversations with his brothers. I heard him on the phone talking with his parents. He said he was doing fine. He appeared fine, so why wasn't I? Why couldn't I just brush this off like he did?

Chrissy's hand touched mine and I looked down at her perfectly manicured fingers on top of my own. I raised my gaze to meet hers and realized that she had been speaking to me all this time. I was just staring off into space like I always did.

"Sorry," I mumbled, though I wasn't really sorry. It was irritating to sit here and pretend that I was okay. I hated trying to hold a conversation with someone when the grief was still so strong that the thought of idle chit chat made me want to scream.

"How's everything at work? Is Charlene bitching because I'm not back?"

"No, she's actually been pretty understanding about it."

I nodded, thinking about how I was supposed to return to work after having time off after the baby was born. She probably would have been pissed at me for taking such a long maternity leave, but somehow losing a baby made people feel they had to be nicer. Would she be nice to me when I finally went back or would she be her same bitchy self? I almost preferred the latter. I wasn't sure if I could take my boss, the woman that hated everyone, to be nice to me.

"How's Eric?"

My eyes flicked up to hers and I realized that yet again, I had missed more of the conversation.

"I'm sorry, I…" I stood without saying anything else and walked out of the room. I didn't have it in me to talk to anyone. It was hard enough having my mom here all the time, but visitors were too much. And I was sure that any day now, I would have half the town descending on me. I walked upstairs and shut the door behind me once I got in my room. Sighing, I laid down on my bed and stared at the ceiling. When would the pain pass? When would I feel like I could function on some level again?

The door opened and my mom walked in, sitting on the edge of the bed. "Chrissy left."

I didn't say anything.

"She wasn't upset. She said she understood that you needed space."

Was that really all it was? Did I only need space?

"Honey, I know you don't want to, but you need to start doing more around here. You're drowning in your own grief. Maybe getting up and doing small things will help."

"Eric said the same thing."

"He's right. You need to start living."

I didn't want to start living. I didn't want to get up and do stuff. I just wanted to be numb to everything. But the only way I was going to get everyone off my back was to actually do what they asked.

"I'll try."

ERIC

It took me twenty-five minutes to leave the office after I stepped onto the sidewalk. Everyone that passed had some kind of condolences to share with me. I gritted my teeth and listened, even though I really wanted to tell them all to fuck off. Didn't they know I didn't want to talk about it? Did they want to see me have a breakdown? Was that the goal?

I got in my truck and headed back home, praying that something was different tonight. I was reaching my limit with Kat's comatose state. I didn't know what to do for her, and I wasn't sure that anything I was saying was helpful at all. It seemed like every time I talked to her, she was off on another planet.

Even my brothers were mysteriously absent around the house. As much as they annoyed the fuck out of me, right now I would give anything for them to be there, just to fill the silence. When Kat's mom left at the end of every day, it was just me sitting with Kat, wishing I could say something to help her. I tried to get her to watch TV, thinking I might be able to distract her even for a half hour. But she just stared at the TV. I knew she wasn't really seeing it. I tried to tell her about my day, but again, she just stared off into space. Her responses were short when she was listening, and I could tell that she was only putting forth half the effort.

I trudged up the stairs to my house. Every day, I hated coming back here a little more. I hated sitting alone with Kat. I hated walking past the baby's room every night. I hated the dreams I had about our baby. The worst ones were the ones where she lived. Because when I woke up, the pain was twice as bad.

When I walked in, I knew today was going to be the same as every other night. I set my keys down and took off my boots, then walked over to the counter where Kat's mom had set my dinner. I ate as if it was the most delicious meal in the world, but in reality, I never tasted anything. It was all an act. My whole world was one large show I was putting on to pretend that I was okay.

"How was your day?" Kat's mom asked as she walked into the kitchen.

"Good. I got a couple new jobs. They're going to keep me busy for a while."

"That's good," she smiled. She glanced into the living room and sighed. "I wish I could find something for Katherine to do. Something to distract her."

"Did she do anything today?"

"She made dinner."

I glanced down at my plate in surprise. "Really?"

"Well, I told her that I hurt my wrist," she whispered. "It was the only way I could see to get her to do something."

"I'm surprised it worked."

Her smile fell. "Well, she's upstairs now. I think making dinner wore her out."

I sighed and ran a hand over my face. "I don't know what else to do for her. I feel like I'm failing at everything."

"It's going to take time. You can't make her better. She has to decide that she wants to get better."

"There's this total disconnect with us. It's like we're strangers living in the same house."

"She's like that with everyone. We just have to give her more time.

Keep pushing her to do things. Eventually, she'll get into some kind of routine. It may take a while, but eventually she'll come back to us."

"But will she still want me?" I asked, laying my fears out for her. "I don't know, I'm just not sure there's any coming back from this."

"Don't give up. You know she loves you. You just have to believe that your love is strong enough to get through this."

That was the kicker of all this. I didn't know that we were strong enough. It's not like we were dating before she got pregnant. Everything we had built was because we were having a baby. I loved her, more than anything in this world, but I wasn't sure she really felt the same way about me. What if she decided that she'd had enough, that we weren't worth fighting for? Would I argue with her on that point? After everything she'd been through, I wasn't sure I had it in me to *not* give her whatever she wanted, even if that included space from me. I just prayed that it didn't come to that.

KATHERINE

I wasn't sure how much time had passed. The days all blended together in one long blur. People came and went all day long. It seemed like I was never alone. Friends from town came to visit and brought me food, and of course, they always made me eat some. Some of the old ladies from town even came out for a visit, though they really only talked with Mom. I just sat there, trying to pretend that I was there. Physically, I was, but mentally, I had checked out. It was the only way that I could deal with any of this.

After Angel's funeral, it was like my mind just shut down. The only way I could deal with the emotions running through me was to not feel them at all. I stuffed all that shit in a sack and tossed it to a very far corner of my mind. But along with that, it seemed everything had left me. I didn't remember what happened most days, but I know that from time to time I got up and did something. One day, I helped my mom with the dishes. Another day, I folded a blanket that I had used and put it on the back of the couch. I knew it wasn't much, but I had promised Eric that I would do something every day.

"Honey?"

I looked up at my mom with a vacant stare, noticing that she had on her coat and had a bag next to her. She was leaving. I wasn't sure how I felt about that. I liked that I wouldn't have to deal with anyone constantly trying to get my attention. But I also worried that the silence would be too much to deal with.

"I have to get back home. Do you think you can handle being alone?"

I didn't have a choice. She couldn't just stay here and babysit me all day. And now that I knew I could do minor things, it wouldn't be too bad. I would probably be fine.

I grabbed her hand and felt her squeeze mine. "Thank you for being here."

Her eyes shone bright as she looked back at me. I knew that this had been hard on my mom, but she had stuck by my side the whole time, doing anything she could to help me through. But it was time for me to start doing things for myself. I didn't want to, but I couldn't just rely on others for the rest of my life. It wouldn't be the same without Angel in it, but I could start off small. That was all I was ready for.

She bent down and gave me a hug. I held her tight, for the first time feeling something. I was sad she was leaving. "I'll call you tomorrow, okay?"

"Okay."

I heard Eric walking her out and then his heavy footsteps came back into the living room. He stared at me for a moment and I lifted my head to look at him.

"Are you going to be okay here alone during the day?"

"Yeah."

He sat down on the couch across from me, rubbing his hands together. "Kat, I need to know that you'll be okay here by yourself. You need to make sure you eat and shower. Can you do that?"

I felt like I was being scolded. I knew how to do all that stuff for myself. I was just sad and overwhelmed with everything that had happened. I needed time to adjust. Didn't he see that?

"I'll be fine."

He nodded, but he didn't look convinced. "It's been three weeks,

Kat. I know this is hard on you, but you have to start living again. Maybe go into town and go to the store, or just go grab a coffee."

It had been three weeks? How had that much time passed without me noticing? I knew that time had been passing, but I didn't really recall anything that happened. And how had my mom and Eric been dealing with me? He was right, something had to change. I couldn't keep putting this burden on Eric to take care of me. But going into town? No, I couldn't do that. I wasn't ready for that. I would do better tomorrow. It would be a new day and I would make sure that I actually accomplished something big tomorrow.

I swallowed hard and nodded. "I'll be fine."

I made a point of getting up when Eric got up the next morning. I didn't want to. All I really wanted to do was stay in bed, but I promised Eric that I could take care of myself. I was still reeling from finding out that it had already been three weeks. Where had Eric been all that time? Had he been off at work? Surely I would have remembered if Eric had been there with me. Did he not feel the loss of our daughter like I did? If he had, wouldn't he have been there with me, grieving for her every day? How could he just go into work every day and pretend like nothing had happened? I was shattered, barely moving from one day to the next, but as I walked downstairs, I saw that he was moving around, checking his phone as if he didn't have a care in the world. Meanwhile, my whole world had crashed around me.

His eyes flashed to mine and he slowly put his phone away. "How are you this morning?"

The question irritated me. Like there was another way to be? "Fine."

"You say that every day, Kat."

"What else do you want me to say?"

He sighed heavily. "The truth."

My eyebrows shot up. "You want the truth?"

"It would be nice. I'm surprised you're speaking at all, so maybe I should take that as a win, but yes, I want to know how you really are."

"I'm...numb. It takes everything in me to move forward every day.

I don't want to get out of bed. I don't want to have these pointless conversations. I hate that you're just moving on with life while I'm stuck here in this painful non-existence. I hate you for being able to shove it all aside like our daughter didn't matter. You're just moving on with life."

"What would you have me do?" he asked tiredly. "Should I sit around here with you all day and feel sorry for myself?"

"You think that's what I'm doing all day?"

"I don't know what's going on in your head. This is the first conversation I've had with you where you actually talked back. Most of the time, you just stare right through me. That's not living, Kat. That's not even trying. I don't know how to help you. I can't make you want to live again."

"Because I don't want to live again!" I shouted.

"And you think I do?" he shouted, pounding his chest with his fist. "I have to go out there every day and get hounded by people that want to know every last detail about how we're doing. I have to listen to their condolences, and you think that's easy to deal with?"

"You say you don't want to live, but you were back to work the day after the funeral. You didn't even take a week off. It was like our daughter died and you just decided that work was more important. You had my mom stay with me, probably so you didn't have to deal with me. And let's not forget about that little comment you made in the hospital."

"What comment?"

"You said *it sucks* when our daughter died. I knew that you were rigid and cold when I met you, but that was low even for you."

He scoffed, taking a step away from me. "Wow, it's great to know that you think I'm even more of an asshole than I had assumed." He ran his hand over his face, and I found myself wishing that his hand was running up and down my back, comforting me like he used to. I wasn't sure how I could be so upset at him, but need his comfort at the same time. "I have to get to work."

He walked past me and grabbed his jacket off the hook by the back door. "That's it? You're just leaving?"

"One of us has to bring in the money, Kat. We can't both sit around here and be miserable."

With that, he opened the door and stormed out. The door slammed behind him, reverberating through my body. For the first time since the funeral, my throat closed up and tears spilled down my cheeks. Nothing was right. I was losing it, and I didn't know how to get myself back.

ERIC

I got off work early tonight so I could go grocery shopping. I knew there was no way I would get Katherine to do so. After our argument the other day, neither of us was speaking to the other. I knew she was hurting, but it had been three weeks and she was still barely functioning. I was supposed to take care of her, to make sure that she would be okay, but I didn't have the first clue how to do that. I thought about bringing in a grief counselor, but she had flat out rejected that in the hospital. I wasn't sure that was the way to go.

I pushed the cart through the grocery store, loading up tons of meat and vegetables. I was going to stock that fridge with so much food that hopefully it would inspire her to at least cook. Hell, I would take a half-assed meal right now if it meant I didn't have to eat peanut butter sandwiches.

"Eric?"

I turned and saw a high school classmate come sauntering over. She was just as pretty as she was in high school, but you could tell the years had filled her out into a classic beauty. Not that it did anything for me. She had never been my type, and I had Kat now. I wasn't sure there could ever be another woman that turned my head.

"Hey, Sheila."

She walked up to me and rested her hand on my arm. "I heard about what happened. I'm so sorry. How are you?"

She tilted her head in that way that people do when they want to show sympathy. It pissed me off. It felt fake. I hadn't seen this woman in years, but suddenly she felt she had to come talk to me.

"I'm doing fine."

"Aw," she said sympathetically. "It must be so hard. How's your girlfriend doing?"

"She's fine," I said with more confidence than I had. The last thing I needed was the town gossiping about Kat.

"I can't even imagine what she's going through." She looked around and then leaned in closer. "I heard that she can't even get out of bed. Poor thing."

My blood boiled. I didn't have the slightest clue if the gossip mill had started because someone had talked or if people were just drawing their own conclusions. Either way, I was stopping this shit right now.

"She's doing fine. She's not stuck in bed, so whoever told you that can fuck off."

She jerked back in surprise at my tone, but I didn't give a fuck. I always tried to be nice to people, but the last thing I was going to deal with was a bunch of nosy assholes spreading rumors just for the sake of something to gossip about.

"I didn't mean-"

"I know exactly what you meant. Do you think I don't see the whole fucking town staring at me anytime I go anywhere? Do you think I don't see their pitying looks or notice that everyone stops talking as soon as I walk in a room? Instead of worrying about what's going on with me, why don't you figure out your own shit? My family is none of your concern. We haven't talked to each other in years, and I'd prefer we keep it that way."

I shoved my cart forward, ignoring all the people staring at me. Shit. I had lost it on a woman in front of a good portion of the town.

How long would it take to spread that shit around? I finished with my shopping and headed to the checkout lane. People moved out of my way, like I was going to snap at them as well. I sighed in irritation. Just because I snapped one time didn't make me a monster.

I unloaded my groceries on the conveyor belt and gritted my teeth as the cashier kept glancing up at me with fear in her eyes. The bagger very gently packed each item, like I would actually snap at someone for how they packed my groceries. I looked over my shoulder to the checkout line behind me. Everyone quickly looked away. Goddamnit, I was ready to just leave the groceries and walk away.

"Um...Mr. Cortell?"

"What?" I snapped.

"Um...your total is one hundred fifty-seven dollars and twenty-two cents."

"Fine." I pulled out my wallet and grabbed some cash, tossing it down on the conveyor belt. I narrowed my eyes at the guy watching my every move two lanes over. He quickly turned around, but kept glancing over his shoulder.

"Um...Mr. Cortell," the cashier said.

"What?"

"Um...it's just that..."

"What?"

"I'm sorry-"

"You know what? I don't want to hear it. I don't need your pity or your sad looks. In fact," I said, taking a step back and raising my voice for everyone to hear. "I would prefer it if all of you would just fuck off." There were a few gasps, but I wasn't even close to being done. "The last fucking thing I need is for everyone to stare at me all the time. How would you like it if everyone was staring at you all the time or discussing your personal life?"

I turned to the woman in the next aisle and grinned. "I'm sure you would love it if everyone was discussing your boob job you had last year. Yeah, didn't think anyone knew about it, huh?"

The woman turned bright red and grabbed her stuff before storming out.

"Or how about you, Gene? How would you like it everyone discussed the affair you had with the Queen of the Corn Fest last year?" He turned bright red, but I wasn't done yet. "Or maybe we should talk about how the only way that your wife gets through the day is by drinking a fifth of whiskey every night."

The manager walked over to me. "Mr. Cortell-"

"Sam, I'm glad you came over here. Does everyone know that you're working three jobs to support your family? Or that you have to do it because you had to put your mom in a mental hospital?"

His face turned angry, but he didn't say anything.

"Yeah, it seems it's not so fun when everyone's gossiping about you. This is why I don't live in town. At least in the country I can get away from all the bullshit in town. You want to know how we're doing? Pay attention, because I'm only saying this once. Kat is doing as well as can be expected. After all, we just lost our first child. I'm going to work, just barely functioning so I don't have to think about the agonizing pain of losing my daughter. Nothing is right between us right now, but I'm sure you can all guess why. After all, you've all been shoving your noses in my business since you found out that I knocked Kat up. So, what else do you want to know? You want to know if we're fucking again? You want to know if she's going to leave me? I know that's what you're all thinking. So," I leaned forward and looked at the cashier's name tag, "Kelly, what was it that you wanted to ask me?"

She looked around at everyone else before clearing her throat. "I was just going to tell you that you're twenty dollars short."

I looked down at the money that she had laid down on the belt and counted it. I was twenty dollars short, and apparently, a giant asshole. I pulled out another twenty and tossed it on the counter. I stalked to the end of the belt and grabbed the shopping cart, walking out of there like I hadn't just humiliated myself in front of half the town.

∽

I slammed the door open and carried in my groceries. I was pissed, mostly at myself for losing my temper. I was normally so level-headed, but right now, I wasn't thinking straight about anything.

"I see you've had a productive day," Joe said, calmly drinking from his cup. I tossed the bags down on the table and marched back out to get the rest. I heard his footsteps behind me. "Did you decide that you just couldn't adult today?"

"You're an asshole," I said, not bothering to face him.

"No, that would be you."

"Yeah? And why's that?"

"Well, you're all over the town Facebook page right now. Apparently, someone recorded your little outburst at the register. Got it all on camera. Talk about spilling the tea. You demolished a few people's lives in the span of five minutes."

"I thought you were over talking like a dipshit."

"See? Right there. You've always been a little salty, but right now, I don't even recognize the man standing in front of me."

"Maybe I'm just sick of your shit."

"My shit? I'm pretty sure that everyone's been taking more shit from you since Angel died than is really necessary."

I spun around and glared at him. "Don't fucking say her name."

"Why not? You don't want people talking to you about her? Or you just don't want to think about her?"

"You have no fucking clue what you're talking about."

"I know you were an asshole in town tonight because people were trying to be nice to you. I know that a bunch of people deserve an apology for the shit you said."

"Fuck you," I spat. "You don't know what the fuck you're talking about."

"I know that people in this town want to help you in any way they can, but you're being an asshole to everyone. God forbid that anyone look at you and feel sad for you. It's not fucking pity."

"That's exactly what it is," I shouted.

"No, it's not. You're just too much of an asshole to see it."

I lost it and dropped my bags, charging at my brother. I slammed into him, tackling him to the ground and then started punching him in the face. He didn't even fight me. He fucking grinned at me with blood dripping from his mouth.

"Go ahead, asshole. Punch me again."

I reared back and slammed my fist into his face one last time before arms wrapped around me and dragged me off him. My chest was heaving and my eye was twitching out of control. My whole body was shaking as adrenaline pulsed through me. I wanted to go another five rounds with him, but the arms holding me back prevented me from going after him.

He pushed up on one elbow and swiped at his lip, taking in the blood that was pouring from his mouth. I might have knocked out a tooth. Then he started chuckling. "You're so fucked up. You can't even see what's going on."

I tried to go at him again, but I was still being held back.

"When are you going to open your eyes and see that these people care about you? Yeah, it's fucking annoying, but we're a community. We grew up here. Hell, half of them covered up the trouble that we got into. When we robbed the bank, they played along with us. They could have thrown our asses in jail, but they didn't. And when you started up your lawn care business as a teenager, how many of them hired you? Do you think Mr. Johnson needed you to do his lawn? You know how fucking picky he is about his lawn. But he hired you because he wanted to help you build your business. And you just went in there tonight and destroyed everything. I get that you're hurting, but destroying everyone else isn't going to make you feel better."

He stood and brushed himself off, spitting out the blood in his mouth.

"You know, I always looked up to you. You were my responsible older brother that I wanted to be just like. Now...I'm sorry to call you my brother."

He walked away, stalking up the stairs to the house. Kat was standing just inside the door, but she turned away when she saw me looking at her. My arms were released and Andrew started walking away.

"Are you pissed at me too?"

"Disappointed." He sighed, shaking his head slightly. "You can't push everyone away, Eric. At some point, you gotta let others help."

I put my hands on my hips and stared at the ground. I went from being the responsible guy that everyone could count on to the man that everyone was disappointed in. I was doing everything I could to take care of Kat and help her through this, but in the process I was destroying us and pissing off the whole town. I didn't know how to make things change, but I knew that I had some apologies I had to make.

I grabbed the groceries and headed inside to put them away. No one was around the house. They had all disappeared to their rooms. Kat was no doubt in bed already, and she would ignore me after what she just witnessed. I sat down at the kitchen table, my whole body drooping in defeat. There was so much I wished that I could change. Nothing in my life was going right. But one thing I would never change was getting Kat pregnant. Even though we lost the baby, I knew a happiness I had only dreamed about. But Angel was in the past now. I couldn't bring her back. Thinking about her constantly would only make this harder. What I needed to do was get Kat and myself back to a place where we could move forward. Because if we didn't move forward, I would lose her.

~

Taking a deep breath, I walked up the steps to Sam's house and knocked. I knew he wasn't working this morning, because I had called the grocery store to find out. It was time to eat crow. The woman at the grocery store knew who I was immediately, and she didn't want to help me out, but when I explained why I needed to see Sam, she sighed and gave me his schedule. That is, after she told me that I was being an asshole, but she still felt sorry for me and wished the best for Kat and I. It made me feel even worse.

MAINTENANCE REQUIRED

The door opened and Sam stared at me in shock, but he didn't slam the door. I took that as a good sign. He stepped out onto the porch, shutting the door behind him.

"Mary said you were coming by, but I didn't believe it."

"Of course she did," I muttered. "Is there anything that goes on in this town that people don't know about?"

"Well, nobody knew about me putting my mother in a mental institution until last night," he said with a slight laugh.

I winced, rubbing the back of my neck. "I'm really sorry about that. I guess I lost it."

"Understandable. I'm sure everyone has been coming up to you a lot lately."

"Worse than when they found out I got Kat pregnant."

He huffed out a laugh. "I don't know, that Facebook group can be brutal. Listen, I know that you may not want to hear this, but everyone in this town cares about you. That's why they're so damn nosy. But you have to understand, everyone in this town has watched you grow up from just a young kid. We've all watched as you've had your successes. They just want to be there to help you with your losses too."

"Is that why you didn't tell anyone about your mom?"

"You know, I've had at least fifty calls since you outed me. Everything from words of sympathy to people offering to help me out in any way they can. Honestly, it was a relief. One of my employers heard about my situation and offered me a different position with better hours and benefits. It'll allow me to quit my third job."

"That's great."

He smiled. "Look, I know you didn't mean any of the shit you said yesterday. I know this is a hard time for you, and everyone else in town knows that too. Apologize to Kelly, Gene, and Big Tits Linda. I'm sure they'll all forgive you."

"Big Tits Linda?"

"What? Did you really think that people didn't know about her boob job? Just because it's not discussed on Facebook doesn't mean it hasn't gone through the rumor mill."

"And everyone else in the store?"

"Trust me, they'll all know that you came to apologize. The minute you hung up with Mary this morning, I can guarantee that she spread it all through the store. It's probably halfway around town right now. By tomorrow, nobody's going to be talking about this."

"So, we're good?"

"There was never a problem, Eric." He shook my hand and smiled. I didn't feel better, but it was a relief that I hadn't alienated half the town. My brother was right, they had always been there to support me. I just had to learn to accept that people wanted to help out.

KATHERINE

After Eric's embarrassing debacle in the grocery store, I was pissed. It was bad enough that people were talking about us nonstop because we lost the baby. Now they were gossiping because he was a giant asshole to everyone in that store. It took several days for me to calm down and finally see that he was just frustrated. He was one the one dealing with the non stop questions while I hid out at home.

So, here I was, making dinner for him, trying to show him that I still stood by him. I was putting in more effort than I had in over a month. The pain was still just as real as the day I lost her, but at least I could function now. I had to. My parents were worried about me and I hated to see them worry.

Every day was a struggle. It wasn't just that I had lost my child. I had lost the life I thought I was building with Eric. He was distant now, never coming too close to me. We didn't snuggle in bed. He never kissed me, not even on the forehead. All affection had disappeared. We weren't acting like two people that loved each other, but two people that were just existing together.

And being in this house was torture. It killed me to walk past the baby's room. We hadn't even gone in there since Eric closed the door sometime after we came home from the hospital. I wasn't sure I ever would. This whole house just reminded me of everything I was supposed to have. I hated it. I wanted to burn it down, and had thought about it several times. The only thing that stopped me was that it wasn't my house. It was Eric's parents' house and they had given it to him.

I rubbed my hand across my forehead, my hand shaking slightly. I was losing it, thinking of burning down houses. Eric would have me committed if he knew those thoughts had crossed my mind. I heard his truck pull in and swiped at my face, making sure that I appeared normal. I needed to make an effort for him. It wasn't much, but it was better than I had been.

Eric walked in the door and tossed his keys on the counter. I stood at the stove, my apron tied around me as I put the finishing touches on dinner. When Eric glanced up, his eyes widened in surprise.

"Hey," he said quietly.

"Hey."

He didn't comment on the fact that I was cooking for him. I had done it in the past, but I was making a real meal with all the fixings. And I was dressed in real clothes, not pajamas or sweats. I had even somewhat done my hair. I was trying to put in the effort here.

"You look nice."

"Thank you."

The awkward silence was too much, so I broke eye contact and finished with dinner. Eric got out plates and glasses, then the silverware. It was like it had been before, except he wasn't as affectionate as he used to be. Maybe he didn't know how to, or maybe he just didn't feel that way.

I put the dish on the table between us and sat down. "How was your day?"

"Good," he said, dishing out some food onto my plate before moving to his own. "Lots of work coming in. Thank God, Robert found Anna for me. She's been whipping the whole place into shape. I'd be lost without her."

It shouldn't bother me that he would be lost without his office manager, but after weeks of feeling desperately alone, it hit me hard. I took a deep breath and picked up my fork. Each movement was forced, but this was what people did after a loss. They pushed through and moved on.

"Is Joe still working with you?"

"Yeah. He's actually a natural, but I'm thinking of telling him to go back to his job."

"Why?"

"Because it's not what he wants to do. He's trying to save up for a tattoo parlor, and instead he's hovering around me."

I nodded, wondering if I would ever want to go back to work. Would he expect me to? "I'm not sure I can go back to working at the hospital," I said tentatively.

"Do you know what else you would want to do?"

I huffed out a laugh. "I just got dressed today and made dinner. Work plans seem like such a big decision."

"You could always join a private practice."

I cleared my throat. Thinking that far in the future was intimidating. I was barely putting one foot in front of the other. What made him think I was ready to switch jobs and just pick up life?

"I was thinking maybe we should go out this weekend."

My head snapped up. "What?"

"It'll be good for you to get out of the house. We could get dinner and go dancing. It might cheer you up."

I couldn't believe it. Was it really that simple for him? Just go out and get some dinner and suddenly everything's better? Maybe that's the way it was for guys, but for me? Just the thought of mingling with other people when I felt so broken made my skin break out in hives. That was my child. I carried her for eight months. I just lost her a month ago, and he wanted me to go out and put a smile on my face.

I put my fork down and pushed back from the table. When I walked past him, he grabbed my hand. "Kat-"

I jerked out of his grasp, my eyes filling with tears. "Is it really that easy for you? Go out to dinner and just forget what happened?"

"Kat, I'm not suggesting that dinner will make this better, but-"

"No. No buts, Eric. You don't get it. I had my little girl for eight months and then she was ripped from me. I had to deliver our dead child and then bury her in the ground. So, no. After a month, I'm not ready to just go out and get some dinner and go dancing."

"You can't just hide in the house all day. Can't you see that this isn't helping?"

"I can see that you're not helping," I shot back.

He stiffened and slowly set down his fork. "What exactly do you want from me, Kat? If you think that I don't feel the pain of losing our child, you're wrong. But I can't just sit around all day. I need to do something. I can't just drown in my misery like you are."

"I'm not drowning in my misery! I'm hurting. I feel dead inside. Don't you get it? There's nothing left inside me to give. I wish I could go out with you and have it how it used to be, but I just can't. I can't give you what you need. I don't want to have sex. I don't want to kiss. I can't even stand to look at you because it's a reminder of what we had."

He stared at me warily. "What's that supposed to mean? You don't want to be with me?"

Tears slipped down my face and struggled to think of what I was trying to say, but I was a mess. I wasn't sure what I wanted. "I don't know what I want. I just know that pushing me to be something I may never be isn't going to help."

He pushed back his chair and stood, taking hold of my hand. "Then tell me this, Kat. Do you still want to be with me, or did we lose everything when we lost Angel?"

"I don't know," I whispered.

It was true. I just didn't know which way was up anymore. Maybe what I really needed was to just be free of any reminders of Angel. Being here in this house, where I was supposed to raise my daughter, was just too painful. To walk past her room every day and know that she wasn't in there made me want to cry every single time. But, the biggest reminder was Eric. I loved this man, but I felt like I had failed. I was supposed to be able to have kids, but I hadn't protected my child. She died inside me. How could Eric ever look at me the way he used to? I couldn't even contemplate having kids in the future, and Eric wanted a family. Maybe this was never meant to be. Maybe it *would* be better if we weren't together. Eric wouldn't have to worry about me every day, and I could maybe move on if I wasn't in this house.

He stepped back from me and shoved his hands in his pockets. He looked defeated and I hated that I was doing that to him, but I didn't know how to move on. Maybe this was the only way. Maybe I needed to get away from him so I could heal myself.

"Eric-"

"It's fine, Kat. I get it."

"You do?"

He shrugged slightly, looking away. "You need more time."

"I need more than time."

He slowly turned back to face me, his eyes filled with trepidation. "What are you saying?"

"I think...I think I need to get my own place."

He stared at me in shock, his beautiful eyes filled with confusion. "What? I thought you just needed more time. Now you're moving out?"

"Maybe it's for the best. I mean, we wouldn't have been together if it weren't for the baby. Look at how long it took us to even be civil to each other."

"Kat, that was then. I love you. Do you still love me?"

My eyes dropped to the floor. I couldn't look at him. I couldn't bear to see the heartbreak on his face. But I couldn't stay here either. "It's not about love. I can't be here. I can't walk past her room every day and know she's not in there."

"So, we'll get rid of the stuff."

"And you think that'll just magically make everything better?" I asked wearily.

"It's better than you walking away."

"It's not just about the house, Eric. We're not the same. This would never have worked between us if we didn't have Angel. Now she's gone. There's nothing holding us together."

He clenched his jaw. "So, that's it. Our daughter is gone and you don't want to be with me now."

"It's not about what I want. It's about what I need."

"And that's to be away from me."

I didn't say anything. I didn't want to be away from him. I just didn't want to feel this pain every time I looked at him. I wanted to go back a year and do things differently. I knew that wasn't possible, but something had to change, and this was the only way I could see to stop the constant bleeding.

When I looked up at him, he no longer looked like the man that loved me. He looked like the man that I had just crushed. I didn't want to do this, but I didn't know how else to move forward.

He nodded slightly, his whole body stiffening. "I'll help you find someplace to stay."

ERIC

I loaded up the last of Katherine's things into the back of my pickup truck and slammed the tailgate. She was inside looking for anything she might have left behind. I leaned against the tailgate, taking a deep breath. I couldn't believe this was happening. The woman I loved was leaving me. And the worst part was, I hadn't fought for her to stay. I didn't know how to. When she looked at me with tears in her eyes and told me that this was what she needed, I just couldn't argue with her. She had been through enough. She didn't need me making this harder on her. But the thought of losing her was like losing Angel all over again.

"Are you ready?" she asked hesitantly.

"Yeah," I said, glad that my voice didn't crack. I was anything but ready for this. I knew the last month and a half had been hard, but I didn't expect this. Now I would have to go to bed every night alone. Even though we hadn't slept wrapped in each other's arms since we lost Angel, I had been comforted by the fact that she was there. I didn't feel so alone. As much as I hated being home because I didn't know how to help Kat, at night, I could lay beside her and pretend that things would be okay. Now, that was all gone. Maybe I should have done things differently. Maybe then she wouldn't be leaving me.

But I couldn't change the past, and I didn't know how to make her want to be with me.

I got into the truck and drove her into town. She had found another townhouse for sale. So, even though she was leaving me, I put a damn deposit down on it and made sure that everything was ready for her. It didn't take too much to have the real estate agent work with me. It turns out, the people in this town really did care about us. Angie, the agent, said that she was sorry that it had come to this, and she would do whatever it took to take care of things swiftly. She had come through a little too quickly for me.

I pulled up to the townhouse and shut off the engine. Glancing out the passenger window, I looked at the cold exterior and sighed. I started unloading the truck as she walked up the steps and unlocked the door. I carried up the first box, but practically ran into her because she had stopped in the doorway. She was staring at the living room, but then turned to me in confusion.

"How did all this furniture get here?"

"I had it delivered yesterday."

"But I didn't order it."

I sighed and set down the box. "Kat, you can't live here without any furniture. I know it's not a lot, but I got what I could for you."

Her brows furrowed. "But...how did you afford all this? I mean, the deposit and now the furniture?"

I didn't answer. It didn't really matter. She needed a place to stay and she had to have at least a little bit of furniture.

"Eric, please tell me you didn't charge all of this."

"No, I...I told the investigator looking into Josh's disappearance to take a few months off."

Tears filled her eyes and she covered her mouth with her hand. "You shouldn't have done that for me."

"Kat, I've been chasing answers for years and I still don't have anything more than the day he disappeared. Taking a few months off won't change that." Her eyes slipped closed, so I hurried on, hoping that it would soften what I told her. "Look, not all of it is new. Mrs. Jenkins is moving in with her son. She gave me her kitchen table. And the coffee table and end tables came from the mayor. He and his wife were getting new furniture, so they sold this to me for cheap. But the bed and the couch are new. I wouldn't sleep or sit on used furniture if I didn't have to."

She shoved her hands in her back pockets and stared at the ground. I wasn't trying to make her feel bad. I just hoped that when she moved in, she would feel a little more comfortable.

"Hey," I said, stepping forward and running my hand up her arm. "I'm just trying to help out."

She swiped at some tears on her face, clearing her throat. "It doesn't seem right to say thank you. After everything that's happened, that just…"

"I wanted to do this, so stop feeling like you don't deserve this."

"I'll pay you back for all this, once I start working again."

"I don't expect you to pay me back. I just want to make sure that you're okay." She nodded and I picked up the box. "So, tell me where to put everything."

Over the course of the next hour, I unloaded the truck and put everything where she wanted it. I thought about staying to help her unpack it all, but there was something about setting up your own house that felt intimate. And since this wasn't my house, and I had no relationship with her, it felt like overstepping to stay any longer.

I walked to the door, each step feeling like a death sentence for me. After this, there was no going back. I would officially be on my own again. And I was letting it happen.

Turning back to her, I shoved my hands in my pockets, but I couldn't look at her. "If you ever need anything, don't hesitate to call me."

"I have to do this on my own," she said quietly.

I nodded, then stepped forward and pulled her into my arms. I wanted to kiss her. Hell, I couldn't remember the last time that I had tasted those sweet lips. I pressed my lips to her forehead and then turned and walked out the door.

Walking into my house, the first thing I noticed was the silence. Even when Kat had been laid up in bed, I always knew she was here. But now, the silence was deafening. My brothers had been mysteriously absent for weeks, only showing up sporadically. I was all alone again. I gripped the back of the kitchen chair and squeezed my fingers around the wood.

The sadness of the situation was replaced with a burning rage. How much more was I supposed to give? I had done everything the way I was supposed to. I took care of Kat. I supported her throughout the pregnancy. I fell in love with her. And then it was all ripped away from me.

I flung the chair across the kitchen as I yelled out. The chair smashed against the wall and the leg snapped off. It clattered to the floor in a heap and I stared at it for a moment. Deciding that it felt pretty good to be the one to lose it, I moved onto the next chair and threw that across the room also. This one smashed into the kitchen cabinets. I moved on and threw the next one, which smashed right through the window, coming to rest half in and half out of the window.

I moved on to the coat rack by the door and swung it like a baseball bat at anything I could. I was like a tornado, ripping apart the house with my fury. After breaking the TV in the living room, I stood there heaving, taking in all the destruction. I dropped the busted up coat rack to the ground and stumbled back into the kitchen, pulling out the whiskey that my brothers kept just in case. I wasn't a drinker, but right now, it sounded like a pretty good idea. I could end this the way it started.

I pulled out the last remaining chair and took a seat, pouring myself a glass of whiskey. I cringed at the strong taste. This probably wasn't a good idea, but I found I didn't really give a shit right now. I finished off the last of the glass with a giant swallow. I must have sat there for a good hour, just numbing myself to the pain. It felt good, to finally let loose and not have to feel in control for once. I poured myself another drink just as I heard a truck pull up. Great, now one of my brothers decided to show up. Perfect timing. I ignored Joe as he walked in with Andrew. I took another drink and stared straight ahead.

"Redecorating?" I looked up as he stared at the chair that was sitting in the window. "I'm not sure company would be comfortable sitting there, but we could try it."

I took another drink as Andrew walked over to the chair laying on the ground. He tried to set it upright, but with one of the legs broken off, it just tilted. He sighed and let it fall back to the floor.

"I take it your bae left," Andrew said.

"She's not my bae," I answered, taking another drink.

I let the whole bae thing slide. When I was drinking, I found I wasn't nearly as irritated by their weird language.

"Where's the coat rack?" Joe asked as he went to hang up his jacket.

I nodded to the living room. He raised an eyebrow at me and headed into the living room.

"Holy shit," he muttered. "I guess we're not watching the game tonight."

I huffed out a laugh and drank some more.

"Maybe you should slow down, Hunty."

I stared at Andrew, his face twisted in concern, and I started laughing. I wasn't sure why I was laughing or what was so funny, but him calling me Hunty just set off something inside me. I couldn't stop laughing once I started. Tears leaked from my eyes and my side hurt from laughing so hard. I poured myself some more to drink, spilling all over the table as my hand shook from me laughing.

Joe crossed his arms over his chest and leaned back against the wall. "So, she left you and you decided that drinking was the way to go?"

I shrugged slightly, laughter still shaking my shoulders. "What else is there to do? Karma's a bitch, you know? I figured I'd finish the way I started."

"You should have fought for her," Andrew muttered.

I raised the glass to my mouth and drank down the whiskey. It was hitting me hard, just like the vodka had that first night with her. If I was lucky, I wouldn't remember any of this day tomorrow.

"Yeah, that sounds like a great idea," I slurred. I stood from my chair, stumbling against the table. I snatched the bottle off the table and took another drink. "The love of my life wants to leave me because it's too fucking painful to be around me, and I should beg her to stay." I huffed out a laugh. "That's sounds like a fucking fantastic plan."

"You need to sit down," Joe admonished.

I spun toward the table and the room tilted sharply. I stumbled and tripped over the leg of the table and went down hard. My face smashed into the floor and I would have groaned, but the alcohol had thoroughly numbed me from feeling anything.

"Should we pick him up?"

"Just fucking leave him. He's on his stomach. If he pukes, he's not gonna choke on it."

I stared across the floor, seeing shards of glass from the broken window. I'd have to clean that up in the morning. I ran my finger over a dirty spot on the floor, grimacing at how dirty it was. I never let my house get this dirty, but I had been busy over the past few weeks, helping Kat get her townhouse. The place she would live without me. How would I keep going, seeing her in town from time to time? Could I really see her and pretend that my fucking heart wasn't breaking? God, I was miserable.

"I just want her back," I mumbled to myself.

"That's not gonna happen if you get drunk and destroy your house."

"Not gonna happen anyway. She doesn't want me."

I heard a heavy sigh and then I was hauled up by both arms. The room tilted all around me and I had to squeeze my eyes shut so I didn't fall over, which only made me feel like I was falling backwards.

"Come on, lover boy. Let's get you upstairs."

"No," I shook my head. Or, I thought I did. "I don't want to sleep in that room. Not without her."

We started moving, but they led me over to the couch where they all but tossed me down. I flopped over and let my arm hang over the edge of the couch. The lights started to dim around me and the hurt faded to a dull ache. This was good. I could do this every night, and just not feel the pain of losing her ever again.

~

My head pounded and my throat felt like it was stuffed with a dishrag. I opened my mouth and worked my jaw, certain that something was going to pop out and explain the lack of moisture inside my mouth. When nothing happened, I peeled open an eyelid and then quickly snapped it shut. The light was too bright and felt like it was stabbing my eyeballs. I groaned and tried to roll over, but ended up landing on the floor with a giant thud.

"And he's awake."

I glanced up slowly to see my brother, Joe, sitting in a chair, drinking coffee. "What are you doing up so early?"

"Early?" He glanced at his watch. "It's nearly noon."

"Noon?" My brows furrowed as I tried to figure out why the hell I had slept so late. I rubbed at my eyes and noticed broken shit all over the floor. The TV had been smashed in and the coat rack lay on the floor completely busted. I scrambled to my feet, swaying slightly as the room tilted.

"Shit, who broke into the house?" I glanced around the room and headed for the kitchen, seeing the chair sitting half in and half out of the window. "Shit. Well, that explains the headache."

"What explains the headache?" Joe asked, walking in behind me.

"They must have knocked me out. Did they get anything?"

He stared at me for a moment and then he busted out laughing. "You think someone else did this?"

My head pounded and I raised a hand to silence him. "Head injury over here. Do you think you could tone it down?"

"Head injury?"

"Yeah, the pounding in my head? Hey, why did you leave me on the floor? Why didn't you take me to the hospital? I could have had a serious injury."

"Yeah, and that serious injury would have been alcohol poisoning, but seeing as how you didn't actually drink that much, I wasn't too worried about it."

I glanced around the room again, struggling to remember anything. "Wait, are you saying *I* did this?"

"No, I'm saying that you got drunk and someone broke into the house just to throw shit around."

I cringed at his harsh tone. "So, did you catch him?"

"Christ, no one broke into the fucking house. You did this!"

I shook my head slightly. "No, I couldn't have. I would remember-"

"No, you wouldn't because you drank whiskey last night. Andrew and I walked in on you drowning your sorrows in a bottle."

"Fuck, I don't remember any of that." I held my head and tried to stop the throbbing. This wasn't like me. I didn't get upset and break shit. I didn't drink.

"Yeah, well, maybe you should find a different outlet for your anger. Ma's gonna be pissed when she finds out you broke her kitchen chairs."

I winced, rubbing at my stomach. God, I felt like shit. I sat down gingerly in the one remaining chair and stared at the damage. I really needed to get to work, but the way I was feeling, I wasn't sure holding a tool or handling phone calls was the way to go.

"Can you call RJ for me?"

"Already done. I told him that you had a meeting out of town."

I nodded, even though it felt more like my head was rolling around on my shoulders. "Thanks."

"Look, I get that you're hurting and this situation sucks, but you need to get your head on straight. The shit you've been pulling lately isn't like you. Now, people are willing to give you some leeway because they know you're going through a hard time, but eventually, they're gonna get sick of this shit and start getting pissed."

I ran my hand through my hair, trying to rub some life back into my body. "I know."

He sighed and yanked the chair out of the window, examining the legs. After deeming that it was still in working order, he set it on the ground and eased into it.

"So, I take it that it didn't go so well yesterday when you dropped her off."

"It went as well as expected."

"Did she sound at all reluctant about living there?"

"No," I croaked out.

He nodded. "Give her time. You can't expect that she's going to be okay overnight."

"I don't need to give her time. It's over."

"You can't be sure. I mean, it's been a little over two months. You can't expect her to-"

"I saw the look on her face," I interjected. "Trust me, it's over for her. Whatever we had, it's gone."

"I'm sorry, man."

"Me too."

We sat in silence for a few minutes before he stood. "I have to go help out on a job. I expect this shit to be cleaned up by the time I get home."

He squeezed my shoulder, making me feel like he was the older brother and I was the fuck up. I was never the fuck up, and I found that I really didn't like it. So, I made myself some coffee and I got to work cleaning up the house. I refused to sit and mope about my failed relationship. If she could move on, so could I.

KATHERINE

After two weeks of sitting around my townhouse, I decided that it was time for me to get out. It had been easier being here, away from all the reminders of what I once had. Sleeping was a little easier, and not having the reminders of my child around me all the time made it easier to heal. Not that I was healed, but I felt like I was moving forward, even if it was only in small steps.

Now, I sat in my car outside the hospital and willed myself to go inside. I wasn't sure I could do this, but I had to start working again. Eric had made sure that I had money in my account to get me through a few weeks. It was nice of him, and if I asked him for more money, I knew he would give it in a heartbeat. But I wasn't about to do that. Eric and I were over. It didn't matter what we once had. I had ended things with him and now it was my responsibility to pick myself up and get back on my feet.

I opened the door and walked into the hospital. I felt a slight panic at being here again, but I had to push on. I needed the income. I bypassed the maternity ward and headed for the children's center. As expected my boss was at the nurse's station, ordering everyone around like she usually did. When she glanced up and saw me, she pursed her lips.

"Hi, Charlene."

"Katherine. Are you ready to come back?"

I swallowed hard, hoping I was right to do this. "I think so."

She raised an eyebrow at me. "Look, if you're not ready, I can't have you coming back here and losing it on the patients. They need a nurse that can take care of them, not someone that will start crying at the drop of a hat."

I felt like I had been slapped, but then her face softened.

"I'm not trying to be cruel, Katherine. I want you to really think about this before you come back. It's not just the patients that are depending on you. The other nurses need to know that you're capable of doing your job. Go home and think about it for another day. If you're sure you're ready to come back, give me a call and I'll put you on the schedule."

I nodded, but before I could say anything, she turned from me and went back to work. I was just turning to leave when I saw Chrissy in the hallway with Casey's parents. I didn't have a right to go over there and talk to them. I wasn't on duty and I hadn't been in months. Still, I couldn't help but wonder what was going on.

Casey's mom turned to me with a big grin as I approached. I put on my best fake smile. "Hi, Cynthia. How's Casey?"

"She's doing great. Her scans came back clean. She gets to go home finally."

"That's wonderful," I said sincerely. Casey had been in this hospital for way too long. She deserved to go home.

"I just can't believe it. All this time in the hospital, I didn't think she was going to make it. Now we can go home and finally start living again. I just didn't think this was going to happen." She shook her head with tears in her eyes. "You know, all those times that I thought I would never see her ride a bike again or even read her a story in her own bed." She swiped at her face and smiled, taking a deep breath. "It really is a miracle."

She kept going, talking about how wonderful it was that Casey was going home, and it was. But the whole time she spoke, it just felt like a punch to the gut. I wanted to yell at her and tell her to stop rubbing it in. I got it, she still had her daughter, but I didn't have mine. How was that fair?

Chrissy gripped my hand, pulling me out of my thoughts. "I have to get back on rounds, but let me know when you're all packed up. I'll bring in a wheelchair for Casey."

"Thank you, Chrissy."

Chrissy pulled me away, my feet feeling like lead as she dragged me down the halls of the hospital. She pulled me into the break room and shoved me into a chair. "I'm sorry. I didn't know you were coming in today."

"Did you hear her?" I asked woodenly. *"My daughter's going home. I never thought I would read her a story..."*

"Kat, she's excited. Casey's been in the hospital for a long time."

"But she knows that I lost my daughter," I snapped. "How about a little sensitivity?"

Chrissy sighed and pulled out a chair, sitting down beside me. "Alright, I'm going to tell you something, but I want you to remember that I'm saying this because I love you." I rolled my eyes, but nodded. "Kat, you're being a selfish bitch."

My mouth dropped open. "Excuse me?"

"You are. I'm sorry, but you need to hear this. I know you lost your baby and that's killing you. But Cynthia has every reason in the world to gush over the fact that her daughter is going home. She's not being rude or trying to be hurtful. Her daughter has been suffering for years. In a way, you got lucky. Yes, your daughter died, but she didn't suffer for years. You didn't have to be in Cynthia's shoes, wondering if she would ever get to hold her daughter again. I know it's still painful, but there are a ton of people suffering in this world, and you need to wake up and realize that you're not alone in this. You've already pushed Eric away, and he's hurting just as much as you are."

"I doubt that," I grumbled.

"Just because he didn't get lost in his mind or sit around moping for months doesn't mean that he's not hurting. Guys are different than us. They're fixers. He needed to fix you, but there was no way he could ever do that. So, he did what any guy would do and he tried to move on, to lessen the pain. You have to stop judging other people for how they're acting. The world moves on, even though you feel like it's stuck in one place and time. Now, you have a choice. You can either choose to take every happy moment and turn it into a sad or angry one, or you can push on with life."

"How do I do that? You don't get it. You don't understand what this is like."

"No, I don't, but I also know that if you continue to mourn your child the way you are now, you're going to lose everything about you that makes you who you are. You're going to lose Eric. You're going to lose the chance to have the family that you could have had."

Tears slipped down my cheeks and I quickly swiped them away. "Eric and I don't fit. Come on, Chrissy. You know we were never meant to be."

"What I know is that you had something great with him, but you let your grief take over and push him away. That man would take you back in an instant, if only you would let him in."

I considered this, but there was still one problem. "I'm different now. Even if I wanted him back, will he like the person I am now? I cry a lot, and I'm not that nice to people."

"He's not that nice anymore either. You make the perfect couple," she laughed. "Seriously, it's only been a couple of months. You can't expect that you're going to bounce back all at once, but you also can't just let life defeat you like this. Take life by the horns and make her your bitch."

I huffed out a laugh and let her pull me into her arms for a hug. I knew that she was right. I just had to let my mind and my heart get on the same page.

"You know what you need?"

"What?"

"You need something to remind you that you're still alive."

I quirked an eyebrow at her. "Chrissy, I think I'm long past my days of acting like a crazy person."

"Well, who knows. If you play this right, you might even convince Eric to do something crazy with you."

I took a few more days to get my head on straight and then I called Charlene to put me on the schedule. She said I could start slow, working half the hours I normally did, which I thought was wise. Considering that I hadn't worked in several months, if I went back full force, I would wear myself out. I took my time, getting my townhouse in order and making it my own, but it never was. My home was with Eric at the farmhouse, where we could sit out under my favorite tree. This place would never feel like home to me, no matter how much decorating I did.

My doorbell rang and I reluctantly went to the door to answer. I didn't want company. I just wanted to be left in peace. It was no doubt some nosy person from town that came to check on me. And I was sick of being checked on. I flung the door open and was surprised to see Andrew standing on my doorstep, holding a box of pizza.

"Is that for me?"

He glanced at the pizza box, seeming to come to a decision. "Well, I initially bought it for me, but then I decided to share it with you."

He held out the box and I took it warily, opening it up to see what kind it was.

"This is cheese."

"Yeah."

"You don't eat cheese."

He rolled his eyes. "Fine, bust my balls about this. I bought the pizza to share with you, and since you like cheese, I got cheese."

I narrowed my eyes at him. "You told me that you would never share a pizza with me."

He snatched the pizza box back and glared at me. "Fine, I won't share it with you."

I took it back and walked into the townhouse, leaving the door open for him to enter. I heard him shut the door as I plopped down on the couch and opened the box. "There's water in the fridge. Sorry, I don't have any beer."

He nodded and grabbed a couple of bottles, then sat down across from me. "Don't hog all the pizza. I said I would share, not give it all to you."

"Then eat faster," I shot back.

He took a bite and glanced around the house, grimacing at my decorations. "This place sucks."

"I know."

"I mean, it's nice, but…."

I shrugged. "I know. It's not the same."

I took another bite and tried to ignore the awkward silence between us. He wiped his hands on a napkin and tossed it on the table. "Look, I'm just going to put this out there. You need to come home."

I sighed and dropped my pizza back in the box. "Andrew, if you came here to try and convince me to go back to Eric, you can save your breath. We just don't work."

"What? What does Eric have to do with any of this?"

I looked at him strangely. "Um…why else would I move back to the farmhouse?"

He sighed deeply. "You know, he's not the only one there. I have no one to do my laundry, and you cook better than Eric. Don't come back for him. Come back for me. I miss you."

I laughed out loud, my first genuine laugh in a long time. "Andrew, you're crazy."

He grinned at me and took another bite. "I'm serious, though. It sucks not having you there. You always folded my laundry so neatly and Eric refuses to fold my clothes, and that's like the worst part about doing laundry!"

"You forget that I yelled at you any time I had to do your laundry."

"I didn't forget. It was kind of hot, even if I think of you as a sister."

I grimaced. "You know, that just sounds disgusting."

"Well, I never said we were a biological family. You can still daydream about a step-sibling or an adopted sibling."

"Please tell me you're joking."

"Of course, I am. As much as I love you, it would never work between us. Frankly, I'm in my prime and you're going to turn into an old spinster, especially dressed in sweats and a t-shirt," he said, nodding to my clothes. I tossed my balled-up napkin at him.

"Be nice, or I'll take the rest of the pizza." I snatched another piece and shoved it in my mouth. "So, did you find a job yet?"

"Nah. I'm just doing side work for now."

"You mean, you're still a hacker."

He shrugged. "It pays good money."

"Eric's gonna be so pissed when he finds out how you actually make your money," I laughed.

"Hey, it's not completely illegal. I still pay my taxes."

I shook my head at him. He was going to have to grow up at some point and get a real job.

"So, when do you go back to work?"

"Tomorrow. I can't sit around here any longer."

"That's because you're not doing it right. You need to watch a movie and relax with some popcorn."

"I don't know of any good movies."

He grabbed the remote and found a movie to watch. I wasn't really sure what it was, but I didn't care. I found that even though I didn't want company, I didn't mind Andrew stopping by. He didn't ask me about how I was feeling or anything like that. He just joked with me and tried to make me feel better.

Andrew moved to the couch, his eyes glued to the TV as he got comfortable. I watched the screen with little attention, more content to just be sitting here with someone and not having to put on a good face or talk about anything. Only a half hour into the movie, I was yawning and ready to fall asleep. Even though I had been sleeping the days away, it was rarely restful. Andrew pulled a pillow from his side of the couch and plopped it against his leg, then patted it for me to lay down. With anyone else, it might be a little weird, but this was Eric's brother. And if I couldn't have Eric, I could enjoy this one simple pleasure of feeling like I was at least close to him. I laid down and it wasn't even a few minutes before I was asleep.

ERIC

Andrew walked into the house at six o'clock that night, grinning like a fool.

"What's so amusing?"

"Nothing. I just spent the afternoon with a beautiful woman."

Will snorted, barely looking up from his cards. Robert and Joe were also concentrating hard on the cards in their hands.

"Figures that you would miss poker to screw a woman," Robert replied, tossing two cards on the table. I passed him two more off the top of the deck and waited for Joe to take his turn.

"Oh, I didn't screw her, but she was laying down on my lap."

"Wait, you spent the day with a woman, but you didn't screw her?" Will confirmed.

"Oh, I'm not saying that it wasn't kinky. I mean, her head was in my lap," he grinned, waggling his eyebrows at me.

"Another bimbo?" I asked. "Where did you meet this one? Another bar?"

"Nope. I've known this one for close to a year now."

"And you haven't sealed the deal yet?" Robert asked curiously.

"You know, there's something so great about having a woman that's so comfortable with you that she'll just put her head in your lap," Andrew said, staring off with a smile at absolutely nothing. "Yeah, she was definitely comfortable with me."

"So, what's her name? Obviously, she means something to you if you've gone a year and haven't fucked her."

He winked at me. "Kat."

We all stopped and stared at him. "Sorry, what did you just say?" I asked, my anger shooting sky high.

"You heard me. I brought her some food and we talked. You know, I know what you saw in her. She's smart, beautiful, and man do I like her head in my lap."

I shoved the chair back, ready to attack Andrew, but Joe stood and held me back, shoving me away from Andrew.

"Why the fuck were you with Kat?"

"Why the fuck aren't you?" he shot back. "Hey, if you don't see what you have, I'll happily move in and take over."

I charged again, barely being held back by Joe. Then Will was there, holding out his hands to calm me down. "Just hold on a minute. This is Andrew. You know he's not moving in on your girl."

"His girl?" Andrew snorted. "Like he deserves to call her that. No, she's not his girl anymore, and since he's made that perfectly clear, it's open season on her."

"The fuck it is," I snarled. "Stay the fuck away from her."

"No, I don't think I will. I'm thinking by this time next week, she'll be my bae, and it'll be me that she'll Netflix and chill with. Though, I'm really hoping for more of the chill than the Netflix, if you know what I mean."

My nostrils flared, because I knew exactly what the fuck he meant for once. But as if he was trying to rub salt in the wound, he leaned forward and whispered, "That means there'll be lots of sex and not so much hanging out."

"You fucker," I growled, lunging forward and breaking Joe's hold on me. Will skittered out of the way, watching as I tackled Andrew to the ground and buried my fist in his face. The fucker smiled up at me.

"I knew she would be worth it."

I threw another punch, slamming his head back into the floor. All I could see was red, his hands on her. Her laying in his lap. She was mine, or she used to be. She could go after anyone else, but not my family. No one in my family was allowed to touch her, to know her intimately like I did.

Will and Robert dragged me off Andrew, and Joe helped him to his feet. "Do you have a death wish?" Joe asked.

"Oh, relax. I went over there to see her because this fucker is refusing to get off his ass," Andrew said, jerking his thumb in my direction. "She's starting back at work tomorrow. I went to check on her and see how she was doing. I brought her a pizza and we talked. Then I got her to watch a movie and she fell asleep because she's fucking exhausted." I glared at him and he rolled his eyes. "I put a pillow against my leg so she could lay down and relax."

"You shouldn't have gone over there," I said accusingly. "She's not yours."

"You're right, she's not mine, but she is my family. We're all her family, and you've just abandoned her."

"I didn't abandon her. She abandoned me!" I shouted. "Did you forget that she's the one that wanted to leave?"

"She's hurting," he shot back. "Everyone else is moving on with their lives. You're going to work and we're all doing our own thing. She's lost, man. She doesn't know how to move forward."

"What the fuck do you want me to do? She wanted out. I asked her to stay and she didn't want to. I can't change her mind one that. I can't make her want to be with me."

He shook his head disappointedly. "There was a time that you were willing to make her see what you could have together. What happened to that man?"

I sighed, not knowing what else to say. When she left, she took that part of me with her. Everything was different now. "That man disappeared the moment she walked out the door."

I headed into the grocery store on my way home. I had been a chicken shit about coming in here since I blew up at everyone for watching me. But I couldn't hide out forever. I had to eventually move on with life, and going back in the fucking grocery store was part of that. I grabbed the cart as I walked in and watched as one of the workers backed away from me slowly with wide eyes.

"I'm not gonna snap," I muttered, more to myself than her. I pushed the cart down the first aisle and started loading up the cart. The stock boy at the other end of the aisle looked up, but when he saw me, he quickly moved out of the aisle, abandoning the pallet of canned goods he was stocking. Tightening my fists on the cart, I pushed on and continued loading my cart. I only had myself to blame. I moved down the next aisle, ignoring the way people hurried past me. I may have been forgiven for my bad behavior, but it was obvious that everyone still thought I was a ticking time bomb.

I was halfway through the store when I turned down an aisle and my heart stopped in my chest. I came face to face with Kat, but I didn't have a fucking clue what to say. She looked better, a little less pale and weak from when I moved her into her house. She was in her scrubs from work, but she had never looked more beautiful. Those green eyes held just a little more life and she didn't look so defeated. But the longer I stared at her, the more the sadness crept into her face. She was sad because I was a reminder of all she'd lost. That's what she told me when she moved out. I was breaking her heart by just existing.

"Hey," I finally said. I couldn't just ignore her and pretend like she didn't exist, no matter how much easier that might be.

"Hey."

Awkward…"You look good."

"Thanks. You do too."

It was like our first date, only so much worse. "So, you're back at work?"

She looked down at her scrubs and then back up to me. "Um…

yeah. It's been about two weeks now. Just a light schedule until I'm ready to go back full time."

I nodded, trying to come up with some magical way to disappear so I didn't have to feel this pain in my chest. Staring at her just made me sad. I wanted to pull her into my arms. I wanted to kiss her and feel her arms around me. I wanted a drink.

"I should..." I gestured to the aisle and she quickly moved aside, brushing some loose hair behind her ear.

"Right, sorry."

I gave a slight smile and slowly moved past her. Each step was torture. I could feel my heart pulling to be with her, like it was leaving my body to be closer to her. I gripped the handle of the cart and kept pushing, staring at the shelves and shoving anything in my cart just so that I could appear normal. When I was about halfway down the aisle, I turned back to look at her. She was gone and my stomach dropped out. My face fell in sadness, but there was nothing I could do. I took a deep breath and shoved the cart forward. I passed an older woman that smiled kindly at me, and I returned the smile to the best of my ability.

I made it through the store, doing my best not to look for her around every corner. I didn't see her the rest of the time I was in there. When I got to the check out lane, I started unloading the groceries onto the conveyor belt. My eyes landed on her through the window, loading her groceries in the trunk of her Jeep. I stared at her, watching as she moved quickly, swiping at her cheeks before she slammed the back door. She got into the driver's side and quickly tore out of the lot.

"Mr. Cortell?" I glanced at the bagger at the end. He looked at me expectantly.

"Sorry, what?"

"Paper or plastic?"

"Anything," I said. "Anything's fine."

But nothing was fine, and it never would be again.

I walked in the door and immediately regretted it. Andrew sat at the table with Will and Robert, and they were all grinning at me.

"What?"

"Somebody's trending on Facebook," Robert grinned, shaking his phone from side to side.

"You don't trend on Facebook. That's on Chirp," Will said.

"Chirp is a book site," Andrew chimed in. "You're thinking of Twitter."

"Twitter. What a fucking stupid name for a company about sharing every fucking thought in your head with the entire planet," Will groused.

"They call it Twitter because it's like birds talking. Twittering or some shit," Andrew informed him.

"Why can't you trend on Facebook?" Robert asked.

"What the hell is the difference?" I asked, taking a seat at the table.

"Trending means you have several people replying to the tweet," Andrew explained.

"Well…how many people are talking about me on Facebook?" I asked.

Robert scrolled through his phone and snorted. "The whole fucking town."

"Well, isn't that trending?"

"Trending is for Twitter only," Andrew explained. "And stop acting like you don't know what this shit is. You may be older than me, but you're not ancient."

"I *don't* know what this shit means," I said, irritatedly. "This fucking hippie millennial generation, with all your made up words and hipster talk. And what's with those fucking jeans? Do you not realize that real men don't show off their ass like that? And get a fucking haircut. You look like you cut half your hair the wrong way."

"You know, you're technically a millennial too," Andrew shot back.

I snorted, snatching a beer from the center of the table. "Not a millennial. You can call it whatever the hell you want, but I don't mind getting dirty, I don't sit with my face buried in my phone, and I definitely would rather be sweating my ass off outside than sitting in that pretty shirt you're wearing," I nodded to his purple button down.

"There's nothing wrong with my clothes."

"Bullshit," Robert coughed into his fist. "No man dresses in purple. And Eric's right. You look..." He examined Andrew's hair, shaking his head slightly. "Like an exotic bird."

I chuckled, trying not to laugh too hard at my brother. At some point over the last ten years, my baby brother had started dressing and talking like an idiot.

"Whatever. Laugh at me all you want, but don't be surprised when I clap back."

"Clap back?" I asked with a grin. "Are you going to cheer me on?"

He shoved away from the table and headed for the stairs.

"Hey, I was joking!"

He gave me the middle finger and went upstairs. I shook my head, drinking my beer. I almost forgot about what happened today. And it was nice, not to have to think about that shit for a while. But then I got angry with myself. I needed to stop thinking about her, and schedule my grocery shopping for when I wouldn't see her. The more I wanted to see her, the harder it would be to stay away. As much as I didn't want to do it, I had to stay far away. I couldn't see her again. It would hurt too much.

I cleared my throat, grinning at my brothers who were looking at me the way they did after we lost the baby. "So, what are they saying about me this time?"

Robert shook his head. "Uh...you know, just town bullshit."

"Okay, so what's the word today? Is this about me losing my temper with the welder? Because that idiot had it coming."

Robert glanced at Will and then back to me. "You know, same old bullshit."

But the way he was being dodgy, I knew it was more than that. I snatched the phone out of his hand before he could react, and then turned so he couldn't get the phone back.

Jeannie Jax

Did anyone else see Eric at the grocery store today? What happened?

Carl Roverton

Katherine was in the store. They ran into each other.

Jeannie Jax

OMG! That poor man.

Carly Summers

I saw her at the deli counter. She was practically in tears. And then I saw him watching her through the window at the checkout lane. You could practically see the man's heart breaking.

Bessy Phillips

I wish they could find their way back to each other. Everyone in town can see how much they love each other.

Carly Summers

I've seen them together. The way he looks at her, you know that they were meant to be together.

Bessy Phillips

But after everything they've gone through, maybe it just won't work out.

Jeannie Jax

I see him every few days in the hardware store. He puts on a good front, but his eyes always look so sad.

Carly Summers

Katherine came into the hair salon about a week ago. She looked okay, I guess, but you could tell she just wasn't anything close to herself.

Bessy Phillips

Maybe we should find a way to get them back together?

Carly Summers

You can't make two people that love each other stay together. They have to do that themselves.

I put the phone down and sighed. It appeared that everyone in the town could see how miserable we both were. It also appeared that everyone could see right through me. I wasn't fooling anyone. I was fucking miserable, and now it was clear that everyone else knew it. And as I looked at my brothers, it was clear that I wasn't fooling them either.

KATHERINE

I was getting used to the whispers as I walked around town. Some people were nice and stopped to talk to me. Others just hid behind their hands as they gossiped. That was what it was like living in a small town. But as the weeks went on, I was finding a new rhythm for my life. It wasn't as bright and cheerful as it used to be, but I wasn't completely miserable either.

Now that Casey was released from the hospital, there were no patients that I was familiar with. I decided that I would play it like Charlene had said, no emotional connection. They were my patients and I was their nurse. Other than that, I couldn't offer anything else. She was right, it was too hard to watch kids go through so much pain when you were personally involved, and since I was still grieving, I didn't need to set myself up for heartache.

I met Chrissy in the cafeteria on our lunch break. I was still on three days a week, but I was working full days. The good thing was, I got to see Chrissy most of the days I worked, which helped me feel like I was getting back to normal. She always had some funny story to tell me about her husband, and I dutifully smiled along. I tried desperately not to think about what stories I might share if I were still with Eric. Those times were over for me.

"So, I saw on Facebook that you and Eric ran into each other yesterday."

"Why does that not surprise me?"

"So?"

"So, what?"

She sighed in irritation. "So, what happened? Did he try to get you back?"

"No. He just…it was awkward. Neither of us knew what to say. He said I looked nice and then he moved on."

"He said you looked nice." I nodded. "In your scrubs."

"He was just being nice."

"Kat, when are you going to wake up and see that the man is one hundred percent in love with you and always will be?"

"When are you going to stop pressuring me about this? And why did you have to take on his nickname for me? I think we need to go back to Kiki."

"No," she shook her head. "Absolutely not. Ever since he said it was a bird's name, that's all I picture when I hear it."

"Well, I don't want to be Kat anymore."

"Should I call you Katherine then?"

I grimaced, thinking of when he insisted on calling me Katherine. No, I couldn't hear that either. "How about we just stick with Katie?"

"Katie? You want to be Katie now?"

I sighed in irritation. "What does it matter? It's just a name!"

"Exactly, you're running from a name. Do you see this? Do you hear yourself? You need to deal with the fact that the man you love is not coming back unless you make the first move."

I picked at the label of my drink. "I don't know how to do that. I said some really horrible things to him."

"Like what?"

"I said that I couldn't look at him because he reminded me of her."

She looked at me sympathetically. "On Facebook, someone said she saw you crying at the grocery store. Was that because of Angel?"

I shook my head. In all honesty, I hadn't thought about Angel when I saw him. I just thought of the pain of losing *him*. "It just hit me hard, you know? I still love him, but I made a mess of everything. I was a jerk to him."

"When?"

"We had this argument before I moved out. He said we should go out to dinner, try and get out of the house. I got mad because it felt like he was trying to make me move on and forget."

"Well, do you feel better now that you're not at home, moping around all the time?"

I glared at her. "Yes."

"So, he wasn't wrong."

"Well, I didn't feel that way at the time. I was stuck in my head. I honestly think that moving out of that house has been good for me. It was hard to walk past Angel's room every day. The distance has been good for me."

"Okay, so why was it wrong when he suggested it?"

I shrugged. "Because it felt like he just wanted to move on. I don't know," I sighed. "I was a wreck and I wasn't thinking straight. I couldn't see that he was suffering. I only saw that I was in pain and he wasn't. I accused him of not being sad over our loss."

She let out a low whistle and leaned back in her chair. "That was harsh."

"I know."

"So, now you've moved out and you're both miserable."

"Yes."

"And he won't come to you because he thinks you don't want him."

"I pretty much told him that."

"Wow, I gotta say, Kat, the bitch factor just went up by ten."

"Well, you can see now how I can't just go get him back. I hurt him, a lot, and an apology isn't going to make everything better. And I'm not sure that I want to try anyway. I was serious when I told you that we weren't right for each other. I think with time, it won't hurt so much and we'll both see that we never should have happened."

"Right," she nodded. "Spoken like a true coward."

I glared at her. "It's not being a coward to walk away to protect someone else. He's going to move on and find someone better for him, someone that doesn't say shitty stuff to make him feel horrible."

"You're right. You wouldn't be a coward if you were protecting him. But you're not. You're protecting yourself from getting hurt again. Kat, you don't get to decide other people's lives for them. You should give him the chance to find out for himself if he wants to be with you or not. And if you don't, you're making yourself miserable. You'll never be happy and you'll never realize that the one person that you're pushing away is the one person that could help you heal."

She stood and grabbed her garbage, staring down at me in pity. But this wasn't pity for my loss. This was pity because she knew that I was making a mistake and she knew that I didn't have it in me right now to make this better for myself.

ERIC

"Dude, you're miserable," Will said, sighing as he took a seat across from me. "You can't keep doing this. It's bad enough you lost Angel, but you can't just let Kat slip away too."

"I didn't let her slip away. She didn't want to be here anymore."

"You really believe that?" He shook his head slightly. "I saw the way she looked at you. I saw how much she loved you. She's scared."

"Scared of what?"

"Of being with you now that Angel's gone. Afraid that you won't look at her the same way. Afraid that you don't want just her." He shrugged. "Take your pick."

I rubbed my thumb on a spot on the table. Sighing, I just didn't know what to say. I wanted her back so much, but after everything we'd been through, I didn't know how to get her back. I didn't have the confidence to get her back. Nothing seemed to function right without her. I pushed through my days, hoping to get as quickly as possible to the next day. But then I still had to deal with my nights, alone and empty in my bed without the woman I loved.

"Go get her."

I snorted. "She doesn't want me."

"She does. She just needs you to go get her and remind her of what you had together. She needs someone else to take the reins on this, because she doesn't trust what she's feeling."

"She never wanted me, Will. She was with me because of the baby. Angel's gone. There's no reason in the world that she would still want me."

"God, you're so fucking blind. You're the fucking stupidest man I've ever met."

My head snapped up to meet his gaze.

"Yeah, you know, if you would pull your head out of your ass for five minutes, you would see that she's loved you from the moment she saw you making that crib. That was just the beginning. And it wasn't because of the baby. It was because she started to see *you*. Everything about your relationship has happened backwards, but her falling in love with you was real, and I know you love her too."

"Of course, I love her."

"Then stop being a pussy and go get her back."

"How? I don't even know how to do that."

"Just be real with her. Tell her that you love her, that you can't live without her."

I shook my head. That sounded like a shitty plan.

"You know she's going to meet someone else." I rubbed at my chest, hating that thought. "She's going to find someone else, and she's going to fall in love with that guy, and he's going to be the luckiest fucker in the world because he took a shot with her, despite everything that's happened to her. He's going to love her, and one day, have the kids with her that you should be having with her. He's going to take her home every night and love her the way you should be."

"Stop," I said, hating the way my voice broke.

"No, you need to hear this. You need to realize what you're risking. The longer you wait, the more she's going to feel like you don't really want her. She needs to hear every last thing you're thinking. She needs you to stop acting like a fucking robot and take her back!"

I sat there for another minute considering this, but then Will slammed his hand down on the table. "Now, you fucking idiot!"

I jumped at the command. "Like, right now?"

"No, tomorrow, asshole. Yes, right fucking now!" He grabbed my jacket and then hauled me out of my chair, shoving me toward the door. "Let's go get her back right fucking now, and if you come home without her, I swear to God, I'm calling Derek to dispose of your useless body."

He shoved me out the door, kicking me in the ass as I stumbled across the porch.

"You're coming with me?"

"You bet your ass I am." He pulled his jacket on and stomped toward the truck. "Somebody has to bring our girl home."

"Our girl?"

He spun around and got in my face. "She's not just your woman. She's our sister and we all miss her. So, yeah, she's our girl and I want her back with you. I happened to like you a lot better when you were happy with her."

I swung my jacket on and walked after him to my truck, but the more I walked, the more determined I became. My heart started racing and adrenaline kicked in. Before I knew it, I was running to my truck, flinging the door open and peeling out of my driveway. He barely made it into the truck before I pulled out. I was going to get her back. I was going to make her mine again.

Dust kicked up behind us on the dirt road as I put the metal all the way down. Will held on to the *oh shit* handle as I took a sharp turn down the next road. My knuckles were white as I squeezed the wheel. Adrenaline flooded my system and I felt an energy I hadn't felt in a long time.

I broke every speed limit driving into town, not bothering to stop at any of the red lights.

"Uh…cops," Will said as we flew past cops that were headed in our direction. I watched in the rearview mirror as the cops pulled a uey in the street and took off after me. I punched the gas.

"The cops are chasing you," Will said.

"I don't give a fuck. I'm not stopping until I find her."

"When I said *go get her back*, I wasn't meaning that you should get thrown in jail to make it happen."

I swerved around a car that was driving too slow, barely making in back into my lane before I plowed into the oncoming traffic. I glanced over at Will with a grin, but he looked like he was about to puke.

"This was not what I had in mind," he said, panic in his voice. "Where's my rational brother that would yell at me right now for convincing him to do something so reckless?"

"You said to get her back. It's now or never."

"It's going to be never, because as soon as you get pulled over, you're getting your ass hauled off to jail."

Two more cop cars pulled into line behind me and I saw another cop car with its lights on off to the right. I punched the gas and flew past the intersection. I was just a minute from Kat's house now.

I jumped the curb as I pulled up to Kat's townhouse, just barely throwing the truck in park as I jumped out and raced up the steps to her door. I pounded, waiting for an answer.

"Hey," the cop shouted, racing up to me. "Eric, what the fuck are you doing?"

I spun around and saw that it was Jack. "I have to get her back."

"What?"

"Kat. I was an asshole, letting her walk away. I should have known that she needed me to step up and take over, but instead, I just let her walk out the door." I gripped him by the arms, a maniacal smile splitting my lips. "But not anymore. I'm getting her back tonight."

I turned and pounded on her door again, leaning over the railing to look in her window. She had a small light on, but it was dark everywhere else. I turned and raced down her steps to my truck. The cops had all parked, surrounding my vehicle. Will was sitting in the truck, wide-eyed and wondering what the hell to do. I would plow through the cars if I had to.

"Hey! Where are you going?" Jack shouted.

"The hospital!" I shouted over my shoulder.

"Wait! I'll give you an escort." I heard him call dispatch, but I was already getting in my truck and pulling out. Jack pulled around me, his sirens on as he drove toward the hospital. I started to notice a line of cars pulling out behind me. People were racing out of their houses and headed for their cars. What the hell?

"I guess these people have never seen a car chase," I snorted.

"Uh...that's not why they're running out."

"Why then?"

"I may have posted this on the town Facebook page," he said sheepishly.

"Seriously? You're doing it now too? Is there no loyalty among brothers? What did you say?"

"In a car chase through Small Town, USA with Eric. On the way to the hospital to #GetKatBack."

I snorted, and then started laughing. I felt crazy. This whole thing was insane; the town, the people, my crazy brothers, and the fact that I was indeed involved in a car chase so that I could get the woman I loved back. And now I had half the town following me, whether to watch for sport or to help me win the love of my life back.

I drove as fast as I could to the hospital, racing through stop lights and squealing to a stop outside the ER. I didn't care if I wasn't supposed to park there. I had only one goal and that was to get to Kat. I ran to the elevator and pressed the button, feeling a little more confident as the crowd gathered. It was like I had a whole army with me to get her back.

"Are you really doing it?" one person shouted.

"Are you going to get her back?" Mrs. Cranston asked. I did a double take and noticed that she had a big smile on her face.

I felt like I should say something really awesome, but all I came up with was, "Yes, I am."

"You're all over Facebook," one man said, holding his phone out to read Will's post. #GetKatBack. I looked at the man's phone and noticed that people were responding faster than I could read.

Will stepped up beside me, dropping the keys into my hand with a clap on the shoulder. "It's gonna work, man."

I nodded and stepped into the elevator, squishing to the front as people filtered in with me. I noticed there were more of them coming, so I hit the button for her floor and hit the button to close the doors. I needed to get to Kat.

When the doors opened, I took a deep breath and stepped out, rushing over to the nurse's station. They told me she was down the hall in the break room. She had just finished her shift.

"You'd better run if you want to catch her-"

I took off, barely hearing the rest of what she said. I raced down to the break room and slammed the door open, but she wasn't there. My heart pounded wildly in my chest. I had to find her. I stepped out of the break room and looked down the hall, but I didn't see her.

"There she is!" someone shouted. I shoved past the crowd and saw her waiting by the elevator.

"Kat!" I shouted, running toward her. She turned to look at me and her eyes widened as she saw me racing toward her with a herd of people behind me. "Kat, wait!"

I ran up to her, stopping just feet from her.

"Eric, what are you doing here?"

"I...I came to get you back."

Her face flushed and she pressed the button on the elevator again. "Eric, we both know that this won't work between us."

"Yes, it will."

"Tell me why it would work this time."

"Because I love you."

She shook her head slightly. "Eric, you loved me because of the baby, and she's gone now. You don't have to do this. You don't have to pretend. I'll be okay."

"You may be, but I'll never be okay if you're not by my side," I said, putting as much emotion into it as possible. "Kat, I fell in love with you, and it wasn't because we were having a baby. It was because of you. You made me live. You made me want to live life for more than just what I had to do every day. You gave me the freedom to be something I've never been. You showed me what true love looks like. You gave me a chance to have something perfect with you. And I know you love me too. It's not just in the way you kiss me or the way you stare at me when you think I'm not looking. I can feel it even standing over here. We have a connection that I never thought I would have with anyone else. When you're not with me, life seems pointless. When I wake up in the morning, I'm sad and alone. I miss your scent on my pillows. I miss knocking your razors down in the shower and stepping on them. I miss cooking for you and seeing your bright eyes when you're teasing me."

The elevator opened and people poured out, all of them staring at us. Then the stairwell door opened and more people ran toward us, all of them with hopeful looks on their faces.

"What happened?" someone hissed.

"He misses stepping on her razors," another person said.

"That's not romantic."

"Yes, it is," a woman sighed.

"Kat," I pleaded.

She shook her head slowly, tears filling her eyes. "Eric, we were good together because of Angel. We had that connection, but once she was gone, she took everything good with her. We're better apart."

"I don't believe that," I argued. "I know that I'm miserable when I'm without you. I know that everything good in me disappeared the moment you walked out my door. I know that you're just as miserable as I am. But it doesn't have to be that way. Whether or not we're perfect for each other is a pointless argument. You and I both know that we weren't just good together because of Angel. We work because...because despite our differences, we're still better together than we are apart." I stared at her beautiful face, watching the tears slip down her cheeks. I was getting through to her. "Kat, we've had a rough road, but I would rather spend the rest of my life knowing we'll have bumps along the way, than spend even one more minute without you."

She huffed out a laugh and she swiped at the tears dripping down her face. "I'm still a mess."

"So am I. We'll be a mess together." I rushed to her, pulling her into my arms and kissing her hard. Her tears slipped down her cheeks, slipping onto my face, but I didn't care. I would take her tears for the rest of my life and make them happy tears.

My hand dug into her hair as I kissed her harder. Her arms were wrapped around me, pulling me close. Catcalls sounded around us. People were clapping and cheering, but all I heard was the sound of her gasps as she pulled me closer.

I broke the kiss and stared into her beautiful eyes. "It's only you, Kat. For the rest of my life, it'll only ever be you."

She gave a watery laugh as the elevator opened. Joe and Andrew ran out, followed by an elevator full of people. Joe's face fell when he saw us together.

"Shit, did we miss it?"

"What happened?" I heard Derek shout, right before I saw his face on Joe's phone. "Did he kiss her?"

We both laughed and then I pulled her into my arms, kissing her slower this time, taking my time to really feel her against me again. I had her back, and there was no way I would ever let her go again.

KATHERINE

I headed for the truck with my arm wrapped around Eric. He had his arm around my shoulder, pulling me in close to him, pressing kisses to my temple every few seconds, like he couldn't believe that I was here. There were police cars parked all over the hospital parking lot, directing traffic. I couldn't believe that the whole town had followed him here, but it somehow fit.

"See?" Will said from behind us. "I told you this would work!"

Eric took the keys out of my hands and tossed them over his shoulder. "Make sure Kat's truck gets to the house."

"No problem."

He took off, but Andrew and Joe were still with us. "So, what does this mean? Are you back together?" Joe asked.

"You're coming home with us, right?" Andrew asked excitedly. "I really need my laundry done."

"It's just not the same without you," Joe nodded.

"Guys!" Eric shouted, cutting them off. "Yes, I got her back, but I think we'd like to be alone tonight."

Joe's face fell. "No reunion?"

"No pizza?" Andrew asked.

"Guys, we can do that over the weekend. Just give us tonight."

"After we rushed all the way over here? We missed all of it!" Joe said, kicking at the pavement.

"It's on Facebook. Someone recorded it," Andrew said, scrolling through his phone.

"See? You can watch the replay," I said with a grin. I couldn't believe this was happening. I had been down all day, wishing that I could find the courage to get Eric back, but it turned out that Eric came to my rescue. He needed me just as much as I needed him.

"You guys find someplace else to stay tonight," Eric said, opening the truck door for me. "I want Kat to myself tonight."

"That's not fair," Andrew whined. "We just got her back!"

"*I* got her back."

"That's not fair. She's our sister too. We should get to spend some time with her after you were an asshole and didn't fight for her."

"Guys," I interrupted. "How about you guys spend the whole day with us tomorrow. I have the day off. We can play poker or something."

Andrew shoved his hands in his pockets and kicked at the pavement. "Yeah, I guess."

"I'll even do your laundry for you," I added for good measure.

"Kat-" Eric started, but I shook my head. If this would get them to back off, I'd gladly do their laundry.

"Yeah, okay," Andrew mumbled. I was just about to get into the truck when he suddenly wrapped me in a hug and pulled me in tight. "Glad to have you back, sis."

My heart melted and I patted him on the shoulder. "Me too."

I got into the truck, not missing the way Eric glared at his brothers in warning. When he got in, he just sat there and stared at me for a moment.

"What?"

He shook his head slowly. "I just…" I watched as he swallowed hard and his eyes misted slightly. "I've missed you, Kat."

I interlocked my fingers with his. "I missed you too."

We stayed like that the whole ride home, and when we pulled up to his house, it felt like a huge weight was lifted off my shoulders. I was home. This was where I was meant to be. He opened my door for me and held my hand as we walked up the steps.

I glanced over at him, his smile warming my heart. He slid his hand through my hair to the back of my head and pulled me in close. "Welcome home, Kat."

His mouth slid over mine, his tongue slipping inside. My body ignited from his touch. It had been too long since I felt him against me. I hadn't realized in my grief how much I needed Eric to ground me. We just drifted apart, and the further I sank into my depression, the less I connected with him in any real way, until there was nothing left between us. But after I moved out and my head cleared, I realized that what my heart needed and what my head was telling me were two different things.

"Kat, I need you," he murmured against my lips. "Is it too soon?"

I shook my head. "No, I need you too."

He pressed his lips to me one last time before taking my hand and leading me upstairs. When we passed Angel's room, I stumbled slightly. With my heart in my throat, I opened the door and looked around the room. I felt Eric slip his arms around me from behind and rest his head on my shoulder.

"Are you okay?"

"It's funny," I sighed. "I thought it would hurt more to look in here. Do you think it's bad that I don't think about her all the time?"

"I think it would be bad if you did, honestly." He turned me to face him. "Kat, when we lost Angel, I felt like we both lost everything. You were drowning and I didn't know how to save you. I wish that I had handled things differently. Maybe we never would have spent months apart."

"No, I think I needed the space. As much as I needed you, I needed to learn how to move forward on my own. Everyone was holding me up. It took moving away to realize that I couldn't just sit there all day. I had moved away from everyone that was taking care of me, and then it just hit me. I had to survive. I had to go back to work and push on. If I hadn't done that, I might have continued to sit around here staring at the wall and blaming you for not grieving the same way I did."

"But I have you back now?"

I smiled up at him. "Yeah, you have me back. I'm not saying that I'm all fixed, but I'm ready to move on with you."

I stepped toward the bedroom, holding his hand in mine. He watched as I slowly took a step back, pulling him with me. When I had him in the bedroom, I slowly pulled my shirt over my head and tossed it on the ground. He stared at me, his eyes blazing a fiery trail over my body as I slowly peeled off my clothes. By the time I was standing in front of him naked, he was clenching his fists hard to control himself. But I didn't want his control. I wanted all of him, the way it used to be.

I stepped forward and unzipped his pants. I could feel his hard erection pressing against the zipper. I wondered for a moment if he had been with anyone else, but I quickly pushed that thought aside. That wasn't like Eric. Deep down, I knew he would never bring anyone else home, not unless he had a connection with her. And I knew he didn't, because he was still stupidly in love with me.

I felt my flush of arousal as I pulled him out and swiped my thumb over the tip of his cock. He hissed when I played with his piercing. Slowly, I jerked him, working his cock in my hand until he was panting.

"Kat, it's been too long. You've gotta stop."

I smiled up at him and dropped to my knees. He shook his head, like he couldn't believe I was really doing this. I flicked my tongue and grinned when he groaned. Pumping him in my hand had never felt so good, but when I slid my mouth around his cock and felt his hips jerk, I felt higher than the first time I did this after his piercing.

"Kat," he moaned. I swirled my tongue around the head and took him deep in my throat, moaning and driving him insane. He didn't last more than a few thrusts before he was filling my mouth with his cum.

He pulled me up against him and kissed me hard. He scooped me up into his arms and carried me to the bed, kissing me with everything he had. When he laid me down, his hands immediately slid over my body, brushing lightly over my breasts and down to the apex of my thighs. He never touched me where I needed him, just drove me crazy with the touch of his fingers gliding across my skin. His lips skimmed over my body until he was there, licking and sucking, giving me everything I needed. I gasped as he pushed two fingers inside me, pumping me until I came hard.

He quickly stripped out of his clothes and then he was over me, pushing inside me. I gasped and gripped his arms, stopping him from moving.

"Are you okay?"

"I'm not…We should…" I swallowed hard, trying to find a way to tell him what I needed. But he must have understood without me saying it.

"I won't come inside you," he promised.

I nodded slightly. "I'm just not ready to risk that."

"I know."

He kissed me lightly, and then he was moving inside me. I wrapped my legs around him, pulling him closer to me. He stared at me the whole time, kissing me and telling me he loved me. It was like the last few months were erased and all that existed was us.

"I'm gonna come," he said, thumbing my clit as he pulled out. I grabbed his cock in my hands and jerked him until he poured his release on my stomach. When I saw his cum splash against my skin, it ignited something inside me and I came hard, riding out my own orgasm against his fingers.

He bent over and kissed me, wiping my sweaty hair away from my face. "Hi."

"Hi," I smiled back. "I missed you."

"Me too." He kissed me and then hopped off the bed, picking up his shirt to wipe the cum off my belly. When he laid back beside me, I saw a flash of ink on his skin and pressed my hand to his chest.

"What?"

I looked closer and saw a set of angel wings tattooed over his left pec. "When did you do this?"

"A few weeks ago."

My eyes widened in shock. "You willingly went to get a tattoo?"

"Well, Joe did it for me. He's actually really good."

I ran my hand over the wings and smiled. "He's very good."

"I was thinking of having him give me another tattoo."

"Oh yeah?" I grinned.

"Yeah, a pussy cat."

I bit my lip as I laughed. "Really. And where would this pussy cat be located?"

He raised an eyebrow and grinned. "Where any good pussy cat belongs."

I burst out laughing, shaking my head slightly. "Do you really think your brother is the person that should give you that?"

His eyes roamed off as he thought about it and then he shook his head. "You're right. I'll have Decker do it."

"That's fine, but I get a tattoo as well, then."

"Yeah? What's yours going to be?"

"I'll let you choose, but I know one thing's for sure. Where I'm getting that tattoo, your brother won't be allowed to see."

He groaned and buried his face in the crook of my neck, kissing me and sliding back inside me again.

ERIC

"Eric, where are we going?"

I gripped her hand tighter and took a deep breath. I was playing it cool, or I thought I was. Deep down, I was terrified. I had never done something like this before, but I knew this was what we needed. I just hoped that she saw it the same way. Shit, I was gonna piss my pants.

"You'll see," I said confidently. "We're almost there."

We had been driving for hours to get here. Andrew, Will, Robert, and Joe all came in the other truck to watch. They wanted to get it on camera. If I died, at least my idiocy would be recorded.

A half hour later, we pulled into the adventure park where I had booked our appointment. Kat looked at me strangely, but didn't say anything as we got out. I gripped her hand in mine, squeezing a little too tightly. She winced and I smiled down at her.

"Sorry. Just a little nervous."

"Eric, what are we doing?"

"We're taking a leap of faith and starting over."

She looked at me strangely. "A leap of faith?"

I pulled her into the office and stepped up to the counter. "Hi, I'm Eric Cortell. I made a reservation to go bungee jumping."

"Let me take a look...Right, here you are. Jimmy will be out in just a minute to take you out to the site."

I nodded and took a deep breath. Kat stood in front of me, staring at me intently.

"Are you sure you want to do this? Eric, this is..."

"Crazy? Insane? The most idiotic thing I've ever done?"

"Well-"

"I mean, this place has a good record. They haven't lost anyone yet," I laughed nervously.

"Eric and Kat?" a man said, stepping out from the back.

"That's me-us. We. I mean, we're here," I rambled.

He smiled at us. "First time?"

"Yes, well, not her. But, yes. You caught me. Bungee jumping virgin."

"Well, it looks like you picked a pretty lady to pop your cherry with. Let's head on over and get you set up."

I nodded, but I felt like I was going to pass out. The guy took us out to the jump spot, or whatever the hell it was. Hell, it looked like a bridge of death or something. My hands were shaky and my knees were weak, but I knew I had to do this. It was like a reset for us, a chance for us to take a leap of faith and move forward. I listened intently as the guy walked through the whole process with us, all the while squeezing Kat's hand like my life depended on it.

Before I knew it, it was time and we were about to plummet to our deaths. But if I went, I was going out with Kat. I just hoped I didn't piss myself on the way down. Kat and I stood together, staring into each other's eyes as we stood on the edge of the bridge. It was now or never.

"Kat, I just want you to know that I love you more than anything in this world. And if we survive this, you know, don't smack the ground and end up flat like a pancake, I don't want to waste another minute of my life. I want to do crazy things with you and...get a tattoo on my ass or whatever." She laughed as I stood there mumbling and making a fool of myself. I slid my hand into my pocket and pulled out the ring that I had picked out with my brothers. Of course, they all had to have a say in what ring I got. I still wasn't sure why.

I held it out in front of me and watched with bated breath as her eyes widened in shock. "Kat, take this leap with me. Tell me you're mine for the rest of our lives, because I know that you're all I want for the rest of mine."

She smiled and laughed, nodding her head. "Yes, I'll marry you."

I slid the ring on her finger and kissed her hard, stumbling over my own feet to get to her. She started to slip and I reached for her. Then we were both flying off the bridge, holding onto one another as we leapt into our future.

ALSO BY GIULIA LAGOMARSINO

Thank you for reading Kat and Eric's story. You can read more about The Cortell Brothers in the next book, coming in December, Collateral Damage.

Are you a new reader? See where it all began with the For The Love Of A Good Woman series. And continue with some of your favorite characters in the Reed Security series! Or follow the individual links down below!

Did you start in the middle? We've all done it! Find your place in the series and start from there! There's no need to question which book to start with. These books are best read in order. All books are available in Kindle Unlimited! For The Love Of A Good Woman:

Jack , Cole, Logan, Drew, Sebastian, Sean, Ryan

Not ready for those characters you love to disappear? You can catch them again throughout the Reed Security Series! These men and women are strong, sexy, and willing to fight for those they love. Sometimes, they fall right into love, while others need a little more convincing. Don't miss out on this exciting series!

Sinner, Cap, Cazzo, Knight, Irish, Hunter, Whiskey, Lola, Ice, Burg, Gabe, Jules, Sniper, Jackson, Chance, Phoenix Rising, Alec, Storm, Wolf, A Mad Reed Security Christmas, Rocco, Coop, TNT, Nightingale, Parker, GoodKnight